NOT THE MESSIAH

J. Butler Cox

Previously published as Providence of Mercy

Cover art by SelfPubBookCovers.com/Burner

Published in the United States of America

First Printing, 2015

ISBN 978-0-9904127-1-7

www.jbutlercox.com

To Dawn and all the members of the Hill City Writers for their support and encouragement.

BOOK I

THE FALL

CHAPTER ONE

The contents of my stomach were staying down only with great difficulty as I swayed in the doorway, my eyes straining to focus on the figure grayed out by the downpour.

"You don't look so good." The little nameplate on his uniform read Lt. B. Devon. "I wouldn't ask if there was any other way."

I zipped the collar of my jacket up around my neck and pulled a baseball cap down over my head before sprinting toward the patrol car.

"Sorry, but regulations say you have to sit in the back."

"Like the neighbors need something else to talk about."

I climbed into the backseat behind the cage and started to shiver. What was it about October cold that made it seem so much worse than the far more frigid temperatures of December and January?

Devon toweled off his head and sat still for a moment before putting the car in gear. In the rearview mirror I saw him close his eyes and move his lips. I think he was saying a quick prayer. "I can't tell you how much I appr—"

"I'm not comfortable with it," I said. "I know the situation and I accept this is the only option, but that doesn't mean I have to like it. I'm not in the habit of turning people down, but sooner or later I'm going to have to make the decision to say 'no.'"

"She's my daughter."

"That's the only reason I'm doing this."

I saw the unasked question on his lips. People—at least those few who know about my so-called "gift"—are always asking me whether I can actually revive a recently deceased person. So far that question has gone unanswered. I have to draw the line somewhere.

Devon fired up the blue lights as we pulled out of the neighborhood onto the congested commercial strip known as Timberlake Road. Like a lot of police officers, he was a large man who'd gotten a little too large for his own good. Though I stood an inch over six feet, he still towered over me. The buttoned-up collar and tie of his uniform made an already round face look bloated. His sunken eyes were perfect studies in worry and exhaustion.

"Her name is Emily. It means 'industrious.' Do you have children, Mr. Townsend?"

"It's Jeremiah. No, no children."

He nodded.

"It's hard to convey to somebody who's never had a child the feeling you have when you hold your own in your arms for the first time. Her mother and I couldn't have children of our own. She got pregnant four, maybe five times, but couldn't hold it, so we adopted. I think for us that made it even more special."

I nodded, aware he probably didn't see me.

"I'll never forget how small and perfect she was. Her fingers wouldn't even go around my thumb. She just completed me in a way nothing else I'd ever done could. I remember how I promised her I would always keep her...safe." He shuddered and snorted, pulling a handkerchief out of his pocket, keeping one hand on the wheel.

"Don't do this to yourself."

"You don't understand. If a cop can't keep his own daughter safe, who can?"

I started to speak then thought better of it. He needed this. I was just glad he kept the howler off. I don't think my head could have stood it. Cars yielded to us at the red light at the three-way intersection of Timberlake, Wards Road and Fort Avenue, where we swung onto Fort.

"She was very artistic, Emily," he continued.

"Is. Use the present tense."

"She liked to draw, I guess all kids do, but then she discovered painting. Horses and unicorns at first, like all girls. You know, pinks and a lot of pastels, that sort of thing. Then she started doing still lifes, and she really started getting good. You should see the new Hilltopper she did for the high school. Damn thing looks like it could come charging right off the gym wall and spear you on its lance."

The rain continued to pound as we veered onto Memorial, where the road narrowed to two lanes. Even on high the wipers barely kept a portal of visibility cleared.

"I guess when it comes right down to it, she is physically very mature for her age."

"Stop it," I said. "You're trying to excuse his behavior. This is not about how big her breasts were or how short her skirt was. It's not about your manhood or how you failed as a father to protect her. It's about an evil man, a disgusting, sick, perverted piece of scum who preys on the young and helpless. Don't make it sound like she asked for it."

"You're right. I know it. That's what we teach in all the rape prevention classes. It's just...we found my daughter's panties, you know. I don't even like to say the word anymore, I call 'em underpants now, it seems more innocent. We found 'em by the side of the road not twenty yards away from where he took her. The bastard couldn't wait to—"

"Don't go there."

"I have to go there, dammit! I have to know what he did to her!"

"Whatever it was, he can't do it anymore. That's all that matters now."

"It's just...I don't know...she was so *trusting*. Always ready to see the good in people. She probably befriended him, felt sorry for him. Look what he did to her. I'd like to take the dullest, rustiest old piece of metal I could find and cut his fu—"

"We need him alive, don't we?"

"Alive, yes. That's all."

The ride ended at the helipad at Lynchburg General Hospital, where the rotors on an orange and white Bell owned and operated by the Virginia State Police were already beginning to turn.

"Hope your head gets better," Devon said, as a pair of troopers pulled me into the helicopter. "There's no room for me, so I'm driving on up."

The pilot, a light-skinned black man who appeared to be in his early thirties, flashed me a quick grin under his headphones. "There's going to be quite a bit of turbulence until we get above some of this, so you'd better hold on. Ever been in a helicopter before?"

I nodded—such rides were almost becoming part of the job—but I nearly lost my breakfast as we lurched into the air. The second officer, a Latino whom I later learned was the paramedic, briefed me as best he could on the situation over the drone of the rotors. The radio rasped and spat with emergency chatter, though it was hard to make anything out above the drone of the rotors.

The story of Emily Devon's kidnapping had been in the news for weeks. There were few leads in the case until an overzealous rookie cop spotted the suspect, a former carnival worker turned drifter, trying to buy beer at a convenience store in Albemarle County, just outside Charlottesville.

"Instead of calling for backup, he tried to be a hero." The paramedic shook his head. "He didn't realize what a psycho this guy was. The desperate ones, they got nothin' to lose, you know. The cop and a customer in the store wound up dead, the suspect shot full of holes and unable to tell anybody where the girl was."

At UVA, about fifteen minutes away by air, another pair of cops grabbed me by each arm and virtually threw me into the ER where the star of the show was flatlining and the shock-paddles were smoking. I had to have one of the officers physically remove the head trauma tech so I could get to the gurney where our boy was breathing his last breath.

There are certain things I can't heal, like addictions. I can't make an alcoholic better. I can't make old people young again. I also can't do anything about abnormal psychological problems. I can't make a pedophile stop lusting after children, although that would certainly be a worthy ability to have, and I can't do anything about food cravings, fear of heights or any of the zillion or so other neuroses that affect people.

Healing a gunshot wound is tricky, especially when the bullet is still stuck in the person's body—or in this case, the skull. Cancer is relatively easy because all you have to do is cure the diseased cells, a cinch if you've really got the gift. Foreign, non-biological objects have to come out, whether by surgery or by some other means. If the bullet is lodged in the center of the brain, things get complicated.

Even for a miracle worker.

I don't like the sight of blood, and with my stomach burning its way up my esophagus, I was absolutely in no shape to be there, but I stretched my arm out as far as I could and laid my hand squarely on the wound.

I don't know how or why, but I could feel the bullet through his skull and all the assorted tissue. I thought about it for a second and the next thing I knew I had the slug in my hand and the machines were all beeping normally again. A muted gasp turned into even more muted applause as the medical team members pinched and slapped each other to make sure they were all awake.

A cloud of officers swarmed the bed, apparently afraid their boy was going to come up shooting, but the poor guy just lay there wondering if the bright lights he was staring at were part of the afterlife. If they were, I'm sure the thought continued, then why did Hell have so many cops?

Although my stomach still fizzed and boiled, my headache had gone away. Little did I know the attorneys of the world would make sure I would never go another day without one.

CHAPTER TWO

"Didn't get married over the weekend, did you, Jeremiah?"

Miss Parker, the receptionist at the nonprofit Hippocrates Foundation, had asked me that question every Monday morning for the past five years, the perennial mother hen watching out for the son she never had.

"Now, Moneypenny, you know my heart belongs only to you." I sounded more like Scotty from *Star Trek* than Sean Connery.

"I thought maybe you and your lawyer-girlfriend would finally decide to tie the knot. It's a shame for a clean-cut, good-looking young man like yourself to stay on the market so long. You don't know how many women would love to have wavy hair and blue eyes like yours."

Though never married herself, Miss Parker was forever playing matchmaker for every unmarried soul who entered her universe. Slightly Rubinesque but always impeccably coiffed and dressed, she had startling cat eyes that could lock a man's gaze in place like a magnet until she decided to break the spell. I couldn't understand why she never made it down the aisle.

"She's not my girlfriend," I said.

"Of course she isn't. I take it you heard about the

kidnapper?"

"I was there in the ER. I was the guy who saved him for the police."

"No, I mean over the weekend. The convenience store… Don't tell me you haven't heard?"

Before I could reply, she handed the morning's newspaper to me, the front page headline screaming the news of the escape, pushing the story about the Children of Darkness doomsday cult below the fold.

Most people who had been jerked right out of the gates of hell would be only too pleased to make sure the next shot they got at life would be better spent, but not this guy.

Soon after learning about his miraculous brush with death, it seemed, but just before being released into police custody, the man, identified as Carlos Daniels, faked an epileptic seizure that got him sent back to the ER. En route he punched out a doctor, broke a female nurse's arm and ran out into the night.

"Dear God." I tried not to look at the photos yet.

A few hours later, the story continued, the cops cornered him at the same convenience store where he'd originally been wounded, but this time he took the owners hostage. Negotiations did not go well and he wound up killing the old man who ran the place, just to make a point. The FBI finally took him out in a cloud of tear gas and several thousand rounds of ammo.

No Miracle Man was going to get to him this time.

The story package was complete with wire service photos and

graphics of the hospital escape and the layout of the convenience store. My heart sagged in my chest at the photo of a police officer comforting the store owner's widow.

"Dear God," I said. "I had no idea. I —"

Miss Parker's intercom buzzed and the voice of Dr. Tom Wheatley asked if anyone had heard from me yet.

"He's right here, sir. I'll send him back."

Dr. Wheatley had established the foundation more than twenty-five years earlier as an alternative to conventional medical research. It was Dr. Wheatley who brought me to Lynchburg in the first place. The foundation provided me with a small stipend and the use of my house and utilities rent-free. In return I accepted assignments which took me all over the country and occasionally out of it. I reported in every Monday, when my bookstore was closed.

At fifty-nine, Dr. Wheatley still had a full head of red hair, though now lined with gray, and an energy those in their mid-thirties often envied. His face bore an uncharacteristically solemn expression as I entered the tiny office he maintained on the first floor of the building.

"I recognize that look. That's your damage-control face," I said.

"Jeremiah, you know we've never tried to restrain you in any way from exercising your abilities to help those in need." He nodded toward a chair in the corner. "I know you've struggled for years with the questions of when you should step in to help someone and when you should refuse."

"So far it's never even occurred to me to refuse someone who was really in need. Are you saying I should have refused to save the kidnapper?"

"No, I can't say that. I don't think the foundation would have sanctioned what you did, but those decisions are yours to make and yours alone. What you do on your own time is up to you. I'm just not sure how or why you wound up saving a dying criminal, especially one who turns around and kills someone else. I guess my problem is really you didn't tell me you had done this. I had to read about it in the papers and read between the lines to guess your involvement, what with the man's 'miraculous recovery from the jaws of death' and all that. I mean, isn't your girlfriend a lawyer? What does she say about all this?"

"She's not my girlfriend." I was weary of repeating the fact. "The how and why was the father of the girl he kidnapped, who just happens to be a Lynchburg police officer who figured me out a long time ago. He came to me and asked me to do what I could for the guy so they could find his daughter. He came to my house, took me to the helipad at General and had me flown to UVA. He promised me it would all be kept out of the papers."

"You know the papers here are absolutely clueless since the one company, what's it called, Mediocre General or something, bought them all up. No, your name isn't specifically mentioned, but there was something about reports of a man who stormed into the ER in Charlottesville and saved the man when doctors had given up on him."

"Have you ever known me to just barge into a hospital and demand to go to the emergency room? All my life I've tried to downplay this, this gift, as everyone calls it, to not call attention to myself. The last thing I need is publicity."

"Well publicity is what you've got now, like it or not, and the foundation is probably going to be cast in an unfavorable light. I'm not saying you did the wrong thing—"

"Then what are you saying? I shouldn't answer my door or my phone? I keep telling you, these things seem to always find me. I don't seek them out, they just—"

"I know, I know. I don't envy you. You've been blessed and cursed with the same hand. Maybe you should take some time off, to let it all sink in, that's all. The foundation will support you no matter what you do, you know that. I've studied you for years hoping to find out how to pass this power of yours on to others, for the good of humanity. I'm not so sure now that would be the right thing to do, even if it were possible. Maybe one miracle man every few thousand years is enough. Maybe man wasn't supposed to have this gift."

"I know I wasn't supposed to have it."

"What makes you say that?"

"Oh…nothing. I've always felt bound to this great destiny that was somehow put before me, but it seems all I do is mess it up. I hate comparing myself to—well, you know who—but every day I think I understand a little more how he felt when he prayed in the garden to have the cup taken away from him. I'm so tired of having this —"

"'This great unfulfilled purpose.' You've said it before. Go home. Take a vacation. Get some rest. Do something that doesn't involve saving the world."

So that was it. I had the day off. As I wandered out into the parking lot under an October sky that seemed several shades beyond blue, I considered the novelty of actually opening the bookstore on a Monday. It was, after all, one of the few places where you could still find a copy of my first, and, some would say, only legitimate foray into the literary world, *A Bullet for My Father's Whore*. I didn't bother stocking my other efforts, a series of detective potboilers written under the pen name Biff Granite, although they did help pay the bills...

I decided I might as well call the lawyer-who-wasn't-my-girlfriend. Amanda and I had been best friends since college and, except for one occasion our junior year, our relationship had remained platonic over the years.

I picked up the cell phone and dialed her office in Roanoke, a city an hour west of Lynchburg, not expecting to actually get to talk to her.

"I'm sorry, Ms. Ogden is with a client at the moment," the receptionist told me. "Mr. Townsend? Just a moment, sir, she told me to drop everything if you called."

I didn't remember ever getting that kind of a response. After a few moments of listening to classical music while I waited on hold, Amanda came on the line.

"Jeremiah? Where are you? Good. Listen, it's important you

do not go home just yet. I have to be in Bedford this afternoon, so why don't we plan to have lunch together?"

I had no idea why she was so emphatic about my not going home, but I had learned to trust Amanda's instincts. Since the morning was still young, I opted to stop by a new gift shop I'd had my eye on in a decaying strip mall not far from Langhorne Road and lose myself among the shelves.

Anonymity, however, was a treasure I was seldom allowed to enjoy.

Several times the young man made eye contact with me across the greeting card aisle, obviously trying to get up the courage to make me notice him and open the door for an introduction. Whatever the strategy, it made me nervous. Over the years I'd learned to make myself scarce whenever someone I didn't know seemed to recognize me. Healers, both the supernaturally gifted and the ones with initials after their names, usually wind up targets of the hypochondriacs as well as the truly sick.

Not that there was any question about this young man's condition. Pale, sweaty skin covered with red sores, swollen lymph nodes, and a cough too loud for anyone without TB—I didn't need the visible symptoms to tell me he was suffering from AIDS. Along with the gift of healing I've developed an ability to diagnose any illness or medical condition at a glance, and I'm seldom wrong.

I also recognized this particular fellow as someone I'd healed some years back at a children's ward in Memphis, while on assignment with the foundation. I'm not always good with names, but I never forget the face of someone I heal. That particular trip stood out as the day a young amputee grew a new leg and outran all the other children to be the first one in the ward to come up and hug me.

I put the card I was looking at back in the bin, stretched and made my way over to the audio books section where I could see the kid from behind. His head swiveled as if he were noticing a bug on the floor, but he was tracking me as I moved into position in the aisle behind him.

I could help him. There was no doubt. My record at that point, with a few exceptions, was unblemished. Cancer? A flick of the wrist. AIDS? Hardly worth the time it took to introduce myself.

What I could no longer stand were the awkward introductions. The measured greeting, the apologetic segue—the polite, "I hate to bother you, but let's cut-to-the-chase," if you will—but most of all I could no longer bear hearing the actual ailment described. I would almost rather go running down the street screaming than listen to another tale of tragedy.

I'm not a hard person. I genuinely grieve for those who are suffering, but I can only take so much of the pain of others. As I stared over my book toward the sickened youth, my course was clear. I would simply walk by him and pat him on the back in an understanding, hopefully non-condescending, way that would avoid any embarrassment or uneasiness for either of us. We could both go on with our lives. I would never have to know his name or his situation; he would never have to know what an ungracious jerk I was.

I closed and reshelved the book and started around the corner, but the moment was gone, and the young man with it. Whether it was relief or guilt I felt, I don't know, but he was not there. The problem had solved itself. Perhaps I had read too much into the situation and was simply paranoid.

I knew better. I knew I had to find him or his blood would stain my hands. Neither procrastination nor pride absolves us of our duty to others, and my duty was to help this young man.

I had taken but a few steps into the parking lot when I saw him standing by a tree in one of those little landscaped islands designed to break up the sea of asphalt. His jaw was set in determination, but his eyes betrayed him.

"It's not for me." His tears pooled in shame. "It's for my partner. I gave this to him. I deserve my fate. He doesn't."

I tried to assure him I was not in a position to judge anyone, but he wouldn't let me touch him. I have learned to overcome many prejudices in my time.

"Just promise me you'll come see him. You'll understand."

He resisted all attempts at conversation as I drove him to a dismal little neighborhood on Norwood Street, perched on a cliff above the James River a few blocks from downtown. He would only tell me his name was Darren, his partner's was Warren. I tried not to notice the battleground of needle scars up and down the insides of his arms.

By every indication, the shell of a house he directed me to

was abandoned. No shades or curtains hung on the windows, no light came from within. The house exuded chill. Beer cans and trash peppered the yard; a two-by-four propped up one corner of a sagging porch.

In its heyday this neglected old Victorian had stood tall above the rest of the neighborhood. Now it sighed and sulked. Grass had long since broken chunks of the sidewalk away and plastic covered windows where there was no glass.

A big-assed, small-breasted blonde in tight jeans yelled something incomprehensible at me as I stepped out of the car. Walking toward us, she smiled and took a drag off a cigarette and said something else, followed by, "Don't you wanna?" Her shirt drooped open just enough for me to see a green tattoo of what had once been a red rose on her left breast.

"She's not right." Darren turned toward the house. The blonde yelled something else and pulled her shirt up, showing her strange black nipples to the world. Chants of "Kimmy, Kimmy, no-no," or something to that effect, followed us into the house.

"There's no power, so it's kind of cold." Darren opened the shredded screen door and pushed through.

"Whatchoowant, Mother Fucker?" A very short, wiry black man in a Redskins sweatshirt stepped from the shadows and slammed Darren against the hallway wall. "What's up now, bitch?"

"Hey, easy, let him go." I pushed the assailant away.

"Who dis white man? Yo, watch yoself, white boy, or I'm—"

"He's cool, Tee, he's cool. He's here to help Warren. He

19

don't got no crack, no drugs, no cash, he's just here to see Warren." Darren took charge of the situation.

"You just better watch yourself, white boy; I'll cut you bad."

I glowered down at "Tee" as he strutted and pantomimed the movements of various gangsta rappers. I didn't want to take my eyes off him, but Darren was tugging at my sleeve to follow him.

"Tee's all talk. He sees himself as one of the neighborhood thugs, but he's just a crackhead loser like all the rest of us around here."

Darren led me down a long hallway to a bedroom behind the stairwell. The light from outside cast long shadows, but I found I could see well enough to maneuver. A small kerosene lamp gave the bedroom—for that was the only piece of furniture in the room, other than a straw padded, wooden chair—a flickering, uncertain amber glow.

"Warren, are you asleep? This man's here to help you." He gently brushed the hair out of the tiny figure's face.

The rage of a thousand betrayals boiled within me when I glimpsed Darren's own features, some ten years younger, on the face of the small form curled up on the bed, clutching only a ragged foam blanket for warmth. Tears sputtered down my cheeks as I sought to reconcile the impossible image before me with all I knew about what was right and wrong. My clenched teeth wouldn't part to let me speak.

"Oh...my...God! Tell me this isn't what I think!"

Darren's voice was small and far away, though I couldn't

bring myself to look at him.

"I didn't know if you would come if I told you."

"How old is he?"

"Eleven."

"How could—"

I actually stomped around in a white hot, righteous rage, shaking with anger and revulsion and shame, shame I was witness to such a desecration.

"Can you help him or not?"

"I don't know! I don't know! Oh, God!"

"God knows what I have done, and he has punished me. Don't let my little brother pay the price of my sin."

Darren's words stung my sense of reason. A glimmer of objectivity flickered as though through a distant window in the fog, and I knew my path.

"I can't do anything for him here, like this, shaking with rage. I've got to get him out of here."

"Take him, then. There's no life for him here."

In any other instance, the tears I shed that day would have shamed me, but as I lifted the tiny form off the mattress, I cried with a vengeance. I cried for all the Warrens of the world, that my tears could somehow wash away the stains of abuse and restore the innocence of their souls.

I cried for the Darrens of the world to be wiped from memory.

Warren was too weak to talk. Tee took one look at my face as

21

I came out the door and stood well clear of my path. The bizarre blonde yelled, "Warren baby better!" and started jumping up and down like a *Price is Right* contestant.

"Can somebody help me get him in the car?" I called, to the general area. Tee ran up and opened the back door of my Mazda as I leaned in with a body that was not much more than a large rag doll.

Something was wrong. The power wasn't working. My very touch should have been enough to have Warren up and dancing, but I was so angered by the wrong that had been done him I was useless. My only thought was to get him to the emergency room at General.

"C'mon, Warren, hang on for me." My tires squealed as I pulled out.

"Did you help Darren?" The voice was so small I almost thought it was in my head.

"I'm more worried about you right now, big guy."

"No, you gotta help Darren. He's all I got."

I pulled the car back to the curb, shaking. Was that what was wrong? My anger, my disgust, my eventual refusal to help the monster who had done this to him? My unspoken—indeed, unadmitted—wish that Darren would die because of what he had done?

I was willing to judge him, and in doing so had also decreed the sentence be carried out. Obviously, it was not my place to do so.

"You're right. We'll go back and help Darren, too." I turned in my seat and took Warren's cold, pale hand. Warmth flowed back into my own hand instantly, and I could see the color returning to his

22

face. "You're both going to be all right."

I circled back around from Cabell Street and parked the car in front of the lot. Leaving Warren in the car, I walked back to the front porch, where Darren stood looking down.

"I don't want you to help me," he said.

"I don't care. Warren wants me to and I promised I would do it." Shoving Tee aside, I took Darren's unoffered hand and dared him to stop me. The change in his condition was remarkable, even to me. I let his hand drop back by his side. I still wanted to slug him.

"I'm taking him away from you," I said.

Darren offered no response. I had no idea where Tee was.

Getting back into the car, I asked Warren if he had any other relatives he could live with.

"My aunt lives in Tennessee. She's a nice lady."

"We're heading to Tennessee, then, but first I have to meet someone for lunch."

CHAPTER THREE

I could only shake my head and grin as Warren inhaled two large cheeseburgers and a double order of fries, then salivated as the waitress asked if he was interested in dessert. We were sitting in a little mom-and-pop café in Bedford, just a few blocks from my bookstore, where the food was good and plentiful.

It took me a moment to realize the stunning woman in the doorway, backlit by the noonday sun so you could see her figure perfectly through her dress, was Amanda, blinking as she stared into the darkened confines of the café looking for me. Never a fan of foundation garments, she appeared almost an x-ray image of a woman in the floral print dress she wore that day.

"There you are. I couldn't see for a moment coming in out of the sun." She made her way to our booth, the dim light making her auburn hair look darker than it really was. "Who's this good-looking young man?"

"This is Warren. We're going to be taking a little trip to Tennessee in a while. I'll give you the details later. Warren, this is my friend Amanda."

"Is she your girlfriend?" Warren squirmed in the booth trying to reach the floor with his feet. "She's hot."

Amanda smiled and handed Warren several dollars he could use to play the video games he had been eyeing in the corner of the café.

"So what's the story there, and why are you taking him to Tennessee?" she said, after Warren ran over to the game machines. As I retold the story of my encounter with Darren, Amanda shook her head. "Jeremiah, Jeremiah." There was a hint of a sigh in her voice.

"Always trying to save the world; you can't even go into a store without being drawn into this quest of yours, can you?"

"How could I possibly say no when—"

"I know, I know. No one can fault you for trying to do the right thing. You have to realize the world we live in is complicated, and there can be consequences for your actions, no matter how noble your intentions. This deal with the kidnapper has lawsuit written all over it; that's why I don't want you to go home just yet."

"What are you saying?"

"All right, look at this from a lawyer's perspective. Specifically, one of those lawsuit-happy, sue-anybody-till-you-hit-blood types who goes beyond chasing ambulances to stirring up lawsuits where none would normally exist. Now let's go a step further and say one of those lawyers picks up the morning paper and sees that picture of the widow of the man killed in the convenience store and wonders who could be sued in that particular situation. Not the kidnapper, he's dead. So whom does that leave?"

"I suppose you're not going to say the kidnapper's family?"

25

"That's a possibility, but the chances of success there are pretty low. No, that lawyer is going to go looking for the man who made it all happen, the Miracle Man who supposedly charged into the emergency room and saved the kidnapper from death just a few days earlier. He's going to come looking for you, with the grieving widow on hand for the cameras. Even though you're supposedly doing all this in secret, he'll find you. You are now in the spotlight. Miss, can I get a menu over here?"

"Wait a minute; I was only doing what the police asked me to do. Besides, the doctors in the emergency room were trying to do the same thing, save his life." I pushed away my plate of unfinished french-fries.

"I'm not saying they'll win, or even that the widow will file a lawsuit." Amanda nabbed a few choice fries from my plate. "Maybe nothing will happen at all. I'm saying the door has been opened, the possibility is there, and once it happens, it could get ugly. You may have to start thinking more critically about how and when you use this gift of yours."

I snorted at the word "gift," a term I was beginning to loathe. "So it's finally come down to this: I really will have to pick and choose who lives and who dies."

"You once told me someone has to die or else the world gets too crowded and we all get sick and die."

"I was drunk."

"You don't drink. And you were profoundly right when you made that statement."

"Why would anybody bother suing me? I don't have any money."

"Maybe not now, but if word ever gets out about you, the tabloids will come around with their checkbooks hanging open for exclusive rights to your story. Not to mention the book publishers. You could very easily wind up with a six- or even seven-figure deal for an authorized biography. That would certainly make suing you worthwhile. Then there's your first book, *A Bullet for My Father's Whore*. This could revive interest in it and cause it to be released all over again. This could be just the thing to revive your literary career."

"My literary career is doing just fine, thank you."

"The Biff Granite stuff? That's so far beneath you that...We've had this dialogue before, haven't we?"

"Monologue is more like it."

I looked around the café. Warren hadn't taken his eyes away from the video screen.

"On a lighter note, what were you smiling about when I came in?" Amanda took a sip of water.

"You don't want to hear about it." I picked out a few remainders from the old fries.

"Sure I do."

"It would just embarrass you."

"Now I definitely want to hear it."

"Well, that dress is a bit on the sheer side and the way the sun was behind you, I could pretty much see right through it." I noticed the flicker of a smile she tried to stifle. "It got me to thinking about that night our junior year when you took your towel off and made a man out of me. Do you ever think about it, wonder what might have happened if we hadn't gone back to being just friends?"

Amanda tried to look wistful, but a flash of hurt in her eyes betrayed her.

"Let me guess. You hated the whole thing and wish it never happened," I said.

"No, it was the most special night of my life. I go back to that night often in my mind. Really often. More than you know, especially when I'm lying in bed at night and can't sleep and wish we could do it all over again for real. I realized that night I had found the truest friend I would ever know."

"Then why did you wince when I brought it up?"

"Look, I didn't come here to rehash old memories. I came to warn you about the possibility of a lawsuit." She returned to the role of a counselor rather than an ex-lover. "I think it would do you well to stay as low profile as possible the next few weeks. Your little adventure this morning with Warren and his brother wasn't the best course of action, but maybe getting out of town to go to Tennessee will do you some good. Can you go straight from here without going home first?"

"Without packing?"

"It's an overnight trip; how much do you need? I just think you need to avoid going home right away. There may be reporters there waiting for you, and the last thing you need right now is more publicity."

Warren's interest in the video games seemed to be waning. He was smacking the machine with his hand as the game ended.

"It'd be nice to have a change of clothes and a toothbrush."

"So go to the Dollar General and pick up some underwear and things. Jeez, here's twenty bucks if it's the money you're worried about." Amanda flung the bill with a clockwise spin.

I tossed Mr. Jackson back. "Thanks, but I'm not indigent just yet, although I do stay on the margins. Okay, I'll take Warren and go." I stood and left a tip for the waitress.

"Wait. There's something I need to tell you and this isn't the way I wanted to tell it to you, but I'm seeing someone. It's getting pretty serious."

"Okay."

"What I mean is, it's a real relationship with real potential. Oh, jeez, I didn't want it to all just burble out like that, but there it is. I thought we'd have a nice, friend-to-friend talk and I could tell you how wonderful it is and I could get all giggly and girly about it, but now I've just blurted it out like spilling wine on the table, and I can't stop talking for some reason even though I really, really want to."

"You don't have to apologize or explain anything to me." I acted more nonchalant than I really felt. "I'm happy for you. I guess I've been holding you back, expecting you to put your life on hold forever while we just palled around. I mean, well, now it's my turn to sputter on, but it seems like we've both just been hanging around waiting for something to happen between us and it hasn't."

"Well, I can't wait forever. I shouldn't have to." She shot

only the occasional glance my way. "I want a life and a family, and you're my best friend in the world, but I'm not getting any younger."

For some reason there didn't seem to be anything more to say, though in reality there were volumes of things that needed to be said. A voice inside my head was screaming at me to grab her and kiss her, but unfortunately not loudly enough for anyone else to hear it.

"Anybody I—"

"Brien Dooley. We started going out for the occasional lunch, then a dinner date, and it just worked its way from there."

I started to blurt something about Old One-Eyed Dooley but couldn't see a positive outcome there. Dooley was an insurance salesman who rented office space next to Amanda in Roanoke and restored antique furniture on the side. He was somewhere between thirty-five and sixty-eight and was in every civic organization in the Roanoke Valley, despite going to bed at 9:30 every night. He'd been a sharpshooter in the Army before an overturned chemical jar caused him to lose the sight in his right eye. Amanda had hinted for years that maybe I should do something about his eye, but as a rule I didn't usually volunteer unless asked to do so. As far as I knew, she had never mentioned my little "talent" to Brien.

"Well, Brien's a good guy. Very stable. I've got to get Warren to Tennessee so I can open the bookstore tomorrow, so I'd better get going."

"Oh, and Jeremiah?"

"Yeah?"

"Don't do any miracles on the way down or back. Unless it's an emergency."

CHAPTER FOUR

"Must be pretty cool bein' able to save people all the time the way you do," Warren said as we headed south toward Tennessee on Interstate 81. "Give you a good feelin'."

"Sometimes."

"Sometimes? When is it not a good feelin'?"

"When something goes wrong." *Like with Monique.*

"How does it go wrong?"

"Sometimes things just don't work out the way you hope they will."

"Like when?"

"Like when little guys like you who need a nap try to stay awake."

"You don't care?"

"Go ahead."

Warren reclined his seat, rolled his body away from me and was snoring in minutes, leaving me to the radio and my thoughts. Though I tried to push her away, Monique often came to me in times like this.

Monique was a transfer student I met during my sophomore year in high school, back in Lee County, the westernmost county in the state, on the Kentucky/Tennessee line. She was a basketball

32

cheerleader and band majorette who made the other majorettes look like middle school girls who had yet to see puberty. She was the belle of the ball no matter what the occasion; yet, for reasons I never understood, she always kept her dance card cleared for me. We dated for almost three years, becoming as intimate as possible without actually consummating our relationship.

Monique had it all going for her, but she invariably missed at least one day of school each month. The day came during our senior year when she asked me to do something about it.

The moment I saw her in the hallway that morning, I knew what time of the month it was. The smile that came so easily the other twenty-some days was forced, and her face was pallid. The lipstick and rouge she employed in a vain attempt to hide her condition only made her look clownish. She even walked with a restrained gait, so different from the carefree bounce that usually carried her through life. Monique suffered from severe, crippling cramps and a heavy menstrual flow. She was often bedridden for at least one day every time her period rolled around.

"Hey, sport! Let's ditch this dump and go to Gatlinburg!" She winced with each step.

"You look like you should be in a morgue." That was the usual tact I employed in those days.

"That bad, huh? Actually, I'm doing pretty good this month. At least I'm up and about. This time last month I was lying in a dark room moaning all day."

I had never understood why women say things like "I wish

33

men would have to get pregnant, just to see what it's like," or "I'd like to see a man have to go through cramps every month," as if such things were somehow our fault (I suppose pregnancy usually is). What they fail to understand is we didn't invent biology, we're part of it the same as they are. We just happen to belong to the part that doesn't include pregnancy and periods, that's all. Monique never said things like that, and I felt bad for her whenever I saw her in this condition.

"I wish there was something I could do for you." I didn't realize the irony of my words.

"Well, from what I understand, there is." A smile began to snake its way around her face.

"I'm not sure I like that look."

"I've already seen you do it. Remember when they dropped me off that pyramid at the Thomas Walker game and I twisted my ankle, and you came running over to me? I thought you were just coming to peek up my skirt, but you actually fixed a broken bone on the spot. On the spot!"

"So you want me to try to make your cramps go away?"

"Not just my cramps. I want the whole thing to go away."

"You want me to heal you of your period?"

"I don't mean just this month, I mean forever."

"You want to have easier periods."

"I want to have no periods. Period. Who needs 'em?"

"I'm not so sure that's such a good idea. Your—"

The bell cut me off before I could finish, and for once I was glad for the interruption. Normally a pack of crazed sled dogs couldn't pull me away from Monique, but this time I feigned being worried about getting to class late and sprinted down the hall, hoping she would forget our conversation. I had no idea what disrupting a woman's period would do to her, especially one so young.

She cornered me at lunch and cooed in my ear about how grateful she would be if I cured her of this plague. She even made suggestive gestures with her tongue and a corn dog.

At football practice I went through the routine of putting on pads and a helmet like always, even though the coaching staff had decided during my freshman year I was more valuable as a "trainer" and I would probably never see any actual playing time. The strategy obviously worked, since *Sports Illustrated* once featured us in an article as the most injury-free school in the nation.

I did a few laps with some of the other backups and headed for the bench, my potential as a defensive back never to be realized.

Monique was waiting for me.

"You're not going to get out of this." For the first time I could see frustration showing on her face. "The worst of it's over this month, but then there's next month, and the next and the next. I've got another forty years of this ahead of me, not counting the times when I'll be pregnant. I wish I could make you see how much I need this."

"Babe, I sympathize, I really do. I—"

"How can you sympathize? You're a guy; you don't even know what it's like. You don't even care."

35

"I do care. I can probably imagine what you're going through. I don't want to see you suffer, but I just don't know what taking away your period would do to you. I don't even know I could do that; it might just fix whatever's wrong with it. Maybe you could have a normal period."

"I don't want a normal period; I want no period. You don't have to put up with one, why should I?"

Of course, this argument of hers was absolutely devoid of any logic. Even the most absurd musings seemed profound when delivered by a goddess of sunshine to a perfectly smitten rube. Eventually I relented, and after practice was over and we were out of sight of everyone else, I laid my hand on her abdomen (instead of putting it under her bra, where it usually wound up) and hoped for the best.

My left arm started to tingle—a warning sign I would learn not to disregard in later years—meaning something was wrong, but Monique assured me everything was all right.

"It's okay. I'm just a little lightheaded. I'm always this way when it goes away."

Her face was actually paler than it had been earlier in the day and she rose off the bench on unsteady legs.

"Well, it's late and I've got to get to bed early," she said.

"It's not even four thirty."

"I've lost a lot of blood this month. That makes you weak, believe me. I'll be okay."

Refusing my protestations and offers of help, she walked

slowly to her old Toyota and leaned against the door for a moment before getting in.

In later years I came to realize she probably refused to let me help her for fear that in trying to heal her I would reverse what I had done and she would go back to her menstrual cycle.

Monique never had quite the same smile after that, and her radiance was all but extinguished. To this day I still don't know exactly what it was I did to her—or took from her. I only know life was never again as magical for this vision who was once kissed by the gods. We drifted apart during that last year of high school, and she sank further from the limelight. Monique barely made it through one semester at community college. She dropped out and married a much older man. I don't know where she is today.

I only know she was unable to ever have children.

CHAPTER FIVE

Greeneville, Tennessee, was a pleasant little town an hour east of Knoxville with a quaint downtown complete with brick sidewalks, Federal mansions and historical markers trumpeting it as the home of Andrew Johnson, the seventeenth president. Just to the south of town the Unaka Mountains loomed like a dividing wall, separating it from the world beyond.

Sightseeing was not on our agenda, however, particularly since we got there well after dark and Warren had no idea where his aunt lived. I pulled over by the sidewalk and tried to gather as much information as I could.

"What's your aunt's name?" I said.

"Charlotte."

"What's her last name?"

He shrugged. "Just Aunt Charlotte and Uncle Ben. That's all I ever knew."

"Does she have the same last name as you?"

"I don't know."

"Let's try this: How is she your aunt? Is she your father's sister or your mother's?"

"I don't know. I just know she's married to my uncle."

"Okay, how is he your uncle?"

"He's my mother's brother, I think."

"Well, that helps a little bit, but we still don't have a last name. Wait a minute, what was your mother's maiden name?"

"I don't know," he said.

"You don't know your mother's maiden name?"

"I ain't seen my mother since I was two, and anyway, I don't know what a maiden name is."

I paused and took a breath. Warren wasn't stupid and he wasn't trying to be difficult. Growing up in a crackhouse with no parents and an incestuous brother, however, he was about as disadvantaged as they came. I would simply have to think differently in dealing with him.

"A maiden name is a woman's last name before she gets married and takes her husband's last name. In the old days a young girl was called a maiden before she got married."

"My mother wasn't married," he said.

"Are you sure? So her maiden name was probably Hairston, like your last name?"

He shrugged again.

"Well, that's something to start with. Let's try to find a phone book."

In the days before cell phones proliferated, phone booths with phone books were everywhere, as evidenced by all the movies made prior to the 1990s in which characters would go to a phone booth and rip a page out of the phone book. Now, however, I

39

wound up going into an all-night pharmacy and asking to borrow one.

I scanned the listings under Hairston as a bored teenage clerk twirled her hair and sighed, never taking her eyes off the clock.

"Don't tell me you wanna use the phone?" she said when I looked up.

"It's a local call," I said.

"All right, but make it quick. I'm expecting a call." The clerk never made eye contact.

"I thought this was a business phone."

"So?"

It was almost 10:30 by this point and I didn't want to risk waking Warren's aunt and uncle, but I also didn't want Warren to have to spend the night in a motel. By the sixth ring I was almost hoping no one would answer, since I really wasn't sure what I would say.

On the seventh ring a grizzled old voice answered.

"Mr. Hairston? My name is Jeremiah Townsend and I have your nephew here who —"

"What? Who are you? I can't hear a thing!"

"My name is Jeremiah Townsend and I have your nephew, Warren, here who —"

"I'm sorry; I can't hear you. We're not interested and we're going back to bed."

"Sir, please don't hang up!" I didn't want to shout in the middle of the drugStore, but I could hear him muttering something to his wife. In the background I heard her asking whom he was talking to. The line went dead before I could shout again.

The store clerk obviously enjoyed my conversation by the look on her face as I handed back the phone across the counter.

"Thank you for letting me use your phone anyway."

"Hey, no problem." She was more upbeat than she had been since I entered the store. Her enjoyment ended as the phone rang.

"Aw, shit," she said. "Twenty-Four Seven Pharmacy. Somebody did what?"

She looked up at me. "I think she wants to talk to you. She must have star sixty-nined us."

The voice on the other end was matronly and pleasant: "Hello, someone called us from this number and my husband can't hear very well. I keep telling him not to answer the phone...You're with whom? Warren Hairston? I don't know any Warren. My sister-in-law had a boy named Darren...Ben, did your sister ever have another boy? Your sister, the one in Lynchburg...Lynchburg! Lynchburg! Lynchburg in Virginia! Did she have another boy? Did she have another son? Oh, why do I bother; you can't hear a thing...You say he asked about us? That does sound like Darren, all right, poor boy had no chance in life with that mother of his, running around with men so she could get more drugs. I wouldn't be surprised if she didn't have more children. It's a wonder she didn't have ten or twenty kids, the way she was going. I'll bet those boys don't even have the same father...Well, of course, you can bring him over; we'll be glad to keep him."

41

Mrs. Hairston gave me directions to go with the address in the phone book. The store clerk, whose name tag said "Tiffany" right above the word "Management," blew an enormous bubble with her gum and stared at the ceiling as I handed the phone back.

"So you're from out of town, huh?" Still no eye contact.

"That's right. From Lynchburg, Virginia." She grimaced, not so much at the word "Lynchburg" as from the fact I actually responded to her instead of grunting.

"Guess it's a nice town." She turned away and crossed her arms.

"Is there any place to eat around here?"

"In this town? At this hour? I wish!"

Warren was asleep under my jacket when I went back out to the car. I found the Hairston home, a tidy, two-story brick house, a few miles away on Highway 70, the road heading toward Asheville, North Carolina. Warren's aunt and uncle had landscaped the front yard to within an inch of its life, but in the dark I couldn't make out exactly what the plants were, only that there were plenty of them. Uncle Ben was obviously not a fan of lawn mowing.

Aunt Charlotte and Uncle Ben were in the driveway to greet us, both in their robes and pajamas. Ben, a big man with a craggy face and long-ago broken nose, extended a meaty hand and slapped me on the shoulders.

"Can't hear a damn thing after thirty years workin' in a metal fabrication plant, but if you're lookin' out for those kids of my little sister, you must be a good man," he said.

42

"Your hearing's fine, Mr. Hairston. There's nothing wrong with it."

"No, I mean it, I can't hear a thing. Used to be I could get by with a hearin' aid, but last five years that hasn't worked, either."

"It seems pretty good to me." I followed him toward the door.

"How would you know what my hearin' is like? When I say I can't hear...wait a minute, when did those crickets get so loud?" He tilted his head from side to side. "Well, I'll be. Charlotte; it's like a miracle! All of a sudden I'm hearin' things again!"

Mrs. Hairston, who had come back out to wave us inside, gave me a wink and took her husband by the arm. "That's wonderful, dear. Now maybe I won't lose *my* hearing with the TV always so loud."

"I heard that. You said, 'Maybe I won't lose my hearin' with the TV always so loud.' What is goin' on here?"

"I think our young Mr. Townsend here had something to do with that, didn't you?" she said. "Strange stories are coming out of Virginia these days about people being mysteriously healed, and they always seem to center around Lynchburg. Your name rang a bell with me because there's a little town not too far from here called Townsend. Their claim to fame is they have an outdoor drama, the *Smokey Mountain Passion Play*, every year."

"I know," I said. "That's where I got my last name from. My real name was Cushing, but I decided I needed to change my initials."

Both Mr. and Mrs. Hairston did a quick mental check of the

43

initials for Jeremiah Cushing and each said, "Oh." Warren, meanwhile, tore into some leftover lasagna Mrs. Hairston had reheated.

"Well, it's a good thing what you did for Warren." Mrs. Hairston patted my arm. "He's definitely Lisa's little boy; he looks exactly the way Darren did last time we saw him, must have been a dozen or so years ago, when he was in that hospital in Memphis. I almost thought it was Darren when I first saw him."

"So what happened? How did you lose touch with their mother, if you don't mind my asking?"

"She was going to move to Virginia and turn her life around, but we didn't hear from her anymore; we certainly didn't know she'd had another child. She'd done nothing but have sex with every man who would give her drugs when she was here. Darren wasn't her first child. Social services took the first two away, both boys, both from different men, and I believe she had two or three abortions before that, all from different men as well. We kept Darren a lot when nobody could find Lisa."

Warren wandered into the living room and plopped down on the floor in front of the television. Mr. Hairston tuned it to a channel with cartoons and the boy's eyes brightened.

"Wow. I haven't seen cartoons since I was a little kid," he said.

"Hey, big guy, tell me something," I said. "You told me your aunt was a nice lady, and she certainly is, but your aunt and uncle both say they never knew about you. How did you know about

44

them?"

"Darren used to talk about them a lot, said things'd be a lot different if we coulda been with them."

Mrs. Hairston wiped a tear. "How did you find Warren?"

"Darren came to me, told me he was very sick. They were living in squalor, a crackhouse. Warren had been...abused," I said. "I doubt he's ever been in school more than a few days in his life."

"I'm not surprised. You don't know where Lisa is?"

"Warren says he hasn't seen her since he was two. That was nine years ago. I didn't ask Darren. I didn't really care for what Darren had become."

Mrs. Hairston's eyebrows shot up, but she didn't look at me. "Well, life can do things to people, especially in those kinds of circumstances. He was a good boy when he was younger, that's all I know."

"Well, I should be going. Warren is definitely in good hands now," I said.

"Nonsense, you're not going anywhere at this time of night." Mr. Hairston had wandered back inside from listening to the crickets. "I just got my hearing back and I want some company. I want to listen to somebody talk, besides my wife here, been listenin' to her for fifty years. No offense, dear."

"None taken." Mrs. Hairston went to the kitchen.

"What do you want to talk about?" I said.

"Anything at all, Son, anything at all. I just want to sit back and hear a human voice."

CHAPTER SIX

Aunt Charlotte and Uncle Ben—they both insisted I call them that—were some of the dearest people I'd ever met. By the time the next morning rolled around and I got ready to go—after a night of talking with Uncle Ben about our mutual hatred of the Yankees—I felt like I was leaving my own family behind.

"Don't let them get you down, dear." Aunt Charlotte hugged me good-bye.

"Who?"

"Oh you don't have to hide things from me. You're a young man and you have a kind face, but I can see by the lines in your eyes you've already been worn down by them. By people who ask for more than you can give and leave you with nothing for yourself. By those who just don't understand."

"If I were Warren's age, I'd ask you to adopt me, too." I was only half joking.

"If you asked me now, I'd do it." She sounded wholly serious. "You did more for Ben than just give him his hearing back, didn't you?"

She was perceptive, this one.

"He was heading for a stroke. His arteries were in bad shape, but I took care of them, too. He still needs to get his blood pressure down. That's what really cost him his hearing in the first place, wasn't it?"

"How do you know all that?"

"That's part of the package," I said.

Aunt Charlotte gave me a plastic tub full of homemade chocolate chip cookies for the trip back and a big hug like she was my own grandmother. Uncle Ben had a handshake that would make a mule cry.

Warren, who had nothing to give, started to cry when I got ready to leave.

"It's okay, big guy. You've got a whole life ahead of you, and it's going to be better than before because you're in a real home now," I said.

"Can you keep an eye on Darren for me?"

"I don't know. He's all grown up and on his own now. He has to learn to take better care of himself."

Interstate 81 heading north into Virginia was a beautiful drive at any time of year. I didn't like to brag, but even though Tennessee was a gorgeous state in its own right, the views along the I-81 corridor got even better in the Old Dominion. I left Greeneville in time to make it to Lynchburg by early afternoon, stopping by the little town of Marion for some lunch before hitting the long stretch through the New River Valley, just west of Roanoke.

A B.B. King CD kept me company most of the way home.

Had I listened to the news on the radio, I likely would have kept driving until I ran out of gas, probably somewhere outside Harrisonburg, then taken to the woods on foot.

A gaggle of reporters camping on my front lawn raised its collective head as I approached, like vultures looking up from a not-so-fresh kill. From the looks of the flattened grass all around, quite a few had not been able to spend the night. By the day-old beards on many of the men, though, a good many had. The lights of the television cameras flared to life as I pulled into the driveway and the whole troupe came running my way. Without benefit of a garage I had to open my door right into the pack and some guy almost choked me with his microphone in my face. Amanda had been right.

The reporters screamed out questions with no particular regard to protocol: "Is it true you miraculously healed the man who killed the convenience store owner?" "How do you feel about the man you healed killing someone?" "Would you have healed him had you known?" that sort of thing. They flung irrelevant queries with the kind of thinly veiled contempt usually reserved for dog droppings on the bottom of one's shoe.

Whenever I had seen footage of reporters, particularly broadcast reporters, shouting those kinds of questions at figures they had just ambushed, it had always seemed they never really expected answers. Now, as I found myself squashed against the front door of my own house with three- and four-part questions being shouted from twenty and thirty yards away, it was obvious they didn't really want answers. They simply wanted the viewers to draw misleading conclusions from the fact those questions couldn't be answered under the circumstances. A person on TV unable to answer questions is always going to look guilty of something, no matter how absurd the situation.

I tried to get into the house before someone shouted the question I knew was coming.

I failed.

"Are you afraid of a lawsuit by the relatives of the slain convenience store worker?"

I don't know who asked the question, but it didn't really matter. There it was. For some reason I had held this pathetic hope that if no one actually brought the matter up, the relatives wouldn't think of it themselves, but that one moment made all my hopes moot.

The light on my answering machine pulsed like a crimson strobe, indicating the message memory was full. I was sure Amanda was on there somewhere, probably Dr. Wheatley as well, but I didn't want to wade through all the calls from media outlets. I picked up the phone and called Amanda at her office. Once again the receptionist put me straight through.

"You were right," I said. "I had a severe infestation of reporters on my lawn when I got back from Tennessee, and one of them asked me if I was worried about a lawsuit."

"Whatever happened to, 'Hello, Amanda, dearest, I just got back from my trip and wanted to call and tell you all about it?'"

"Sorry. The trip went well. Aunt Charlotte and Uncle Ben

were great people, just like Warren hoped they would be. Listen, I'll tell you all about that later. What am I going to do about this lawsuit?"

"A reporter asking a hypothetical question is not the same as an actual lawsuit, but the idea is obviously out there floating around in the ether. I'd say now since the question has been asked, the odds of it actually happening have gone up substantially. Even if the widow doesn't come up with the idea herself, either a relative will suggest it to her or some lawyer will come after her with dollar signs in his eyes. You need to stay out of public view for a while. Don't talk to any reporters, but most of all don't answer any questions about a lawsuit. Listen, I'm going to be tied up with a murder trial for some time, so I won't be able to be of much help to you. You didn't do a bunch of miracles in Tennessee, did you?"

"Well, no..."

"Oh, Lord. Jeremiah, what did you do?"

"Nothing much, I just —"

"I know you too well, what did you do down there?"

"I fixed Uncle Ben's hearing and saved him from an impending stroke, that's all."

"Well, that's not too bad. Pretty low-key. Look, just stay out of sight, okay? Promise?"

"Okay."

Three days later I found myself staring at a hastily filed complaint handed to me by a deputy sheriff, even as the cameras rolled.

"Sorry to have to do this." As he offered the document to me, I recalled pulling Deputy B. Templeton out of a coma after he wrecked his cruiser in a pursuit three years earlier. "Isn't your girlfriend a lawyer?"

"She's not my girlfriend," I said. "What do I have to do, put it on a T-shirt?"

My head reeled as I closed the door. For days I had hardly eaten, yet the meager food supply I kept on hand was rapidly dwindling. I had not dared to even open the blinds, much less venture out for food, so I was doubtless suffering from paranoia and/or cabin fever.

The first day of house exile I laughed and took pity on them. I was the one holed up in the house, I told myself, but they were the real prisoners, forced to prostitute themselves for a public which abhorred them. They were prisoners of a lecherous, voyeuristic culture they had created themselves.

Besides, I needed a day off, a day to myself to soak in the tub, to straighten up the house, to catch up on a little reading. Maybe even learn to play the guitar, a task that had always eluded me. In the back of my mind I worried about not opening the bookstore.

Day Two I looked forward to a little more self-indulgent loitering, but I was already beginning to feel a bit restless. I've always been one of those people who suffered from seasonal affective disorder, so forcing myself to stay indoors all day under blue skies was like trying to bottle a hurricane. No matter how much I tried to calm myself by telling myself how much I really enjoying getting to

51

do nothing, my mind kept racing back to the outdoors and all the things I could be doing. Each time my mind wandered out, my pulse quickened a bit and I could feel the adrenaline beginning to build in the old fight or flight response. I tried to eat a sandwich at lunchtime but found myself chewing a piece of ham until it spewed out of my mouth.

I began to pray for rain.

CHAPTER SEVEN

The dream seldom varied. The stench of sickness was always in the air, cutting through even the smell of the burning bodies. I could taste it through the filters in the contamination suit. I felt greasy, unwashed.

I didn't even know where I was. Somewhere in Africa was what I'd been told, but the whole situation was highly classified. I saw mountains in the distance not unlike the Appalachians I once called home, but they were obscured by the smoke as the village burned, eradicating the nameless disease that claimed the entire town.

I was too late, of course. All I saw around me was death. My limbs were weighted with sadness. I wanted to sit down and cry but I went on staggering through the village, hoping, praying, wishing I could find someone alive, but the houses had all been burned. Most of them still smoldered; a few flickered and blazed whenever the wind stirred.

The livestock were all dead, too. Birds, dead; reptiles, dead. Whatever they unleashed here, whomever they were, was brutally thorough and nondiscriminatory. Even the plants looked brown.

"Jeez-Us," I heard a man in a similar bio suit say. "What the hell kind of a pathogen was this?"

I never saw his face but at times I felt as though he was someone I knew. I always woke up just before he removed his helmet. I often thought of my brother, Isaac, with whom I had not spoken in years.

Back in the real world the clock indicated, in dull green digits, it was six thirty-seven. A bit too early to get up, perhaps, but too late to go back to sleep. I hadn't been by the foundation headquarters in better than a week, but the lawsuit dominated my waking thoughts. It smacked of hurt and a need for revenge. It also cited me for causing, among other things, "...the loss of companionship and conjugal relations between husband and wife...," giving it a real ambulance-chasing feel, courtesy of the firm Baker, Tinker & Carpenter.

I was going to have to get a lawyer of my own, and though she was my first choice, I did not want to burden Amanda any more than I already had. She had a full caseload already. I also wasn't sure if there was some possible conflict of interest there, due to our history. I decided to call in Sid Lockstein, an old friend from high school who represented me when I attempted to sue the producers of that TV abomination allegedly based on my book.

Sid felt he owed me a favor dating back to the 11th grade when I paid him a visit while he was hospitalized with mono. I remember he tried to get his parents to call me in the first place, but they thought he was delirious.

The day I stuck my head in the door of his room, Sid grinned and made a lame attempt at hiding his face. His bed was nearest the door, with one of those big rubber curtains separating it from the bed by the window.

"Man, I could have saved you some serious cash if you'd called me last night instead of lettin' them bring you here." There was a certain youthful bravado in my voice. "I healed three broken ribs on you last week against Powell Valley and you think I can't handle a case of mono?"

I wasn't really that obnoxious, but I couldn't avoid rubbing my buddy's nose in it a little.

"So you've come to lay hands on me, eh preacher man? 'Repent and heal ye!' and all that crap?"

"You probably need to repent of something. I'll bet you got caught with your hand up a cheerleader's skirt and this is your penance."

I had no idea who was on the other side of the curtain in the hospital room, but I could feel an icy wind beginning to blow from that direction. A man and a woman had been chatting in low voices when I first went in the room, but all was silent now.

I nodded my head toward the curtain and winced. Sid rolled his eyes and slowly mouthed the word "freaks."

I felt embarrassed to have come in and offended some unseen party right off the bat, but the deafening silence, I knew, was worse than continuing to talk.

"So how long do you have to be in here?" I was hoping to steer the conversation away from my "talent."

"They said probably ten days to two weeks; I don't know. You can fix me up, can't you, Jeremy, old boy? You can have me out of here today."

I shrugged, wondering if it was wise to pursue this topic.

Sid slung a disgusted wave toward the curtain. "Who cares? I want outta here. If you can fix me up and get me on my way, it's better for all concerned."

The most indignant silence I have ever heard suddenly came from the other side of the curtain. It's impossible to explain in words how it was in reality any different from the previous silence, but it was sort of like when your ears suddenly stop ringing and you become aware of the fact they had been ringing in the first place.

"Well, you don't seem to have too much of a fever." I put my hands on Sid's forehead. "My medical opinion is you're ready to go home."

He was. Checking for a fever was all the ruse I needed to heal my friend. He knew it right away.

"Man! How do you do that? This is better than the days when Angela doesn't have her bra on!" My friend had his usual grace and tact. "My God, I'm really healed!"

That was all our silent sufferers could take. The big rubber curtain crashed back with a vengeance and a middle aged, round little woman with long, straight hair glared at us, the eyes in her unadorned face lined with dark circles. Her torpedo-shaped breasts were uncomfortably large, extending almost a full arm's length from her body, straining the fabric of the blue dress which hung almost to her ankles.

The man on the bed had a prominent face and a

preposterous belly that revealed no love for the salad bar. He was curled up in a fetal position facing toward us, his salt-and-pepper hair unkempt, his pinstripe pajamas wrinkled and reeking with the sweat of the sick.

"You young men are blaspheming God's name and I won't have it in my husband's presence. What do you mean by claiming you've healed this man? Are you claiming to have the power to heal or do you just think you're being funny?" the woman said.

"I'm sorry, ma'am. We meant no disrespect. We certainly didn't mean to offend —"

"My friend here has healed me. I don't care whether you believe it or not. He can heal your husband here of his colon cancer, too, if you'll just let him," Sid said.

"Sid, I wish you wouldn't..."

"Look, you've seen how weak I was. I had to have a nurse help me get to the bathroom. Now look at me." He hopped out of bed and immediately dropped to the floor and began doing military style push-ups. Then he leapt back up on his feet, bobbing up and down on rangy calf muscles.

"Get behind me, young Satan," the woman said. "The devil's in you, that's what it is, and I can smell the fires of Sodom and Gomorrah from here. I'm not letting you near my man."

The man opened his mouth to speak, but only a rasp came forth at first. On a second effort he managed to rebuke his wife.

"Be still, woman. I'll decide. Young man, if God give you the power to heal—for only God can heal, they's no one else can—then

I'd be debted to ye if you'd help me. That doctor wants to take out almost my whole colon. I'll gladly let you heal me, but only if you say the power comes from God. Otherwise, it comes from Satan, and I'll have nothin' to do with that."

The man could not bring himself to look me in the eye. He was obviously a humble man but in desperation had dared cross his wife. The wife and Sid, however, could do nothing but stare at me.

Then the woman spoke again, "I see by your silence your power—if you ever had it in the first place—does not come from God."

That smug bitch. She would rather see her husband die than accept help from me. The thought raced through my head that he'd probably be better off dead than living with her.

I focused instead on the man and his pain.

"Sir, do you believe God can heal you?"

"With all my heart, Son."

"Then you are healed."

The woman took a deep, deep breath in preparation for the wrath she was about to unleash upon me, but her husband's hand over her mouth stopped the words in her throat. He stood behind her grinning like a kid at Christmas.

"Son, you are a miracle worker. Praise God, I am healed! Econdolashova!" A litany of bizarre words danced and erupted from his lips, and his wife quickly took up the chorus, spewing gibberish in a sing song rhythm of pure joy.

Sid, who had been unable to take his eyes off them, finally

shook his head and leaned and whispered to me: "You didn't even have to touch him? Damn, you are good!"

"His faith healed him." For the first time in a long, long while, I believed it. "He didn't need me at all."

"How come you didn't ask me that?" He turned his back to the chanting couple.

Growing up my mother had always told me to tell people it was their faith in God that healed them, and I tried to always do that. I couldn't remember the exact moment I stopped, but I suppose it must have been in high school with the football team. On the sidelines there wasn't always the time or the opportunity to ask a guy who'd just had his bell rung if he had faith in God or Jesus, especially while the referee was looking at his watch. Frankly there were a few guys I was afraid to ask those questions of and they would have at least resented my doing so.

Before I could answer Sid's question, the man had me in a bear hug that nearly popped my eyes out of my head.

"Praise God! Truly you are a man of God!" he proclaimed, though through my squinted vision I could see the doubt in the woman's eyes. Her joy had faded the moment her husband turned away from her, and her eyes now narrowed and beamed pure poison into my soul.

In healing her husband over her protests. I could have committed no greater sin.

CHAPTER EIGHT

Although Sid was far from the most competent attorney in the world, I suppose I felt some responsibility for the direction his career had taken. After I had hired him to sue the movie producers, he had packed up his practice and moved to Lynchburg to be my attorney and literary agent, a move which had done little for either of us. After a brief phone call during which we went through the obligatory catching up, we arranged a meeting at his office, a little one-man shop down on Jefferson Street.

Sid's office was several blocks from where most of the "reputable" lawyers hung their shingles and had at one time been a taxidermy shop. As I stepped over several boxes of files to get to his desk, I was surprised—well, maybe surprised is too strong a word for someone who still wore a Members Only jacket—to find he still had that old poster of Farrah Fawcett (the one with the red one-piece swimsuit) hanging on a door.

"It's not too good, pal." He glanced up from a copy of *TV Guide*.

"I gathered that from the look on your face." I was hardly able to recognize that face through the extra jowlage he'd accumulated over the years. His hair still had that white-boy Afro look popular in the late 1970s, though it had retreated up his forehead slightly.

"Well, it's probably not as bad as it looks on the surface." He rose to shake my hand. "Man, you look almost exactly the same as you did in high school. Wish I could say the same. Anyway, I thought I could just get the whole thing thrown out, since you were in a hospital setting trying to save a man's life, which is exactly what all the doctors and nurses there were trying to do. Seems pretty cut-and-dried to me, but their lawyers came back with additional complaints about you practicing medicine without a license."

Sid leaned back in his chair and pressed his fingertips together in a not-too-successful attempt to look relaxed. "I thought I could get around that under the Good Samaritan law, but some other parties have joined the suit, including a population-control group making a case some of the people you've saved are going to go on to have children that should never have been born, and so on and so forth. They're saying you're going to tilt the population balance toward overpopulation."

I'm sure the blood must have drained from my face because Sid was offering me a Coke before I realized a period of time had elapsed.

"This is a little hard to believe," I finally said. "I've never tried to play God and decide who lives and who dies, but it seems like that's what it's coming to."

"Well, there's another group saying that's exactly what you're doing. This thing is getting pretty big, bigger than I expected."

"What am I supposed to do? Tell the young wife, 'Sorry,

61

ma'am, but you and your husband dying of cancer are still likely to reproduce, so I'm going to have to let him go?' Should I only save people too old to have children? Make them sign a pledge promising if they live they won't have kids?"

"Hey, believe me, I sympathize. I wouldn't want to be in your position. I remember all too well what happened with Monique, so I know this power of yours has caused a lot of problems for you. There are a lot of angry people with bizarre, unfathomable grudges out there and unfortunately some of them want a piece of you. I don't understand it myself, but they see you as a threat to the natural order of things."

Sid winced as the pager on his hip went off. His darting eyes told me he was not comfortable not answering the page.

"Go ahead. I need some air anyway," I said.

"Look, we've got a principle on our side. No one can make you not use your power; that's like telling a bird not to fly or sing. We'll fight this thing and we'll win."

"Look, if you feel this is a little out of your league, I understand. I've got some people I can call in..."

I don't think I could have hurt him any more deeply if I'd burned the place down and told him his dog had died. I swear his pupils constricted to minus infinity and his shoulders fell a foot. Healing a shattered spirit was much harder than mending a broken body, but what I said turned out to be true. Had I waited only a few more days, the nonprofit Committee Against Frivolous Lawsuits would have taken my case pro bono, but at the time I didn't know that.

"I was just going to say I still had a good feeling about all this." He tossed my file onto a four-foot tall stack of papers on the floor behind his desk and slumped into his chair.

"Hey, I'm sorry. I'm not firing you; I'm just saying let's get some backup, okay? There's an organization with plenty of lawyers willing to step in here. I'll make sure they know you're the point man here." I knew the CAFL group wouldn't want a cartoon like Sid working with them; in fact, he was exactly the sort of lawyer they were working to get rid of.

But now he was *my* lawyer.

CHAPTER NINE

October eighteen would have been Mama's birthday, had she lived. It's hard to explain to other people why your mother is no longer living when you're supposed to be this all-powerful healer of all the world's ills. It's harder still to make them understand the choices you sometimes make. Some people, like my brother, Isaac, never understand and never forgive you. Now my secret was in the open, I wasn't sure if he would ever forgive me.

My sister, Rachel, always called me every few weeks, but I hadn't heard from her since the story broke about my supposedly healing the kidnapper. Each year on Mama's birthday she and I visited the grave and placed a wreath against the headstone, but since we hadn't spoken for a while I figured this year I wouldn't go.

Finally, two days before the annual pilgrimage, she called.

"I just want to know one thing." She didn't even say hello. "Is it true what they're saying about you being able to cure people like that?"

"Pretty much."

"How long have you been able to do this?"

"Since the year Dad died, the summer the old man was with us."

"What old man?"

64

"You remember, the old man Mama took in for the summer. He helped out around the house when Dad died and Isaac ran off."

"I don't remember any old man. What was his name?"

"I never knew his name, but you remember him. He fixed the porch swing when the storm broke it off its chain, mowed the yard, did all kinds of chores around the house."

"The neighbors helped around the house. Old Man Shoefly fixed the porch swing. Nobody stayed for the summer."

"That's right, Shoefly did fix the swing. But there was an old man who helped out; he helped clean the house, and he slept on the cot on the back porch until just before school started."

"Nobody ever slept on that cot. You must have invented an imaginary friend to help you get over Dad."

I couldn't understand how Rachel couldn't remember the old man being with us for almost three months. Could she have blocked it all out somehow? Or was I really making it all up to the point where I actually believed in a fictitious father figure? I couldn't remember much about what the man looked like, only that he and I spent a lot of time together talking about life and the world in general.

I couldn't have made all that up. Could I?

"So you're saying you could have saved Mama?" she said. "Please tell me that wasn't the case."

"Mama knew about my abilities. She made me promise not to save her."

"She asked you to let her die? Why would she do that? Why

65

would you listen to her? You know she wasn't in her right mind."

"You know she was. She was calm and lucid to the very end. Believe me, I tried and tried to convince her to let me help her. She said she knew too much, she'd lived too long. She said she saw the coming storm and couldn't bear to see me go through it, whatever that meant."

"So she foresaw some coming danger for you and just abandoned you? That doesn't sound like her at all."

"That sounds exactly like her. You know she could never stand to see one of us suffer."

"Least of all you. That's very true."

There was a long silence.

"Anyway, are you coming down this year?" she finally said.

"There's just too much going on with the lawsuit and all the reporters following me around. I don't want them swarming all over Mama's grave."

"Would they really follow you all the way to the cemetery here?"

"Who knows? They might think I'm going there to try to resurrect the dead and stomp all over the other graves trying to get footage. Besides, this whole ritual is getting to be too much for me."

"Do you want me to ask Isaac?"

That made me straighten up. "Have you heard from him?"

"I call him every other week whether he wants me to or not. He knows we do this every year."

"So he doesn't come because of me?"

She sighed. "Jeremiah, Jeremiah. There's more to it than you're aware of. I don't approve of this grudge he holds against you, but I understand it a little better now than I used to. Maybe someday it'll all make sense to both of us. I just hope it won't be too late when it does. Now that he knows that...well, that you could have saved her...I don't know it will ever get any better. He holds grudges for a very long time."

"I thought you, of all people, would understand I was only respecting her wishes," I said.

"I do understand. I also understand where Isaac is coming from and why he blames you the way he does. I just don't happen to agree with him."

"Women are always better peacemakers than men."

"There's going to be no peace between the two of you until you both open your minds up. You have to know the whole story, which you don't know yet. Look, if you don't want to go, I'll go alone."

I relented. The press contingent had waned a bit over the past few weeks anyway, so I figured I could get away without attracting too much notice. Besides, her grave was located almost five hours away from Lynchburg, giving me the opportunity to drop out of sight for a while. I threw a few bags into the back of the car and headed back toward I-81, bound this time for the most remote corner of the state.

As I tooled down U.S. 460 out of town, my cell phone rang. It was Amanda.

"I know what day it is. If it's not too late, why don't you pick me up on the way and take me with you?"

I was startled. Though I could certainly use the company, I had never even considered inviting her along for something quite so personal as this.

"Sure. It's a long drive, though. Can you get off from work?" I wanted to ask what "Brien"—if that was really the way he spelled his name—thought about the situation but managed to fight down the urge.

"It's my practice. If I have no court appearances scheduled, I can do whatever I want. Besides, I've always wanted to visit your hometown. Just stop by the office on your way through Roanoke and I'll be ready."

The thought of having Amanda along brightened what had been shaping up to be another tedious journey to appease my conscience for a decision made fourteen years earlier. Though I disliked having to deflect all the questions which invariably arose as to the nature of our relationship, I suppose I knew deep in my soul she was the woman for me—even if she didn't feel the same way. Deeper still, I realized we both felt exactly the same way but were each afraid to be the first to admit it. Brien was certainly complicating things a bit.

As I swung by her office, she hopped in the car, wearing a pair of khakis and a sheer blue blouse which gave away the goods.

"That doesn't look very lawyerly," I said.

"I'm wearing a bra."

"Yeah, black underwire demibra, to be exact, twenty-four ninety-nine at Belk's. I've seen it in the fliers."

"Just what are you doing looking at the bra ads?"

"With my love life the way it is, that's as close as I'm ever going to get to the real thing."

"Poor Jeremiah. Never gets the girl." She put her hand on my thigh. She kept it there for the next one hundred and fifty miles, Brien be damned.

Lee County is located at the very edge of the Virginia coalfields, with the western portion of the county opening up into farmland along the Cumberland Gap, Boone's famous passage to the west. U.S. 58, 58 Alternate and U.S. 421 are the only highways in or out, well away from the nearest interstate. Amanda was curiously silent as we wound around the mountain roads that led us past mobile homes shored up with cinder blocks on tiny plots of land gouged into the hillsides.

"You read about Appalachian poverty all the time," she said. "Yet these people have a better life than the poor people living in ghettoes and tenements in the cities where the drunks are pissing in doorways and throwing up on the sidewalks. At least these folks can grow an ear of corn."

"You should read the stories in the papers, though," I said. "Every fifteen or twenty years or so someone from the Richmond or Washington paper 'discovers' Southwest Virginia, like they've just found tribes of wild people living out in an uncharted territory. They send a reporter and photographer down to take pictures of the ricketiest tarpaper shack they can find, one that has two or three old refrigerators on the porch or in the yard, and present that as the typical house. It's almost like they have a yellowed old map of the state on a scroll that ends at Roanoke and the words 'Here be sea monsters' beyond it."

Amanda laughed and put her hand back on my leg. "Tell me about your mother."

"I've told you about her lots of times."

"Tell me again. I like hearing you talk about her."

***

We stopped by Rachel's house, a little brick ranch in a farm valley called Woodway, an hour or so before dark. After introducing Amanda and giving the old "she's not my girlfriend" disclaimer, we headed out to Rachel's van for the short trip to the cemetery. Rachel, three years older than I, was already going seriously gray. The gray hair, coupled with the weight she never lost from pregnancy, made her look a good ten years older than she really was. The seventies-style polyester pantsuit called way too much attention to her hips and thighs.

"I've been so busy with two of the kids in high school and driving them back and forth to football practice and cheerleading I barely had time to make the wreath this year," Rachel said, more to Amanda than to me. I've always admired the way women can instantly bond with each other, bumping any man who happens to be around to the outskirts of their attention.

"You mean you actually *make* the wreaths?" I drew instant,

70

identical, indignant stares from the two of them. "It's just they look so good I always assumed you bought them."

"Men," they both said.

The sun was disappearing behind the mountains as we made our way through the little cemetery where most of my family had been buried over the past hundred-plus years and a chill crept into the air. After we laid the wreath against Mama's tombstone, Rachel spoke a few words as Amanda and I stood at a respectful distance.

When my turn came, I could only stand and cry.

"It's so hard, Mama," I said, as silently as possible. "I respected your wishes. I did what you asked of me. I could have saved you if you'd let me. I tell myself every day I did the right thing 'cause it was what you wanted, but I'm not sure I believe it. You could have been here with us and we wouldn't have to come here to talk to you. I hope you got what you wanted. I hope it's everything you thought it would be."

I don't know quite how long I stood there, but eventually a woman's hand touched my elbow and led me away. It could have been either Rachel or Amanda.

"You know, she's not really here," Amanda said. I wasn't sure how she meant that, but I nodded and started to get into the van. Over by the edge of the cemetery, against the old wire fence that sagged around the perimeter of the property, I caught a glimpse of Isaac sulking with a cigarette between the thumb and forefinger of his right hand, his usual pose. He wore an old black leather jacket and jeans, virtually the same attire I'd seen him in last time. I lifted my hand in a gesture of acknowledgment, but he pretended he didn't see it.

"Is there any point in my trying to speak to him?" I said to Rachel.

"Probably not, but who knows? The longest journeys —"

"Begin with a single step, I know, I know. I've made that first step repeatedly. I've offered my hand to him in peace more times than I care to remember. Well, no more. He knows how to find me."

We climbed back into the van and buckled in. Amanda and I were content to not say anything for a while, but Rachel was never one to let a moment of silence go unchecked.

"So have you two ever thought about having kids? I mean, not necessarily with each other, but in general? Oh, never mind. I should just keep my big mouth shut."

Rachel's husband, Donnie, brought home several large pizzas for us and their three children, who arrived home from their various after-school activities in quick succession starting around six p.m. Amanda delighted in hearing stories about how awkward and geeky I was as a child, as opposed to the awkward, geeky adult she knew.

As the evening wore on, Rachel abruptly stood up and stared at us.

"I hadn't really given much thought to the sleeping arrangements." She looked first at me, then at Amanda. "Jeremiah usually sleeps in Todd's room and Todd sleeps on the couch. I'm not sure what you would be...comfortable with."

"Oh, I could just—"

"We'll be fine in Todd's room, if he doesn't mind. He still has the bunk beds, if she wants to get away from me, doesn't he?" I didn't dare look at Amanda, but I could tell her mouth was open.

"No, he got too big so we got him a full-size bed this year," Rachel said. "Is that a problem?"

"We'll be fine. In fact, we should be turning in; we've got a long drive ahead of us in the morning." I took a stunned Amanda by the hand and led her into Todd's room.

CHAPTER TEN

Our meetings with the Committee Against Frivolous Lawsuits attorneys always left me feeling as if my life was proceeding without me. Having to go to Richmond, two-and-a-half hours east of Lynchburg, at least twice a week, didn't help, but after a while I realized getting away from the constant requests now made of me actually provided a chance to relax. The bookstore was becoming all but abandoned.

The firm of Beeker, Beeker and Berkman worked out of a high-rise office building in downtown Richmond. I believe Sid actually bought a new suit to meet with the CAFL lawyers. It was the first time I had seen him in something post-1986. With the new haircut as well, he was starting to look like someone who practiced law successfully. As we walked into the Beeker suite on the seventh floor of the Klein Building, he pulled in his stomach and took on an air of competence and, dare I say it, arrogance.

"Gentlemen, I'm Cassidy Yeatts. I'll be the point-man, so to speak, in our defense." A thirtyish blonde in a grey business suit strode up to meet us, arm extended. The hand she offered was tiny, the grip was not.

"There's a great deal of buzz about this suit starting to hit the papers, and we're getting requests for interviews." Cassidy ushered us into an oak-paneled corporate meeting room. She proceeded to introduce us to five men in identical grey suits, all roughly between 32 and 47, who were all part of the team.

"Given the nature of the debate, we think it's important to get public opinion on our side," Cassidy continued. "We want you to do the interviews. You're a photogenic young man, Jeremiah—you do go by Jeremiah, don't you—and you're very articulate. We think it's important for people to see you doing what you do."

"Of course, you can't comment on the suit directly," added Corey Hargis, the number two man on the "team." "We don't want you to speak to the merits of the case. We just want you to talk about yourself and what it is you do."

The phrases about "doing what you do" and "what it is you do" were making me feel like some sort of closet sex offender, but discretion forced me to stay silent. I was noticing, however, they hadn't so much as looked at Sid.

"Now, we'd like to take a deposition from you," said Cassidy, "for all the pertinent facts in the case."

"My office provided you with a full account of what happened, Jeremiah's deposition, as well as the police reports." Sid, not about to be shut out of the biggest case of his career, added a belated introduction: "Sid Lockstein, attorney-at-law."

"Yes, Mr. Lockstein, Sid, you're a valuable part of the team here, I assure you." Corey wasn't assuring Sid of anything positive. "What we had in mind was more of a demonstration of exactly what it is Jeremiah can do."

Sid turned toward me and made an obscene gesture with his tongue pushing against the inside of his cheek. Though I have no idea why, I almost chuckled.

"What did you have in mind?" I said.

"You claim you have the ability to heal people," Cassidy said. "No, that's not the way I meant to say that. Let me put it this way: Your ability to heal is what sets you apart from everyone else. So far we've had to take it on face value you do indeed have this ability, this gift, as some would call it. We need to quantify for ourselves this ability does exist."

"So you want to test me?"

"After a fashion, yes," said Corey. The other men nodded whenever someone else spoke. Cassidy always nodded more vigorously than anyone else.

"We've arranged for a demonstration; let's call it that, rather than a test. Do you need time to prepare? We can do it some other time, if you prefer," said Cassidy.

"I hope you haven't brought in some terminally ill person just to see if I can really 'do what it is I do.' I would resent using someone that way."

"Oh, no, it's nothing like that. We wouldn't do that." Cassidy suddenly looked as though her bun were about to explode from being knotted too tightly. "Just something simple, really. Our founding partner is a D-Day veteran with an old war wound. He was shot in the leg at Omaha Beach and has had difficulty walking ever

76

since. Do you mind?"

I certainly have no problem with helping war veterans, but the idea of being subjected to a pop quiz with someone's health was distasteful, to say the least. Still, I saw no way I could in good conscience refuse.

"I'll see what I can do. Is he here now?"

Cassidy pulled a small walkie-talkie out of her purse. I was a bit surprised a large firm such as this didn't simply use office intercoms, but I suppose a more mobile means of communications conveyed a high-powered, "on the move" image.

"Janet, can you send J.B. into the large conference room? We're ready for him," she said.

Janet answered in the affirmative, and for the next several minutes Sid and I were forced to endure small talk with six head-nodding, image-conscious individuals—well, there really wasn't much *individual* about any of them—who had no real knowledge of or interest in anything that wasn't in the current headlines. Just as I was about to scream and kick some chairs over, the door opened and a tall, gray-haired man with a booming voice lumbered in and thundered, "Where-in-the-hell-is-that-healer?

"So this is him. Well you don't look dangerous to me, but let's see what you can do, boy. Damn is it hot in here." J.B. Beeker was a man who obviously didn't need to wait for introductions. The hand he offered me for shaking was big and warm and leathery, a sharp contrast to the crypt keeper's hands of the rest of the men around the table. I was warming up to him quickly.

"I'll get right to it. I got a piece of shrapnel in this leg gettin' out of the boat at Omaha and had to crawl my way up the cliff. Killed nine Germans anyway, wish it coulda been more but it's hard to shoot straight when you got a chunk of bone knocked out of your leg." He whacked one of the "team" members on the back. "They pulled out a chunk of a Marine's helmet later, that's what was stuck in my leg, and sewed me up and sent me right back out there, the bastards. I didn't come home till after the Airlift in forty-six. I been limping around with this thing ever since, but I never asked nobody to feel sorry for me, least of all these young fellas. I can still outlast any one of 'em in the courtroom." His claim brought much nodding of heads.

J.B. leaned over, propped one foot in the chair beside me and hiked up his pant leg. His right calf bore an ancient scar and there was a good chunk of muscle missing. I noticed for the first time his shoe sole had been built up several layers.

"If you can do anything for that, you're better than any doctor, surgeon or physical therapist I ever been to."

"That's a pretty old wound." I put the heel of my left hand against his calf. J.B. cried out in pain and jerked away, flailing his arms. Several of the men around the table shrieked and, presumably, wet themselves.

"Just playin' with ya, Son," A grin spread across J.B.'s face. Color was returning to the faces of the six other attorneys besides Sid, who was doubled over with silent laughter. "Try again."

Again I touched his leg. When I pulled my arm away, the scar

78

was still there but the missing muscle was in place. J.B. was silent for a few moments.

"Damn and thunder." He put his leg back on the floor. "That leg feels better'n it's felt in almost sixty years. I've got my full range of movement back. Not only that, my trick shoulder feels better."

A small round of applause made its way around the table, instigated by Cassidy.

"Well, I think we've seen exactly what you can do and are ready to proceed," she said.

"The hell you are. I'm taking this case over personally," J.B. said. "You, there, are you his lawyer?"

"Sid Lockstein, yes, I represent Mr. Townsend."

"Good, you and me are gonna win this thing," J.B. said.

"But, Dad..."

"No buts, Cassidy. This boy is the real deal and we're not gonna let anybody run roughshod over him, not as long as I draw breath. You're still with me, but the rest of you pantywaists can get outta here. Go find something to keep yourselves busy. Chase an ambulance or something."

The room quickly cleared to a chorus of "Yes, J.B.," leaving Sid, J.B., Cassidy Beeker Yeatts and me.

"Now, then, we've got the real team in place," J.B. said. "We're gonna knock those bastards on their asses."

CHAPTER ELEVEN

Judge Martha Reynolds Remington scheduled a preliminary hearing in my case for the first Monday in June. From the moment she walked into the courtroom and the deputy commanded, "All rise," it was apparent who would be in charge in her court.

"Gentlemen, let's get right to it. I have reviewed all the pertinent facts in the case, and I'm going to dismiss the wrongful death suit forthright," a proclamation which provoked an expression of disbelief on the faces of the opposing counsel. "It's apparent to the court Mr. Townsend was simply acting at the request of law enforcement when he revived Cornelius Stinnett, aka Carlos Daniels, at the emergency room on October fourteen of last year. Mr. Townsend was no more responsible for the deceased's actions following those events than were the other medical personnel on hand in the emergency room that day. I am dismissing that suit with prejudice, which means it cannot be brought again in this court.

"Furthermore, a request has been made by the plaintiffs to arrange some sort of public test of Mr. Townsend's abilities to prove to the court he can indeed heal people. While there may be some merit in such a demonstration, I am denying the request. Based on the large volume of letters and e-mail I have received since word of this case first got out, it is apparent a great many people do indeed believe Mr. Townsend possesses such power. While I am sure a demonstration would ensure high ratings for the various news organizations covering this trial, I am not interested in putting on a show for the viewing public. The substance of this case, as I understand it, is not whether Mr. Townsend has the ability to heal people but how he chooses to use that ability and what effect it has on those he encounters."

I was beginning to like this judge a lot. Old man Beeker and Sid were trying hard not to grin too obviously, but so far things were going their way. Judge Remington cast a sharp eye at the opposing counsel members as they shuffled and banged reams of paper on the table and dropped them into their briefcases.

"Is something wrong, gentlemen?" She paused to take off her glasses.

"No, Your Honor. We simply wanted to clear some space here by getting rid of the papers we will no longer be needing," replied the lead attorney, Marcus Stipanovich.

"Very well. I anticipate this could possibly be a rather lengthy trial due to the large number of witnesses both sides plan on calling, so we need to set it for the docket, blocking out an appropriate amount of time." She put her glasses back on. "One more thing. Mr. Townsend, until this case is resolved one way or the other, I'm going to have to direct you to refrain from engaging in the practice of healing or treating anyone for any sort of malady, either real or imagined. Do you understand?"

Sid was on his feet quickly: "Your Honor, our client receives a large number of requests, almost more than you can im—"

"Not so much as a Band-Aid, Mr. Lockstein, do you understand?" Remington said. "If this were a malpractice case against a physician, I couldn't very well let him or her go back out and continue practicing medicine until the case was resolved, now could I? This case is very similar, only Mr. Townsend doesn't even have a license to practice medicine, as I understand. Mr. Townsend, do you understand what I'm telling you."

I nodded my consent.

"You need to speak up in my court, Mr. Townsend."

"Yes, ma'am," I said into the microphone.

"Very well. If I hear of you laying hands on someone or so much as prescribing an aspirin, I'm going to have you arrested for contempt of court," Remington said.

"What about CPR, Your Honor?" Sid said. "Does my client have to stand by and possibly watch someone choke to death until the court makes a ruling?"

"You make an interesting point, Mr. Lockstein. All right, I'll amend my order to allow for saving the life of someone who is on the verge of death or serious injury. That's it. Unless it's absolutely life-or-death, it's hands off for you, Mr. Townsend. Do I make myself clear?"

"Perfectly, Your Honor."

Judge Remington stood and walked out without fanfare. You could feel the barometric pressure in the courtroom rise as attorneys on both sides let their breath out. Old Man Beeker leaned on the table and rubbed his eyes. Sid looked as though he'd been chased from the gates of Hell.

"We're in for a long, hard fight, buddy," Sid said. "We got a couple of wins there at first, but we're going to have to battle for every stretch of ground we hope to take."

"I'm too old for this," Beeker said. "This is my last case. After this I'm retiring."

"What am I supposed to do in the meantime? I'll go nuts turning down all the people who ask me for help," I said.

"Your best bet, young man, is to get out of town. The judge didn't put any travel restrictions on you. You're not under arrest. I'd rent an apartment, go to the beach or find a cabin in the woods if I were you."

"That's good advice but make sure we can find you," Sid said. "We're going to be summoning a hell of a lot of witnesses. You need to make a list of everybody you can think of who's been positively influenced as a result of being healed by you. Remember, those guys over there are going to try and tear you down. They're gonna be turning over rocks and garbage cans, if they have to, to make you out to be a menace. You need to get some rest and stay in touch. Read a book or something."

"Yeah, I'll break out the John Grisham stuff. Who's that other guy that writes the lawyer novels?"

"Scott Turow?" Sid said.

"That's the one. Actually, I think I'll read Perry Mason

instead. His clients were always innocent and the real killers always broke down on the witness stand and confessed. That's the kind of thing I need."

As we stepped outside, a little girl, who couldn't have been more than eleven, came up to me on the front steps of the courthouse holding a Samoyed puppy.

"Mister, can you make my dog better? He's been real sick." She held the dog up toward me with both hands.

"I'm sorry, honey, the judge told me not to. I hope your dog gets better, though." My left arm tingled and flinched.

I heard the sound of a camera clicking repeatedly as the girl's face turned into a frown. The following day, the headline in one of the tabloids screamed "Miracle Man tells little girl to stuff it."

CHAPTER TWELVE

Laying low once your face has been on every wire service, network and cable news feed is like trying to run naked but unnoticed through a crowded school playground. Old friends—in one case a guy I bought a pair of shoes from—suddenly began trying to reestablish communication with me. Reporters turned my yard into a campground without the plumbing, and neighbors started to complain about all the satellite-uplink trucks parked along the street and in their driveways. A restraining order and "no trespassing" signs moved them physically off my property, but I couldn't keep them away from the sidewalk or the street.

I did, however, enjoy—at least for the first week or so—watching all the analysts who tried to describe exactly what both sides were going to try to prove in court. You would think the fate of civilization itself rested on the outcome of my trial, based on some of those gasbags who were only too happy to speculate, postulate and pontificate about my situation.

"Well, Peter, the decision of the court could have wide-ranging ramifications for all those in the practice of medicine, from those in the medical establishment right down to the people who practice New Age or holistic methods," said one commentator, a young woman who kept tugging at her skirt and crossing and uncrossing her legs. "Jeremiah Townsend, in many ways, represents an idealized version of what the medical establishment should be able to do in that he can seemingly, magically cure anything and everything that is wrong with you, but at what price? What sort of Faustian deals do the people who come to him enter into in return for being supposedly 'healed,' and what price do they pay in return?"

I didn't like where that was heading, so I switched channels.

"The strange, bizarre case of the Miracle Man of Virginia—"

Click.

"Who is Jeremiah Townsend, this phenomenally gifted healer with the propensity for wrecking—"

Click.

"… who many are calling the Second Coming of Christ while others refer to him as the Antichrist—"

Click.

"Somewhere, wanderin' loose around Mayberry, is a loaded goat."

Good old Mayberry. If ever there was a town I needed to visit, that was it. Spending half an hour with Andy and Barney wasn't going to take my mind off my troubles for long. The cabin in the woods Old Man Beeker suggested was sounding better and better, but the beach was calling to me. A retired judge I had once helped owned a time-share in South Carolina and had offered it to me whenever I needed it. As I recalled, his week was somewhere around the middle of June.

The phone rang. The number that came up on my caller ID

was not one I recognized, but it was from a Lee County exchange. The voice from long ago was instantly familiar.

"Hello, Jeremiah," Isaac said. "I been thinkin' about callin' you since I saw you at the graveyard."

"That was eight months ago," I said.

"Yeah, it was. Rachel's been after me to call the whole time. Took that long to get up the nerve to do it."

"So now you have."

"Yeah. I guess we got a lot to talk about."

"Over the phone?"

"I don't know. I could come see you. I got some time. I got laid off is what happened. Mines ain't doin' too good these days, and I had the seniority, but a lot of the younger fellers need the work a lot worse'n I do, so I let one'a the ones below me take my spot. I got some money saved up."

"That was very big of you. I hope you get back to work before you eat up too much of your savings."

"Anyway, I'd like to see you if you got some time."

"I'm thinking of going to the beach. Why don't you drive up and we'll go down together?"

"I'd like that. I, um, guess I need directions to your house."

I called Judge Miller and made the arrangements for the condo. Isaac came up the next day. Reporters' Row by this point was nothing more than a pair of satellite trucks parked in front of my house for a couple of hours a day. Even the local reporters had gone back to calling once or twice a week for updates, so Isaac was able to

87

get to the house unmolested.

Five years older than I, Isaac looked like he was in his mid-fifties rather than his early forties. Decades of working underground in the coal mines and smoking cigarettes had stolen years from his life. Though still tall and thin, he had a high, protruding belly I recognized at once as a benign tumor. The hair on top of his head had grown thin, though male pattern baldness didn't run in our family. His skin was leathery and brown, unlike that of the young man I knew years earlier.

"Well, look at you, little brother. You finally outgrew me." He noticed I was now an inch taller than he was.

"I haven't grown; you've shrunk. All that stooping underground can't be good for your spine."

"There ain't much about the coal mine that's good for you, 'scept the money, when you're workin'. Two'a my buddies got killed in the last five years."

"I heard about Ricky. What happened?"

"Stuck his head outside the miner as he was backin' it up, hit it against the wall, that's what happened. Took it clean off. He knew better, just got careless that's all. We all get careless sometimes. He just got caught."

If our conversation was awkward, the silence was worse when we ran out of chitchat, so we loaded up his van and headed south. Because of the age difference between us, we didn't really know many of the same people growing up and shared few common interests. This was promising to be a long few days, indeed.

"So whatever happened to that chick you knew in college?" Isaac broke a silence of some forty-five minutes, when we were within shouting distance of the North Carolina border.

"Amanda? She went on to law school and started a practice in Roanoke. We're still good friends. Everybody assumes we're dating, but she's seeing someone else now."

"I still don't know why you never got married," he said. "You wouldn't be havin' to go to the beach with your grumpy old brother if you'd found you a good woman."

"Look, it's a lonely life I lead. I never said I wanted it to be this way; it just is. It's hard to meet women when you spend most of your time as a guinea pig in a research lab or out on assignments to hospital wards. That's the road my life has gone down."

"What about that girl from high school, Monique? Now *she* was a looker."

"Don't ever bring *her* up. That's a part of my life that's closed, a door I do not wish to open."

"Okay, okay. It's just I don't even know what to talk about with you. It's not like we got anything in common or even talked to each other in the past, what, fifteen years?"

"You're trying to force the conversation, for God's sake. Let's just hang out, be together as brothers, talk about whatever comes up. If nothing comes up naturally, then there's nothing wrong with a little quiet time."

He thought about this for a while. "I guess you're right. Bein' married with kids you just get used to havin' somebody talkin' all the—hello, what's this?"

Traffic along the interstate was slowing, slowing, stopped. The line of cars ahead of us stretched into the distance but there was no forward motion we could see. Then we noticed there was no traffic in the northbound lanes.

"Whatever it is, it's shut down traffic in both directions," Isaac said.

"Is that smoke or haze in the distance?" I couldn't tell. The closer you got to the beach the more gray and dull the skies naturally became.

Isaac put the van in park and shut off the engine. The driver in the oil tanker rig in front of us climbed down to talk to a group of people who had gotten out of their vehicles. Horns barked from all directions but nothing was moving.

"I might as well stretch my legs and see if they know what's going on," I said. "I can't imagine a wreck stopping six lanes of traffic both ways for this long."

I sauntered up to the cadre that was forming at the rear of the oil tanker, where everyone seemed to be more in the know than either Isaac or I.

"Big chemical plant explosion about six miles ahead." The driver acknowledged a newcomer. "They're bringin' in the biohazard units. We're not going anywhere for a long, long time. Probably gonna route us all over into the northbound lanes and make us detour out of here."

"Anybody hurt?" I said.

"Radio said there was bodies all over. Blew a whole side of the building out, sprayed some kinda stuff hundreds of feet into the air, real mushroom cloud kinda thing," the driver said.

An older man in the group with a windbreaker and sharp blue eyes glinted hard at me, and I could see the realization crawl across his face.

"Say, ain't you that Miracle Man that's in the news, the one that heals people?" the man said.

I nodded.

"They could probably use you up there, if you could get up to it," he said.

"I'm not supposed to do anything like that until after my trial, unless it's absolute life and death."

"Sounds to me like that's exactly what they got goin' on up there," the trucker said. "I could call in and tell the state police you're back here and they could get somebody to come get you, if you're willing to help."

"Sure. Why not?"

Of course I knew exactly why not. This smacked of precisely the sort of meddling I was not supposed to engage in. Destiny never stopped to ask what was convenient and what wasn't, however, so within twenty minutes a state police helicopter was hovering above the highway dropping a rope ladder, since there was no place to land.

Climbing a rope ladder while dangling from a helicopter wasn't covered in Miracle Man 101, or for that matter, anything I knew of outside of military special operations. Suffice it to say after multiple false starts, all of which sent the ladder spinning wildly and my own sense of balance whirling out of control, I made it into the craft, thanks in part to an EMS tech who reached down and grabbed the back of my belt and hauled me in the way one might pull a suicide jumper from a bridge.

"Ever worn a biohazard suit before?" the co-pilot said over the sound of the chopper.

"As a matter of fact, yes!"

As we turned and flew into the haze and smoke, I carefully pulled on the protective gear, wondering just how and where we were going to land. As it turns out, we didn't. I departed via the rope ladder, the bulky suit making the descent even more difficult than the initial climb.

The whirling blades of the helicopter cleared some of the smoke away, enough to where I could see the ground well enough to drop from the rope ladder. Other biohazard-suited personnel immediately grabbed me and ushered me to the perimeter command area, a staging area set up a good half mile from the plant.

"We're not sending you into the plant because the fires are still burning and there's a chance of explosion," the guy in charge radioed to me. "Stay out here and we'll bring people to you to see what you can do."

At least he didn't say "Do what it is you do."

Within a matter of five to seven minutes, ambulances, the ones which hadn't gone directly to hospitals, began pulling into the command area. Most of the people I saw that day suffered from smoke inhalation. Those who had been burned had already been taken away, so I didn't do anything spectacular, but I still felt good about it. In a span of an hour and forty-five minutes, I kept more than 200 people from flooding the local hospitals. Not a bad day's work on your way to the beach.

Before I could feel too good about myself, however, I turned to face the sheriff's deputies who were there to arrest me for violating a court order.

CHAPTER THIRTEEN

Over the next few days I heard a lot of hate-to-have-to-do-this-just-doing-my-job types of disclaimers from deputies and jailers. I was given my own cell in the county jail, a Spartan cubicle with a stainless steel sink/toilet combo and a cot bolted to the wall. No request I made was refused, while in turn I took care of two abscessed teeth, a broken arm and a nasty case of shingles among the inmate population, in return for a promise not to let Judge Remington know what I was doing.

I couldn't complain about the jail food because I didn't have to eat it. The staff members pooled their resources and bought me a steak dinner from one of the best restaurants in the county on my first night, and every meal wound up being some form of takeout. One enterprising deputy even brought in a spare TV, although there was no cable jack—and no place to put the TV, except in the floor, although I didn't complain. I would rather have had a good book but this wasn't a hotel.

I had no idea what became of Isaac, although he was there when my three days were up. The default sentence was actually ten days, but Judge Remington made allowances for the fact the North Carolina state police did give me a lift for my violation of her order.

Also, she hadn't explicitly said whether her order applied outside Virginia.

The jail staff gave me a commemorative coffee mug and calendar upon my release, neither of which, I'm sure, is standard fare for the newly discharged. There were also the requisite apologies for having to do their jobs and a lot of best wishes.

As Isaac and I walked out the front door onto the concrete landing in front of the county courthouse, however, I had my first encounter with the masses.

A sea of faces several hundred strong, many holding signs which said things like "Free the Miracle Man" and "Where's the crime in doing good?" flowed downward from the front steps, all along the sidewalks and into the parking lot in front of the building. Television cameras stood out among the parade of humanity and reporters were trying to shout questions, but I could not hear individual voices above the din. The sheriff and district attorney had walked out with us and descended the steps in front of us, hands in the air, somehow trying to clear a path the way Moses parted the Red Sea.

"Do you feel the judge's order was just?" someone shouted.

"Can you heal my daughter?" I heard from afar.

"Can you give us some words of wisdom, some food for thought?" That seemed to quiet the throng to a discordant murmur.

I wasn't confident speaking without my attorney. Where was Sid or, for that matter, Old Man Beeker? What was I supposed to do, deliver my Sermon on the Mount before the TV cameras?

Before I could turn and run back into the building, a tiny old man with thick glasses and pink hearing aids looping out of both ears maneuvered an even tinier woman, bones grating like old hinges inside her paper-thin skin, out of the jumble and up the steps in front of me, graciously steadying her forearm.

"Please," he said. "My wife and I drove here all the way from Vermont."

"I'm sorry," I said. "The judge was very clear—"

"No, no, we're not asking to be made well, nothing like that," the woman said, her head unsteady from Parkinson's. "We want you to tell us what we should do."

"How we should live our lives," the man said.

"Should we give to the church, to charities, or save it for our daughters," the woman said. "What is the way to salvation?"

The cameras were right in our faces, awaiting my reply. How could I tell them I had no answers to give them, that I wasn't sure in my own life what was right and what was wrong?

"Live a clean life," I said, never doubting they had already done just that. "Be kind to others. Love without expecting anything in return. Temper all your remarks with kindness. Be true to yourselves."

I was out of my depth here. That sort of bland rehash wouldn't even make the *Chicken Soup* books, but it was all I had. It brought smiles and tears to the couples' eyes, however, and they hugged each other to subdued applause. The crowd rolled in tighter around me. I lost sight of Isaac, the sheriff and the district attorney and had to back up the steps to the top landing to better scan the scene.

Questions about sin, salvation, heaven, hell, Jesus, Mary, Moses, Abraham, Mohammed, the Second Coming and a barrage of rhetorical, theoretical and theological conundrums cascaded around me, each more obscure than the one before.

"Are you the Messiah?" I heard. "No," was the reply I quickly offered.

"Do you have the Mark of the Beast?"

"Are we in the thousand years of darkness?"

"Is the Antichrist alive today?"

"Why does God allow babies to die?"

"Are the streets of heaven really paved with gold?"

Suddenly, to my own salvation, out of the chaos came order.

"Ladies and gentlemen, my client cannot speak in public like this until after the trial." Sid had appeared behind me. "Mr. Townsend is involved in ongoing litigation and cannot comment at this time."

The wave of disappointment surging through the crowd was as draining to my spirits as the bolt of fright that hit me when I first saw the assemblage. Crestfallen, the throng melted away like snow over a manhole cover.

"We need guidance!" someone said.

"Go to your local clergyman or woman," Sid said. "You need to find answers in your own communities, not from headline-of-the-moment celebrities."

I'm not sure whether Sid meant that to sound the way it did, but I wasn't offended. I wasn't cut out to be a messianic figure or even a self-help guru.

"Thanks, buddy," I said, as we turned and ran back inside the courthouse. "What took you so long to get here?"

"You can expect a lot more of this kind of adoration now that you've been wrongfully arrested, at least in the minds of most people. Like it or not, people look up to you as some sort of messenger from above."

CHAPTER FOURTEEN

The salt air cleared my sinuses as Isaac and I continued heading south to a small condo not far from Myrtle Beach, sunshine streaming through the windows and classic rock music from the seventies and eighties vibrating through the metal structure of the van.

It's amazing how two nearly middle-aged adults can revert to their childhoods on a long, dull car trip, resorting to such old time-killing standbys as "punch Bug" or straining to be the first to spot a particular sign or exit. Here on the open highway that snaked through the Carolinas, a blanket of anonymity enfolded me, hiding me among the infinite procession of drones that wound its way along the blacktop.

We talked about the grandiose and the grandly insipid, digressing at length as to whether breasts or legs were most attractive in a woman (we came to no definitive conclusion; I'm attracted to librarian types in tight skirts and glasses while Isaac likes T & A) and whether women should be coy and demure or mount you the way a gymnast hits the pommel horse.

"I still prefer a woman with big tits. At least that gives me something to do with my hands," Isaac said, for perhaps the ten-thousandth time in his life.

After our discourse on the opposite sex ran its course, we settled into a comfortable silence. I didn't care; I felt like I had discovered a brother I never knew I had. The miles wore on along the great winding sea of asphalt. I yearned to hit the back roads and wander through the small towns largely forgotten by the great highways, but Isaac was strictly an interstate man.

"I know you liked that movie *2001*, but I never got the ending." Isaac mused, apparently triggered by a billboard touting a movie theme park in Florida. "I mean, the guy winds up in somebody's kitchen. Then there's the old man and the baby in the bubble, and it's this great movie and nobody ever admits they don't get it."

"You have to read the book to really figure it out. The old man and the baby are both him at different stages in life, and he's reborn as the Star Child, a messenger to do the aliens' bidding."

"That's how he comes back in the next movie."

"Right."

We pulled in to one of those highway rest stops to stretch, walk, whiz and load up on junk food. Ever the babe hound, Isaac was lusting over the women in shorts and tube tops as they walked their dogs behind the snack annex.

"I hate those skort things they wear now." He watched one such specimen pass. "You see a woman from the front, you think she's all hot and sexy in her little miniskirt, then she walks by and she's wearing a damn pair of shorts. It's like a breach of promise.

Where's the intrigue, the mystery in that?"

"You mean where's the remote hope she'll flash her panties at you as she's getting out of her car, or as she trips and falls and has to get back up, don't you?"

"Or if there's a sudden gust of wind, a nice updraft," he said. "Or maybe she won't be wearing panties at all. It could happen. Oh, don't roll your eyes at me. You'd look, same as me."

"Sorry, but with all the diseases going around now, I think wearing panties is a good thing, skirt, skort or whatever."

"Yeah, but you can cure anything they might have."

"Let's not go down that road. I don't like the mental image you're giving me."

We sat at a concrete picnic table and noshed on M&Ms, Hershey bars, barbecued potato chips and soft drinks, a nutritional nightmare worthy of a surgeon general's warning. We took turns belching at each other, just like we had as kids. I could still burp the vowels—even going so far as "and sometimes Y"—but Isaac could do the entire alphabet, followed by half the preamble to the Constitution, as sung in that little ditty we learned watching Saturday morning cartoons. He was lewd and crude, but he was still my big brother.

"I know you don't understand why I didn't save Mom." I wasn't sure why I wanted to spoil an absolutely perfect moment, one I'd waited almost two decades to share. "There are times—hell, more times than I can imagine— when I wish I'd saved her, too, even over her objections. I wish you could understand what I went through.

Please believe me when I tell you there was no right choice. It was either save her against her will and have her resent me for the rest of her life, never enjoying a moment of the time I'd bought for her, or watch her die, spending my remaining days grieving, knowing I could have saved her."

I stopped, feeling as though I had ventured out onto a bridge that was collapsing at both ends. I strained to keep the tears behind my eyes. Isaac just nodded his head, never looking up from a bag of peanuts that was suddenly more than he could finish. The color trickled from his face and he looked like the forty-something man with a wife, no job and too many kids that he was. Mentally I cursed and beat myself all across the boundaries of my brain, feeling like a drunken father who'd just insulted his child and told him there was no Santa Claus.

"It's raining," Isaac said. "We'd better get going."

As soon as we made it back to the van, an angry purple sky unleashed everything it had, hurling blinding rain, hail, lightning and high winds as if pissed off at the world. This was one of those rains you didn't bother driving in. Instead we sat in the van and watched the sidewalk storm sewer regurgitate the river of water that overwhelmed it. Outside people ran for shelter in their own cars, many scooping up small dogs in their arms to avoid dragging them along on leashes. Hail the size of billiard balls—it's always the size of some type of ball—smacked and shattered against the windshield, giving us another reason to stay where we were.

Inside the van we fogged the windows with our breath. Isaac

turned on the engine and started the air conditioner, clearing the mist. A reporter on the radio babbled about the possibility of tornadoes in the area before continuing with the regular newscast.

"Yet another party has joined the list of plaintiffs in the Virginia trial against the so-called Miracle Man," said a woman with the homogeneous Midwest diction all broadcast reporters were evolving toward. "The group Citizens for Death With Dignity has taken up arms against Jeremiah Townsend, who reportedly has the power to miraculously cure any ailment. Lawyers for the embattled Townsend had no comment earlier today, but in Lynchburg a group of people took to the streets to show their support for a man they say has done no wrong. The—"

"Do you want to listen to this?" Isaac had his hand at the switch.

"No. I just want to go to the beach and never come back."

If I'd felt like hell for bringing up Mama, I felt even worse now. Such a perfect day for losing myself and now here I sat, heart ricocheting against my rib cage as if I were running for my life. In a way that was exactly what I was doing, only there was no foreseeable end to this race.

CHAPTER FIFTEEN

Like most coastal resort cities, Myrtle Beach had the feel of one long shopping mall/amusement park complex, a place that existed only to serve tourists all too willing to hand over two months' pay for spicy food, brand-conscious T-shirts and any sort of beachwear imaginable. If you looked real hard you might find the occasional authentic seafood restaurant—and by authentic I mean ones which served seafood caught locally that day— nestled among the beachfront hotels and water parks. You had to look harder still to convince yourself that anyone not associated with the retail trade sector actually lived and worked there.

Our destination, a small private beach away from the mayhem of summer, lay some twenty miles outside Myrtle Beach proper. I sensed restlessness from Isaac as we left the heart of the strip, away from the allure of young women in bikinis who had grown up watching the *Girls Gone Wild* videos and who, one might reasonably or unreasonably assume, would behave in the same fashion given the proper stimulus, i.e. music and alcohol. The beach we headed toward, however, was more for retired folk out for a quiet good time. The only women we were likely to encounter probably wore heavily structured, one-piece bathing suits with skirts and lots of ruffles—the beachwear equivalent of skorts, as far as Isaac was concerned.

I didn't care. Unlike my married brother, I had long since given up the bizarre hope of making it with twins, triplets or any other combination of swimsuit/lingerie model college students looking for a night of debauchery with older men who had no money. Turning off the TV once in a while helped starve out some of those dreams before they could draw nourishment.

The stark white condo building, set well off the highway and jutting out at an odd angle toward the beach, was as devoid of character as a sidewalk. Though the architect had plainly tried to accomplish something with the variety of angles, textured exterior walls and tall wraparound windows throughout, it reminded me of something a bright child might build with an erector set with most of the pieces missing.

"Looks like it was designed by Frank Lloyd McWright." That prompted a snicker from Isaac—the first sound I'd heard from him since my ill-timed comments about Mama.

"It's by the beach and it's free. What more do you want?" he said.

Indeed. As we staggered out of the van and tried to regain our land legs, we could hear and smell the ocean, thanks in part to a warm wind that washed over us with an abrasive quality. Dozens of seagulls hopped along the parking lot while others glided through the air. It was the beach and it was good.

We unloaded the van without speaking. Isaac found the judge's unit on the second floor around the side of the building facing the beach. Once inside I dropped my bags on the floor and jerked open the blinds, subjecting myself to the same sensory overload we all experienced when we first glimpsed the infinite waters of the ocean.

Isaac hit the shower as I stepped out onto the deck. The wind blowing in from the sea lifted my shirttails and blew my sunglasses off from atop my head. I could see less than a dozen people walking along the beach below. One man ran behind a Labrador retriever who romped through the surf as if he'd never been out of the house before, clearly enjoying life to the hilt.

"I'm going to wander down to the beach and get my feet wet." Isaac looked fresher than he had in days. "Why don't you catch a shower and find me later?"

I nodded, feeling unusually agreeable. He could have said, "Hey, let's run through a plate glass window" and I would have checked my watch to be sure I had time to get back from the hospital before dinner.

After a sinfully long shower, I hit the sand wearing a pair of flip-flops but chucked them almost immediately. My life at that moment held no purpose outside of walking to the ends of the earth along the edge of the water, observing the jellyfish and other creatures that washed up at intervals, stopping occasionally to pick the seaweed out of my toes.

In reality we weren't that far from the crowds. As I glanced up the shoreline, just at the edge of my vision, thousands of bodies clustered together along what appeared to be the tiniest outcrop of beach, a sea of humanity that littered the shore like some form of pestilence.

Whoa, there I go, thinking along apocalyptic lines again. Better to enjoy the serenity at hand than curse the chaos ahead.

The surf was rolling in around my ankles. I paused to reel in the giddy feeling of the suction created as the water suddenly washed back out from under my feet, taking some of the sand and muck with it.

I don't know how long or how far I walked, but a slight gnawing sensation in my belly finally brought me back in the direction of the condo as the full moon shimmered atop the waves. It had been dark for some time.

"Hey, little bro, glad you didn't walk into the sea and drown." Isaac was sitting around a fire with two of the loveliest Asian women I had ever seen. They were twins, it seemed, with dark hair that fell to their shoulders and matching floral-print bikinis. "I kept promising them I had a brother, but I think they were beginning to doubt me."

He introduced me to Tomoko and Tanasha, down from Maryland for a visit. His arm hung limply over Tanasha's shoulders in a drunken frat-boy sort of way, but his wedding band was conveniently absent. "Tasha—excuse me, Tanasha—is in computer science and Tomoko is into germ warfare or something, I don't know what the hell she said."

"Microbiology," Tomoko said, as if she had been correcting Isaac all his life. "I don't do germ warfare."

She offered me her hand, fingers pointed downward, and I

kissed it like the perfect gentleman in the script. Her smile was big and friendly and she wasn't afraid of eye contact. Apparently the more modest of the two, Tomoko wore a silky sarong that offered only the occasional glimpse of leg as she walked.

"Your brother and Tanasha seem to have hit it off. I was afraid I was going to have to call it a night." She took my arm and led me away from the fire and back toward the beach. I was getting a bit chilly from the wind and would have enjoyed a fire at that point, but I didn't complain, particularly when she nestled her warm, petite body against me as we walked. I didn't care if it was too good to be true.

"I take it you're at least second generation." I hoped I hadn't struck a nerve. "I mean your English is perfect, no offense. I assume by the names your ancestry is Japanese."

"Our grandparents were held in the Japanese internment camps during World War II and our parents were born then, so I guess that makes us third generation." She was still smiling. "A lot of people we meet expect us to say things like, 'Ah, so, thank you vewy much,' or, 'Thanka you, most honorable fatha.' It gets old, especially when they think all Asians read fortune cookies or eat nothing but dogs and cats and rice. What really burns my biscuits is when people call us Oriental. We're not rugs, you know."

"So what's a nice girl like you doing at a beach like this?"

I really *was* out of pickup lines.

"I didn't think people really said things like that." She gave my arm a playful squeeze. "I'm just trying to stay out of the way while your brother puts the moves on my sister."

I'm sure that would have been the perfect opportunity to bring up my brother's marital status, namely the wife and kids, but some clandestine sense of loyalty—coupled, I suppose, with the growing hope I was going to score here as well—forced me into silence. Instead I wrapped my arms around Tomoko's waist from behind and rested my chin on top of her head as we stared at the moon, now hovering well above the ocean.

There are moments in life when time as we know it does not matter. It does not march ever onward, nor does it retreat like some stricken animal skittering away into the underbrush. It simply becomes irrelevant, a subset of values that do not factor into the present equation, a side street not taken. For Tomoko and me time ceased to exist.

We kissed in the sand, lay in the surf and fell asleep in the judge's condo. In the morning I awoke to screams as the woman beside me gasped for her last breath.

CHAPTER SIXTEEN

I leaped out of bed and pulled the sheets around me as the woman I had gone to bed with, savagely beaten until she was almost unrecognizable, choked on her own phlegm. Her sister screamed and called me a murderer, taking pictures of the crime scene as Isaac came running in from the other bedroom.

"For God's sake, do something, Jeremiah." Isaac tried to put his hand over the other woman's mouth and pull her away from the bed. "Don't let her die!"

My head swam in disbelief at the sight before me, a woman whose face had been beaten to the point the skull no longer matched the swollen, pulpy tissue around it. My hands shook so hard I didn't know if I would be able to help her before it was too late, but I forced myself to speak in a calm voice.

"It's all right, Tomoko, I'm here. I can help you." I ran my hands through the bloodstained tangle of hair that clung to her head in a patchwork puzzle. "I'm not going to let anything happen to you."

First I put my hands on her chest and concentrated on keeping her breathing. I could feel the broken ribs mend themselves, pulling away from the lung they had punctured. Then I moved to her throat, where her windpipe had collapsed. Lastly I moved to her face and head, where bones and tissue moved back into place and the bruises went away. I grabbed another sheet and wrapped it around her.

"You bastard!" Her sister had broken away from Isaac and was now striking me in the back and pulling at my hair. "Don't think this makes up for what you did to my sister! You think you can beat a woman half to death and then make it all right? What kind of sick, perverted pleasure do you get—"

"That's enough." Isaac grabbed her in a half nelson and dragged her away from me. "Jeremiah didn't beat this woman and until we find out what happened, you are staying out of here!" He threw her out of the condo and locked the door.

"You've been set up, little brother," he said.

The savagely beaten sister sat up in bed and hugged her knees, refusing to let me comfort her. Great, mournful sobs came wailing out of her chest and she took deep, gasping breaths before crying more.

"Tomoko, as God is my witness, I did not do this to you. I don't know what happened, but you're all right now. You're going to be fine."

She motioned me away from her. "Where's my sister? What did you do to her?"

"She's outside," Isaac said. "She was getting a little hysterical."

"I don't even know where my clothes are." She stood and pulled the sheet around herself like a toga. I handed her the clothes she had pulled off the night before and she walked quietly to the door, clutching them to her with the sheet. Isaac opened the door for her, where her sister was still standing outside. The sisters embraced and turned away from us, Tanasha throwing a last glare my way.

"What the hell was that all about?" said Isaac. "What happened in here?"

"I don't know. I woke up when Tanasha screamed. What was she doing in here, anyway, and with a camera to boot?"

"She got up to go to the bathroom. I guess she just wanted to look in on you two."

"With a camera? Her sister's in bed with another man and she brings a camera?"

"It sounds bad. Somebody's trying to frame you. We'd better get out of here before they call the police."

"Run from the police? That'll look real good. I'm in enough trouble already without becoming a fugitive. No, I have to stick it out, see what happens. There are too many things here that don't make sense."

We didn't have to wait long. I was too nervous to eat so I went ahead and took my shower. I was dragging an electric shaver across my face when the local police knocked on the door. I soon found myself at the sheriff's office, confronted by a very puzzled looking detective in a tiny interview room with no windows. A sign on a table indicated the room was normally used to administer polygraph tests.

"There's not a damn thing that makes sense here."

112

Investigator Darren DuPre was a fiftyish, thick-necked man with bulging lips and a headache you could feel from down the hall. He was well beyond overweight and his necktie hung away from him at a garish angle. "You wake up because this one woman's screaming and you find the woman you went to bed with's been beat half to death. Only there's no evidence of that 'cause you healed her right away, which I suppose could be considered tampering with the crime scene."

"The sister took some photos." I wondered at once how that statement was supposed to help me.

"Ah, they didn't come out. What was she doing with a camera there, anyway; that makes no sense. We just have the word of the two eyewitnesses, the two sisters, that you beat the hell out of one of 'em, but there's no wounds and no bruises. About all I can charge you with is misdemeanor assault."

I leaned back in the rickety old chair beside the desk and rubbed my eyes. There was something I was overlooking; it had been nagging at me for hours. I could see it, but I couldn't focus on it. DuPre stared at the paperwork in front of him, then at his computer screen, moving with the speed of a narcoleptic snail. He obviously saw something wasn't right, but I had a glimmer of insight he had no access to. There was something about the twins themselves I had overlooked during the morning's crisis.

"Did they do a rape kit at the hospital?" The fog in my brain began to lift. I had a thread of an idea but couldn't yet see where it led.

"She's not accusing you of raping her. If there was sex, it was apparently consensual, at least as far as she's concerned. I don't know if they'd do a rape kit in a situation like that."

"I think you should see to it they do a rape kit. Do a DNA analysis."

"You're not listening to me. She's not accusing you—"

"We didn't have sex," I said, "at all, consensual or otherwise. I'll bet if you do an analysis on that woman, you'll find she had sex last night. The DNA may match mine, or at least it'll be close."

"You're obviously getting at something. So who do you think had sex with her last night, your brother? He was with the other woman."

"That woman *is* the other woman. They switched on us last night. They're supposed to be twins, remember?"

Lt. DuPre had that "go on with it" look on his face, so I continued.

"Look, this is hard to explain, but along with the ability to heal, I also have the ability to diagnose, to sense exactly what's wrong with a person. It's something that developed more slowly than the healing power, but over the years I've gotten pretty good and it's never let me down.

"I see you're not exactly following me," I continued. "For example, just looking at you, I know you have high blood pressure, have high cholesterol and are borderline diabetic."

DuPre rubbed his eyes under his glasses and sighed. He was clearly not impressed.

114

"That's hardly remarkable. Most people could guess those conditions just by looking at me. I'm not exactly the picture of health, I realize. I'm overweight, probably obese, when you get right down to it. Anybody who's fairly observant or even conscious could probably guess I have high blood pressure and cholesterol, and diabetes is not much of a stretch from there."

"Yes, but could everyone guess you also have a faint arrhythmia, macular degeneration in the left eye, blood in your urine, a herniated disc in the lumbar region, erectile dysfunction and—well, it's none of my business what else you have."

This perked him up a bit.

"Go on. What else do I have?"

"It's none of my business. You no doubt are familiar with your own health conditions."

"What else?"

"All right. You have an aneurysm in your brain. It's apparently been growing for some time. I doubt it's operable." I hated that kind of matter-of-fact delivery when pronouncing a death sentence on someone, but I wasn't exactly in a position to give him a hug.

DuPre tried gamely not to look crushed, but at the same time it seemed as though he wasn't entirely surprised.

"I have been having a lot of headaches lately. A lot of them." He shuffled papers with no purpose other than avoiding eye contact with me. "My vision has been affected. The doctors seem to think it's sinus pressure, but one guy I went to did suggest doing a CT scan.

115

It's inoperable, you say; are you sure?"

"I can't be entirely sure about that, no. If I were placing a bet, I'd say yes, it's inoperable."

"I suppose you could probably help me."

I shrugged, not sure what else I was supposed to do. I've always been uncomfortable whenever someone in a position of authority over me tries to hint around for help without asking for it.

"If you ask me—"

"I'm asking. Not for me; I have a daughter I'd like to see grow up, at least get through college. I'll still have to charge you with the misdemeanor assault, of course, although I think it's pretty damn clear you've been set up. If that means you can't help me, fine, I still have a job to do."

"Take off your glasses and close your eyes."

He did as I told him. I placed my right hand on his sweaty forehead and closed my own eyes. I could feel the aneurism shrink and disappear.

"Your blood pressure and cholesterol have gone down a few points, I believe, but since you're still way over on the heavy side, I can't promise they won't go back up." I settled back into my chair on the other side of his desk. "I can't cure bad health habits. If you lose the weight, they'll probably stay down. It's the same for the diabetes. The macular degeneration, blood in the urine and the aneurism are gone, however."

"My God, I can see." He opened his eyes again. "I don't even need my glasses. I can read the numbers on that chart over there."

116

"Well, that's a nice side effect. I've ruined a lot of business for a lot of optometrists. Now can we get back to my problem?"

DuPre blinked and looked around like a man just awakened from a coma; I should know, I've seen that happen before.

"Oh, yeah. You were telling me how you can diagnose illnesses. Obviously pretty well."

"Right. As I was saying, the woman I was with the night before, Tomoko, was overall a very healthy person, although she was in the middle of her period—"

"She told you that?"

"Later, yes, but I already knew it because I sensed it. It's part of the whole ability to diagnose and has a lot to do with why we didn't have sex. Anyway, the woman I woke up with had a very different medical history, in addition to the obvious injuries. For starters, she suffered from asthma and was, I believe, in the early stages of emphysema as well. She also had a sort of blood toxicity I've never seen before, possibly from heavy drug use, which was leading to imminent organ failure. She also seemed to be several years older than her twin, probably from all the health problems. I doubt she would have lived more than five years."

"Without your help, you mean."

"Without my help. I took care of all that when I healed her injuries."

"So the sisters, you're saying, agreed one of them would get beaten nearly to death in exchange for being healed by you to save her from an early death?"

117

"That's pretty much it, yes."

"That's so fucked up. Why couldn't she just approach you for help outright instead of going through all this? Who beat her up?"

I could see Lt. DuPre was already forming his own answers to those very questions, but I helped the process along.

"My brother. He's the answer to both questions. The first question is simply a matter of accessibility. The sisters didn't know me or how to get in touch with me so he arranged for them to meet me."

DuPre took a deep breath. He had already figured it out, of course, but hearing it said aloud took something out of him.

"Look, I know it sounds absurd, but he's always carried an insane sort of grudge against me. First I think it was because he was jealous of all the attention I got that he didn't. You have to understand it's only recently become public I have this ability to heal; that's something I've never shared with him. Now he realizes I could have saved our mother from dying but didn't. I allowed her to die, at her own request. She didn't want to be healed; she was just tired of living and I respected her wishes. In a way, I've hated myself every day of my life since then for letting that happen. No matter how much I hated myself for letting it happen, he's always hated me even more, without even knowing about it. When he finally did find out, I think that pushed him over the edge."

The telephone startled me. DuPre answered and gruffly dismissed the party on the other end.

"So your brother arranged all this, is what you're telling me."

He returned to our conversation. "He convinced the two girls to go through with this in exchange for the one getting healed. He did the beating?"

"Absolutely. I noticed his knuckles were raw. No doubt he took out all his rage and frustration toward me on that poor girl. Then he carried her into the room and put her in bed with me, while the other sister grabbed a camera and screamed so I would wake up in time to save her."

DuPre turned away from me and started accessing a database of some sort on his computer.

"You said earlier one twin seemed to be older than the other?"

"She seemed to have aged more rapidly, that's all I know."

"Well, according to these records, they're not twins at all. In fact they're eight years apart. One's thirty, the other's twenty-two, although there is a remarkable resemblance, especially since they both wear their hair exactly the same. You really only saw them together at night, by the light of the fire on the beach, until the one had the hell beat out of her, right?"

"That's right." I suppose I was feeling somewhat relieved since DuPre seemed to be believing my story.

"So exactly how long has your brother been trying to set this up?"

"Probably his whole life. I suspect he did the bulk of it while I was in jail after the chemical plant explosion on the way down here. That's probably when he ran into the two girls."

"What I still don't understand is what he hopes to gain by all this. It's a pretty fucked up job of framing somebody, if that's what he wants to do. We would have figured it out. Did he really think this would work?"

That question made me think for a moment. I had been so busy trying to unravel the whole thing—and the motive was certainly never in question—that I hadn't stopped to consider how far ahead Isaac had thought things out.

"No, I don't think he did. Isaac knows he isn't the smartest person in the world, and I don't think he ever saw me going to jail for this. I think he probably realized he would wind up going to jail himself once you figured the whole scam out. I think all he really wanted was to publicly humiliate me before my trial this fall. Once word of this gets out, I'm going to look like some bad-tempered, whore-hopping jerk."

DuPre was again working at his computer. "What year did you say your mother died?"

"Nineteen eighty-six."

"What was her name?"

"Sarah."

DuPre looked even more puzzled than usual and said "hmm" a lot as he clicked through a number of screens.

"Have you ever seen a copy of your birth certificate?" he said.

"No, I've never really needed to."

"Well, I think you need to look at this."

CHAPTER SEVENTEEN

Upon his arrival at the sheriff's office, Sid gave me what our old high school football coach used to call a "juicy verbal chewing" over my comments to DuPre. He was none too fond of the candor with which I discussed my situation with an investigating officer without an attorney present. In hindsight I can see his point, but I knew DuPre was on the verge of figuring out the whole sham— which wasn't that cleverly concocted, after all—without my help.

Still, after getting hauled away by the police for the second time in three days, I was in no mood for a lecture from my lawyer and I let him know that, waving away all attempts at making me see things from his point of view. Finally, he sighed and gave up.

"So where do you want to go now?" He looked at his watch. It had been a long drive down from Lynchburg and the air conditioner in his car obviously hadn't been working.

"Where's the nearest hospital?" I said.

"I saw one on the way—why, what are you thinking of doing? You're not sick, are you?" No doubt he saw the look of determination to do something stupid.

"I'm going to do exactly what everyone says I'm supposed to be doing. I've been accused of being too selective in who all I help, so I'm going to go help everybody. We're going to put that hospital

121

out of business."

"I don't think that's a good idea. You're still under a court order not to heal anyone. Remember the judge's comment about practicing medicine without a license?"

"I'm not practicing medicine and I'm not accepting any kind of payment for my services. All I've ever done is try to help people, and I'll be damned if I'm going to stop now just because people can't understand what I do or how I do it. They want to know why I don't heal more people, or how I decide which ones to heal? Fine. I'll heal everyone in sight. Are you with me or not?"

"You're insane. I've never known you to go looking for trouble like this. What has gotten into you?"

"She wasn't even my real mother."

"Who?"

"My mother. The woman I thought was my mother. I've felt so guilty all these years for letting my own mother die, and she wasn't really even my mother."

"Okay, now I know something's up. If she wasn't your mother, who was she?"

"My grandmother. My maternal grandmother, who was only sixteen years older than my mother. My real mother died the day I was born, probably from complications from childbirth. So I guess I killed her, too. Here's what really gets me: nobody ever told me. I had to find out from a cop doing a computer check."

Sid didn't even bother trying to look reassuring. He was as stunned as I had been when I first found out hours earlier.

"So your brother —"

"He knew all along. He's five years older, so he probably remembers our real mother. That's why he's hated me since before I could remember; he blames me for killing her. Now he knows I let our 'other' mother die when I could have saved her, so he blames me for killing both the mothers in his life."

"Your sister?"

"She probably wouldn't remember her, but she must know. That's what she meant when she said she understood the situation between Isaac and me better than I did and that I didn't know the whole story."

"I'm not even going to pretend I understand how you must feel or what the hell's going on here. This is pretty messed up," Sid said.

"So are you going to take me to the hospital or not?"

"Not. As if destroying my case weren't bad enough, now you're trying to wreck my career as well. If I help you, as your attorney, by helping you disobey the judge's order, I'll never be able to practice law anywhere again."

"Fine. I'll take a cab."

That's exactly what I did. Sid bellowed and fumed and stomped off. I took a taxi to the county hospital, hitting the doors running, ignoring the twinge in my left arm. I went straight toward the ER, where there wasn't a whole lot going on, and healed two car wreck victims, both complaining of neck and lower back pain. The doctors there weren't quite sure what to do with me, so they

123

apparently decided the best course of action was to simply step aside and gape at me. My arm was tingling more but the adrenaline rush helped me ignore it.

"Which way to the patient rooms?" I demanded. An orderly pointed me toward the elevator.

On the second floor I took a deep breath and started going room by room. A cancer patient in room 202, gallbladder in 204, hernia in 206—I would hit the odd-numbered rooms on the way back down the hall. I was flinging my left hand hard by this point, the way one shakes a limb that has fallen asleep. Several security guards were summoned to keep an eye on me, but they generally stayed out of my way as I made the rounds, hardly stopping to speak as I visited each room.

Word of my arrival began to spread along the floors and the more mobile patients dragged their IV stands to their doorways to watch my approach. I brushed past a nurse administering an enema to an elderly woman in 317 and healed the woman on the spot.

"Get that damn thing out of my ass!" the woman shouted to the nurse as soon as she felt what I had done. "Oh, God, that hurts! Get it out!" It might have been funny if I'd had time to stay, but as my left arm curled up against my body in a tight clench, I began to worry time was running out.

A 75-bed, four-floor facility isn't particularly large as far as hospitals go these days. In fact, that's about average for a rural, county hospital, but as I made my way to the fourth floor on my insane, ill-conceived quest to prove whatever in God's name I was trying to prove, the entire left side of my body was beginning to draw up tightly, and I was staggering badly against the hallway walls, gripping my right hand against the handrail to keep myself upright. A crowd had gathered behind me like some legion of disciples.

"What's the matter with him?" I heard a woman say.

"He looks pretty bad. Why doesn't somebody stop him?"

Somebody finally did. When I could no longer continue moving forward, when I could no longer hold myself in a standing position and both knees sagged to the floor, still clutching the handrail with my good right hand, I heard a man's voice say, "All right, that's enough."

Enough indeed. The entire left side of my body, including my mouth and jaw, was gnarled and locked into a wretched position like some twisted oak tree in a horror movie.

The Miracle Man's pride had gotten the better of him and this was his penance.

CHAPTER EIGHTEEN

A neurologist handed down the diagnosis: cerebrovascular accident caused by spontaneous intracranial hemorrhage, resulting in hemiplegia. In other words, I had suffered a crippling stroke of the right hemisphere of the brain, disrupting or shutting down the neurological functions of the left side of the body.

I, of course, knew better. Instead of genuinely trying to help my fellow man, I had stormed into the hospital out of spite, ignoring the tingling sensation acts as an alarm whenever I am on the verge of misusing this power.

It's easy to be reflective from a wheelchair or a nursing home bed. After being institutionalized, I had ample opportunity to ponder and learn a sense of respect for those who do what they can to make life more comfortable and worth living—without miraculous abilities. Far more incredible than the ability to instantly heal someone is the courage it takes to face the most wretched among us, day after day after day, with a smile and a commitment to do whatever it takes to help them—to help *us*—get through the day.

So, I have learned to pass my time at the Central Virginia Regional Rehabilitative Center, where I am writing this manuscript on a laptop computer using my still-functioning right hand. In fact

126

the entire right side of my body works as if still under warranty, very fortuitous for someone who is right-handed.

The left side, however, is a wreck. Doctors discontinued the use of muscle relaxants, as they rendered the right side floppy and useless while providing little benefit for the other side. Eventually, one enterprising physician found a way to locally administer the relaxers without affecting my good side, allowing the physical therapists to move my gnarled limbs into more aesthetically pleasing positions.

Speech, however, remains troublesome. Although my tongue was unaffected by the seizure, it's difficult to be articulate when one side of your jaw is essentially frozen and part of the lip is curled into a sneer. I generally shun all reflective surfaces.

Mobility is not as great a problem thanks to a motorized wheelchair. With one good hand available, I can drive it anywhere within the grounds and find myself spending most of my non-therapy time in the outside gardens.

Naturally, word of my plight hit the news the very night of my collapse. Judge Remington put my trial on indefinite hiatus and mail began to pour in from all over the world, from the famous and lesser-known alike. The correspondence was overwhelmingly positive and encouraging. From all indications, a sizable portion of the population was praying for me, although there was the occasional, gleeful "ha ha, got what ya deserve" missive.

Some clearly understood what I was experiencing better than most. Stephen Hawking, who is physically far worse off than I, sent

127

me a copy of *The Universe in a Nutshell,* his follow-up to the brilliant *A Brief History of Time.* Though I don't pretend to understand much of it, it remains one of my most cherished possessions. Christopher Reeve, meanwhile, started a correspondence with me which continued until his death. He eventually sent me DVDs of every movie he ever made, including a rare *Superman* blooper reel. I also, for reasons I will not go into, now own the complete line of Superman-themed underwear.

There's little else worth mentioning during my stay at the rehab center, where one day melts and reforms into another, nearly identical day. A few stand out in memory, however, such as the day Old Man Girardi—I believe his first name was Quentin, but no one ever called him that—challenged me to a table tennis match. Old Man Girardi, it should be noted, was also paralyzed along one side of his body. His misfortune, however, was due to your everyday, aneurysm-induced stroke, rather than the bizarre punishment-of-the-gods thunderbolt thrown my way. He was also 78 at the time, whereas I was not yet 40.

The match was awkward at best, tragically futile at worst, but it was good for quite a few laughs from the other residents and staff. Girardi was clearly the more accomplished player, but in light of our circumstances, that mattered little. After a marathon match that will no doubt be recalled with howls of laughter for decades—hell, it'll probably become legend, the stuff of misty-eyed reminiscences and eventually a "that-couldn't-really-have-happened" kind of dismissal— I finally triumphed, beating him in straight sets. My victory was due more to the fact I still had use of my preferred side than to any exceptional skill on my part. Girardi, a southpaw by birth, was forced to depend on his right hand after his stroke.

He took his "defeat," as it were, with dignity. He rolled his chair over to shake my hand, but the instant our hands clasped, I saw a startled look in his eye, the type you would expect from someone who suddenly realized he had left the stove on. He stretched out his formerly useless left arm and flexed his hand as if trying on a new glove.

"Dear God," I heard him say, the most clearly articulated words he had spoken since the stroke. He braced his arms against the chair to stand, but a pair of nurse's aides swarmed him in an attempt to stop him.

"No, no, don't stop me! I can do this." He gained altitude as he lifted himself into a standing position. "It's all over. The nightmare is gone."

People flooded the recreation room to see Old Man Girardi on his new legs, but he fixed his eyes, now leaking freely, on me.

"God bless you, young man. Whatever I can do to help you, I will. I pray you'll be out of your own chair soon."

Then the residents, those who were most able, were washing over me. I don't know how much business the center lost that day, but everyone who came to me was healed. This was not at all like the situation at the hospital, where I swaggered through the doors to stroke my own ego. I had been humbled like a whipped dog and was left to reflect on my fall. The last of my power went that day to free the residents of the rehab center from their own prisons of flesh.

Today I have the longest tenure of anyone here. The ones who didn't make it to be healed that day eventually went to their own rewards while I remain, wondering when the miracle will come for me. I suppose I will eventually leave this place, though I do not know when or how or what the circumstances of my leaving will be. I only know I am ready to go, one way or another.

As I sit here now and read back through the pages of my story so many of my earlier concerns seem distant and trivial in comparison to my present situation. If I had it to do all over again, there are certainly some things I would do differently. For starters, I wouldn't have gone within five miles of that hospital. Even more importantly, I would certainly have seen my relationship with Amanda for what it was. I wish her the best in her marriage and hope she will forgive me.

BOOK II

HOPE

CHAPTER ONE

In my dreams I am whole. I stand and walk in the golden light of dawn, the grass cool and smooth under my feet, the air fresh and damp with the sweet smell of honeysuckle. Somewhere off camera people murmur and talk about my remarkable recovery and how it was really all a terrible dream. My steps are light and gentle, prancing and running, ready to burst into flight.

Then I awaken to the dull, thumping realization my world is the stark, sterile walls of an institution where they put you away to be forgotten. I wish the dreams would stop. They give me a false sense of hope, then cut me somewhere deep in the soul the moment I wake up.

Early on I had a lot of visitors. Some were just people drawn to the ironic fate of a miracle worker trapped in a frozen body. In time the novelty exhausted itself and I became one more anonymous soul who dropped out of all knowledge. Eventually only Amanda and Rachel stopped by. Of the two, Rachel actually bore my situation better. Amanda could merely cry and shake her head.

Then the angel came.

Not an actual supernatural being, of course, but one no less heavenly, whose hair shone and sparkled like the surface of calm waters in the late afternoon sun. She wore a translucent yellow sun dress that fluttered and flowed as if accompanied by its own personal breeze. A majestic white dog was at her side.

Her eyes were deep pools that belonged to a much older face, but her smile was as young and full of hope as a spring morning. I was smitten.

"I heard you were here." She smoothed her skirt against her thighs. "I've wanted to come for some time, but I was afraid you wouldn't want to see me. I didn't know if you would even remember me, but I wanted you to see Admiral, to see that he's okay."

She indicated the dog who was wagging his tail lazily as he licked my useless left hand. Slowly the fog lifted from my eyes and I remembered, as if the images came from a great distance.

"You're the little girl from outside the police station in North Carolina." I was startled by the sudden clarity of my own speech. "This is the dog you asked me to heal. He was just a puppy then. I turned you down."

"Because of the judge's orders. I remember reading in an interview somewhere you said that was the first time you ever turned anybody down and how bad it made you feel. I just kept thinking you'd probably feel better if you knew things worked out all right."

"You have no idea." I pulled myself up onto legs that felt rusty and old but which now, for reasons unknown, worked.

"What just happened here?" I stretched and flexed muscles as stale as month-old socks. "How did you do this?"

"I think it had something to do with that day I saw you at the

133

courthouse. I had a cold that day, and as you patted my arm, I got better. Then a little while later I realized I could heal other people, too. I think you must have passed some of your powers on to me."

"How long has it been?"

"I was eleven years old then and I'm fifteen now. Admiral here is four years old."

"Four years." I held out my hand to the girl. "I'm Jeremiah."

She stepped right past my hand, wrapping her arms around me in an embrace of forgiveness and understanding.

"I'm Hope," she said.

As if I didn't already know that.

CHAPTER TWO

I don't pretend to understand how I could possibly have passed my abilities on to Hope; although it is uncanny, she was the same age I was when I first acquired the gift. Then again, I don't fully understand what put me in the rehabilitation center in the first place—or where the ability to heal came from or why I was chosen to bear it.

I kept scant belongings at the rehab center, outside of a few changes of clothing, books and a laptop computer, so checking out—something almost no one had ever done prior to my table tennis match with Old Man Girardi—didn't take long. The staff bought me a large basket of flowers and some candy and there were a great many hugs to go around. It was an oddly bittersweet moment, though I can't say I wanted to stay. The thought I had spent the last four years of my life there reminded me my days on this Earth were dwindling.

"You sure you don't want to go around and set the rest of 'em loose?" Barney Gillespie, my physical therapist for the past three-and-a-half years, was a large, fortyish black man who made you smile on the gloomiest of days. I wasn't sure if he really wanted me to send

135

all his patients home, but the point was moot since I no longer had the power. Even if I could have done so, the lesson learned from my hospital fiasco was still too fresh.

"No, it doesn't work that way. That's sort of what got me in here in the first place. What it really comes down to is they have to come to me. I don't know why it works that way, it just does."

"Well, then, I guess I got a confession to make." Barney looked at his feet rather than at me. "Me and the wife wadn't gettin' along so well in the bedroom when I started workin' here. I was having some problems down there, with the equipment and all, and when I found out who you was, I was hopin' you could fix things, only I was too embarrassed to ask."

"Are you asking now?"

"No, actually, the first day I worked with you, I was wonderin' if you could help me or not, and while I was working with your arm there, I started feelin' somethin' stirrin' down below. We've had two kids since then and one's on the way." He grinned so hard he couldn't look at me.

"Well, congratulations. I'm glad I could be there for you." I gave him the obligatory punch on the arm. "I always like to hear success stories. I think sometimes I focus too much on the things that go wrong."

"What could go wrong with healin' somebody? I mean, that's about the most beautiful thing anybody could do. I do my part here every day to help people, but what I do only goes so far. You, man, you make a difference. You give them back their lives."

You give them back their lives. I don't think anyone could have paid me a higher compliment. For the first time in a long, long while, I felt like my life had a purpose after all. As if maybe, just maybe, I hadn't screwed everything up.

Rachel and Donnie were there to pick me up. She had put all my belongings into storage for me while I was away, holding onto the hope I would someday need them again. I lost my house in the interim, but she found a small house in Lynchburg for me to rent.

She kissed my cheek as we hugged and I felt the sobs within.

"What's wrong, Rache?"

"Nothing. I'm just so glad to see you well again."

Never a talker, Donnie shook my hand. "Good to have you back."

As Donnie carried my duffel bag to the car, I pulled Rachel aside and demanded she tell me what was wrong.

"I haven't had the chance to tell you; Isaac committed suicide."

The words slapped me. Isaac hurt me badly and I tried, all the while I was in the rehab center, to hate him while I felt sorry for myself. Sometimes I succeeded, though seldom for long.

"When? How?"

"Two days ago. Just before you got well. Took Dad's old service pistol to the basement and put it in his mouth, Jenny and the kids upstairs. They heard the shot and ran down to find him there."

Most men would have cried, at least a little. I couldn't find a single tear.

"Did he say anything about why, or leave a note?"

"No. Isaac's always been a hard man, hard to understand, hard to love, hard to forgive. He was always finding ways to hurt people, right down to the bitter end. Jenny knew he cheated on her. I don't think he cared. He gave her something, you know."

"What, like VD?"

"Syphilis, I think. She cried when she found out. He just shrugged. Said they had drugs for it now."

I finally asked the question I really didn't want to know the answer to: "Did he ever say anything about what he did to me at the beach, say he was sorry at all?"

"I don't think he ever thought he did anything wrong. After those two sisters confessed to what they did, they all three got charged with filing a false report or trying to defraud the police or some other minor something-or-other, but none of them did any time. It didn't even make the front page of the local papers."

"No, but I'll bet my arrest made it."

"Naturally, you were all over the papers. You're probably better off—well, I guess I can't really say what happened to you was better than the publicity."

We drove back toward Lynchburg in silence, not even discussing Isaac's funeral arrangements. Finally I had to ask.

"Why didn't you tell me the truth about Mama?"

"How much do you know?"

"I know the woman we called Mama wasn't our real mother. That our real mother died the day I was born, I have to assume from

138

giving birth to me. I also have to assume that's why Isaac hated me so much, not just because I allowed the woman I thought was our mother to die. Do you know how I had to find out? A cop showed me the information on my birth certificate, showed me Sara wasn't my mother, she was my grandmother. I had to go find a death certificate for Doris Cushing, our biological mother."

Rachel winced and looked out the window for perhaps a mile or so.

"I've only known it for a few years," she said. "I don't remember our real mother, either. I was too young. Isaac remembered her, though, and he thought you killed her. He also remembered everyone in the family making him promise never to tell you about her, never to even talk about her, and I think that made him very bitter. Eventually he came to accept Sara as his mother, but when you allowed her to die, albeit at her own request, that was just too much. He thought you killed his mother twice."

"I always thought our parents were—I don't know, I guess 'distant' is the word—for a married couple, what with the separate bedrooms and all. The age difference, although Sara certainly looked younger than she was. I still don't know why they deliberately played out this fantasy for us."

"They didn't want you to feel guilty about our real mother," Rachel said. "I agree it wasn't the right thing to do, especially making poor Isaac live out this lie. You have to realize Sara was only sixteen or seventeen when Doris was born, so she was very, very close to her daughter. Close enough to raise Doris' children as her own, literally as her own."

***

Rachel tried to get me to come to Pennington for a while, but I didn't want any sort of big homecoming that would get me back in the papers and get interest started up in my case all over again. I was much more anonymous in Lynchburg. The newspaper there was more interested in running long, rambling special series—the type no one read but which drove the press association contest people into ecstasy—than in covering people stories. With any luck I could settle in and generally lose myself for a while.

"So how are you on money? Do you need any?" These were the first words Donnie had spoken since shaking my hand.

"You know, I don't really know. I haven't seen a bank book in so long." I was ashamed I had given this no thought. All my assets—mostly the inventory from the bookstore, my car and what little furniture I owned, along with my meager savings and the cash value in my life insurance policies—had been liquidated to help pay for my stay in the rehab center.

"You might be better off than you think," Rachel said. "A lot of people around the country donated money to pay your medical bills once they found out what happened to you. Didn't you know that?"

I shook my head, mouth open. How could no one have told me this? I had assumed Medicaid had taken care of my long-term care. I never knew about any donations.

"You may well have thousands and thousands of dollars set

140

aside just for you." She beamed at this bit of what seemed, on the surface, like good news.

"If it was for medical bills, and I no longer have any, then I'm going to have to give it all back, whatever might be left," I said.

"Why would you do that? It's yours, enjoy it. You deserve it."

"You don't understand. My life is governed by a bizarre set of unwritten rules that don't apply to anyone else. I just spent four years as a semi-invalid for breaking some of those rules. I don't dare take money that was set aside for a single purpose and use it for something else!"

I knew that explanation made no sense to anyone but me, but my pulse was thundering like hoof beats coming down the backstretch at the thought of what recrimination lay in store for me if I wound up living off money meant to pay medical bills. How much money were we talking about? Where was it? How would I find who all had donated it?

What was worst of all was giving it all back would put me on public display again.

CHAPTER THREE

The house Rachel rented for me was a two-bedroom frame affair on a road called Wards Ferry. The traffic count there was extremely high because it was located behind a new series of shopping centers and provided a shortcut between two of the busiest roads in Lynchburg. After four years in the rehab center, however, all that mattered to me was the roof didn't leak and I could get a few pieces of old furniture from Rachel and Donnie's basement into it. The landladies also allowed me to have a dog, a necessity since Hope had given Admiral to me, albeit over my vehement protests.

Donnie and I did the grunt work of moving everything from a storage unit a few miles away while Rachel cleaned and put everything in place. By eight o'clock that evening the house looked reasonably ready for occupancy.

"I can't thank you guys enough. I'll pay you as soon as I find out how much money I have in the bank," I said. "Where do I find out about this fund that was set up?"

"It's all in Eastern Federal Commerce Bank," Rachel said. "Where your regular account is."

Then, seeing the look on my face, she added, "I guess no one told you your bank was bought out a couple of times while you were away."

Eastern Federal Commerce, or EastFed, as it was becoming known, had indeed taken over all the familiar branches of my old bank. The downtown branch was located in Lynchburg's only skyscraper, often called the Bank of the Week building or even Bank duJour by some because of the rapid buyout rate among the building owners. When I walked in, Special Customer Accounts Manager Pat McArdle had a manila file folder full of documents I had to sign before she would even discuss the account with me.

"It looks like you have a balance of seventeen thousand, two hundred fifty-eight dollars and seventy-seven cents. There hasn't been a donation for about two and a half years." She peered at a computer screen turned away from me. "That's a nice little coming home present, isn't it?"

"It certainly is. Do you have a record of who the donors are? So I can thank them all properly?"

"No, I'm sorry; we don't keep that information on file. Typically, donations to this sort of fund come in twenty to twenty-five dollar increments, usually no more than about seventy-five dollars, max, so we're talking about quite a number of donations. I don't think people really expect to receive personal acknowledgments when they give to this type of fund; it just becomes too much to keep up with, especially when you don't have any administrative staff assigned to it. As I understand, quite a few businesses around the country set up jars on countertops, labeled 'Miracle Man Fund,' then sent them in when they were full, so, of course, all that would be impossible to track."

"What about my regular accounts, checking and savings? Do I have anything left in them?"

Ms. McArdle attempted, unsuccessfully, to mask her annoyance at having to return to her computer again. "No, those accounts were emptied and closed. Anytime someone is institutionalized in a nursing home-type environment, the institution has the right to claim all the person's assets before turning to Medicaid. They took pretty much everything you had."

She studied my face carefully. "You feel guilty about using this money to live on, don't you? I mean, it's really none of my business, but —"

"The account was supposed to help pay for medical expenses, wasn't it?"

"Let me see; hmm, no, it doesn't seem to specifically say anything about that. It says 'supplemental and/or living expenses' associated with your residence there, which could mean almost anything, including extra snacks or recreation or whatever else you want. Whoever set this up was very careful to make sure you could use the money however you saw fit."

"That brings up another question: exactly who set this account up?"

McArdle leafed through the files some more, pausing for a sip off a lipstick-stained straw in a large Styrofoam cup.

"It was signed off on by Isaac Jacob Cushing."

CHAPTER FOUR

I tried to tell myself I would have gone to Isaac's funeral even if he hadn't set up the account for me, but I never really succeeded. All the way back to Lee County I kept wondering if he would have gone through with the suicide if I had recovered from my paralysis just a few days earlier. If he was feeling guilty over what he'd done to me—and with Isaac there was no way to tell—it might have made a difference.

Mortimer's Funeral Home was housed in a quiet little brick building tucked away on a hilly side street in the shadow of the mountain ridge that made up the town's southern boundary, directly across from the old 1940s-era hospital. As I pulled into the parking lot just prior to the visitation, I noticed a fair assortment of vans and sedans already there. Several men in jeans and flannel shirts stood outside and smoked while their wives, presumably, were inside.

Inside I recognized quite a few faces I hadn't seen in years. Isaac's coffin, a metallic gray tube with a tremendous, symmetrical floral arrangement, sat almost unnoticed in the corner of the chapel, as if it were nothing more than an extraneous table. No one seemed much interested in viewing the body.

"Not a bad turnout," Rachel said, as I stepped into the reception area. "For Isaac, I mean."

"They're here because of Jenny and you and the kids, not out of any sense of respect for Isaac. I don't see any of his drinking buddies here. Where is Jenny?"

"She's in the family room. She's not handling it well at all," Rachel said. "I'm really worried about her; she can't even dress herself. I had to sit her on the bed and pull her pantyhose on her. Just losing him would have been bad enough, but finding him the way she did, the way he was...I don't know why he had to do that to her. The kids are staying with me. Maybe you could do something for her, cure her or something."

"I don't have that power anymore, and even so, I never had the power to just magically make grief go away. I can't wave a wand and make everything in the world all better. Besides, I don't even know if she would want to see me after the spotty history he and I had."

"Well, you need to—"

Before she could finish, a small contingent of glad-handers, speaking in the requisite low tones with appropriately stern faces, recognized me and inserted themselves between us.

"Jeremiah Cushing, I mean, Townsend, after all these years," said a teapot of a man I believed I had seen around town years ago. "I thought you'd forgot all about us hill folk."

"No, I get back a few times a year." I shook his sweaty hand. I still couldn't recall his name, but he seemed to be wearing the same clothes he had worn whenever I had last seen him.

"Too bad you weren't here when it happened. From what I

hear about you, you might have saved him." His teapot-ish wife held out her arms and puckered her lips for the obligatory cheek peck.

"Well." I bent down so she could buss me.

"Say, maybe it's not too late. Or does all the embalming fluid mess everything up so you can't bring him back?" From the look on her face it was apparent she really thought she was on to something. "Does it matter how long he's been dead?"

I don't know how long I stared at this absurd little woman before Rachel led me away by the arm to a quiet kitchenette with a TV and vending machines.

"Did you hear what she asked me? She thinks I could actually bring him *back*."

"Now, dear, people don't really understand this power of yours; you know that. A lot of people probably think you can bring the dead back to life and walk on water, for that matter."

"If I could changes loaves into fishes, I'd slap her with a mackerel."

The low hum of a pipe organ indicated the service would be starting soon. I still hadn't had a chance to talk to Jenny, but Rachel and I made our way to the front pew on the left side, reserved for family members. The other visitors stood on either side of the center aisle and allowed us to pass, nodding in recognition as we walked by.

Jenny sat in the far corner of the pew nearest the wall, her gaze fixed upon some point on the speaker's podium. Black was not a color for someone with such pale skin, but society dictated widows wear it in quantity. With her blonde hair tinged with gray and her

147

eyes bloodshot and swollen from days of crying, she could have passed for a homeless drug addict, albeit a well-dressed one with perfect posture. Rachel sat next to her and held her hand, but Jenny seemed not to notice.

I glanced at Isaac lying in the coffin. I never did buy the argument about how good dead bodies looked or how the deceased always looked as though they were merely sleeping, because it just wasn't true. The figure in the casket looked like a cheap wax replica of my brother in a bad suit. Additionally, dead men always seemed to swell up somehow. I'd never noticed this with women, but men always looked bloated when lying in state.

"When I think of someone passing on I don't like to think of it so much as us losing a friend or a loved one here on Earth, but rather Heaven's getting a new voice for the choir." The eulogist was a balding young man who had obviously never met my brother. "Isaac may have left his loved ones here on Earth, but he's rejoined those who've gone before him. They's a reunion in Heaven right now and Isaac's the guest of honor."

I suppose at such times it would be appropriate to look back on the happy times I spent with my brother but there had been none. All I could seem to come up with was an endless series of recollections of him pushing me down, twisting my arm behind my back until I cried throwing away my favorite toys. I remembered the time when I was nine and he was fourteen when he hit me in the stomach so hard I vomited for hours. Mama—my grandmother, actually—believed him when he told her I swallowed an entire pack of chewing tobacco. The best moment came when I was fifteen and finally big enough to knock him on his ass and pound his head into the floor. He never touched me again.

Before I could mentally torture myself any more, Rachel whispered in my ear, "Jenny wants you to say something."

"You must be out of your —"

"Just do it."

After going on at length with the scribbled platitudes people had handed him about Isaac and offering his own interpretation as to whether suicides do indeed go straight to hell, the eulogist paused.

"Would anyone here like to say anything on behalf of Isaac?"

Rachel dug an elbow into my rib. Wincing in pain, I acquiesced.

The minister stepped aside as I approached the podium, my heart pounding so loudly the mourners surely heard it. I gripped the lectern and searched for words. If Jenny hadn't been there, I would have verbally blasted the hide off his sorry-looking corpse.

"Isaac and I used to roughhouse a lot growing up." I had no idea where I was heading with this track. "As the older brother, five years older, he usually got the better of me."

No, he used to beat the hell out of me.

"I suppose there are life lessons to be learned from those kinds of experiences. I learned a lot from my brother, mostly about...about..."

I was floundering. The mourners were staring at me. Jenny's eyes were still blank.

"...About forgiveness, I guess is the biggest thing. Isaac was never a forgiving man, never able to forgive me for something he blamed me for from a long time ago, and I've never really been able to forgive him for despising me, until now. Even now I'm not sure I can, but I guess I should. Look where his hate and bitterness got him. God knows I don't want to end up like my brother. I guess maybe this is a wake-up call for all of us. I'm going to try to learn from this, try to forgive him for the pain he caused me. There are those of you out there who have to let go of your hurt and anger, too, and forgive him for the pain he caused you."

Jenny was looking down at the floor nodding her head. Now it was Rachel's turn to stare; her eyes were widened with shock. No one else in the audience was making eye contact with me.

Strangely enough, I felt better than I had in years.

CHAPTER FIVE

I resisted the temptation to take out an ad in the papers thanking the public for the donations, opting instead to try to stay as far out of view as I could. I had enough money in the bank to give myself some time to get reacquainted with the world of the able-bodied and think about what I wanted to do without having to rush out and find a job. The bookstore was long gone; I had originally opened it with some of the money earned from my own novel, but that little revenue stream had been long since derailed. I suppose I could eventually have gone back to the foundation, though without my healing ability, I was of little use to them. The small retainer they paid was nowhere near enough to live on.

I shuddered at the thought of returning to journalism; the local paper was so bad the high school English classes routinely dissected it for errors. No one on staff seemed to have any idea about subject/verb agreement, the difference between "its" and "it's," or, for that matter, the difference between the uses of "site," "cite" and "sight."

One thing I had to do was get myself back in shape. Although all symptoms of my mysterious paralysis were gone, there was very little muscle tone in the left side of my body and scarcely more in the right, despite Barney's vigorous therapy. I started taking long walks in the various city parks while carrying hand weights, then worked my way up to jogging and bicycle riding with Admiral at my side. I had forgotten just how reassuring a dog could be.

After five weeks, I ran a mile on the local track in under six-and-a-half minutes, though Admiral lapped me twice. He sat and whined as I lay in the grass gasping.

"I miss her, too, big guy." I rubbed his head. "She's a little young for me, though. Jail bait is what I think they call it." Still, it was hard to get the picture of Hope in that sundress out of my head. I drank in every detail while she was there with me and now could recall each button and hem, as well as the curve of her hips, the outline of her panties through the dress and the way the slit in the skirt parted when she sat and crossed her legs.

I shook my head and bit my lip when my mind wandered to the way the dress had fallen open when she first leaned forward to talk to me as I sat in the wheelchair. I definitely had needs that had to be met.

Back at the house, after a fair amount of pacing, grumbling and talking myself into and out of the next step, I finally picked up the phone and dialed the number I had stashed in my wallet. There was one person in my life who had been absent since my recovery, and I needed to at least hear her voice again.

The line on the other end rang six, seven, eight times. On the ninth ring, as I prepared to hang up, a voice answered.

"Amanda, hey, it's —"

"Jeremiah! I called the rehab center to check on you and they

152

told me you'd been discharged! They said you suddenly got better. That's wonderful. How did you do it?"

"It's kind of a long story. Well, actually, it's not that long, but it's not really much of a story at all. I was just miraculously healed, that's all, kind of the way I've been healing other people all these years."

The conversation from there was pretty mundane, as I relayed the details of moving into a rented house in Lynchburg and trying to regain my health. Amanda told me how the grind of her law practice was wearing her down. She made no mention of Brien.

"Sometimes I think I just want to give it all up and —"

"I'd really like to see you." My right hand was white-knuckling my T-shirt. "Soon."

I heard a sudden intake of breath on the other end of the line.

"I can be there in an hour," she said. "Just tell me how to find you."

I spent the next hour straightening the house and changing the bed sheets. As I stood in the shower, my mind kept replaying those last few words and the subtle way the pitch of her voice had risen. She had almost squealed.

Amanda pulled her Subaru into the driveway precisely one hour and seventeen minutes after we hung up and emerged wearing a black cocktail dress with spaghetti straps and shoes with four-inch heels.

"I brought some oysters. To help you get your strength back," she said. I grabbed her under the armpits just in time to keep her from falling as her ankles buckled on the wobbly shoes she was unaccustomed to wearing. As I did so, the heels of my hands grazed the sides of her breasts, which had been slammed together inside a push-up bra. The effect, on me at least, was electrifying and, shall we say, uplifting.

"It's so good to see you well again." She wrapped her arms around me. The moment we embraced, as our bodies touched, there was no hiding what was on my mind.

"It's not much." I broke away from a hug that was beginning to linger dangerously long. "It's plenty big enough for me. Oh, I see you've met Admiral." I realized the dog had stuck his nose up her skirt.

"It's cozy." She stepped into the living room, which had a couch, one recliner and a 19-inch TV on a microwave cart. "We'll work on getting you some more furniture."

I caught her as her ankles gave way yet again and insisted she step down off the stilts before she seriously injured herself.

"I can't heal you anymore if you bust your butt." I patted her on the aforementioned posterior, something I had never done. "Though it certainly is a nice butt."

I don't know why my hand lingered there, but she made no effort to remove it.

"Maybe I should take these to the kitchen." She indicated the oysters. I reluctantly released my grip.

As she disappeared with the food, I reminded myself she was a married woman now, now I was finally ready to open up for her and let her all the way into my life. I cursed myself for all the years of missed opportunities. The chances to make things right had all been there, too numerous to recall, though at that moment my brain was making a valiant effort to remember every one.

As I paced the living room, I became aware of another presence in the room. She had returned and was sitting on the couch staring at the floor. I started toward the other chair but a small, girlish voice said, "Sit with me."

The couch creaked under me; the instant I sat down my weight created a depression that rolled her toward me.

"I hope to get some more —"

"Tell me how good I look tonight," she said.

"You are more beautiful than all the glimmering reflections on all the quiet ponds on the face of the Earth." I touched her lightly on the shoulder, trying not to notice how her skirt was slowly riding up her thigh. "Your hair is more luxurious than the finest silk; your eyes shine with a love and kindness not seen in all the world today; your breasts..."

I dared not go further.

"Go on. My breasts..."

"...Are right where they should be. They are touched, caressed, fondled, licked, sucked, by another man. They are his domain, not mine." I drew my arm away.

"They are mine, to enjoy with whom I please, and tonight you will touch, caress, fondle, lick and suck them to please me." She took hold of my wrists and placed my hands on her breasts.

"You're married." I seemed to be unable to withdraw my hands.

"To the wrong man. We've endured a lot of wrongs, you and I. It's time to start making things right."

"I can't do that."

"Then take your hands off my breasts."

"I can't do that, either."

"Then you have a choice to make; either take your hands away and I'll leave, or make love to me here and now, on this couch, on the floor, in the bedroom, I don't care, one way or another you will make love to me tonight. We've wasted too many years with the wrong people, with foolish pride and indecision. I intend to make the most of whatever time I have left on this Earth and I intend to make it with you. I don't intend to let a wrong decision stand in the way."

She leaned forward and kissed me as my hands slid down her sides to her thighs and slowly made their way up her skirt. Moving with a will of their own, my fingers slithered over the waistband of her panties and slid them down to her knees. Amanda shucked them from there.

I struggled for the zipper I thought was on the back of the dress as she straddled me on the couch and kissed me long and deep.

"Fuck the zipper." She pulled the dress over the top of her head and flung it away in one swift motion. "No, fuck me."

She repeated that last phrase—or, specifically, the last two words—constantly over the next hour, turning it into a kind of mantra, changing the emphasis on the words from time to time, as we relived that night from college all those years ago, but with even more pent-up gusto now.

I'm not sure how we got there, but we wound up naked on the floor of the kitchen, Amanda reclining in my arms, my face buried in her hair. There was so much to say and it was all so wrong.

"I can hear you back there," she said.

"I didn't say anything."

"I can hear your thoughts. The sound of you overanalyzing everything."

"You said the same thing that night in college."

"You just committed adultery. You violated another man's wife. You stole the fruit of another man's garden."

I tried to release her, but she wouldn't let me.

"Don't you dare ever let go of me again. I'm leaving him, Jeremiah. He was a mistake; that's all there was to it. I just got caught in my own trap."

"I don't understand what you mean."

"Of course you do. I was trying to force you into action. I never planned to go through with marrying Brien, dear sweet man though he is. I thought if you saw time was running out to have me, you'd finally come forward and admit you loved me. I didn't count on you going ballistic in that hospital and having a stroke and winding up in a nursing home. I was crushed; I didn't have the will to break off the engagement, and I was tired of being alone. I wanted a husband and a family, so I went ahead and married him. I figured I would learn to love him, eventually. A safe husband, I thought, was better than no husband."

I stood and wandered in search of my clothes. I found a sweatshirt and sweatpants for Amanda and brought them to her.

"I can't be part of this. I love you and want you more than anything in the world, more than life itself, but I can't be part of some sordid affair, and I can't ask you to leave him for me." My stomach twisted and my heart almost came up my throat at those words.

"You don't have to ask me. I'm leaving him anyway, whether you'll have me or not. It's not fair to him to keep this facade going, and it's not fair to me, either."

"How can you just throw away the last four years like that?"

"Four wasted years. I'd like to forget them almost as much as you would. I don't love him, and I don't think he really loves me. It just became convenient to get married to each other, that's all. If I wanted to be really nasty, I could cite breach of promise in the divorce proceedings. He knew I wanted a family, yet he's all but sterile, and on top of that, he's impotent ninety percent of the time, which he knew all along. So how honest is that?"

"You could always adopt." By this time I was making us some tea.

"I might eventually do that. I want children of my own. It's important to me, as a woman. I've done everything I wanted in my career, and now I want to be a mother. I want to bear my own child and suckle it at my breast. That's not something you could understand."

"I understand I want you so badly I could explode, but I can't have you. I don't know that I could live with myself knowing you left your husband for me. I already feel disgusted with myself for what just happened, no matter how wonderful it was at the moment."

"I'm not just leaving him for you; I'm leaving him for my own sake, and his as well. I would have left him eventually even if you were still in that nursing home, because I never should have married him. Oh, God, don't you see? This is it, our last chance. If we don't take it now, we'll never be together!"

The voices in my head were screaming, shrieking so loudly anyone in the vicinity must have heard them, imploring me to grab her, to kiss her, to fall on my knees and profess my everlasting love.

They never made it to my tongue.

"I can't do it." I turned away. "I can't take another man's wife. What just happened here was wrong, a slipup, the result of putting ourselves in a situation that never should have been allowed to happen."

I heard her slump backward against the wall and slide to the floor, sobbing and gasping for breath. I was crying, too.

I walked into the living room and stood in the darkness, shaking, on the verge of vomiting. Everything I could possibly have wanted in life was there in the kitchen, there for the asking. I had only to say the word and it was mine. All the years of missed opportunities, all the nights of emptiness and longing, all could be erased with a single gesture.

A gesture I could not make, all for some misplaced sense of

nobility and respect for an institution that had already been destroyed, a bond that had already been broken, and a covenant that had already been desecrated.

Amanda walked into the living room behind me, still crying, and found her dress and shoes in the dark. The tears on her face reflected the streetlights from outside as she gave me one last glance. My heart burst as she turned toward the door.

Don't go. Stay. I love you. The words were all there; I just could not voice them.

She pulled the door open. A soft rain pattered outside. All the comings and goings in my life seemed to happen in the rain.

"Jeremiah?"

"I'm here."

"I could be pregnant."

She closed the door behind her and disappeared into the rain.

CHAPTER SIX

Of course I bolted after her, catching her at her car. The sky had now unleashed itself and the rain was rolling across us.

"Are you sure?" The rain washed the tears from my face. "How can you know this soon?"

"I'm ovulating. I know. Just like I knew last time." Her eyes moved from mine to her feet. "Look at me, barefoot and pregnant, don't have sense enough to get in out of the rain. If my mother could see me now."

"You can't drive home in this. Come inside."

Back in the house I found the only two bath towels I had and we both dried off. Fortunately I had a spare robe as well.

"Sounds like you need to fess up," I said.

"Whatever happened to those oysters I brought?"

I retrieved them from the refrigerator. We obviously hadn't needed their other, more-heralded qualities that night.

"We've always been honest with each other, haven't we?" she said, after we had finished eating.

"I know I have."

"I know you have, too. I haven't been entirely honest with you." She looked at me for a reaction. She found none.

"What I never told you about was the miscarriage," she

161

continued.

I sat up a little straighter. This was a new topic indeed.

"You mean you got pregnant when we did it in college?"

"I was ovulating and horny, that's the only reason I would have been prancing around like a stripper, only I didn't realize it at the time. Women get smarter about these things over the years, but at that stage in life we aren't always as aware and careful as we should be. Anyway, it was in the spring so I didn't realize I was pregnant until the school year was over. During the break I didn't call you and tell you because I didn't know what I should do. Having a baby at that point would have ruined any shot at graduating on time, of going to law school. It would have changed the character of our relationship forever. Abortion was an option, I suppose, but I never wanted to be one of those girls, those women, I mean, who have to resort to taking a life because of a careless mistake."

"So you were scared and confused." I was displaying my usual mastery of the obvious.

"More than you'll ever know. I cried all night, every night, after my mother went to bed. There just were no good answers. I'm not an overly religious person, but I prayed a lot then."

"Then you lost it."

"I won't go into details, but the old saying about being careful what you wish for is true. I was relieved and crushed all at the same time."

"So when we went back to school the following year, you made sure our budding romance never bore fruit. Wait, that's not the

162

way I wanted that to come out."

"That's all right, I know what you meant. No, I couldn't take a chance on getting pregnant again, so I kept it platonic."

"So you became a born-again virgin. Why didn't you tell me?"

"I saw no point in it. Honestly, do you feel better knowing it now?"

"I don't know. At least it helps explain why things were different between us that next year. Although there was no real reason it had to stay platonic all these years."

"You've had plenty of chances to make it otherwise." She slid her tongue around her lips with the expertise of a porn star.

"You always said your law career had to come first."

"Yes, but I wanted you to come, too. Just like you did tonight." She straddled my lap and licked my left earlobe.

All I could do at that point was moan.

"Anyway," as she got off my lap and went back to her own chair, "the point is, I know when I'm pregnant. I'm pregnant now. So now Brien has grounds to divorce me. Of course, it's going to be a bit embarrassing for a married lawyer to be caught getting pregnant behind her husband's back, but he couldn't do the job and, frankly, I'm running out of eggs."

"You're awfully nonchalant about all this."

"No, I'm scared as hell. I'm well into the latter stages of my childbearing years, so anything could go wrong, and you can't heal the fetus anymore if something is wrong. Plus, I don't know exactly what all this is going to mean for my career, for us."

163

"I just realized. Judge Remington is going to be retiring before long, and you're one of the leading candidates to be her successor."

"Where did you hear that?"

"Sid told me. It's true, isn't it? You are one of the top candidates, aren't you?"

"I was. An out-of-wedlock pregnancy resulting from an extramarital affair will pretty much wreck any chance of being chosen now. Judges are supposed to be upstanding citizens, examples of high moral character and all that. Now I'm just a cheap floozie who couldn't keep her skirt from flying up."

"You're taking this awfully lightly."

"I love the law and I've wanted to be a judge since I was a little girl, but it isn't going to happen now. It can't happen. That's all there is to it. I still have my career, I'm going to have a baby, and most of all, I finally have you. I do have you, don't I?"

I didn't know what to say, except, "You're still a married woman."

"I know, and in Virginia it still takes forever to get a divorce, even a no-fault, no frills one. I have to go out of state if I want to speed this thing up. It's much quicker in Tennessee, that's pretty close."

"You're moving to Tennessee?"

"I have to. I want this baby to have his father's last name, and I want there to be no doubt about that."

"This is nuts. You can't just go running away to Tennessee!

What about your clients?"

"Let me worry about that. I'll take a leave of absence. Maria and Carlton will have to shoulder the extra caseload. I have to establish a minimum residency. It'll probably be about ninety days, and I'll file for divorce from Brien."

"So we finally get each other, we finally commit to a relationship, and boom! Just like that you're leaving?"

"That's the way it has to be if we want to do this thing right." She climbed back into my lap and put her arms around me. "Hey, come on, some things are worth waiting for. We've waited all these years to get to this point, what's a few more months?"

She glanced around the kitchen. "We're definitely not living in this dump."

CHAPTER SEVEN

Our lives finally began falling into place over the next few weeks, in spite of Amanda's absences while she temporarily moved to Tennessee. We pooled enough of our resources to go screaming into debt to reestablish my bookstore, opting this time for Bedford, since it was almost centrally located between Lynchburg and Roanoke. Fortunately my old supplier was still in business and gave us some pretty deep discounts on inventory.

Another concern of parents who create a blended household is whether the existing children from the two worlds will adapt to each other. Fortunately, Admiral and Tam-Tam, Amanda's orange tabby, agreed to a standoff, each pretending the other didn't exist. Tam-Tam learned very quickly not to sleep on Admiral's bed, and he, in turn, stopped chasing her up trees after the first week. He spent most of the time down at the bookstore with us anyway, where Amanda helped out on weekends.

"This is just the sort of store this town needed." Mrs. Creasy, a Daughter of the American Revolution, was one of our first customers and chatted up business for us all around town. "The people in that mall bookstore don't really enjoy books the way you all do. I also don't like the feel; this is very homey, especially the big comfy chairs and the little reading lamps."

"Well, my wife wouldn't allow me to keep any of my furniture, so I had to find a suitable home for it." I still enjoyed the way the words "my wife" rolled off my tongue, even though we weren't yet married.

"How long have the two of you been married?" Mrs. Creasy glanced at Amanda's tummy. Though she had not yet begun to show, she had already started wearing maternity tops.

"Two-and-a-half months." Amanda handed her a cappuccino. "We got pregnant right away."

"Well, it happens that way sometimes." Mrs. Creasy took her cappuccino with her out the front door.

"That woman would like nothing more than to jump up and declare us fornicators," Amanda said.

"Well, we have to be nice to our only customer. Otherwise you'll never be able to quit your day job."

That threw a blanket over her mood. We were running seriously low on cash, what with her maintaining a small apartment in Tennessee, the start-up costs of the bookstore and the fact her high-income lawyer job was on hold.

"You could call the foundation and start working with them again. It's not a lot, but it would help."

"I know; it's just I've managed to lay low for over six months now and I'm getting the hang of it. Besides, without the healing powers, I don't know what I could do for them anyway."

"You could always start writing again. You've had so many experiences you could write a memoir," she said.

167

"I'm not really into first-person writing. For your information, I am writing. I never really stopped."

"I mean real writing, not the Biff Granite crap, you don't even carry it in your own bookstore. Oh, don't get all defensive, you know what I mean. You're better than that. You have a gift. Your first book was brilliant; you could have been one of the preeminent voices of your generation, but you settled for that formulaic hack stuff because you were scared of success. You were afraid of becoming a one-hit wonder, so you took yourself out of the game, blamed that God-awful TV movie for wrecking your career because it was a cop-out, an easy excuse. It's always easier to look back years down the road and say, 'I could have been one of the great ones if not for so-and-so,' than it is to actually be one of the great ones."

All I could do was stand and stare. Nothing cut quite so deeply as the truth.

"Look, I'm sorry, it's the hormones talking —"

"No it's not. You really do feel that way, don't you?"

"You could have truly been one of the great ones. It's still not too late, you know."

I returned to rearranging the display in the front window, studying how best to keep the Harry Potter and Stephen King books from overshadowing the W.P. Kinsella collection we were spotlighting. I hardly noticed the old man looking through some of the books in the metaphysics/New Age section.

"Can I help you, sir?" I said.

"Oh, I'm just an old man, wandering around."

"Nothing wrong with that. Let me know if you need anything."

"Now that you mention it, my shoulder hurts something fierce." He rotated his right arm around.

"I'm afraid I can't help you there."

"You can't? I thought you could fix things like that." He froze me with a look of recognition.

"I used to be able to do things like that. Not anymore." I was trying not to delve too deeply into this thread of conversation.

"Why not? What happened?"

"Sir, that's a bit personal. If you must know, I messed it all up. I had the power, and I misused it and had to pay dearly for it. The whole thing was a mistake anyway."

"Why do you say that?"

"Because I was never supposed to have that sort of power in the first place, that's why. Now if you have a question concerning a book, I might be able to help you. Otherwise, I have things to do."

"Oh, there was no mistake. These things aren't passed along lightly. You were the right person at the right time."

"How would you know that?"

"How does anyone know anything? You're probably right, and I'm just an old man who must be going. Sorry I troubled you. My shoulder is much better, though."

With that he bowed his head and walked back out the door.

"Silly old coot."

"Who's a silly old coot?" Amanda said.

"Oh, that old man who just left."

"What old man?"

"The guy I was arguing with in front of the store; he said my having the healing power was no mistake. What does he know about it?"

"I didn't hear you arguing with anybody."

Amanda went back to doing inventory at the back of the store, and I started arranging books in the front window. I remember seeing the white sedan as it went careening through the stop light near the front of the store. I even remember thinking, "He's going to hit those people."

I've often heard people say that sudden, catastrophic events seem to happen very slowly in front of them, as if they were somehow removed from the time stream. Not only do I remember having time to realize the car was going to hit the group of school children crossing the street, I even remember the horror on their faces as they, too, knew it, yet stood frozen in place. For the tiniest moment of time imaginable, I felt like I could actually run out there and grab them before the impact.

I will hear the screech of tires in my dreams as long as I live, the shrieks cut short, the dull thud of the blow.

"For God's sake, Jeremiah, run out there and help them!"

It took a Herculean effort to pry the stubborn door open, swollen as it was from the humidity. A crowd had already gathered around the car, now sitting skewed in the middle of Main Street. People were screaming from both sides of the street, and in the chaos it was hard to find where the victims had landed.

One girl of about twelve was sprawled over the hood of the car, her head sticking through the bloody, spider-webbed windshield, already dead.

Now how did I know that? I instinctively knew the answer. Suddenly it seemed as though the past four years had never happened; I knew exactly what to do.

I managed to get to four children lying around in various positions on the pavement, arms and legs bent and twisted in ungodly formations. Despite being unable to heal anything more severe than a boo-boo for better than four years, I found myself running to each child and pouring out the healing power. I watched as one by one they came around at the moment I touched them, each one breaking out into a wail of sobs at the sight of a classmate on the hood of the car.

"Get the girl on the car! Save her!" a woman shouted.

I ran instead to check on the driver, slumped forward on the steering wheel in a diabetic coma.

"Never mind him! Save the girl!" the shouts were coming from all along the sidewalks.

The driver woke with a start at my touch, saw what he had done and passed out again.

"The girl! Save the girl!"

The girl, I knew, was beyond even my help. I was startled, however, as her body jolted and shivered at my touch, as if I were running powerful electric currents through it. Perhaps the tiniest spark of life remained, but it was too faint to reach, even with my suddenly replenished abilities.

"Help her!"

"It's too late!" I shouted back. "She's gone!"

"You let her die! You could have saved her while you were helping that murderer. You should have done her first!" A rather obese woman, maybe five feet tall, waddled off the sidewalk to confront me. "I recognize you from when you were on the news before!"

"She was already gone." Obviously, I wasn't convincing the woman at all. "I couldn't do anything for her."

The whoop of an ambulance interrupted us and I saw flashing lights everywhere.

"Officer, this is the man who used to heal people, and he let that girl die," the woman said to a town policeman who came up to us. Two members of the emergency medical services team, meanwhile, put a sheet over the dead girl and laid her onto a stretcher. Other EMS personnel shined flashlights into the other four children's eyes and checked for injury. On the sidewalk I saw more than two dozen other children crying and hugging each other.

"Sir, I'd like to get a statement from you, if you'll step over here with me." Officer B. Shelton applied a gentle push to my elbow.

"I couldn't help the girl, officer. I tried. She was too far gone."

"I'm sure she was. I'm not accusing you of anything. Were you a witness to the accident?"

I recounted seeing the car lurch through the intersection into the crosswalk, filled with children whom I later learned were on a field trip. The clicking of camera shutters as the officer questioned me indicated my anonymity was blown.

Three television cameras, one from each local news station in the Roanoke-Lynchburg market, glared at me as I finished with Officer Shelton. The newspaper photographers crouched and snapped in that unique, duck-walking style they all seemed to master.

The questions, as always, seemed to fling themselves at me.

"Are you Jeremiah Townsend, the Miracle Man who mysteriously disappeared a few years ago?"

"When did you get out of the nursing home?"

"Was it a deliberate decision to try to help the girl on the hood last?"

"How does it feel to not be able to help the dead girl?"

That was the one I always hated. The old "how-does-it-feel" query is the most thoughtless, useless, and downright inappropriate of all the questions reporters ask. It's a lazy question used by reporters who can't—or who don't bother—to come up with something more intelligent. It's almost always asked when the answer is as obvious as a smack in the head.

"How do you think it feels?" I gave the answer given 99 times out of a hundred when the question was vomited.

The crush of people trying to get a look at me quickly washed the reporters somewhere downstream. Someone shoved a pad and pencil in my hand and asked for an autograph. People stuck their arms out to touch me.

"I've got cancer."

"My little girl has cerebral palsy."

"Can you make it rain?"

Like I told Amanda earlier: People always seem to have a way of finding me.

CHAPTER EIGHT

Amanda and I had to lock the doors to the bookstore to keep the crowds of people wanting to be healed of various ailments, both large and small, from overwhelming us in such a small space and possibly walking away with some, or all, of our inventory.

"We had two hundred forty-two dollars and seventy-eight cents in sales today before the accident. We were on our way to a pretty good day." She rang up the "No Sale" button on the antique mechanical cash register we had restored. "If all these people wanted in to buy books," she indicated the faces pressed up against the windows, beating on the glass, "We'd have to close tomorrow anyway just to restock."

I fidgeted with an unopened box of books, pretending not to notice the riot that was forming on the sidewalk. I knew the people in front of the mob could see me.

"You could duck out the back door, into the alley." Amanda noticed the look on my face. "It's not easy ignoring them, is it?"

"I have no business ignoring them. I should be out there with them, helping them."

"They'd tear you apart. This isn't like the old days back in Pennington, where you were just a local curiosity. You've become a worldwide phenomenon, a legendary messenger of God. Now you're

175

back from exile in that rehab center, it's almost like you're back from the dead. Some people think you're the Second Coming—"

"Which I'm not..."

"Others think you're the Antichrist."

"Quite a few think I'm a fraud."

"Most think you're simply a gift from God, a sign everything's going to be all right. Don't forget that. No matter how many loonies there are out there that want to tie you to some end-time theology, the vast majority think of you as a blessing, a benevolent soul assigned to help those you can. Still, I think you should slip out the back door."

"Where would I go? There are probably reporters already at the house."

The beating on the glass ceased as the mob became preoccupied with something else. We saw people in the crowd turn to face soldiers in riot gear who forced them away from the windows.

"Oh great. They've called in the National Guard. You'd better go talk to them," Amanda said.

My heart sank as I saw the crowd scuffling with the soldiers. A sergeant was demanding I open the door for him, so I complied.

"Mr. Townsend, do you need protection, sir?" said Staff Sgt. J. Lowry.

"My wife and I just need a passage to get to our car safely."

"We'll provide it. Come with me now, sir."

For the first time in my life I walked the streets of a U.S. city, in this case a small town of 7,000 people, under armed guard, clutching Amanda's arm. Guardsmen forced the mob away from Amanda's Subaru. The crowd was booing us. It must have looked like we were abandoning them. In a way, I suppose, we were.

We drove home and pulled the car straight into the garage, closing the automatic door behind us before we were even out of the car. No one was at the house waiting for us, but we wanted to take no chances.

"I'm glad we went to the grocery store last night," Amanda said.

The garage was attached to the side of a small brick ranch we bought in Bedford County, just outside the city limits. We entered the kitchen through a glassed-in breezeway between the house and the garage.

"The answering machine is lit up," Amanda said.

"I thought we were supposed to have an unpublished number."

The messages were mostly from the foundation, trying to get me to come back, wanting to know why I never told anyone I was out of the rehab center. A few were from my sister, who had seen something about the morning's events on the crawl at the bottom of the television screen on CNN. The word was definitely out about me.

"Why don't you go back to the foundation? At least there you were shielded from the public and they gave you room and board and a small stipend."

"I don't want to be a lab rat anymore. My dream is a normal life, with you and our child, working in the bookstore. These past six months have been the happiest of my adult life, just living life as an ordinary citizen. I want to kiss my wife and go to work in the morning, then come home and make love to her at night."

"I suppose you want me to make cookies and have supper on the table?"

"If it's not too much trouble."

She hugged me as best she could before wincing.

"Jeez my titties are sore." She gave her breasts a little boost with her hands.

"I could probably fix that, since I seem to be back in business again."

"No, that's all right. Don't waste it on a little thing like sore boobs. How did you suddenly regain your powers?"

"It's the old man. It had to be. I first got these powers after he visited us that summer, and I got them back today after he popped into the bookstore. I didn't recognize him from before because I could never really remember what he looked like, but it had to be him."

"You mean the old man neither your brother nor your sister remember," she said.

"He was there, I'm telling you. Mama, grandmamma, whoever she was, and I both remembered him."

"Of course, I couldn't see or hear him, either. Sounds a bit dubious to me, but something obviously gave you this power. So who is he, and how come no one else can see him? How could it be the same man all these years later if he was as old as you say he was

178

when you were a child? He'd be long dead by now."

"I wish I knew, but if I ever see him again, I'm going to shoot him on sight. Who is he to mess up my life like this?"

"You mean who is he to go around playing God?"

"I didn't say that, but why not? People have accused me of doing just that, and it's all because of him. I'm sick of him thrusting this responsibility at me. I should have been suspicious this morning when he made that statement about how my being chosen was not a mistake."

I looked out the window. We hadn't been followed. We hadn't lived in the house long, so our whereabouts weren't common knowledge yet.

The look I saw on Amanda's face made my heart stop. "Are you all right?"

"I just had a thought, oh God, it makes my skin creep. Why did the old man pick today, right before the accident, to give you your powers back? Did he somehow know what was going to happen? Or did he cause the accident to happen, just so you would be forced to go public again? Dear God, Jeremiah, who is he?"

"He's no friend of mine, that's for sure. Now that I've been outed again, we're never going to have any peace. The bookstore is a bust."

"You have to go back to the foundation. We're still together; I'm still going to be your wife. I'm still going to have your baby. We'll have lots more, if we want. That won't change."

"What are you going to do? I can't leave you to face the

mobs."

"I can go back to my apartment in Tennessee. I'll stay out of trouble."

She turned in my arms and leaned against me. My hands found their automatic resting place on her breasts.

"Ouch! Careful, those are—wait a minute, that feels a lot better. Oh, yeah, the soreness is gone. In fact, that feels really, really good. Ooh, that feels so good you're going to have to do something about it."

She led me gently into the bedroom.

She had been right about one thing. These weren't the old days anymore. They were, in fact, much better than the old days.

Now, at least, I had someone else to draw strength from.

CHAPTER NINE

We got up early the next morning and drove to Amanda's house in Roanoke where we could be assured some degree of anonymity. That evening on television we saw live remote broadcasts from our front yard in Bedford, where reporters had set up tents and were camping out for the night.

"As you can see, the house behind me is dark and it appears that no one is home." The male reporter, in his late twenties, was dressed as though he was leaving to hike the Appalachian Trail in a few minutes. "We've knocked on the door a number of times and no one has answered, but we're staying put to bring you any new developments."

We couldn't help but chuckle in spite of the fact this man was trespassing on our property. As much as I sometimes despised reporters, particularly TV reporters, I felt a twinge of pity for those poor souls wasting their time and embarrassing themselves in front of an audience for a non-story.

The phone rang. It was Sid.

"Jeremiah, why don't you tell anyone when you get home? It took me a while to find this number."

"If you'll turn on your TV, you'll see exactly why I didn't want anybody to know I was back," I said.

"I didn't mean you had to call a press conference, just call a few old friends to let them know how you are."

"How many times did *you* visit me in the rehab center?"

"Hey, I tried to talk you out of going to that hospital in South Carolina and walking in like John Wayne, all swagger and bravado, in the first place. I even refused to drive you there. If you'd listened to me, you never would have wound up in that nursing home."

"I guess you're right about that."

"Damn right I'm right. Listen, I didn't call to start an argument. I just wanted to let you know Judge Remington's office has informed me your case is still considered active and this little stunt with the kids in the car wreck is in violation of her order, which still stands."

"It wasn't a stunt. At least two of those kids would have died if I hadn't gotten to them as quickly as I did. One of them was dead before I got there. The judge's order did specifically allow me to intervene to save someone's life. That's really not the point here. Her order is wrong; morally, categorically, rhetorically, however you want to put it, it's just wrong. I can't obey it."

"Then I can't stop the case from moving forward again if the plaintiffs wish to pursue it."

"If they don't pursue it then her order becomes pointless, doesn't it? I mean, the order was only in effect as long as the trial was moving forward, wasn't it?"

"I suppose so. To tell you the truth, I don't know if the plaintiffs will want to start it all up again or not after four-plus years.

I'll talk to the judge to see if I can get the order rescinded, at least until we can determine if there is going to be a trial. Otherwise, you're just on indefinite hold."

"Attaboy, Sid."

"By the way, what's up with Amanda? The last time I tried to call her office they told me she was on a leave of absence."

"She's taken up temporary residence in Tennessee so she can get her divorce. She said it takes too long in Virginia."

"She's a billion percent right about that. It's taken me the better part of three years and I'm still waiting. *I'm* a lawyer."

"Wait a minute, when did you get married?"

"Oh, you remember Tanasha, don't you?"

"Tanasha? Good God, Sid, after what she did to me? Is there nothing to which you will not stoop?"

"Well, she was quite a looker."

"Quite a hooker is more like it. I can't believe you're sleeping with the enemy."

"Well, not since Tomoko came into the picture I'm not."

"My God, Sid, Tomoko, too? Even my sleazy brother didn't do them *both*."

"Actually, he did. They were quite fond of him, to the point they even agreed to a threesome. Tanasha wasn't willing to share me, however. Now they're not speaking to each other."

I had to hang up at that point. I began to wonder if maybe I hadn't been adopted and Sid and Isaac were the real brothers.

"Any good news?" Amanda said after I hung up.

I started to tell her about Benedict Sid but saw no real use in it.

"Judge Remington knows about what happened today, but I reminded Sid she did say I could use my power to save someone's life."

"Well today's events certainly fell into that category. You saved four lives. The fact one girl actually died proves the severity of the situation."

"Yeah, but now the word's out about me again, there'll be more requests to heal people of routine, non-life threatening types of things. Then I'm back in the same boat of either refusing their requests, thus misusing the power, or defying a court order."

"Maybe she'll reconsider. I could prepare an appeal..."

"No, that's Sid's job. I don't want to put your career in the spotlight here or you could be ruined. I've done enough damage in that area already."

Amanda sighed and dropped to the couch. A few random gray hairs around her temples glowed in the waning light of the sun and the crow's-feet around her eyes seemed to take on more prominence. She rested her hands on her belly.

"They're never going to let us have any peace, are they?" She didn't look up.

"I'm sorry. This is the life I lead. I should never have brought you into it."

Her stare almost knocked me off my feet: "Don't ever let me hear you say that again. This child growing in my abdomen exists only because you brought me further into your life. *We* are not a mistake and *we* are not the problem here. The problem is with a world that doesn't know how to treat a gift from God when it comes to them."

"Please don't start with the messianic imagery again."

"You'd be better off rejoining the foundation, at least for a while. They can treat you fairly and objectively. As long as we try to go it alone, we'll keep fighting the same battles."

I didn't sleep well that night. Several times I awoke and had to sit up in bed and take deep breaths.

"The Africa dream again?" Amanda began rubbing my neck.

"Yeah. I've been having it more and more frequently of late."

The following morning Amanda drove me back to Lynchburg to foundation headquarters, a nondescript two-story gray building that refused to stand out among a series of equally bland structures. The building bore no sign nor any indication of what it actually was. We parked in the back parking lot. I kissed Amanda before getting out of the car, not knowing when I would see her again, then walked across the parking lot to a metal door that blended so well with the building's design it was practically invisible. I couldn't believe my old door code still worked.

"Jeremiah! The Prodigal Son returns home!"

"Dr. Wheatley, it's good to see you." I braced my hand for his renowned bone-crushing handshake. "Looks like nothing much has changed."

"I wouldn't be too sure of that. In spite of the bad economy,

185

we've picked up beau coups of new equipment thanks to some grants that were never before available to us. We're doing some groundbreaking work on electromagnetic fields and their effects on human health. We were the first to categorically, beyond a shadow of a doubt, prove that cell phones and electric shavers are absolutely safe to use."

He guided me into a room with a large rotating metal ball in the center and banks of computers all around. Each computer had a graph of sine (or cosine, I wasn't really sure) waves on the screen. A low hum seemed to emanate from the walls themselves.

"The equipment in this room alone cost more than the entire annual economic output of most Third World countries," he said.

"That's wonderful, but I don't see very many people. Don't tell me you had to lay everybody off to afford this stuff."

He laughed and slapped my shoulder: "Heavens no. We've expanded so much we had to open a new research facility over on Candler's Mountain. This is only one quarter of the people who work with us now."

We updated each other on what had happened over the past four years.

"I still wish you'd come to us instead of going to that glorified chiropractor's office. We might have been able to do more for you than park you in a wheelchair and wait for a miracle."

"The miracle did come. The girl might not have been able to find me if you'd taken me in."

"That's true. We are pretty low profile. Still, we're glad to have you back. I'm willing to double your previous stipend if you're prepared to go to work with us again. I already have your first assignment, if you're willing to accept it."

"Is the tape going to self-destruct?"

Dr. Wheatley chortled that goofy, honking laugh of his, and I felt like I was home at last.

"I'm relieved but a little surprised you want to send me back out into the field so soon. I figured you'd want to plug me into some new imaging machine to see what makes me tick."

"No, I realized long ago your gifts are beyond the capability of contemporary science to understand. In fact I doubt we'd ever be able to quantify the forces at work here, even if you were still around a thousand years from now."

"Well, I don't plan on going anywhere."

This time he blew coffee out his nose. I'd forgotten how easy it was to make this man laugh.

"So what's this assignment you have for me?"

"I want to send you to Africa where a plague of unknown origin is threatening to wipe out a small village. You'll be accompanied by a team from the World Health Organization and the CDC, as well as some of our own people. So far the plague has resisted all attempts to—Jeremiah, what's wrong? You look like you've seen a ghost."

CHAPTER TEN

I didn't bother telling Dr. Wheatley about the dream I'd been having for years now, though of all the legitimate scientists in the world, he would probably be the most likely to accept the possibility of clairvoyance.

I focused instead on preparing for the mission: attending briefings, learning what I could of the language and customs of the natives we'd encounter and getting my inoculations.

The World Health Organization sent a team to present a slide show of conditions in the village. As we sat in the boardroom, we saw image after image of bodies in the streets. The pathogen, they said, appeared to be airborne, highly contagious and always led to an extremely high fever before death.

It was also, to date, 100 percent fatal.

"What about the blood work?" Dr. Wheatley asked Carl, the WHO man conducting the presentation.

"Inconclusive. The only thing we know at this point is the pathogen does die with its host, so there's little risk of infection from the bodies. Carl rubbed his glasses on a handkerchief at least every two minutes. "The fevers are beyond anything we've ever seen. It's almost as if the body is trying to burn the pathogen out. Unfortunately, the fever always claims the victim before eradicating it."

"Is this a naturally occurring pathogen or is it manmade?" I said.

"We don't know for sure but there is certainly always the possibility it could be artificial in origin. You're the healer, aren't you, the one they call the Miracle Man?"

"Jeremiah is an important and trusted member of our organization, and he may be the only hope these people have," Dr. Wheatley said.

"Well, this is one crisis that should put him to the test, if he's really as good as they say," Carl said.

After Carl sat down, a woman with a French- or Belgian-sounding accent named Renee went through an exhaustive analysis of the village's water supply. At the end of an hour and fifteen minutes, she concluded that while the small creek which ran through the village did test positive for giardia, there was nothing there to cause the illness which was threatening to exterminate the village.

"I think we need to get going." That drew angry looks from the presenters who had yet to take their turn at the podium. "While there's someone still alive."

We took a 20 minute recess. Dr. Wheatley put his arm around my shoulders and took me off to the side.

"Jeremiah, you're awfully anxious and not usually this blunt. Is there something we need to know about?"

"It's nothing I can explain quantitatively, as you might say, but I've got a bad feeling about this mission. I'm afraid we're already too late, but I'd like to get going as soon as possible, now if not sooner."

"There's still some red tape to be worked out, but we've got people in the State Department doing their best to clear the way for us. I know you mean well; you've always had the best of intentions for everyone, but there are channels we have to go through. We aren't some vigilante rescue organization that can just storm the village out of helicopters."

"Then I'm going to go take a nap. I can't sit through any more of these briefings when I know people are dying."

The building had several tiny rooms not much larger than library carrels set aside with cots for exactly that purpose. I found the one farthest from the briefing room, turned on the white noise machine and dozed off. I figured perhaps if I had the Africa dream again, I might learn something.

Dr. Wheatley must have found a way to get the so-called red tape cleared up because within a few days we were boarding a charter plane at Lynchburg Regional Airport, ready to set out on the first leg of our journey. I had just enough time to hug Amanda, who came racing in from Tennessee to meet us on the tarmac.

"Seems like all of a sudden all we do is say good-bye," I said.

"Yes, but you've got your sense of purpose back. I see it in your eyes."

"That's silly. I've been happier in the four months we've been together than ever in my life."

"Contentment and drive are two totally different things, my

190

love. It's one thing to be full, quite another to have a fire in your belly."

"Whatever that means."

"You'll figure it out soon enough."

The flight from Lynchburg to Dulles was little more than a hop. At Dulles we boarded another charter and lifted off on the long voyage across the Atlantic.

Though I was initially afraid to fall asleep, the droning of the engines gradually lulled me away. I dreamed not of Africa but of mundane vignettes with those from my past: sharing ice cream with Monique, hiding a friend's jock strap in the football locker room during high school, taking a dump in the only toilet in town, which happened to be under a willow tree in the middle of the town square with everyone watching. Nonsensical as they were, these unlikely scenarios were oddly reassuring, as if telling me nothing was ever really what it seemed.

"We're getting ready to land in Cameroon," a man's voice said, though it seemed to come to me from the mouth of a cow.

"What?" I opened my eyes and looked around. There was no talking cow to be seen.

"We have to land in Cameroon." Carl, the man from the slide show, was now sitting beside me wiping his glasses. "We've been denied permission to fly through Mimbutu airspace. We're going to have to drive across the border. There's no airfield within two hundred miles of the village we're going to, anyway."

I groaned. My neck had been twisted backward for far too

many hours and my entire body was numb. Memories of my stay in the rehab center washed across me in waves of fear, but I soon realized I still had movement and feeling. I was also soaking wet.

"The air-conditioning isn't working so well in this plane." I now noticed Carl was dripping sweat from his nose. "Boy, you were really out of it there."

"I could have sworn a cow told me we were landing in Cameroon."

"Well, I am a little overweight, but —"

Our bodies lurched forward without warning and thumped against the seats in front of us. Everything that wasn't secured in some way went skittering down the aisle as the nose of the plane lunged downward in a zero-G descent I don't want to experience again.

"What the hell is—"

"Jeremiah, the pilot's having a heart attack! You've got to help him or we're all dead!" Dr. Wheatley practically crawled over the seats to get back to where I was.

"What do you mean—oh, never mind!" I climbed over Carl and staggered down the aisle, holding onto the backs of the seats to keep from flying into the cockpit door.

The ground was spinning up toward us while the pilot, who was unconscious but alive, slumped against the yoke. There was no copilot. With one hand against the instrument panel to steady myself, I put my other hand over the man's chest and concentrated on reviving him. He stirred slowly, smacking his lips, the stupor not fully

192

dissipated.

"You've got to wake up and pull us out of this dive!" I screamed and slapped him awake.

"Ff-uuu-ck!" He grabbed the yoke and pushed forward. "Grab the other yoke and push it forward!"

I clambered into the copilot's seat and seized the u-shaped control, then leaned it forward, praying the hydraulics were working. In a matter of moments, our flight path was again parallel with the ground, though we were only a few hundred feet up.

"You can relax a bit now." His voice was strained and wispy.

I loosened the death grip I had on the yoke. My hands still trembled.

"Are we still landing in Cameroon?"

"I have no idea where we are just yet. It'll take me awhile to get my bearings."

I pulled myself up onto shaking legs and made my way back toward my seat. Applause and whistles greeted me as I stepped out of the cockpit.

An announcement sounded over the intercom: "This is the pilot speaking, and I'm feeling a lot better now, as I'm sure most of the rest of you are, too. Folks, you've all just been part of a miracle, and we have our own resident Miracle Man to thank. We missed our target in Cameroon, unfortunately, so we'll be landing at the first friendly airport we can find."

Carl squinted at me with a newfound sense of respect as he rubbed his glasses on his shirt. "I guess you're the real thing, after

193

all."

"This definitely wasn't in the job description," I said.

The rest of the flight was uneventful, right down to landing at a tiny airfield in some isolated locale that wasn't on any of our maps. The problem at this point became one of ground transport and the fact there was none to be found.

We took turns visiting the bushes behind the all-purpose wooden shack that served as control tower and administrative office whenever there was anyone present to work the airfield. In its present state it appeared as though no one had manned this facility for several years.

Though we were all sick of being aboard, the plane itself offered the only relief from the heat and mosquitoes. Eventually everyone climbed back in and sat, staring morosely.

"Well, the good news is I've located some transportation." The pilot popped back into the cabin. "At least one Land Rover and some other vehicles are on the way. Also, according to the global positioning units, it seems we ended up landing much closer to the village than originally planned, so the drive there won't take nearly as long from here."

"What's the bad news?" Carl said.

"The airport seems to be closed for business today."

CHAPTER ELEVEN

A few of the team members managed to get the door to the airfield shack open, but it was so hot in there no one could stand to be inside for more than three or four minutes at a time. It also reeked with a stale, baked-in stench of urine that had been left to fry for however many years since the place was last used.

Whomever sealed the place up removed any equipment that might be usable, leaving a wooden counter with a cutout where the radio once sat. A few stained maps of the surrounding area still hung on the ramshackle walls, only to be appropriated by our pilot, who carried them back to the plane for study.

"It really, really, really stinks in here." Renee began giving a detailed rundown of exactly what all kinds of disease-causing agents probably thrived inside the shack, concluding with, "If we had a bulldozer here, our best bet would be to just knock it down and burn everything."

After a great deal of wandering throughout the general vicinity, the consensus among the group was this was the most remote airfield anyone had ever encountered. More than one person pronounced the pilot's ability to raise anyone at all on the radio as nothing short of a miracle. Eventually we surrendered to the heat and climbed back aboard the plane, where the climate control system was functioning.

The miracle of the Global Positioning Satellite system, however, meant when the pilot finally did find someone on the radio who spoke a language he spoke, he could relay our exact coordinates to within a few feet of our actual location. Just a few years earlier, this would not have been possible and we might have had to resort to using the stars. With a number of handheld GPS units among the members of our team, however, we could accurately determine the location of each person within the body of the plane itself. I'm not sure how this would ever come in handy outside of a scavenger hunt or hide-and-seek, but it was nice to know it was possible.

"So is the plane actually flyable?" I heard someone a few rows ahead of me ask.

"I think I heard him say we were low on fuel," someone in another row answered. "We apparently used up a lot of fuel pulling out of that nosedive we were in. Besides, where would we go? Other airfields are probably just as remote as this one."

Waiting can be interminable in and of itself, particularly when you have no idea when the party you are waiting for will arrive. Throw in the heat, frustration and overall sense of helplessness you feel in such tight, uncomfortable conditions and you have the potential for tempers to ignite. Fortunately, the members of the team seemed to take everything about as well as could be expected. This was, after all, a humanitarian mission, above all else, and the people aboard the plane were there to save lives if at all possible, not make themselves comfortable.

I wish I could say I took our situation as well as the others. Instead, I became more anxious by the minute, knowing somehow time was getting away from us. Most of the incidents up to this point, even our near crash and the emergency landing, gave me a sense of hope things would not turn out as they had in my dream since none of those things happened in the dream. Now, as the minutes crawled forward, my heart hung in my chest, knowing what we would find.

CHAPTER TWELVE

By the time vehicles arrived from the closest possible village, we had spent some thirty-six hours either aboard the plane or wandering within a two-mile radius. The pilot found a spring less than two miles away. Renee tested the water and determined it was potable, though I noticed she drank only water we had brought with us.

Potable or not, it was just dandy for bathing, something we all sorely needed by the time relief arrived in the form of the promised Land Rovers, four in all, driven by UNICEF workers.

The pilot, an ex-Air Force captain named Scott Robertson, took charge of our group as long as we were in and around his plane. He determined just which parties went in what direction and what time they had to be back, thus eliminating the need to send people out looking for someone else who hadn't gotten back yet. The day and a half passed without major incident, though I don't think that would have been the case had we been there another four or five hours.

A tall, thin African man named Martin N'Tende got out of the first Land Rover and shook hands with Capt. Robertson.

"Another truck with fuel and parts is on the way." He spoke with a very formal, very British-sounding dialect. "They are perhaps two hours behind us. They must drive slowly over this terrain."

"Captain, you're welcome to come with us if you don't want to wait here," Dr. Wheatley said. "I hate the thought of you having to remain here any longer than necessary."

"Thanks, Doc, but I will stay with my plane, if it is all the same to you. She is the only plane I have, and I do not want to leave her alone with these 'mechanics' on the way. I would like to still have an engine when we get back."

We all thanked Capt. Robertson—again—for pulling off the incredible landing he made and loaded our gear into the waiting vehicles. Our equipment, which included biohazard suits and medical supplies, competed for space with large cans of spare fuel in each vehicle. Apparently gas stations were spaced a good ways apart out here.

I climbed into the backseat of one of the vehicles with Renee, Carl and Dr. Wheatley. Other team members hung off the sides of the four trucks, but no one complained. No matter how heavily laden with people, equipment and gas the vehicles were, we were at least moving, moving somewhere away from the airfield and the plane.

That somewhere proved to be a meandering road, not much more than a ditch, that at times was indistinguishable from the rest of the terrain. We lurched our way through mile after mile of arid climate surrounded by weeds, weeds and more weeds.

"Not many villages on our route, eh?" Dr. Wheatley tried to make himself heard above the sound of the engine and ceaseless creaking of the vehicle's aging suspension system.

"What?" The driver was not a native English speaker.

"I said, not many villages along the way, are there?"

"Once there were many," the driver said. "Now very few. The water dry up, the animals die, the plants die, the people move on."

"It's a shame, really." Dr. Wheatley now confined his conversation to the backseat, where he could be more easily heard. "Jeremiah here could probably do a world of good for the starving and diseased people of this region, if we come across any."

I shook my head: "Dehydration and starvation are long-term conditions that can't be waved away. I could probably temporarily help someone dying of starvation or thirst, but without adequate food and water, that person would soon go back to dying a slow death. I can't make people immortal."

"You're right, of course. Sometimes I let my optimism get the better of me. Hello, we seem to be stopping."

Our little convoy, of which we were the third vehicle back, had halted at some sort of checkpoint with a tiny white booth just big enough for two people and a large orange and white gate not unlike those you normally see at toll roads. Two soldiers in white uniforms walked around inspecting the first Land Rover. Then, with a minimum of fuss, they raised the gate and let the first two vehicles go through before lowering it again in front of our car.

"Some sort of security checkpoint?" said Carl.

"I think we're passing into another country," said Renee.

One guard and our driver exchanged what sounded like angry

words in a language I did not understand. Then the guard opened the door and pulled the driver out by the collar while the other guard motioned the rest of us out of the vehicle.

The two men didn't carry rifles but both wore sidearms. Between the two remaining vehicles, we had enough people to easily overpower them, but I recalled Dr. Wheatley's words about us not being a vigilante rescue team.

The driver gesticulated wildly and spat on the ground in front of the guard several times, then showed him some papers. The guard went back to the little booth and studied the papers for perhaps five minutes before raising the gate again and allowing both cars through.

"That's it?" said Carl, as we passed under the gate and on our way. "They didn't even search the vehicles! What a waste of time!"

"It's called boredom, my friend," said Renee. "They have next to nothing to do all day. Four vehicles in a row amounts to probably the busiest day they've had in quite a time. They wanted to make the most of it without working too hard. That's why they only spoke to the first and third vehicles and let the other two through."

"You've seen this before?" I said.

"Many times. In your country as well," she said. "Americans call it trying to be the big fish in the small pond."

We were amazed the road could get any worse, but once we crossed the border into whatever country we were in, the ditch became a rut. We were bouncing so hard in our seats now items began falling out of our pants pockets. I began to worry about the folks outside the vehicle holding on. The grinding of the transmission

201

pierced our ears as the driver shifted into the lowest four-wheel drive gear he had.

"I am going to be sick if this does not stop soon," Renee said. Carl seconded her. I knew I could keep them from getting physically ill, but there was nothing I could do for myself.

The bouncing stopped so abruptly we thought we had fallen off a cliff. The rut turned into an actual road. Not a paved road, but one with a smooth, level surface nonetheless. Here it was a superhighway.

"Does anyone know where we are?" I didn't want to grumble but I was becoming very weary of all this driving. My butt was sore and my legs were cramped. Ever since my four-year incapacitation, any numbness of limbs was unbearable, putting me close to panic.

"We are very near the village you are going. Very near now," the driver said.

"Very near" turned out to be another forty-five minutes, during which the entire convoy stopped to fill up with gas from the containers each vehicle carried. Fifteen minutes outside the village, the road shrank back to a single lane pitted with rocks, but it was still far better than the studded wagon-wheel track we'd gone through earlier.

As the first signs of a village appeared on the horizon, the convoy stopped. Smoke rose in the distance. A bad sign.

"We have to suit up and walk from here, I'm afraid," Dr. Wheatley said. "It's going to be extremely warm inside the suits, so I want everyone to drink plenty of water."

"Extremely warm" would be an appropriate term for someone wearing long pants while hiking in the sun. What we experienced wearing the enviro suits was more akin to sitting in a car with all the windows rolled up in the middle of summer while covered from head to foot in multiple layers of plastic garbage bags. We were stinking miserable hot as we trudged along the road. The suits had built-in cooling units; without them we would have died within 100 yards, but we still suffered beyond measure.

My own pulse echoed in my helmet as I walked, beating faster and faster, not so much from the exertion as from the anticipation of what I would see. Then, off to my left, there it was—the same mountain I had seen in my dream. The ramshackle houses scattered haphazardly along the lane were identical to those I had unwillingly visited on so many anxious nights.

"We're not going to find anyone alive here." I hadn't realized my helmet radio was on.

"What was that?" said Dr. Wheatley.

"I said we're not going to find anyone alive here."

***

I was too late, of course.

My limbs were weighted with sadness. I wanted to sit down and cry but I went on staggering through the village, hoping, praying, wishing I could find someone alive, but the huts had all been burned. Most of them still smoldered; a few flickered and blazed whenever the wind stirred.

The cooling unit in my suit had worked sporadically at best. I wanted to yank my helmet off and breathe real air, but the smoke and scent probably would've killed me.

At this point I didn't really care. No one even noticed me. It was a myth, by the way, you got accustomed to death when you saw enough of it. The men on this biohazard team had seen death and all of the masks it wore, staring at it stoically. Yet I saw the burdens they bore in the steps they took, in the hollows of their eyes when they looked into the distance. They wandered aimlessly, crying shamelessly, as did I. For it was when you became hardened to death and suffering you lost your soul.

The livestock were all dead, too. Birds dead; reptiles dead. Whatever they unleashed here, whomever they were, was brutally thorough and nondiscriminatory. Even the plants looked dry and brown

"Jeez-Us," I heard a team member say. "What the hell kind of a pathogen was this?"

This was not a U.S. sponsored test, or so they told me. We didn't use biological warfare, nor did any of our allies. The results were just too unpredictable. There were no safeguards, no way to safely inoculate against whatever a particular disease strain might mutate into, no telling what it would do to the environment or the long-term survival of our species. No way to keep it from getting loose, going where you didn't want it to.

So why the secrecy? It was a question I had asked again and again. Why were the people of the world not allowed to see this carnage, to rise up with righteous indignation? To go after those responsible?

"Who would do this?" I said, to no one in particular.

No one in particular responded.

This wasn't the first time I had been sent into a death zone to save whoever was left, but it was the first time there was no one left to save.

I didn't know what this would do to me. What it *was* doing to me. I only knew I had to get that helmet off.

Air. Thank God. It felt so good to breathe real air, even as putrid as it was. I didn't care if I did catch whatever it was that killed those people. My will was gone.

"It should be all right for you to take off your helmet." A man behind me had likewise popped the seal on his own headgear and twisted it out of the gasket. "The spore has gone dormant."

"This was caused by a spore? Like a mold?"

"Yes, or a mushroom. It attacks the respiratory system of anything that breathes. That's why the birds and animals, right down to the lizards and insects, are all dead, too. All in all, I'd say it was a pretty impressive test."

The man could no doubt see my anger rising. Though he stood a good three inches taller and outweighed me by better than 50 pounds, I was building a rage. I'm sure he could see it in my eyes; I saw a momentary flicker of concern.

"Easy, Son. I didn't say *we* were testing it. We just came here to observe and try to save a few of these folks if we could. We're testing you, too, in a way, to see if you can neutralize artificially created diseases. By God, if I could have gotten you here in time for these people, I would have."

I felt the blood lust pass, but I still was wary of this man with the ready answers.

"Just who is we, anyway? If we didn't do this, then who did?"

"We are a tactical U.S. biohazard/medical squad attached to a UN crisis deployment team. That's about as specific yet generic as I can be. We really are the good guys, trying to clean up the messes made by the bad guys."

"And the bad guys are?"

"We have reason to believe it's a doomsday cult that calls itself the Children of Darkness. They want to hasten the end of the world, taking out as many people as possible. This was a test, a trial run, to evaluate the power of their weapon before taking it on to a bigger stage. You know, a terrorist organization is one thing, but a doomsday cult—how do you deal with people like that?"

I had no answers for him.

"The world is an increasingly scary place," he continued. "I was a Marine before joining the Navy SEALS, and it scares me. Look around you; I don't want my daughter growing up in a world where men can do this to their neighbors."

Before I could venture another question, our beepers both went off with instructions to return to the base camp for decontamination proceedings. I've been through these exercises before and can tell you they are unpleasant at best, something akin to the Inquisition at worst. I've been probed, prodded, scrubbed,

206

sprayed and exposed to more radiation than the average convenience store microwave jockey. Though fair-skinned in my youth, I've had more than a healthy tan for a number of years now.

Col. Wesley, that was the name on the outside of his containment suit, anyway, was already disappearing over a hill when I saw the figures standing in the trees watching me. Somehow I knew I only saw them because they wanted me to.

You have to be careful how you approach various people. I stared at the two men for several moments, then looked toward the ground as a sign of respect before reestablishing eye contact. That was what I was told to do in the debriefing.

Apparently it was the correct sequence. One of them motioned me toward them with his spear and I stepped forward, slowly. They were a good thirty yards away, so they had several seconds to size me up.

They were both tall men, lean yet muscular. Their skin was much darker than that of the average American black man I had met. As I came closer, I realized the one on the left was older than I first realized. His skin hung a bit more loosely than that of his companion, and he bore the eyes of wisdom. He was slowly graying. Initially I perceived him to be the medicine man for this tribe, but something in his eyes told me otherwise. No, these men were not from the village, probably not of the same tribe. They were onlookers, curious and concerned.

Language was not a barrier. The old man lifted a scrawny arm toward the village; I shook my head and made the word "no" with my lips. Their eyes brightened with shock and they shared a worried look. Their demeanor changed to one of agitation. I fought off the urge to shrug my shoulders. The stare they gave me could have burned the flesh from my bones.

Then the younger man did something the older man did not seem to expect. He motioned me to follow them back to their village. It was a trail which apparently only they could see, for I didn't know where I was and had to keep up with them every step or I would've fallen behind and become lost. It was hot, but with my helmet off, it was bearable, though just barely.

Hours later I stumbled back into the base camp, fully suited. I raised my hands at the protestations of everyone in the camp, all demanding simultaneously to know where I'd been.

"Second village," was all I could manage. "Also infected."

"Were you able to help them?" Dr. Wheatley asked, stepping out of the semicircle that had formed around me.

I nodded. "One hundred seventy-five in all. All clean now."

"That's wonderful news." Then, as if the light bulb has just been turned on, he added, "Oh, my God! I just realized why you're wearing your helmet!"

"I'm infected, too."

CHAPTER THIRTEEN

I remember very little of what happened next. I know Dr. Wheatley screamed something about getting me back to the foundation headquarters in Lynchburg ASAP, flying directly from Africa, refueling in the air if we had to.

Then I was somewhere in a bed, burning with fever. The images are still scattered: waking up, screaming in pain, strangers looking down at me, occasionally it was Amanda, then sleeping again. The pattern was consistent, the intervals were not: sleep, wake, scream, sleep. Gradually the waking periods begin to last longer and longer.

In what I was told was my fourth week back, I woke without screaming. For the first time I was able to look around the room and take stock of where I was. I recognized Clinic Room 213C at the foundation in Lynchburg. A television on the wall was chattering away.

"You're still slightly warm, one hundred point one, nothing to be too concerned about," a voice said.

"Hey, darling. I knew it was you I'd been seeing whenever I woke up."

"The way you were screaming, we weren't sure just how lucid you could possibly be." Amanda's belly was now beginning to bulge slightly. "Dr. Wheatley was afraid you were in some sort of fevered delusion and saw us all as demons here to torment you."

"No, that was only when somebody had the TV tuned to Jerry Springer," I said. "You'd scream, too, if you had to sit through one more segment of 'My Mother is Sleeping with My Brother and Having His Baby.'"

"Humor. That's a good sign." Dr. Wheatley was standing in the doorway.

"No, somebody really did keep leaving the TV on the Springer show."

"That was my idea. I figured if you were forced to listen to something really wretched, you might force yourself to wake up," Dr. Wheatley said.

"So how'd you do it? How did you get the fever to destroy the virus without killing me?"

"First of all, it wasn't a virus, as we first thought. It was a spore form, which I believe someone on one of the other teams told you after we arrived at the first village, too late for those poor souls. Secondly, we couldn't have done anything at all for you without a great deal of help."

A nurse brought in a tall black man with nervous eyes, glancing from side to side like a rabbit ready to flee. I recognized him as the younger of the two men who led me to the second village.

"Wait a minute." The fog was slowly burning away from my brain. "There's no way I could have found my way back to the base camp alone. This man led me back, but all I could remember was

210

stumbling and staggering all the way back in my enviro suit."

"That's right. He came with you, leading you by the arm," Dr. Wheatley said. "He also stayed with us and offered his life for you. He told us how you saved his entire village. Oh, and by the way, the number you gave us was a little low. From our best guess, based on what he told us, the number of people in the village you saved was closer to four hundred fifty, not one hundred seventy-five."

I smiled at the young man. He returned the gesture, though eye contact seemed to make him nervous.

"Tell him what else happened." Amanda, squeezed my hand.

"Oh, yes, of course. When you cured the villagers, including this young man, you apparently created antibodies in their bloodstream which absorbed the spores. By taking samples of his blood, we were able to recreate those antibodies to treat you. Ours weren't as effective as yours, of course, which is why it took so long to cure you. If you hadn't cured this young man, we wouldn't have been able to help you at all. Perhaps the best news of all is we now know how to treat this particular plague should it appear again. We'll keep samples of both his blood and yours on hand should we ever need it. We may have lost the battle of the first village, but in the long run, we're going to win the war against this particular epidemic. I've got a few protocols in mind now should we ever encounter it again. We have some new evidence this girl Hope may not be the only person you've passed some of your abilities on to."

"There are others?"

"It would appear that way. This is a very new development,

something we've only become aware of in the past twenty-four hours, or else we might have been able to use one of them to help you. There will be time to talk about all that later."

Tears poured freely down Amanda's cheeks.

"Did you thank him?" I indicated the young man.

"Oh, yes. Many times. I've even offered to adopt him or to sponsor his whole family should they ever want to move over here. He told me, through an interpreter, he prefers to remain in his village with his family."

I looked again at this young man, whose age was impossible to determine due to the hardships he had seen. Twice now in the same year, after a lifetime of healing others, a young person had stepped in to restore my own life.

"Tell him I'm grateful beyond words."

The nurse relayed something to that effect, though it seemed to take a while to say it in his native tongue. The man shook his head and responded in a lilting, singsong voice.

"He says you made great magic that day. His gratitude will be with you always. He also says should you ever need him again, he will come," the nurse said.

"You know, I don't even know his name," I said.

"Oh, I know that," Amanda said. "I can't pronounce it very well, but it translates roughly into 'One Who Has Great Faith.' They call him Faith."

CHAPTER FOURTEEN

Faith stayed with us for a few weeks in our Bedford home in case I relapsed and needed more antibodies than the foundation could replicate. My stipend from the foundation included a generous bonus that month, and the United Nations wanted to fly me to New York to accept a special humanitarian award.

"Do you want to go?" Amanda said.

"I could always beg out and say I'm still feeling weak."

She looked out the window at the infestation of media on our lawn: "Yes, but if you left town again, it'd at least help these people get their lives back. I think the whole neighborhood would be grateful if you got them out of here."

"This, too, shall pass." I pulled the curtains closed again. "I've been through this before. They can only stay after you for so long if you don't actually do anything."

"Have you ever given any thought to just setting up shop and having regular office hours, like a doctor's office? Lining 'em all up and letting 'em come? Wouldn't that be better than the random way you've been doing it?"

I peeled a banana as I thought of the best way to phrase my reply, one I'd worked out in my head years ago.

213

"Sure I have. When you get right down to it, most people don't need me that badly." I took a bite of the banana to let her think about that. "I don't think I was put here to heal the bunions and runny noses of the world, although I'm frequently asked to do just that. There are some things in life you just have to live with, or at least treat in more conventional methods. I don't mean to sound cold here, but look at me. With the exception of the girl in the nursing home, no one's ever just miraculously healed me of anything. I had to suffer for four years waiting for that particular miracle. When I'm sick, I just have to treat it and wait it out like everybody else. Most of the people who come to me are not dying or suffering all that greatly. I've had women ask me to give them bigger breasts or make their butts smaller. I've also seen men who've wanted to be taller, old people who want to feel young again. I can't tell you the times obese people have asked me to make them thinner."

"What do you do then?"

"I tell them to see a doctor, go on a diet, exercise more. The point is, I don't feel like I'm obligated to make everyone feel better, especially with trivial, lifestyle kinds of conditions."

Amanda held her belly and backed herself onto the couch. "So then why were you put on this Earth? You can't save everybody who's dying."

"That's the question I still can't answer. Maybe it was for that village in Africa. Maybe for the young HIV-positive boy I took away from his brother. Maybe there was no reason at all. Maybe it was all just an accident. Maybe somebody else was supposed to have this

214

power."

"Maybe it was to make love to me and make my babies," she said. "Albeit twenty years too late."

I chuckled. The doorbell rang.

"That's the first time in a while one of them has gotten the nerve to do that," Amanda said.

I opened the door and recognized Sid's "good news-bad news" face immediately.

"What a pleasant, pleasant surprise. We were just not talking about you." I closed the door in a reporter's face as Sid stepped inside.

"Amanda, you look...big," Sid said.

"I'm having a baby. I've been having sex with my husband. You should try it sometime."

"With *your* husband? You don't mind?"

"Nyuk nyuk there, Moe. What brings you out to run through the gauntlet here?" I said.

"Well, I've got —"

"Good news and bad news, we know. We can read you like a menu."

"Okay, the good news is, the lawsuit's off. The plaintiffs have pulled out and Judge Remington has dismissed the case. You can go back to healing whoever and whatever you want, as much as you want."

"And the bad?"

"You know, you're very rude hosts. I come out here to see

you, risking life and limb through the crush of reporters out there, and you don't even offer me a—oh, thank you, Amanda. Where was I?" He took a sip of lemonade.

"As much as I want."

"Right. What does that mean? Oh, yeah. The bad news is, the Senate has taken the whole thing up. They're going to hold special hearings looking into your activities. Apparently there's been a whole wave of copycat healers, charlatans all, but it makes you look extremely bad, like you're bilking people all over the country out of their life savings."

"The Senate? That's ridiculous," Amanda said.

"Of course it is. This is a big election year and there's a whole lot of posturing going on. Healthcare reform is in the toilet, the Republicans and Democrats are both basically standing around with their thumbs up their—sorry, forgot there's a lady present. So anyway, along comes all these healers making people pay them money for dubious miracles, and some junior senator sitting on a useless committee somewhere says, 'Aha! Let's show the people how concerned we are! Let's get that miracle guy out here and rake his fanny through the coals!'"

"So what you're saying is, they're trying to court the anti-miracle man vote?" Amanda said. "What do they hope to accomplish?"

"Posturing, my love, it's all about the posturing. They can point fingers and say 'Harrumph!' a lot and make it look like they're actually doing something about a problem that doesn't even exist,"

Sid said.

"In the process drag my life and reputation through the mud all over again," I said.

"That's about the size of it."

"Wait a minute, what committee is this?" Amanda said.

"It's a special subcommittee of the health and education committee, the full name of which, interestingly, is the acronym HELP," Sid said. "Anyway, this subcommittee, the name of which I don't know yet, was formed just this year to deal with all the instances of so-called healers that have been operating—for a fee, I might add—in the wake of Jeremiah's return. Since Jeremiah is the granddaddy of them all, they want to talk to him."

"Isn't that just my luck," I said. "I get out of the lawsuit only to be hit with Senate hearings This will be on C-SPAN and CourtTV."

"Well, that's the bad news. The even worse news is our own dear Senator Cordoba is on the panel. As we all know, he always has an agenda of his own, but at this point I don't know what it is. He gives opportunists a bad name." Sid paused to drain the rest of the lemonade. "You may remember he was a Democrat for years before switching parties when the Republicans took control of Congress in ninety-four. What I don't understand is why he remains such a powerful figure when pretty much everybody, Republicans and Democrats alike, all hate him. I don't just mean they dislike him or occasionally disagree with him, I mean they really, really loathe him."

"Blackmail," Amanda said. "At least that's the rumor."

"I've heard that, too, but nobody can ever seem to prove it," Sid said. "Somehow he has the goods on pretty much everybody in Washington."

"He has the goods on them because he sets them up, that's how." Amanda settled back onto the couch beside me in that wide-legged sprawl she'd adopted of late, even though she really wasn't that big yet. "He supposedly sends women of, shall we say, low moral repute, to sleep with other senators, then threatens to expose them if they don't go along with him. He uses different tactics on the women in the Senate, of course, but he seems to hold some power over them, too."

"Which means there's a lot more going on here than we realize. I just can't figure out what he hopes to gain from it," Sid said.

"Why did Remington dismiss the case?" I said.

"My guess would be Remington somehow got wind of all this and dismissed the case so it wouldn't be dragging on when the hearings came up in the Senate. In fact, I'll bet the plaintiffs didn't really pull out at all, did they, Sid?"

"Well, now that you mention it..."

"Anything else you've been withholding you'd care to share with us?" Amanda advanced toward him with eyes blazing.

"Well, it looks like the plaintiffs will probably have their day after all. Word has it they'll all be subpoenaed to testify before the subcommittee, so they'll all have their say."

"So there really was no good news at all," Amanda said.

"Hey, don't shoot the messenger. You can bet these yard

apes outside haven't heard about it yet or else they'd all be banging on your door instead of being content to work on their tans. That won't last long, though. You need to either get out of town and hide somewhere or call the sheriff and have him enforce a no-trespassing order. You can at least keep them off your property, but not out of the road."

"As much as I hate to admit it, he's right," I said to Amanda. "What other options do we have? What happens if we go to Canada?"

"Either they'll extradite us back or arrest us the next time we set foot in the country. We also can't expect to hide at my house in Roanoke anymore. They'll figure that out pretty quickly. No, the thing to do is not run. You haven't broken any laws, this is not the same as a civil or criminal trial. It's merely an inquiry."

"An inquisition, you mean," I said.

"No, it may seem like that, but it's just a hearing. It's like the old 'sticks-and-stones' mantra; they can call you names and say nasty things about you, but they really can't do anything to you. They have no power over you. That's why there's no need for us to run. You just go on and open the bookstore tomorrow morning, and I'll go to work and we'll live our lives. So what if they get clips of us ignoring reporters every day? Like you said, 'This, too, shall pass.'"

"I really could have used some good news right about now."

"Actually, there is some extremely good news," Sid said. "All this new publicity has revived interest in your book. Your first book, not that silly Biff Granite stuff."

"See? Even he thinks it's bad," Amanda said.

"Yeah, well, Barnes and Noble has reported a seventy-five percent increase in demand, Amazon's and Borders' numbers are up about the same, and Scribner is preparing a tenth anniversary limited edition with a new cover, new forward, the whole thing. Hey, that's great news; that's money for you! Lots of money!"

"Scribner? What happened to Pinetree?" I said.

"Where've you been? Pinetree Press went belly-up three years ago. Well, I guess I know where you were then. Anyway, their assets were liquidated. Scribner got your book and most of the self-help stuff, and all the do-it-yourself stuff went to other publishers."

"So what's the bad news?"

"Hey, try to contain your enthusiasm there, big fella! Did you hear what I said? You stand to make a lot of money here! Did I mention you're in demand for lectures and guest signings all over again? Oh, and they want to talk to you about doing a sequel."

I thought at that point I must have drifted away in thought, because there was no way I could have heard what I thought I'd heard.

"A sequel? Are you nuts? The story centered around a once-in-a-lifetime occurrence. How could you possibly have *A Bullet for My Father's Whore II?*"

"Then how about a prequel, something that takes place before all that?"

"A prequel? Sid, did you ever actually read that book?"

"Well, I mean, I saw the original synopsis, and I was in on

most of the meetings with the Pinetree people, but no, not the whole thing."

"Well if you had paid attention during any of that, you'd know the whole thing is told in flashback, meaning —"

"The whole thing *is* a prequel, I know, I know. You need to get involved, because the She-BS people are interested in doing a movie sequel, with or without you. That's the bad news."

"How can they do that? I still have the rights to —"

"To all film and video adaptations during the first five years. The five years are up, so it reverted to Simecon, which made the first movie, and She-BS bought the rights from Simecon."

"You were supposed to watch that for me. You're my agent *and* my lawyer."

"Okay, okay, I was asleep at the wheel on that one. So sue me; on second thought, don't sue me. I'm telling you now. She-BS is shopping for a script. The buzz is they want to turn Helena, in this one, into some type of she-vigilante who packs heat and fights violence against women with violence, while wearing a miniskirt and high heels, of course. Rumor has it they're considering it as a pilot for a series rather than a standalone movie. Jeremiah? You there?"

Sid could have stuck nails all the way through my body at that point and I wouldn't have noticed. Although the book had been as integral to my being as my own skin during the five years it took to bring it from conception to publication, I had jettisoned it like a diseased, amputated appendage once that wretched movie came out. Indeed, it *was* diseased after that debacle, but here it was again, like a rotted limb someone had fished from the garbage can and was now dangling before me.

"Can't you stop them?" was all I could say.

"Stop? No. Delay? Possibly. It's probably going to happen, unless the interest in you and your book suddenly goes away. The best you can reasonably hope for is to get in on the ground floor as early as possible with your input. Look at it as your chance to right the wrong done to you the first time out. If the end result isn't what you want it to be, then you can cry all the way to the bank. Make them pay with their checkbooks."

CHAPTER FIFTEEN

At Amanda's urging, I agreed to accept the humanitarian award from the United Nations, although it sounded like too much horn-tooting to me. While at first it looked as though she would not be able to accompany me, a rescheduled trial enabled her to take a few days off to fly up.

Again I boarded a plane from Lynchburg to D.C., though this time the destination there was Reagan National. After a forty-five minute layover, it was on to LaGuardia, where security promptly pulled Amanda out of the line for no other reason than her number came up. After a good deal of pointless questioning, they finally let her go.

"This is so ridiculous. I ask you: how many pregnant women in really expensive shoes blow up planes?" We squeezed into a taxi. "I mean, no woman alive would commit any kind of violent act in three hundred dollar Blahniks."

"Did you know they pulled an old lady out of line the other day because she had a pair of knitting needles?" I said.

"You're kidding."

"No, really. They were afraid she would try to make an afghan."

She groaned as the taxi pulled out.

I had not been to New York since before Sept. 11, 2001, and I wasn't sure how I would react to seeing the Twin Towers missing. Though I never lived there and never planned on moving there at any time in my life, I still was not prepared for the empty ache I felt in my chest as I glanced out over the Manhattan skyline. Even years removed from the event, it somehow seemed so—

"Unreal, isn't it?" Amanda looked out over the bay. "I never thought I'd feel nostalgia for a place I've never been."

We rode in silence the rest of the way to our hotel, where a small bevy of entertainment reporters hung out by the curb and in the lobby for glimpses of celebrities.

"Think we're going to have trouble from them?" Amanda said.

"Nah, we're in a cab, not a limo. I don't think we're all that familiar to this crowd, anyway."

I opted not to try the obvious fedora-and-trench coat disguise, which tended to call attention to the wearer, who invariably looked as though he was trying to hide. We were dressed so much like tourists, I doubted anyone would give us a first glance, much less a second.

Our room was opulent, palatial even. The heart-shaped bed alone was the size of a small swimming pool.

"Well, I can certainly get away from you in this bed," Amanda said. "Though from the looks of my belly, it's a little too late for that."

The brochures described the decor as a "sort of retro-Parisian with a Bohemian afterthought," whatever that meant. On the walls hung lots of paintings that looked like they were drawn by starving sidewalk artisans with bad eyesight, competing with bright, Renaissance-themed wallpaper. Big, heavy drapes, the kind one would expect at an old Southern plantation, seemed, to my untrained eye, absolutely out of place with the motif. I simply headed for the "his" bathroom and soaked for a long, long time in the whirlpool tub.

"You'll enjoy this," Amanda said from outside the bathroom door. "You're not on a single news channel here."

We enjoyed an afternoon stroll and a light meal at a sidewalk café, an amenity Lynchburg had too little of. The array of people one could see at any given moment on a New York City street was nothing short of dazzling. Gradually the sounds of angry voices somewhere down the street began to rise.

"What's going on over there?" I said to the waiter.

"UN protesters." He made no eye contact.

"What are they protesting?"

"Who knows? They're always protesting something over there." He walked away.

"You don't suppose this has something to do with the awards ceremony, do you?" Amanda said.

"I sort of doubt it. I doubt they even know about my award, but there are other people on the program, too."

"We'd better get going so the committee people can meet

225

us," she said.

Back at the hotel we dressed and waited for the committee liaisons to meet us. At 7:15 a matronly woman in an elegant, floor-length ball gown, surrounded by a pair of recently crowned beauty queens adorned with tiaras and sashes, met us at the door and walked us down the hall.

"I didn't even know there was a Miss Goodwill Appeal to the Masses pageant," Amanda said, leaning into my ear.

"Heaving bosoms always appeal to the masses. Look at the knockers on Miss World Famine Concern here."

"Yeah, those are real."

"You're just jealous. I find her very uplifting."

A polite smattering of applause greeted us as we stepped out of the elevator into the lobby, but I quickly realized a number of other award recipients were there as well. Our hostess, the woman who retrieved us from our room, timed all the arrivals perfectly. Smiling pageant queens, all garbed in the attire of the trade, flanked each recipient. There were enough teeth on display to solve a world enamel crisis.

"Ladies and gentlemen, we are so delighted to have such a distinguished cast of luminaries in our presence," the hostess said. "Truly these are people who have answered the call to duty in a multitude of ways across the globe. Each person, in his or her own unselfish way, has made our small globe a better place to live and brought us all a good bit closer together."

As she rattled off the list of recipients, I realized I was in distinguished company indeed. World leaders, political, civic and religious, were among us, as were philanthropists, artists, businesspeople and ordinary citizens who had done extraordinary things. Amanda squeezed my arm and made no attempt to hide the moisture pooling behind her eyes as the roll was called.

A fleet of limousines waited outside to take us to UN headquarters. Miss Goodwill Appeal to the Masses helped us into our vehicle and got in after me.

"I think it's so great what you did there in Africa, with all those people dying in that village and all," she said.

"Um, thank you. My name is Jeremiah Townsend, and this is my wife, Amanda."

"Amber Kendrick, Greeneville, Tennessee. I'm glad to meet you."

"I'm Mistique Topknot, Clemson, South Carolina," said Miss World Famine Concern, she of the inflationary assets. "Actually, my real name is Misty Carroll. Mistique Topknot is just a stage name I use when I act. I don't usually use it in ambassadorial situations."

"What sort of acting do you —"

"Leave it alone, dear," I said. "So, what role do you play in the festivities?"

"To be honest, we're pretty much window dressing," said Amber. "I think they think pretty girls make people happy, so they pick beauty queens from all these different pageants. I want to go into broadcast journalism, but I do a lot of volunteer work with children's organizations."

"I've been in a few movies," said Mistique. Then, as if only Amanda could hear her, "To be honest, I've had to have some surgery to further my career. Can you tell I've had my breasts augmented? Are they too much now?" She cupped her hands around her balloonish trophies and moved them up and down twice.

"They're a little bit much, maybe, but they seem to fit you," Amanda said.

"I would never get my boobs done just to get a job," Amber whispered in my left ear. She was also by now holding my hand and had wrapped her right ankle around my left. "I mean, it's hard enough for an attractive woman to be taken seriously in this world without people like her calling even more attention to their breasts."

I eased my hand away from hers and put my overcoat over my lap, trying to hide the fact I was unmistakably aroused.

"Look at my wife," I said to Amber. "Do you think she's an attractive woman?"

"She's beautiful," she said, and I think she meant it. "She's even beautiful pregnant, and that's not something everyone can pull off."

"She's also very successful and extremely intelligent. She's earned everything she's ever gotten on pure ability and drive, not what's swelling up out of her chest. She's never had to have a tiara and a sash to prove who she was."

"I know; I know; I'm vain." Amber whispered. "I guess a lot of little girls like me just want to be princesses, even if it's only for a while."

228

"There's nothing wrong with that." Amanda had obviously heard everything we had said. "All little girls want to live in a fairy tale. Just don't confuse the fairy tale with the real world."

"I think we're slowing down," said Mistique.

"This looks bad. There've been more and more protesters every week," said Amber.

Several thousand people in the middle of the street forced traffic to stop. Some of them appeared to be rocking the limos further up in our convoy. We couldn't read the signs they carried.

"What's this all about? What are they protesting?" said Amanda.

"Social conditions in developing countries," Amber said. "Capitalist economic policies in general. U.N. aid to dictators in particular. HIV funding. You name it, we're seeing it."

"I'll bet a bunch of people in tuxes and evening gowns riding in limousines really set their dials," I said.

"Oh, it doesn't matter anymore who you are. These aren't all true protesters," Amber said. "A lot of people these days are just thugs drawn to the violence and chaos. Two nights ago a group of so-called 'protesters' pulled a couple of college girls out of a car and raped them right on the sidewalk. There were so many people around it was impossible to identify who did it. The really ironic thing is, it was supposed to be a protest against sexual assault, date rape, that sort of thing."

"We should never have come," I said.

The situation unfolding before us deteriorated into anarchy

when a man in the limo in front of us jumped out of the car and started struggling with someone in the crowd. Amber and Mistique shrieked as the man's head exploded in front of a large semiautomatic weapon.

Over Amanda's protests, I crawled across Amber's lap and pushed the door open against the encroaching crowd, only to find myself pinned against the car and pummeled by fists. By allowing my body to sag back against the car, I ducked under the onslaught and rolled myself onto the hood of the limo, leaping over the heads of the people immediately in front of us to get to the fallen man.

I was too late. He was dead. Looking up, I saw the shooter, a wildly bearded man in fatigues and a cutoff T-shirt, dancing and firing into the air. From a crouched position I sprung into the man, hitting him in the head and kneeing him in the chest with everything I had. I wrested the gun away from him, an act which immediately cleared a wide swath around me.

"This is insane!" I said, over the now muted din. "A man is dead for no reason at all! What kind of statement are you trying to send here?"

Two slender sets of arms took hold of my own and slowly pulled me away from the crowd. I turned to face Amber and Mistique, tiaras ripped from their hair, leading me toward the sidewalk. I dropped the gun. Amber's red silk gown was torn completely away from her body, leaving her only in bra and slip; Mistique's green sequined dress was in tatters and she hobbled on one high heel. The flow of the sidewalk crowd carried us a good ways away from where we started out.

"Where's Amanda?"

"She's still in the car. She's crying pretty badly," said Mistique.

"Where is she? I've got to get to her!" No longer able to see the limo, I jumped up and down and stretched my head to try to see over the crowd. I left the two women and plowed through a sea of arms and legs to get back to the street, where the limos all looked alike.

I hadn't noticed how far back in the convoy we were. I beat on the tinted windows of each car, begging someone to let me see inside. I gasped as I noticed an ambulance pulling up along the sidewalk, parting the people before it, then ran, pushing and pulling bodies away.

A large policeman rose up before me and held up his hand, daring me to go further.

"Please, that's my wife back there," I said. "She's pregnant and this may force her into labor."

"Then the medics are her best bet. They'll take care of her."

"You don't understand, I can fix her, I'm the Miracle Man—"

"Buddy, I don't care if you're a tub of Miracle Whip, there's enough people out here impeding the medics as is."

"I can help her! We won't even need the medics if you let me get to her!"

"That's enough out of you. One more word..."

I didn't wait for what followed. I spun out of his grasp and tried to plow into the crowd again, only to find my arms cuffed and pinned behind me.

"This is for your own good," Officer J. Parker said. I kicked and screamed and made what would have been quite a scene in almost any other city. In New York City, however, I was about as unruly as a firefly. Two other officers showed up to help escort me away.

After chucking me in the backseat of his cruiser, Officer Parker radioed in to find out if I had any priors. Not only did the check come back clean, it indicated I was a guest of the United Nations in town to receive a special award.

"Sorry, buddy, but you did look kinda crazy back there," he said. "Tell you what, I'll drive you to the hospital where they took your wife. Everything'll be okay."

"Please hurry."

With lights and sirens flashing, Officer Parker got me to the hospital far faster than I could have made it on foot or even in a cab. He escorted me to the ER, where I was shuttled straight to the maternity ward. I ran to the desk and demanded to see my wife.

"She went into premature labor, Mr. Townsend," the nurse said. "You understand it was *very* premature, don't you?"

"What are you telling me? How is she? How's the baby."

"I'd better let you speak to a doctor." She picked up a phone to page someone.

My options seemed limited at this point. I thought about

bursting in after my wife and child myself, but with such a large maternity department, I didn't even know where to look. I also recalled what happened to me the last time I went charging into a hospital four-and-a-half years ago. Then there was the prospect of being arrested.

"Tell them to please hurry," I said.

She picked up the phone again: "Dr. Watkins to the front desk, stat. Please have a seat, Mr. Townsend; it's been a very busy evening for us, full moon and all."

"I'd rather stand, thank you." At that point a blood pressure cuff would have blown off my arm with a resounding bang had anyone tried to test me. Some inane show about strangers living together in a sealed house, content to whine away their days, blared from the television on the wall.

Minutes ticked away. The cooped up strangers on the TV continued to whine, argue and whine some more. Finally, when I reached a point where no blood pressure cuff was safe within ten feet of me, an ER doctor in green scrubs came through the swinging door.

"Mr. Townsend, I'm Dr. Watkins. Come with me, please."

"How's my wife? How's the baby?" I put on a mask as we practically sprinted down the corridor.

"We're trying to stabilize your wife, but we're having trouble controlling the bleeding. Quite frankly, if you were any other man, I wouldn't even let you back here. The infant was extremely premature."

233

"I know that. What are you saying? Is the baby alive?"

"It depends on your definition of alive. We have the infant, really still a fetus at this point, on a respirator, but the heartbeat's very faint, almost gone. We're looking at less than a ten percent probability it'll make it through the hour."

"Let me see him," I said.

"Have you ever healed a premature newborn?"

"No, but it sounds like we've got nothing to lose. I've got to try."

I never got the chance. The tiny form was flatlining as we entered the room, and a team of doctors and nurses was trying to fibrillate the heart.

"What's he doing in here?" a nurse snapped upon seeing me.

"This is the father. He's been known to work miracles," Dr. Watkins said.

There was no miracle for this child. My hands seemed monstrously large, like baseball gloves, as I reached inside the plastic tank of the respirator and touched the wrinkled corpse of my son.

Two nurses pried the body from my fingers, and a third caught me before I fell backward. My entire being sagged with a grief that weighted me like an anchor. Breathing no longer seemed automatic.

"Where's..." My voice failed me.

"Your wife is still in surgery. They're doing all they can. We've got to get you out of here, get you some air," someone said.

"I need...see her."

"Mr. Townsend, you're in no shape to help anyone."

"No, take him to her," Dr. Watkins said. "Maybe he can save one life tonight."

Numb to the world, I allowed two nurses, one on each arm, to lead me to the O.R. where Amanda lay dying. Nothing was real to me at this point. I was watching someone else's dream from afar.

"Put my hands on her," I said.

As consciousness drifted away from me and the world went black, the last words I heard were those of my wife, "You left us."

CHAPTER SIXTEEN

Physically, Amanda made a startlingly complete and instantaneous recovery unlike anything anyone at that hospital had ever seen. Emotionally and spiritually, however, she sank into a void where no miracle of mine could touch her. The doctors attributed it to postpartum depression.

"We've put her on antidepressants, but there's really nothing more we can do at this point other than keep her here for observation," Dr. Eudora Wade said. "The shock and grief of losing a child combined with the boiling cauldron of postpartum hormones can bring a woman to an all-time emotional low point. I can't stress enough she is suffering from a dangerous depression. She could be a danger to herself or others, even loved ones."

The wreckage lying in the hospital bed bore only a passing resemblance to the strong-willed woman I married. Clutching her pillows as she curled into the fetal position, she looked very old and tired.

"How long will she sleep?" I said.

"Excessive sleep at this point is an escape mechanism as the body and mind try to shut themselves down to flee the pain and sadness. It's certainly better, at least at this point, than pacing the floor and staying up all night crying. I'd let her sleep as long as possible."

So I began the lonely vigil, hundreds of miles from home, of watching my beloved sleep and cry out. The stranger who occasionally sat up and stared around the room through distant eyes was certainly not the woman I knew. That woman, it seemed, was lost somewhere inside this curiously tiny, fragile form that writhed under the sheets and wailed in its sleep.

On the third day, the doctors discharged Amanda, though she was still uncommunicative outside of the occasional mumble of "You left us."

Unable to put her aboard a plane, I rented a car and drove us the 600 or so miles back to Bedford. At rest stops I had to ask other women to accompany my wife into the restroom and to make sure she came back out. For two nights of the journey we slept in motel rooms.

The silence and vacant stare the entire trip were hell multiplied by a factor of ten. Not knowing whether I should speak or leave her alone, I opted to play the radio, usually staying with the local public station until the signal faded.

When we finally pulled into our garage, Amanda gave no indication she knew where we were or that the car had stopped. I had driven 600 miles with a zombie.

"Honey, we're home."

"You left us."

I opened the passenger door and she stepped out and walked straight to the bedroom, locking the door behind her.

CHAPTER SEVENTEEN

I don't know when Amanda could possibly have filed for divorce and a restraining order, confined as she seemed to the bedroom. There it was, delivered by certified mail even as she lay in the bed. I had twenty-four hours to vacate the home.

"You can't mean this," I said, to the figure undulating under the sheet. "You don't seriously want to divorce me. You're not even in your right mind."

A moan and a grunt answered me.

"I can easily prove you're not competent to make this type of decision."

Several moments of silence followed. Then, "You left us."

"I know I did, dear, and dear God, do I regret it. Every day. At the time, though, the only thing I could think of was getting to that man and saving him. I know I should have thought of you and the baby, but it seemed if you just stayed in the car, everything would be fine for you."

"You left us."

"The really horrible part about it is I couldn't even save the man. I was too late. I really should have just stayed in the car. Because then we lost the baby. Now I've lost you, haven't I?"

Silence.

"Amanda, please, you're all I've got left right now. You've been my hope and my inspiration since I got out of the nursing home. You can't do this to our marriage, our union, our bond, our lives."

Silence.

"Amanda, I lost the baby, too. I'm grieving, too. What good will it do to split up? Then we're both alone. Nobody wins. Nobody wins."

"You left us."

I preferred the silence.

With an ultimatum to clear out, my only immediate option was a cot in the back room of the bookstore. I tossed a few clothes and toiletries into a bag and started out the door.

"Leave the car." Those were her first words other than "you left us" since the emergency delivery.

I took a cab into downtown Bedford and went into the store through the back alley. The back room was even smaller and grimmer than I remembered. The cot, I knew, was probably teeming with life, so I wrapped a hastily chosen old sheet around the mattress and tried my best to ignore the smell. Boxes of books and assorted flotsam lurked precariously along the walls, themselves in need of new plastering. A lone, bare lightbulb hung from the ceiling.

It's best I don't mention the carpet in that room.

After not sleeping all night, I rose with the sun and splashed water from the bathroom sink over my face and hair. With soap and a minuscule vial of shampoo liberated from our New York hotel, I did the best I could to wash my hair and upper body. I wanted to be fresh to greet the day's customers.

With our erratic operating hours, it was probably too much to expect anyone to patronize the store, but by 9 a.m. my first customer walked through the door.

"About time you decided to come to work," said Harley Hairston, an old man whose days were spent primarily in the barber shop down the street, though he seldom actually got his hair cut. "Wish I could get a job with the kinda hours you got."

I started to ask him just what sort of job he'd ever held but thought better of it. Business had been a bit slow and the store had been closed a while.

"We were out of town."

"Didju go to Richmond?"

"New York."

"New York City?"

"Yes."

He whistled. To Harley, New York might as well be Paris or the moon.

"Never been there." I doubted he had ever been to Charlottesville. "Whadja go there for?"

"I was supposed to get an award."

"Was it nice?"

"I didn't make it to the ceremony."

"That's too bad. You got a book?"

"I've got lots of books."

"I know that; I'm not stupid. I'm lookin' for a perticular book, a book for my grandniece. You got Harry Potter?"

"Which one?"

"The one about the boy that's magical or somethin'."

"Which one? There's seven in all."

"Seven? I didn't know they's *that* many!"

"Does your grandniece have any of the other Harry Potter books yet?"

"I don't know. She just said she wanted the Harry Potter book. She didn't say they was seven. Never mind that. Have you got Dr. Seuss?"

"We've got lots of Dr. Seuss. Anything in particular?"

"Don't tell me they's seven'a them, too!"

Harley finally walked away with a pop-up book about turtles, although I tried to convince him it was not age appropriate for a nine year old. I think the price became the deciding factor and it was the cheapest children's book I had.

A bookstore is guaranteed to generate walk-in traffic, though that doesn't always translate into paying customers. The old cowbell on the door clanged repeatedly as the "just lookers" wandered in and out. About two-thirds of them actually put the books or magazines they thumbed through relatively close to where they found them. Some wandered around dropping off my merchandise about as discriminately as a bird decides where to defecate.

Two elderly women in particular walked around frowning and scowling at each and every shelf.

241

"I don't know why they bother with this place. It's never open and you can never find anything," one woman said to the other. "Oh, he can't hear me. There's nothing in here anyway. Look at that." She stared at the cover of *Cosmopolitan*, as if she'd never seen it in the supermarket. "Trash."

The second woman, having given up on getting the first to lower her voice, finally walked up to the counter, her perm still smelling like sour chemicals.

"Pardon me, but do you carry anything by V.C. Andrews?"

"Well, the real V.C. Andrews has been dead for quite some time, but they're still putting out books under her name. We have the whole series over here." I showed her to the proper shelf.

"Well if she's dead, how do they keep using her name?" she said.

"The publishers seem to have trademarked that name. The Andrews books are all written by other authors now."

"Do you have to keep this trash just lying around?" The first woman brandished a *Cosmo* magazine she had already rolled into a tube. "Children can see this."

"Ma'am that magazine is on display in every supermarket and convenience store in America. I don't try to tell my customers what they should and shouldn't read."

"Well I don't want anything to do with it." She dropped the now-tubular magazine onto a table with a display of word puzzles for children. "I can't believe you sell that trash. I'm leaving."

"Well I wasn't through looking." The second woman

watched the first walk out the door. As she scurried out onto the sidewalk after her companion, I got the feeling this argument had taken place many times before.

"I thought she was going to hit you with that rolled up *Cosmo*."

"Sid! I didn't hear you come in."

"I was in the alley and decided to come in through the back door. Listen, I heard about what happened in New York. I'm so sorry. How's Amanda?"

"Not good." I poured him a latte. "She's home in bed suffering with a severe bout of postpartum depression."

"Then what are you doing here? Shouldn't you be home with her?"

"Can't. Threw me out."

"She can't throw you out. It's your house, too. She probably doesn't know what she's doing."

"She's filed for divorce. I slept, or rather, tried to sleep, on the cot in the back room there last night."

He let out a whistle. "I thought you looked more like hell than usual this morning. So what's the deal? How did she lose the baby?"

I really didn't want to go into the whole tragic tale again, but some cultures believed by telling a story you could either give it more power or take away some of its bad magic. Hoping for the latter, I recounted the events from the night of the awards ceremony.

Sid shook his head as he listened.

"Jeremiah, Jeremiah. Always the crusader, rushing out to save the world without tending to your own house first. You really, literally, always forget to look before you leap, don't you?"

"That's funny. Amanda always tells me my biggest problem is I'm afraid to take chances."

"So what are you going to do? You are going to try to patch things up, aren't you?"

"I don't know I can, at least not right now. She's been in bed the past five days. She doesn't eat or speak to anyone. She has a restraining order against me."

"How could she do that? She has to be able to prove you pose some sort of threat to her."

"I don't know how she did it, but here it is." I pulled it out of my pocket and handed it to him.

"Jeremiah, this isn't even legitimate. I've seen these before. They come from a Web site with quasi-legal documents you print out. Look, the signature is completely illegible, but it doesn't represent any judge or magistrate around here. This thing's bogus."

"It was delivered by certified mail."

"So she caught the postman one day when you were downstairs and gave him some money and he brought it back the next. I'll bet the envelope was from her own law firm."

I left Sid while I waited on some customers who were looking for books for their daughter, who was returning to college. Although I didn't carry any of the textbooks they needed, I did sell them a collegiate dictionary and some writing supplies.

"So if this restraining order is bogus," I returned to Sid, "what's she up to? Does she just not know what she's doing or what?"

"It sounds like she's really in a diminished mental state. Any attorney looking at this document knows it's not real. Amanda, in her right mind, would certainly know it wasn't binding. She's one of the best lawyers in the state, for God's sake. This is a cry for help."

I looked at the clock. It was only 11:30.

"Go on home. I'll watch the store," Sid said.

"Don't you have real work to do?"

"Nothing scheduled. Tanasha can take messages. She's got my pager number if she needs me."

"Tanasha? I thought —"

"Long story short, I hired her to do my laundry, we became best friends with benefits, then I hired her to be my secretary."

"I don't know..."

"The merchandise is all marked, isn't it? Then go, I'll keep the store open, try to help you keep from losing your business."

"I need to call a cab."

He flung me his keys. This was above and beyond the call of duty.

As I pulled into the driveway, I noticed all the curtains were still drawn. I would never have left Amanda alone in this state if she hadn't kicked me out. If I'd been just a little bit smarter, however, I never would have let her kick me out.

I opened the door and saw her crumpled on the floor in front of the couch. Blood was everywhere. I dove to the floor and rolled her over.

"My God, honey, what's wrong?" Then I saw the large slit in her abdomen. A butcher knife lay just off to the side.

"The baby." Blood was running out of her mouth. "Somebody already took the baby. I tried to get the baby. Where's the baby?"

Cradling her head against my chest, I reached out with my right hand and closed the wound. It was deep. I couldn't believe she was still alive, much less conscious.

"Where's the baby?" she kept saying.

"The baby's fine," I said. "We already got it out, in New York, remember?"

"New York? Where's my baby?"

I shushed her and continued to rock, clutching her head against my chest. I couldn't just swoop in and heal this wound. I needed help.

I carried her back to the bedroom, realizing as I hoisted her into my arms how much weight she had lost over the past few days.

"I'm going to call your mother." I stroked her hair. "She'll want to come see you."

"Mama? Does she know where the baby is?"

"The baby's fine. You need your sleep now."

I called the local crisis help line. Within fifteen minutes an ambulance was at the house. The EMTs sedated Amanda and loaded her into the vehicle, then took her to Bedford Memorial for observation. I followed, dialing her mother in Roanoke from the cell phone.

After an interminable time in the waiting room, a doctor came out to speak to me.

"We'll watch her for a few days, but she may need to be placed in an institution if her condition doesn't improve. The Central Virginia Training Center in Madison Heights is the next step from here."

"I think her family would prefer she be closer to Roanoke."

"Well, CVTC is the closest state facility to Roanoke, it's about 55 miles away. Marion would be at least twice as far."

"What about in-home care? Could we get a nurse, just to make sure she doesn't hurt herself?"

"Let me think about it."

While Dr. Levine turned away to "think about it," Amanda's mother, Samantha, came out of the elevator. A beauty queen in her youth, Samantha was still stunning in her late 50s. She could almost pass for Amanda's twin, give or take a few wrinkles, being just nineteen years older.

"Where? How is she?"

"She's heavily sedated. She'll be out of it for hours. The doctor wants to keep her here to watch her for a few days. If she doesn't improve, he wants to put her in an institution, but I'm pulling for an in-home nurse."

"You'd better believe we'll get her an in-home nurse. My daughter is not going to one of those places. Why did you leave her at home all alone in the first place? Do you all need the money that bad you had to leave her all by herself with a giant butcher knife so she could —"

"Mrs. Ogden, she threw me out of the house. I had no choice but to leave. She also filed for divorce."

"What? When did this happen?"

"Sometime this week."

"While she was bedridden and out of her mind with depression? How could she do that when she couldn't possibly have gotten to a lawyer?"

"She is a lawyer."

"She didn't go up to her office to draw up the papers, did she? How could she have filed for divorce?"

"I don't know how to answer that question. I just don't know. All I know is a package came to me by certified mail with a petition for divorce and a restraining order, giving me twenty-four hours to get out. So I got out and slept at the bookstore overnight, then opened the store this morning. I thought if she had the wherewithal to draw up those papers she must be in better shape mentally than I thought."

"She obviously isn't. If she's not in her right mind, then there's no way any of that stuff could be valid."

"I know that now. My attorney stopped by the bookstore this morning and said the restraining order was a fake, printed off the Internet."

"What about the divorce papers?"

"I didn't show them to him. They looked real."

She fired off a look that had "you dumb ass" written all over it. I found interesting shapes in the floor tiles and fiddled with the lint in my pockets.

"We'll worry about that later," she said. "Right now we have to see about getting an in-home nurse."

Samantha followed me back to the bookstore so I could drop off Sid's car, then took me home, leaving Sid to close up the store, where he was having a record sales day. Walking into the living room, she tossed her purse into the big corner chair where Amanda always put her own bag. She then plopped down on the couch and stared at the floor, looking eerily like the wife I just left at the hospital.

"So what are we going to do?" she said.

"I'm supposed to go to D.C. in a few days for the Senate hearings. I don't know if I can get them postponed or not. I have no idea how long they'll last."

"Fine. I'll take her to my house."

"I don't mean it like that. I just can't get out of this.

"I know. I'm not trying to play the part of the angry mother-in-law here." She came over and sat on the arm of the chair I was sitting in and started to rub my shoulders. When I closed my eyes she even sounded like Amanda.

"You're very tense."

"It's been a long, long day, and I didn't get any sleep last night."

She kneaded my shoulders for a while, then repositioned

herself so she was facing me, with both arms resting on my shoulders and her forehead leaning against mine. Physically she had become her daughter.

"You've been good for my daughter. I see why she married you."

She kissed my forehead. Then kissed it again. I was surprisingly relaxed; it was almost as if Amanda herself was sitting there. The facsimile was so real, in fact, without realizing what I was doing, I allowed my hands to float up and caress her breasts. It wasn't until she moaned and said, "That feels good" the spell was broken and she jumped out of my lap.

"We won't ever mention this to her." She pulled her blouse back down over her bra. "Or to anyone else."

I just sat there feeling as though I had eaten something out of the trash can. I couldn't believe I had just felt up my own mother-in-law.

BOOK III

BETRAYAL

CHAPTER ONE

Neither one of us could look the other in the eye for several long, awkward minutes. I tried to look engrossed in the day's mail, while Samantha readjusted some of the knick-knacks on the mantel.

"Right, right. Well, as I said, it'd be easier on me if I could take her to my house instead of leaving her here," she finally said. "She grew up in that house, so it'd be familiar to her. Plus we have family all over town, so there'd be lots of familiar faces and people to help out."

"That sounds like the best thing. I hope she comes out of this funk she's in pretty quickly, because I can't sleep thinking about it."

"You can't do anything for her, with all the miracles you do?"

"No, this is something she has to work out for herself. Some depressions are the result of a chemical imbalance; *that* is something I can fix. This comes from somewhere deep within, a place I can't touch."

"I just..."

Samantha started to cry, and it was obvious she'd been holding back for far too long. Great, wailing sobs burst forth from her collapsing diaphragm. I took her in my arms and she burrowed a wet face into my shoulder.

252

"That's okay. Let it all out," I said.

She did exactly that.

***

Samantha Ogden was a strong woman, there was no question of that. After a long, productive cry, she wiped her eyes and went to work calling around for home care nurses to look out for her daughter. In a fit of efficiency, she even cleaned our house, did the laundry and packed my bags for my upcoming trip, all in less than the time it would have taken me to load the dishwasher.

"I've got a nurse lined up," she said, after forty-five minutes. "We're going to bring Amanda back to Roanoke the day after tomorrow and get her well again. You two are going to get back to work on giving me a grandchild."

She kissed me on the cheek.

"Please don't ever tell Amanda what almost happened," she said.

I never did.

Two days later I had just enough time to help get Amanda set up in Samantha's house before bolting for the airport in Roanoke to catch my flight to D.C. I tried to say good-bye to my beloved, but she could only stare through vacant eyes, with no discernible hint of understanding.

"You've got to catch your plane," Samantha said, as I lingered to stroke Amanda's hair. "She'll be waiting for you when you get back."

Samantha drove me to the airport and hugged me before

leaving. I was both relieved and disappointed she did not try to kiss me, but my life was complicated enough without turning it into a Greek morality tale.

The Roanoke Regional Airport was a good bit larger than Lynchburg's, but it was still tiny by most standards. Within a relatively short time, I was seated on my plane and left to sort through the rubble of my thoughts. Amanda's illness had pushed the Senate hearings to the outskirts of my consciousness for the past couple of weeks, and then there was the bookstore, which would be closed again for an undetermined amount of time. The in-flight magazines offered little to occupy my time. Fortunately it was a short flight.

We touched down at Reagan and I got from the airport to the hotel with the minimum amount of frustration one could expect these days. The cab driver apparently still carried a grudge against the Washington Senators baseball team—the *original* team, not the one that became the Texas Rangers—for leaving town in the early 1960s.

"Sorry, I wasn't even born then," I said.

"So am I blamin' ya? Did I say I was blamin' ya? Everybody acts like yer blaming 'em when ya make a simple observation."

He was silent for a moment.

"So I got nothin' against the Orioles, you unnerstand. Great team, they got a wunnerful, beautiful ballpark to play ball in, that Camden Yards place. They just ain't the hometown team, ya know what I mean? I mean, a hot dog don't taste no better just cause it's from some high-class caterer instead of a guy with a cart on wheels."

"We've got a class A team in Lynchburg. They play in a little ballpark built in nineteen forty across from a cemetery, and they do pretty well," I said.

"That's the kinda thing I'm talkin' about. Grassroots baseball, bringing it back closer to the local level, where ya can just pop over and catch a game or even a couple o' innings and leave if ya want to, without feelin' like yer goin' to Disney Freakin' World or sumpin'."

"Well said."

After helping unload my bags, Rick, the cabdriver, promised to look me up someday in Lynchburg and go to a Hillcats baseball game with me. I told him I looked forward to it.

My room was only slightly more Spartan than the one we had in New York. The bathroom was barely the size of the entire room you'd get at a Motel 6 and the bed was merely a king size.

I showered and plopped on the bed. It was only 9:30 p.m., but I figured if I was going to lay awake all night, I might as well get an early start.

***

Somewhere deep in the woods where I seemed to be hunting an aardvark. I heard a phone ringing. I could find no phone anywhere in the deep woods, so it had to be on the nightstand.

Lights. Clock. It was almost five a.m. I had been wandering the shadow world for seven-and-a-half hours.

"Jeremiah? It's Samantha. Did I wake you?"

"Don't worry about it. What's up? Is anything wrong?"

"No, there's not much change here. Amanda did mutter a

255

few words last night, but they made no sense."

"What were they?"

"She said, 'You left us.' That was all. Does that mean anything to you?"

I sighed and sat up in bed.

"It means she blames me for what happened to her and the baby. We were in a limo on the way to the awards ceremony … well, you know what all happened then. I left her in the limo to try to save a man who'd been shot, and she went into the early labor."

Nothing was said on the other end of the line.

"Mrs. Ogden, I'm so sorry. I never should have left them."

"Did you save the man who was shot?"

"No. He was dead by the time I got to him. I couldn't save anybody that day."

"Well, you tried. You did what you thought you had to, I guess. I almost want to be angry with you, but sitting here looking at Amanda, I can't help thinking about you. I know she loved you—"

"Loves. Please don't use the past tense like she's already dead."

"I'm sorry. I know she loves you very much. You made her so happy, and I love you for that. I just can't stand the thought of what they're going to do to you there, of you having to face that hearing committee all alone. You won't even have a lawyer to represent you, will you?"

"No, it's not like that. It's not a trial. I will be tossed to the lions, in a manner of speaking."

"Well, you won't be alone, not really. We'll both be there with you, in spirit, if nothing else."

"Thank you."

This threesome was getting to be too much, especially with only two of us present. I got up, having slept rather well in spite of myself, showered again and wandered downtown, looking for a place to have an early breakfast.

***

It's interesting how nothing ever looks as big in real life as it does on TV, with the exception of the ocean and the Grand Canyon. Outside of C-SPAN I had never seen the floor of the Senate chambers, but as I stood there in that storied hall and took it all in, I realized it was cozier than it seemed on TV. Sure the ceiling was almost ridiculously high, but I didn't have the feeling I was standing in the middle of Yankee Stadium.

A number of people approached and briefed me on how the hearings would proceed and who the players were, but their voices and images were so fleeting I could just as well have been in the dentist's chair under the gas. I made eye contact and nodded a lot but took in very little of what was said.

These hearings had actually been going on for several days. Numerous people had made complaints about paying people to be healed, only to be left worse off than they were before.

I took my turn at the table in front of the microphone, facing a six-member panel of the Senate Subcommittee on Healthcare Fraud. The panel was evenly divided between Republicans and

Democrats, all of whom came up for reelection in the fall.

"If everyone is ready, we're set to begin," said the chairman, Sen. Schmelling of New Hampshire. "Mr. Townsend, I would like to thank you for taking the time to be with us here today. We have a number of questions to ask you."

"It's my pleasure, Senator." It never hurt to be polite.

"Could you begin by telling us your full name and your occupation?"

"My name is Jeremiah Jerome Townsend, and I am currently the co-owner of the Paige Turner Bookstore in Bedford, Virginia."

"Are you also not currently associated with or employed by a private foundation, a New Agey, holistic healing association known as the Hippocrates Foundation?"

I wasn't so sure I liked his tone.

"I am a member of the foundation, and I am paid a small stipend to participate in their research, yes, sir. However, I would not characterize it as 'New Agey,' for they do legitimate scientific research there."

"I meant no disrespect to the foundation or the good work they do there. My point is you are paid by them for your services, are you not?"

"As I said, I help with their research and I do accept assignments from them, but I am not an actual paid employee there. It's just a stipend, a token of their appreciation, really."

"You do, in a sense, charge for your ability, your services as a healer, do you not?"

"No, sir, I have never charged anyone a fee to heal them. The stipend is just what I said, a token of their appreciation. In return I've done everything from operating the gas chromatograph to weeding the garden and sweeping the kitchen."

"So you're saying you're more like the janitor or the all-purpose go-fer?"

"If the senator wishes to put it that way."

"Mr. Townsend, is it not true that Townsend is not, in fact, even your real name?" said Sen. Cordoba of Virginia.

"My given surname was Cushing. I legally changed it to Townsend when I was eighteen."

"I see," said Sen. Cordoba. "Why?"

"I liked the way 'Townsend' sounded."

"Was there nothing more? Did it, in fact, not have something to do with the particular set of initials you had with your given surname? Do you understand the significance the initials 'J.C.' must have for a man of your particular abilities?"

I had already heard enough "in facts" and "is-it-not-trues" for one day.

"Yes, Senator. I knew all along some people would equate the initials 'J.C.' with Jesus Christ, so I felt it best, therefore, to avoid the comparison."

"What was it you found so distasteful about the association with Jesus Christ?" Sen. Cordoba said.

I rubbed my eyes. *Why don't you just ask me if I've stopped beating my wife, you bastard?*

"Senator, I've worked very hard all my life to not make it seem as though I was claiming to be Jesus returned to Earth. I am not the Second Coming of Christ and I have never said I was. I'm just an ordinary man blessed, if you can call it that, with an extraordinary gift."

"Why would you not call it a blessing? Are you saying there's something wrong with what you do?"

"A poor choice of words on my part, Senator. I am very blessed, indeed."

Sen. Schmelling again leaned into the microphone. As far as I could tell the other four senators had been doodling the entire time.

"Mr. Townsend, are you aware of the purpose of these hearings?"

"It's my understanding, Senator, that a number of people have purported to also have the gift of healing and are charging for their services, though I have no actual knowledge of this."

"No actual knowledge of it?" said Sen. Cordoba, in one of those "gotcha!" tones of voice. "Are you aware, Mr. Townsend, many of these people claim to be healing *in your name?*"

Why didn't somebody tell me this?

"No, Senator, I was not aware of that."

"You have heard of the Internet, haven't you, Mr. Townsend? The World Wide Web?"

"Yes, sir. I have a computer."

"Then you must be aware there are no less than five dozen Web sites out there that mention you or are devoted entirely to you or have some form of your name or your title, as the Miracle Man, in their site name?"

"No, sir, I suppose I assumed I was mentioned on some of the newsgroup sites, but I was not aware of any sites devoted entirely to me. I assure you they were created without my knowledge or consent."

"I see," said Sen. Cordoba, though clearly he didn't.

Sens. Cordoba and Schmelling leaned back in their chairs to whisper to one another while the other four doodled away. There was one thing that had to be said for C-SPAN—it gave you all the endless paper shuffling and irrelevant pauses the networks, even the cable news channels, always cut away from. If the hearing consisted entirely of four people straightening paper clips, you'd see it all on C-SPAN.

"Mr. Townsend, tell us about your family," said Sen. Webber of Oklahoma, one of the four doodlers.

"My wife is currently under the care of an in-home nurse. My sister lives in Lee County, Virginia, with her husband and two children. Those are my only living relatives."

"Really?" said Sen. Webber. "That's a little ironic, don't you think, someone who purportedly has the power to heal any and all ailments has only one healthy, surviving family member?"

"I never said I had the power to heal any and all ailments. There are limitations on my abilities." I could have really used an attorney to jump up and object somewhere along the way, but that wasn't the way these hearings worked.

"So do you mind telling us exactly what happened to your mother and father? Unless it's too painful to recall, of course," said Sen. Cordoba, who appeared to be playing the Bad Cop here.

"My father drove himself into a tree at one hundred and ten miles an hour when I was eleven. He was highly intoxicated at the time. My mother died giving birth to me."

I saw the frown move from face to face across the members of the panel, almost like the senators were doing The Wave with their lips and eyebrows. Sen. Cordoba, who reminded me of Alan Greenspan straining out a stool, put his glasses back on and rifled through the dossier before him.

"Mr. Townsend, it says here your mother died when you were twenty-two of terminal cancer. Would you care to enlighten us as to which version is the truth?" Sen. Cordoba said.

"It's a little complicated, sir. I only recently found out, in the last five years or so, that the woman who raised me was not my biological mother but my grandmother. My mother died during childbirth, so her mother, my grandmother, came to live with our family and acted as mother to all three children. My two siblings, who were both older than me, were told to never tell me about my real mother."

Two senators rubbed their chins and a third scratched his ear. The other three stared unblinkingly.

"That's a rather strange thing for the family to do, wasn't it?" said Sen. Cordoba. "Why on earth did they do that?"

"Because the principle parties are all dead now, with the

exception of my sister, who was young enough she probably doesn't remember anything about it, I can only guess it was to keep me from possibly blaming myself for my mother's death. I grew up calling my grandmother 'Mama,' as did my brother and sister."

"So tell us about your brother. You had a rather strained relationship with him, didn't you?" Cordoba said.

"We didn't speak for most of our adult lives, if that's what you mean. He was always belligerent to me growing up and stopped speaking to me altogether when our mother, that is, our grandmother, died, so I thought he must have blamed me for her death. I now know, however, he may have blamed me all along for the death of our real mother, though as a child I didn't know anything about that."

More shuffling of papers and whispering followed. The senator at the far right end facing me, Sen. Danning of Georgia, looked as though he were asleep. I heard a C-SPAN cameraman cough.

"So if your mother died giving birth to you, you obviously couldn't have done anything about that," said Sen. Schmelling. "If you were twenty-two, an adult, when your grandmother, the woman you say you thought was your mother, died, couldn't you have done something about that, if you do indeed have the power you say you have?"

"She hid her disease from me as long as she could. My ability to sense illness was not fully developed at that point. When the time came she could no longer keep it from me, she asked me to honor

263

her wishes and not intervene. It was the most difficult decision I have ever made and still feel it in the pit of my stomach to this day."

"That must have been very hard for you, indeed, but I admire you for having the courage to respect her last request," said Sen. Schmelling. "I'm not sure I could have done the same thing. Have you been put in that position any other time, when you had to let someone go?"

"Yes, sir. There was a lady evangelist near my hometown."

"Would that be a Francis Claremont, age sixty-two, of St. Charles, Virginia?" Sen. Schmelling looked deep within the stack of papers. I had no idea where they pulled these files from, but I was beginning to wonder why they needed me at all. "Apparently you made her enemies' list."

"She was a deeply religious woman who felt I was committing blasphemy by healing her husband. I might add I did so at his request. I was, I believe, a junior in high school at the time."

"Getting back to your brother, Mr. Townsend, what became of him?" said Sen. Cordoba.

"My brother committed suicide after attempting to frame me for assaulting a woman. I think he tried to redeem himself in the end by setting up a trust fund for me while I was institutionalized in a nursing home after suffering a stroke."

Sen. Schmelling let out a whistle. "Your wife is also currently suffering from a severe, crippling depression. That's quite a history of tragedy in the family for a man with your powers, Mr. Townsend. Your whole life, in fact, reads like a soap opera plot."

264

I shrugged, not knowing what else I was supposed to do.

"Strange, indeed, Mr. Townsend, that so much, shall we say, bad luck, seems to have afflicted everyone you touch," said Sen. Cordoba.

I was running out of subtle gestures. What was I supposed to say? Who is John Galt? They probably wouldn't have gotten the reference, anyway.

"I think we should take a ninety minute recess." Sen. Schmelling tapped a gavel one time. "We'll meet back here at one-thirty sharp."

I took a deep breath and let my shoulders sag. This was like the old *This Is Your Life* show as it might be done in Hell.

"Boy you certainly, like, made somebody's shit list up there." An attractive young blonde in a blue blazer and a business skirt offered her hand to shake. "I'm Corrine, I'm a transcriptionist for the Senate, but today's my day off. Would you care to get some lunch with me?"

I accepted. A friendly face, especially one right out of a shampoo commercial, was exactly what I needed now. Corrine took me to a little Italian café a block away where we sat and ordered breadsticks and salad. For the most part I watched her devour her food while I chewed the same piece endlessly until I had no choice but to swallow. Wiping the fairy dust from her mouth, Corrine leaned toward me and offered an analysis of the morning's events thus far.

"I think your strategy up there may, like, have been a little risky, but it might just pay off for you in the end."

"What strategy? They're hammering me like a nail."

"You've answered every question directly and quickly, really on the mark. I'm getting, like, a 'let's get this over with, I'm taking no shit off anybody' vibe from you. I think the rest of the gallery is getting it, too."

"That's good?"

"Sure it is. Most of these things are, like, so boring you just want to go, 'Hello, this is very, incredibly dull. Don't you people have anything better to do?' It's usually some hearing where they go through a report, word-for-word, and then ask questions. You've actually got a story to tell. Are you going to eat the rest of that?"

I gave her my breadsticks. "So then why is what I'm doing also risky?"

"Well, the thing you want to be careful about is not coming across as being, like, too belligerent. They hate that. Not really rude, maybe, but kinda testy. I don't think you're in danger of doing that, but you want to make sure you don't show them up. They don't want anybody to come across as being, like, smarter than themselves."

"That wouldn't be all that difficult." That brought a guffaw from Corrine.

"I like you. You seem like someone who'd probably be really cool to hang with."

"Not really. I'm actually pretty dull."

"I don't believe that. You're funny, without being the class clown, lampshade-on-the-head kind of guy. Those kind of guys are, like, jerks and the act wears thin after a while."

"Yes, but I don't even have an act. I'm just exactly what you see across from you in this booth."

"Well, what I see is an intelligent, disarmingly handsome man who is polite and goes out of his way to help people. You're a regular knight from King Ahab's Round Table."

"King Arthur."

"I knew that, silly. I just wanted to see if you had the balls to correct me. Do you want the rest of your tea?"

Corrine took my arm as we walked back toward the Capitol, humming and kicking her legs up as she walked. Her hair bounced with each step as if buoyed by the sheer joy of an early fall afternoon.

"I live in an apartment not too far from here, in case you wanted to know," she said. "In case you get bored with the usual sightseeing tour kinda stuff and want to see some of Washington's wildlife."

"Just how many married men do you invite up to view the wildlife?"

"Just you. Besides, I noticed you aren't wearing a ring, Mr. Married Man. What's up with that?"

The ring was indeed missing from my finger. "Well, what do you know about that? I didn't even realize I didn't have it on."

"Oh, sure. Like all married men don't let their rings slide off into their pockets when a babe like me comes into view on their chick radar." The self-deprecating laugh that followed was goofy yet charming at the same time. "You should laugh more yourself, you know."

"I'm sorry. It's just I haven't had much to laugh about lately."

"No, but you're smiling. That's a start. C'mon, I'll show you how to get past security."

A mound of messages awaited me as I took my seat in front of the microphone. The Senate pages had been busy while I was out. Several were little notes of reassurance from congressmen not on the panel who had evidently watched the televised proceedings. Most were printed e-mails from viewers around the country encouraging me to hang in there.

A woman from Kansas wrote in thanking me for healing her son at a veteran's hospital in Philadelphia. Quite a few said they were never, ever going to vote for anyone on the panel ever again.

I chuckled at some of the quotes sent in. As I went through the stack, the panel members reappeared and sat down.

"Mr. Townsend, thank you again for agreeing to speak to us," said Sen. Schmelling. "Just recapping some of the events in your role as a healer, did you not recently undertake a humanitarian mission of sorts to central Africa as part of a team made up of people from a number of organizations?"

"Yes, sir, I went as a member of the Hippocrates Foundation, along with representatives from the World Health Organization, the Centers for Disease Control and a government agency which remains unknown to me. We were sent to investigate a sudden plague that had struck a small village."

"What did you find?" Schmelling said.

"There was no one left alive, out of more than two hundred

people, when we got there. Members of the government agency were burning the bodies and all the houses. The air was toxic with smoke."

"So you weren't able to save anyone?" said Sen. Cordoba. "The mission was a complete failure from your point of view?"

"No, sir, I wouldn't say that. I was able to save more than four hundred people in a nearby village, infecting myself in the process. By taking samples of my blood, after I survived the plague, as well as one of the village men who donated blood to help save me, the Hippocrates Foundation was able to create an antidote of sorts that will be kept permanently on hand in case this particular epidemic should ever hit again."

I took a sip of water. Cordoba was leaning back in his chair with his chin in his hand. Schmelling was drumming with his hands.

"All right, those are all the questions we have for the moment, Mr. Townsend," Schmelling said. "We would like you to remain available to us, as we have a few other people we're going to be calling upon. Is a Ms. Monique Hardaway here?"

The sound of that name startled me so badly I spilled the entire pitcher of water right there on television. I hadn't seen Monique since high school; as I twisted in my seat to look toward the aisle behind me, I could not believe the figure slowly moving forward.

With leathery skin stretched taut across fallen cheekbones, the tall, wispy woman who shuffled and limped toward my table looked to be in her late sixties. No creature from my darkest nightmare could have chilled me the way that apparition did. I stood as she approached, more out of fear and an overwhelming urge to run than from any sense of chivalry.

Her chest was flat and almost hollow under a knitted blouse. The legs that protruded from the calf-length plaid skirt were ashen and dry. Perhaps most startling was the mouth, drawn into a permanent "o" shape over toothless gums.

There was no mistaking the eyes, however. This was indeed Monique. She stumbled to the table and, with the assistance of one of the pages, eased into a chair beside me.

Her breath came to her in long, struggling rasps, like wind rattling dry leaves across plastic. What had happened to this young woman whom even the goddesses once envied?

"Sen. Schmelling, Sen. Cordoba, distinguished members of the panel, my name is Monique Maria Esterhaus Hardaway, and I was once the girlfriend of the man beside me." She said it all in one agonized exhalation, exhausted by the effort. I realized I was still standing at that point and sat down.

"Ms. Hardaway, did you ever ask Mr. Townsend here to perform any of his healing abilities on you at any time?" Sen. Schmelling said.

"Yes, sir, what I am today is a result of that." I heard the collective gasp all around the floor. Cameras flashed from all angles as she fought to regain her breath. "When I was in high school, I had an extremely heavy menstrual flow and I asked him to do something about it."

"What exactly did he do about it?" Sen. Cordoba said.

"He placed his hands over my ovaries and I felt a sudden, cold pain. My menstrual period for that month immediately stopped and I never had one again."

"How old were you at that time?" Schmelling said.

"I was eighteen." Again a gasp from the crowd.

"You mean to say you haven't had a menstrual period since the age of eighteen? What did that do to your ability to have children?" Cordoba said.

"It destroyed it. I could never have children." Tears were in her eyes, but Monique apparently didn't have enough wind to cry.

"What other effects did this cure have on you?" Cordoba said.

"I suffered from severe fatigue from that day forward. I lost my teeth in my mid-twenties, lost both breasts to cancer at twenty-nine. I lost this—" she pulled off her wig and set it on the table, exposing a smooth, hairless head—"at thirty-seven. I have no collagen in my skin, giving me the appearance of being much older than I really am."

She coughed for almost two minutes straight as I sat there, on television, afraid to touch her.

"Where was I? Oh, yes, I suffer from advanced emphysema, although I never smoked, and I have been unable to perform sexually for more than ten years due to extreme dryness."

That set the gallery buzzing. As I sat there inches away, my diagnostic abilities were running wide open. I knew she did indeed suffer from everything she said.

271

I could fix it all but dared not try to do so.

"What effect has all this had on your marriage?" Cordoba said.

"My husband divorced me nine years ago. I never remarried. Who would want me now?"

"Ms. Hardaway, you said you were Mr. Townsend's girlfriend in high school. Were you lovers?" Cordoba said.

"What do you mean?"

"Were you sexually active?"

"Yes. Well, not exactly."

"How exactly?"

"We never had intercourse. We...touched each other a lot. We experimented with oral sex."

"Did you ever bring each other to climax, orally or otherwise?"

"Yes."

Well, she hadn't lied so far. I wished they would move on.

"How did you feel about Mr. Townsend, I believe you knew him as Mr. Cushing, at the time?" Cordoba said.

"I loved him. He was my world. I wanted to marry him."

"Tell me, Ms. Hardaway, were you attractive as a young woman?" Cordoba said.

"Yes. At least I'm told I was very pretty."

"So you did well with the boys? Very popular?"

"I was prom queen and homecoming queen my senior year, Miss Lee County and a Miss Young Virginia. Older men as well as boys asked me out all the time."

"You stuck with Mr. Cush—, er, Mr. Townsend, all the while you could have had basically just about anyone you chose. Why was that?"

"I loved him. He was different, smarter, funnier. He seemed like he was going places."

"So as a young girl you were the belle of the ball, so to speak. You had the world in your pretty little hands. What is that world like now?"

Monique stared at the table in front of her for several seconds before looking up and making eye contact—for the first time—with the members of the panel.

"I know I am ugly. I don't like to look at myself. I don't even keep mirrors in my apartment." It seemed about all she could manage in one breath. "Because I am disabled, I am unable to work. I don't go out. I have no friends. I order my food delivered to me. If I died today, no one would know until my rent came due."

The nerves on my arms and neck told me every eye in the building was on me.

"So do you blame Mr. Townsend for what your life has become?" I believe Sen. Cordoba would have laughed and pointed at me had the cameras not been on him.

"Yes. No. Sometimes. Sometimes not."

"Why not?"

"I asked him to do this."

If one more collective gasp had hit the room, we would all

have passed out from the decrease in air pressure.

Way to go Monique.

"Could you elaborate?"

"It wasn't fair the way I put it to him, the problem I had. I didn't just ask him to fix my menstrual problem, I asked him to eliminate it all together."

"What do you mean by that? Eliminate what?" Schmelling said.

"I asked him to remove my menstrual cycle all together. I didn't want to ever have a period again. He did remove it, somehow, and this is what it did to me. I suppose, in a way, I asked for exactly this."

"So you don't feel badly toward him?" Schmelling said.

"Of course I feel badly toward him. He should have refused to do what I asked of him. If he'd known this was going to happen, I know he would have refused. I had a way with him then, a way with all boys, really. I got whatever I wanted from boys in those days."

"Do you still get whatever you want?" Cordoba said.

"Of course not. I'm a hag and I know it. I've had a lot of time to think about what my life was like in those days, and I don't always like the person I was." Another pause for breath. "I was beautiful and I knew it. I used my looks for everything. In time I suppose I would have had to do more than bat my eyes; I would have had to start sleeping around to get the things I was used to getting. I was probably on my way to becoming a whore of some sort."

That raised the ambient noise level a notch. I tried to readjust my position in my seat without calling attention to myself.

"Senators, I sit before you an ugly woman with a beautiful soul. Twenty-five years ago it was the other way around. I was not a good person, I was a vain little bitch who looked out for number one. Jeremiah kept me grounded in many ways, even before this happened. Today I manage to volunteer at homeless shelters when I am able. I write poetry and songs and visit children in the hospital. I get respect without showing my ass, and I mean that in more ways than one, if you'll excuse my language."

Another long pause as Schmelling and Cordoba put their hands over their microphones and whispered while the other four, I can only assume, moved on from doodles to still lifes. Finally, Schmelling scooted back up to the microphone: "So you're saying you had an overall positive experience from your encounter with Mr. Townsend."

Monique sighed, as did everyone else in the building not on the panel.

"No, Senator, I'm saying I more or less brought this on myself. I took a personally devastating experience and turned it around. I survived. In the long view- of things it may be said my experience with Jeremiah taught me a painful lesson, but I can't say that just yet. Maybe I'll leave that for someone else to decide long after I'm gone."

"Mr. Townsend's actions are what caused this devastating experience, are they not?" said Cordoba.

"I'm not ready to say that, Senator. I'm saying we make our own destinies. Now if you'll excuse me, I have to rest." Monique put her wig back on and struggled to her feet. "May I be excused?"

Schmelling "by-all-means"-ed her away with a sweep of his hand.

I sank back in my chair, emotionally exhausted. Monique never once glanced my way after sitting down, never so much as leaned and whispered to me. I didn't blame her. If she'd decided to forgive me, she certainly didn't want me to know about it.

"In light of the lateness of the hour, I think it appropriate we adjourn for the day," Schmelling said. "Mr. Townsend, could you be here again tomorrow morning?"

"Yes, Senator." I stood and stretched, then saw the reporters heading in my direction.

"C'mon, I can sneak you out." Corrine, now wearing a knit shirt and short skirt, ran up to grab my arm. I followed her out through a restricted area, then down a passageway reserved for congressional employees. We emerged into the late afternoon sun, far from anyone with a pad, pencil or camera.

"Well that was an interesting exchange." She held my hand as if we were long-time lovers. "One thing I don't understand is how you could, like, remove her menstrual cycle at her request. I thought you could only fix what was wrong with somebody, not alter them entirely and create new problems."

"That's the way it's supposed to work, but you're right, I shouldn't have been able to stop her cycle altogether. Believe me, I've had plenty of time to wonder about that over the years. I think that was meant as a warning to me I shouldn't go beyond true healing. That's why I don't try to help bald men regrow their hair or help women get rid of cellulite."

"That's too bad." Corrine turned to look at the backs of her legs, pulling her skirt up slightly as she did so. "I'm going to be needing that sort of help before too much longer."

"Your legs are absolutely perfect. I wouldn't touch them."

"Now that's *really* too bad," she said. We stopped at a park bench and sat down, watching the squirrels scamper across the immaculate lawns.

"Something else I don't understand." By now she was practically in my lap. "If she was really as bitchy as she says she was, what did you see in her? You don't seem like the type to be drawn to the selfish, princess chick."

I studied this undulating nymph nuzzling herself against me before answering. With rose-smelling hair that cascaded gently around her shoulders and smooth, firm skin still untouched by age, she was almost in the same league Monique once inhabited—almost.

"It's not something I can explain. I knew, of course, she was selfish and vain, but at the time it didn't seem to matter. Guys are funny like that, especially when they're young and stupid, in that they'll do almost anything or put up with almost anything to be around a beautiful girl. We can be used just as easily, in fact, probably more so, as girls can be used by guys."

"You probably know better now, right?" She traced circles in

277

the palm of my hand.

"That's right." I closed my hand and pulled it away. "I know how to say 'no' to beautiful women now."

"Do you think I'm a beautiful woman?"

"I think you're a tease."

"Oh I'm no tease. A tease just gets you all worked up and leaves you there. I follow through."

"Then yes, I think you're a beautiful woman. And I'm a married man."

"I know that. I'm just having a little fun on my day off."

"I'm really hungry now," I said. "I didn't eat much lunch."

"Tell you what, let's go back to my apartment so I can take a shower; then we'll go out to get something together. You can meet my roommate. She's a riot."

I considered the prospect of eating alone and accepted. Corrine's apartment was three blocks away in an old stone house that had been converted into four units. We mounted the back steps to a second story unit and came into a surprisingly large kitchen, where a stunning young black woman in a T-shirt and panties giggled at us.

"Girl, what you bringin' home now?" The young woman moved with an alarming slowness.

"Girl, I know what you been doin'!" Corrine laughed. "This is my friend, Jeremiah. He's part of some Senate hearings going on now. Jeremiah, this is J.J. Girl, at least go put some pants on!"

J.J. tried to speak but couldn't stop giggling. She pulled on a pair of sweat pants and flopped on the couch, just outside the kitchen. I watched as Corrine disappeared into a back room, leaving me with a stoned idiot.

I sat in an easy chair as far from the couch as possible, looking through a stack of magazines in an effort to distract myself from J.J.'s buzz. The magazines ran the gamut from *Cosmo* to *Glamour*, but I picked one at random anyway and buried my head in it. J.J. giggled at the Teletubbies on the tube. I could hear the shower and was silently urging Corrine to hurry.

After a few minutes I heard J.J. say, "I'd better go check on that white girl, make sure she didn't fall in." She giggled at that and went into the back room.

After twenty minutes passed I knew something was wrong. I wanted to bolt but curiosity kept me in that chair. Finally, a sniggering Corrine staggered into the room still wearing a bathrobe, loosely knotted at the waist, her hair wet and uncombed

"I thought you'd come check on me." She climbed into the chair with me, facing me with her knees down, her robe open to reveal her breasts. "You could have dried me off. Hey, is that a roll of coins in your pocket?"

She found this unbearably funny and slid laughing onto the floor, her robe almost completely off her body now. "You know what's a funny word, Jeremiah? Titter! 'Cause it sounds like titties, get it? Oops, look at that. I'm naked."

"I'd better go." I stood and stepped over her.

"Hey, don't be so uptight." She got up and grabbed my arm. That was funny, too.

"You're stoned. I'm not. You do the math."

"Hey, we can fix that."

"I don't do that stuff."

"Well I do. What ya gonna do about it?"

"I'll show you what I can do about it." I put my hand against her forehead and jerked it away, causing her to wobble backward.

"Goddamn it! That was a good buzz!" She pulled her robe closed, suddenly fully sober. "That buzz cost me eighty dollars!"

"I'll send you a check," I headed for the door.

"No. Wait. I'm sorry." She grabbed my arm and turned me around. "Look, I don't always do this. I don't usually do this. Okay, sometimes I do it. It just relaxes me, okay? Look, I really like you and I don't want you to go away like this."

"I've already seen you naked. What else is in it for me?"

"Lots more. There's lots more of that, if you want it."

"You've already shown your ass. Frankly, I didn't like what I saw." I turned and was out the door.

Monique was right. That expression could have more than one meaning.

CHAPTER TWO

I found a little bistro and ate at a table on the sidewalk that evening. I wondered if possibly I had been too harsh on Corrine. After all, she had befriended me and kept me away from the reporters. I supposed that was certainly worth letting her get stoned, if that was what made her happy.

The real problem was not the fact she had gotten stoned; it was I was sexually attracted to her and she was coming on to me. I should never have gone to her apartment at all, knowing full well we could have ended up bedding each other. In fact, I now silently admitted, that was really why I went there.

I wolfed down a steak sandwich, trying not to look at the people around me. I had no idea what I was going to do with myself the rest of the evening, but I still didn't want to be alone. As if in answer to my plea, a female figure slid into a chair across from me.

"Okay, I'm not stoned. Will you accept an apology?" Corrine obviously had given up on trying to seduce me, judging by the T-shirt, cargo shorts and sandals. Her hair was now up in a ponytail.

"Why do you even care what I think? You're a grown woman, very attractive; you must have guys digging under the fence to get at you. You don't need an old fart like me to make you a woman."

"They're all jerks. You, you're just so, I don't know, like, decent, I guess. I haven't met any guys like you, outside of my dad, my uncles, and my brother. Really my whole family, I guess. I don't like the way they're treating you up there at the Senate, and I hate the thought of you wandering this town alone. This is a very cold town. It doesn't take in strangers very well."

"I'm just visiting, I'm not staying."

"Look, if you want me to go..."

"No, I didn't say that. The truth is I need a friendly face tonight. Yes, I was very turned on by you earlier."

"Well, duh, I could see that. I mean, hello, there it was in my face. That's one thing guys can't hide. They think we don't see that thing sticking out when they don't want us to, but believe me, we do."

"Okay, now that we've got that out of the way, what do you want to do? Are you hungry?"

"I ate a bag of pretzels at the apartment. Your little de-stoning trick didn't cure me of the munchies, you know."

"I wasn't trying. Hey, I've got an urge to see an Orioles game. Can we still catch a few innings?"

"The Orioles? They suck since Ripken retired. Besides, traffic's a bitch up that way. We could catch it on TV, though."

"Not the same thing. How about a movie?"

"You're on."

"No chick flicks, though."

"Damn, I was hoping to let off some excess estrogen."

The movie, a summer action blockbuster ready to retire to the video stores, was entirely forgettable and exactly what I needed. Corrine sat with her feet on the seat in front of us in the way only under-25 females can do and still be adorable doing it. She blitzed her way through a jumbo buttered popcorn, with only minimal help from me, and two Cokes, while I finished off some M&Ms and a small drink.

After the movie she walked me back into the hotel lobby, pausing at the elevator.

"I had a great time." Her gaze shimmied toward the elevator. Her body was angled slightly toward me in a stance that told me she was ready to go either way. The silence was so painful both of us wanted to cough just to break the spell.

"Yeah, it was fun," I said. Neither of us moved.

"Well, I guess I should—"

"Oh, what the hell. Come on up." I was relieved to have made a decision, any decision.

Corrine actually squealed and bounced ever so slightly. She continued to bounce on her toes, ponytail bobbing, as the elevator ferried us up.

Lord, keep me strong.

"Man, this place is huge." She opened her arms wide as we crossed the threshold.

"You should have seen the one we had in New York."

Good. I used the word "we." Remember "we."

"Yeah, I never did hear what happened to you there." She

leaped onto the couch and put her feet on the glass top coffee table. "Weren't you there to get some sort of humanitarian award?"

I sighed. There were many stories about my life I did not like to tell. That one was the worst.

"Let's just say it didn't go well for any of us."

We talked for hours about life, love and the world in general. Corrine became surprisingly articulate when relaxed, even dropping the incessant "like" that peppered the conversations of her generation. I was unaware of time until the phone rang.

"Jeremiah? I tried to call you earlier but you were out. I watched the hearings on TV this evening."

It was Samantha. I couldn't see a clock anywhere so I had no idea what time it was.

"So what did you think?" I found myself wondering why I had a young woman in my hotel room while my mother-in-law was on the phone.

"I thought it was awful. That Cordoba was trying to railroad you. What were the others even doing there, most of them didn't even speak."

I did a double take. Corrine's T-shirt was off. I shook my head violently and mouthed the word "no."

"I think they're doing their best to make me look bad, although I'm not exactly sure what they hope to get out of it. Tomorrow should be an interesting day."

Corrine's bra and shorts were off. There were no visible tan lines. I shook my head even harder and held my hand out in the universal "halt" sign.

"So how's Amanda?" I said. *Stay focused.*

Corrine was on the couch against me, sliding her panties down over her knees.

"No change. She still doesn't know anyone. Jeremiah, I just don't know what to do."

"You're doing about all you possibly can." My pulse was already quickening and my voice had gone up a notch.

Corrine was naked and on top of me.

"I just feel like there should be more I could do, like there's something I'm missing. What's wrong with her?" Samantha said.

I couldn't answer her.

"I know they're saying it's postpartum depression, but that just doesn't seem right at all. There's something else at work here, something so fundamentally simple we just can't see it."

I could barely hold the receiver near my head.

"Jeremiah, you're breathing awfully fast. Is something wrong?"

"What? No..."

"You're out of breath. Have you been running?"

The receiver hit the floor. After a few moments I leaned over and picked it up.

"Hello? Are you still there? No, I'm fine. I just spilled something all over the chair; that's all."

CHAPTER THREE

Corrine rose and snuck out of the hotel room very early the next morning to make sure the reporters wouldn't see her. I wasn't sure what I would say if that happened.

Hello. No, this pretty young woman is not my wife. She's just someone I ran into who came over and got naked and started doing me while I was on the phone with my mother-in-law, who is lamenting that her daughter, my wife, is nearly comatose. Oh, yes, we made a mess all over the upholstery in here.

I shuddered. The best thing for me would probably be to start a regimen of cold showers every day from now on. I relented, however, and took a nice, relaxing hot shower before consuming the complimentary breakfast of bacon, eggs, sausage, juice and milk.

A rabble of reporters awaited me in the lobby as I stepped out of the elevator. Although there hadn't been much interest in the hearings the day before, Monique's appearance generated a fresh take on things.

"Mr. Townsend, what did you think of Ms. Hardaway's description of you yesterday? Was that an accurate account of your prior relationship with her?" asked someone from *USA Today*.

"Do you plan on a stronger defense of your activities thus far at today's hearings?" That was from NBC News.

"I have no comment at this point. I'm not on trial here. I'm simply answering whatever questions the panel has of me. Good day."

"Who was the young woman you were seen with last night?"

"Pardon me?"

"Liz Fauber, *National Confessor*. Who was the young blonde with the ponytail you were seen with last night? You were spotted dining at an outdoor café with her, then going to a movie. She also accompanied you back to this hotel, where she got on the elevator with you, presumably to go up to your room with you. She was not observed leaving all night. Did you have a sexual relationship with her?"

More than a dozen microphones rose up to stare at me like foam-faced cobras.

"She was a very nice young lady who felt sorry for me and agreed to escort me around town for the evening," I said.

"Did you sleep with her?" said Liz Fauber.

"That's not really an appropriate question, is it? Now, if you'll excuse me, I must be going." I turned and loped out the door.

"Mr. Townsend..." said the chorus.

I would have preferred to walk the few blocks to the Capitol but chose the sanctuary of a cab.

Way to go. You were spotted with your little tart.

Oh, well, I had another day of innuendo and accusations to look forward to. That should take my mind off the affair I'd had.

Another bevy of reporters greeted me on the steps of the

Capitol, but no one mentioned the cradle-robbing tryst from the night before. I waved and nodded and made my way up the steps, glad for once to have security to run interference for me.

On the floor a couple of people again approached me to brief me on the day's events. This time I was determined to pay attention.

"You probably won't be called upon for a while this morning so you can sit back in the gallery if you like," said a young woman named Marcia, whose title I failed to grasp. "The panel has some other people lined up for the morning session."

I nodded and took a seat away from the front table, afraid to look around for fear of seeing Corrine. Just where did she work, anyway? She said she was a transcriptionist, which meant she probably worked in an office somewhere transcribing tapes from— oops, no, there she was, right there on the floor with one of those little magic typing machines the court reporters use. She looked fetching in her business jacket, scarf and pleated skirt. I should know, since I fetched her the previous evening. Her legs were even silkier than I remembered. How could she eat the way she did and stay so trim? Looking at her from across the floor, I realized why I couldn't say no to her advances.

At least she had taken her hair down from the ponytail.

Sen. Schmelling's voice opening the hearing shook me from my trance.

"Is Sergeant Lionel Lucas here today?" Schmelling said.

The name meant nothing to me and at first I didn't recognize the tall young Marine striding up to the table. His steely blue eyes never strayed from the panel as he took his seat before the microphone. There was something in the way he carried himself that seemed familiar.

"Sergeant Lucas, I understand you had a most remarkable encounter with our Mr. Townsend," Schmelling said.

"Yes, sir. I grew a new leg thanks to Mr. Townsend."

Oh *that* young man. A murmur made its way around the floor.

"He grew a new leg for you, is that what you said?" said Sen. Cordoba.

"Yes, sir. Twelve years ago, sir. I was in an automobile accident and lost my right leg. I was in a children's hospital in Memphis when Mr. Townsend came to visit our ward. I was eleven at the time."

"I suppose he put his hands on you and you sprouted this leg?" said Schmelling.

"No, sir. He never even came into the room with me. He just walked by and I felt this tingling sensation. At first it really hurt, but then I realized the bone was forming, the skin was stretching and something was happening. Before I knew it, this new leg was in place and I stood up. Without even thinking, I ran to meet him, along with all the other kids in the ward."

I shuffled in my seat. I had to admit, that day was remarkable, even by my standards.

"So you ran to meet him and you've never really stopped

running since, have you?" Schmelling said.

"No, sir. I played football and ran track in high school, where I set the state high school record in the one hundred meter dash and ran the anchor leg on a state champion four hundred meter relay team. I joined the Marine Corps after high school and now hold the record for the one hundred meters across all branches of the service. I also became an alternate on the U.S. Olympic team for the games in Sydney."

That was the first I had heard of all that. I was happy for him.

"Doesn't this magic leg of yours give you an unfair advantage over other athletes?" Cordoba said. "I mean you weren't born with it, you got it through apparently supernatural means, if all this is to be believed. Perhaps it wasn't meant to be used in competition against others."

"The way I see it, sir, my left leg has to run just as fast as my right to keep up."

"I see," said Cordoba. "So it does. So you haven't had any negative effects from this leg?"

"Sir?"

"You know, unexplained bad luck or tragedy for you or others associated with the leg," Cordoba said.

"No, sir. I don't see how regaining my leg could be anything but positive. The tragedy for me was losing it in the first place."

That derailed Cordoba. He sat back in his chair and chewed his pen. The other members of the panel moved little.

"Well, if there are no other questions, Sergeant Lucas, you are free to go. Thank you for your time."

"Sir? If I may?" Lucas said.

"By all means, Sergeant."

"I don't really know Mr. Townsend except for what happened that day. I was absolutely ecstatic when I ran up to meet him when my leg reappeared, but there were a lot of other kids around him that day, all of them wanting his attention. He didn't have to take the time to say anything to me, but he stayed until he'd had a chance to let every one of us thank him. He said to me, 'Just be sure you do something good with that leg.' I know that's not very profound, but it stayed with me. When I get out of the Marines, I plan to help rehabilitate others who've lost limbs or mobility. My life is entirely different because of him and I owe him a debt I can never repay."

You just repaid it, Sergeant.

"Well said, Sergeant Lucas, and thank you for your time," Schmelling said. "Now we have another young man here, I believe, a Darren Hairston. Is Mr. Hairston here?"

That was a name I hoped to forget. There he was, older but still rangy and shaggy. He looked far healthier than when I first saw him, however. He took the seat vacated by Lionel Lucas.

"Mr. Hairston, I believe both you and your younger brother had some dealings with Mr. Townsend, is that correct?"

Darren mumbled something inaudible, well out of microphone range.

"You're going to have to speak up, Mr. Hairston. Please lean

291

toward the microphone," Schmelling said.

"Yeah. Me and my brother, Warren, was both dying of AIDS," Darren said. "I didn't want no help for myself. I was just gonna let whatever was gonna happen, happen. I went lookin' for Mr. Townsend there to help my younger brother."

"Was he able to help your brother?" Schmelling said.

"Oh, yeah. At first he was real uptight about it but then he felt sorry for us and he was cool about it."

"Uptight about what? What are you talking about?" Cordoba said.

"I guess 'cause of what I done to Warren. He got over it and he helped me, too, even though I didn't want no help."

"What did you do to Warren?" Cordoba said.

"I wuz the one that give him AIDS."

Every member of the panel leaned back and rubbed his eyes. The chatter level throughout the hall rose.

"I'm afraid to ask how you did that," said Sen. Jameson of Texas, the first words he had spoken.

"It wuz through sexual contact, Your Honor," Warren said. "It wadn't his fault, though; it wuz all me. I forced myself on him."

"How old were you and your brother at the time?" Jameson said.

"I was twenty-one. Warren was eleven."

That set the place in chaos. Books slammed to the floor, people cursed. Darren flinched in his seat from an imaginary blow.

"Mr. Chairman, I don't want to hear anything else from

292

this...man," Jameson said. "I have nothing but disgust for him and his situation."

Darren's posture did not change.

"I sympathize with your feelings, Senator, and I feel the same way, but we need to get through this. Mr. Townsend, would you mind answering a few questions in this situation?" Schmelling said.

I stood and walked toward the table, taking the seat beside Darren. He nodded without looking at me. I didn't return the gesture.

"Mr. Townsend, how did you enter into this squalid tale?" said Schmelling.

"Mr. Hairston recognized me in a card shop and asked if I could help his partner. I agreed to do so and drove him back to where they were staying."

"Were you aware that his 'partner' was actually his eleven-year-old brother?" Cordoba said.

"Not at the time. I assumed it was an adult."

"What did you find?" Cordoba said.

"I drove Mr. Hairston to a very rundown old house with broken windows and no electricity. It wasn't until I got inside I saw his 'partner' was indeed a child. I then realized the child bore a strong resemblance to Mr. Hairston. In fact, he looked exactly like him, only younger."

"Your reaction, as Mr. Hairston put it, was to get 'uptight'?" Cordoba said.

"It was more than that. I wanted to kill him, that is, the older brother. I was so angry I couldn't even heal the boy, Warren, at first."

"So your power doesn't work if you're angry?" Cordoba said.

"Apparently not if I'm *that* angry. I was more than just mad; I was seething with hate. It wasn't until Warren pleaded for Darren's life I realized what I had to do."

"Which was?"

"I had to find some way to calm myself down, to tell myself it wasn't my job to judge Darren for what he had done. I won't sit here and tell you the anger just melted away, because it didn't, but I did manage to establish a sense of perspective. As soon as I told myself I was going to go back and heal Darren, whether he wanted me to or not, my rage subsided enough to help me heal Warren. Then I went back for Darren."

"You told us yesterday you refused to heal your own mother, er, grandmother, against her wishes," Schmelling said. "What then made you heal this man, this incestuous sexual predator, when he clearly did not want your help?"

"Senator, the situation with my grandmother was entirely different. No one else's life depended on her being saved. She had lived a good, long life and wanted to go on her way. For her the race had been run. In this case, in order to save Warren's life, I had to also save Darren. My grandmother had no regrets over her life, whereas Darren was eaten up with guilt. Perhaps it was part of his punishment to go on living knowing what he had done."

"Did he go on living with Warren?" Schmelling said.

"No, Your Honor, I haven't seen Warren since that day,"

Darren said. "I don't know what became of him."

"I took the liberty of driving Warren to Tennessee where he had an aunt who agreed to take him in and raise him."

"*You* did that, Mr. Townsend?" Jameson said.

"Yes, Senator."

"Did you report Mr. Hairston here to the authorities?" Jameson said.

"No, Senator, I wanted Warren to be able to get on with his life in a new home without first going through the court system."

"There are channels you must go through, Mr. Townsend. We can't just go around playing God, as you of all people should know," Cordoba said. "How do you know Warren received adequate care at this aunt's house?"

"They have sent me Christmas cards every year since then. On two occasions they drove to Lynchburg and visited with me. Warren always seemed quite happy."

"My aunt's a good woman. She'd take good care of the boy," Darren said. "If he says Warren ended up with my aunt Charlotte in Tennessee, then I know he's in good hands."

"How has your life gone since you were healed, Mr. Hairston?" Schmelling said.

"It's just my life, you know, not no better and not no worse than before. Well, I guess it's better 'cause I stopped shootin' up with needles; that's how I got the AIDS in the first place," Darren said. "Let me say for the record, I'm not no homosexual, just 'cause I gave my brother AIDS, no sir. I'm a lot of things, and I may have had sex with my younger brother, but I'm not no homo."

"Mr. Hairston, I'll have you know I am a homosexual, one of the first to openly serve in the Senate, and I find your conduct appalling beyond belief," Schmelling said. "Your insinuation that simply being homosexual in and of itself is somehow worse than the crimes you committed against your own brother is insulting and degrading to every gay person in America. You, sir, are nothing more than a rapist, a sexual predator without shame, both a pedophile and committer of incest. If no one has any other questions for Mr. Hairston, I for one would like to see him removed from these august chambers."

"Hear, hear. I hope to never see him again," Cordoba said.

"Amen and seconded," Jameson said. "I feel like I need to take a shower just being in the room with him."

Darren didn't wait for security to remove him. He stood and slunk away. Even the television cameras parted before him.

"Mr. Townsend, you are to be commended for stepping in on young Warren's behalf, as you did," Schmelling said. "I think the consensus here is he needed to be as far from his brother as possible."

We recessed for lunch. Corrine again caught my arm and took me through the private exit out of the chamber, back to the park.

"Well, that was quite a morning," she said, after we found a bench away from the tourists. "You've certainly had a colorful life with your various adventures."

"Believe me, I've tried to forget Darren."

"That Marine was so good-looking. Not that I'm not still crazy about you, though."

"Somebody saw us out together last night," I said. "A reporter asked me about it this morning. They know you went up to my hotel room with me, apparently to spend the night."

Corrine smoothed her skirt and stared at the ground. "What did you tell them?"

"I told them you were a kind local who agreed to show me around town. That doesn't really explain why you were in my room all night, though."

"I'm sorry. I just really needed to be with you. I thought you needed to be with somebody, even if it wasn't me. I hoped it was me."

"I did need to be with somebody, though not necessarily in that way. Well, physically, I suppose, I needed it to be that way. Emotionally, too. Oh, hell, what I needed was to be with my wife."

"If she can't be with you, then why can't I?" Corrine appeared to be making every effort not to cry.

"Because it doesn't work that way. She's still my wife. How would you like it if you were the one lying there, unresponsive, and some other woman, young and beautiful, was all over your husband?"

"I'd want you to be happy, no matter what, even if I couldn't be the one doing it." She was shaking with tears. "You don't understand how I feel about you, Jeremiah. I'm in love with you. I

297

would do anything for you, give up anything for you. I would do absolutely anything, anything, you asked of me. Just please don't ask me to go away, out of your life."

"My God, you're twenty-three years old. You don't know what you want; you sure don't know it's me. You just met me yesterday. You don't know anything about me. How can you—"

"Because you just know when it's right. I know it's right. You're right for me. I know you are. I'm asking you again, I'm begging you; please don't send me away."

I sighed. Young love is always so blind yet determined.

"All right, we can spend some more time together, as long as I'm stuck here in this town. I want no repeats of last night. My only redeeming grace here, if you can even call it that, is I didn't initiate it. I suppose I should have resisted harder. I guess I'm grasping at something to take my mind off the guilt. Listen to me: if—when— Amanda comes around, that's it, it's over. She's my wife, the love of my life, and she'll be my choice. There can be no doubt about that."

"What if she never wakes up? Are you going to deny yourself the pleasure of a woman's love for the rest of your life because you're waiting for someone who may never return? When you're eighty years old, are you going to look back and say it was all worth it, all those years alone?"

"If she wakes up next week am I going to say, 'Look, dear, this is Corrine. She's here because I couldn't keep my pants zipped for two weeks while you were unconscious. Oh, and by the way, she's having my baby.'"

"That's not fair."

We walked back to the Capitol in silence, without getting lunch. Though I could feel angry rumbles boiling up in my stomach, I knew it would be useless to try to eat. Useless to try to shake this smitten little wench who had no idea what sort of man she would want next month, much less years down the road.

Again Corrine took me in past security, where we parted ways. As soon as I could no longer see her, I snagged a young page rushing between the chambers.

"Is there any way I can get a quick sandwich?" I handed a ten dollar bill to the young man in the blue blazer.

"I'll, er, see what I can do," he said.

Though I had few hopes he would actually come through, within fifteen minutes he came back with a roast beef sandwich and a soft drink. I let him keep the change.

I had just enough time to down the sandwich before Schmelling called the hearings to order again.

"Is Dr. Tom Wheatley here?" Schmelling said.

Dr. Wheatley came from somewhere behind me and took his seat at the table beside me.

"Dr. Wheatley, you are the founder and chairman of the Hippocrates Foundation, are you not?" Schmelling said.

"I am," Dr. Wheatley said.

"Can you fill us in just briefly on how you came to create this foundation and its purpose?" Schmelling said.

"During my travels throughout the world I had the

opportunity to observe the medical practices of a number of different cultures, and I began to realize our methods in the Western world weren't always the most effective or efficient in all situations." He paused for a sip of water. "We've made remarkable progress in eradicating a number of diseases, but our treatment regimens are becoming increasingly more expensive and often out of the reach of the average person. We have chosen to ignore many simpler, less expensive forms of therapy in use in many other cultures. There is a great deal of conventional wisdom in other areas of the world that is lacking among modern physicians and researchers."

"How did you come to be associated with Mr. Townsend here?"

"I had heard of Mr. Townsend's abilities for some time through accounts of his exploits in the media. I must admit at first I dismissed the accounts of this 'Miracle Man' as tabloid fodder, but as the stories about him continued to pour out, I decided to put him to the test."

Dr. Wheatley stopped and grinned at me before going on.

"Mr. Townsend probably isn't aware of what I'm going to tell you, but I sent two members of the foundation to find out if he really was as remarkable as he was being made out to be. I sent a husband and wife team out to meet him in Southwest Virginia. The husband pretended to have a broken leg and even had a fake plaster cast made. Mr. Townsend took one look at him and told him his leg wasn't broken at all but he did have a cracked rib, which was true; he had cracked it the day before when he fell in the bathtub, but the man thought he had concealed it well with a bandage around the chest. Mr. Townsend touched the man on the rib and instantly made the pain go away. There was no sign on the x-rays later the rib had ever been damaged.

"Mr. Townsend also told the wife she was pregnant with twins, something she didn't even know herself. She had only conceived them two days earlier. Nine months later she gave birth to a healthy pair of fraternal twins. That was enough for me. I drove to the far western end of Virginia to visit Mr. Townsend and asked him to become part of our foundation."

"I understand at first Mr. Townsend was a sort of guinea pig, was he not?" Cordoba said. "Didn't you study him to try to find out what made him tick?"

"Oh yes, but to no avail. Mr. Townsend graciously consented to having literally bucket loads of his blood drawn. We tested it ourselves; we sent it to every research facility in the world to try to find out if there was anything unusual there. All we ever learned was he is type A positive with a mild allergic reaction to ragweed. Oh, and he shouldn't eat shellfish."

That elicited a chuckle around the room. "We also ran a number of spectroscopic scans, CT scans, x-rays, MRIs, you name it. We had Mr. Townsend actually heal people while his body was attached to every sort of diagnostic equipment known. We studied the patients after they were healed to see if we could divulge any clues as to how these miraculous abilities work, but to date we have come up with nothing. We have analyzed his DNA. We know exactly how tall he is to the micron, how much he weighs down to the microgram, what his resting heart rate is and what his lung capacity is, but we don't know how he does what he does."

"What about you, Mr. Townsend?" Cordoba said. "What's your explanation for your ability?"

"I have none, Senator." I chose not to mention the old man. "It first manifested itself when I was eleven years old. I assume I'll die with it, unless I can somehow pass it on."

"Dr. Wheatley, I'm interested in the financial arrangement the foundation has with the defen—, er, Mr. Townsend," Cordoba said. "Do you or do you not specifically pay him for his services?"

"Well, in a sense, we have an arrangement with Mr. Townsend. We pay him a small stipend, but what it really amounts to is a retainer for his services as needed. Until his illness a few years ago, we also let him stay in some foundation housing we acquired for our members. It was a medium-sized, two-bedroom ranch home with a garage and all utilities furnished, nothing extravagant, I assure you. He also ran a small bookstore which, I suppose, earned him a modest income, and he received some royalties from the publishing industry for a book he wrote some years ago."

"So with the free housing, the stipend, as you call it, would be enough for a single man to live on?" Cordoba apparently chose to ignore the parts about the bookstore and the book royalties.

"Not in style, but yes, if one were frugal one could manage to live on that amount. It would certainly be next to impossible—no, strike that, it would be quite impossible—to try to go out and rent a house or apartment and still have enough left to live on with what we paid him," Dr. Wheatley said.

"You're saying he never received any money to specifically go out and heal someone or perform any sort of miracle?" Cordoba said.

"Not through the foundation," Dr. Wheatley said.

Schmelling excused Dr. Wheatley and called for a recess.

"I think I see what they're trying to get at and I don't like it," Dr. Wheatley said as we stood together and stretched. "They're trying to make you out to be either an opportunist or a fraud. One thing they can never say about you is you're a fraud. I know you too well to believe you'd take advantage of anyone."

"I'm getting numb to the whole thing," I said. "I can't believe how much time I'm wasting here when I should be with Amanda and keeping the bookstore open."

Out of the clutches of that vixen at the transcribing table. Look at her tossing her hair back, stretching in her chair, arching her back, breasts thrust forward...

"Well why didn't you say you needed someone to run the store for you? We could get someone from the foundation to keep it open for you until you get back," Dr. Wheatley said.

Now she's standing up. She's always smoothing that skirt. It's pleated, for God's sake, it's supposed to have wrinkles in it.

"Jeremiah?"

"Oh, I don't know. I'd hate to ask someone to give up what they're doing—"

"Nonsense, you're a member of the foundation and we're all

part of the same family. We stick together and do whatever is necessary to help one another. Just give me a key and you're in business," he said.

"If you're sure it's all right..."

"Of course it is."

I dug in my pants pocket for my key ring and performed the necessary separation surgery. The correct key made it around the loop and was free.

"Remember, Wednesday is senior citizens' day. They get a ten percent discount on all purchases," I said.

"Only ten?"

"We're struggling, okay?"

"By the way. The protocols we discussed earlier are in place." He handed me a headset with a microphone attached. "If we ever need to institute them, you know what to do. It turns out you have more help than either of us realized."

Corrine was talking to the page who brought me my sandwich. Her right hand flirted with his forearm while her left twisted the hem of her skirt in a girlish twirl.

I wasn't jealous. After all I was married. She was nothing to me. A regrettable fling. She could put her hand on anyone she wished. What did I care?

She saw me and winked. Why did she assume I would be looking at her? Was she so self-assured she figured I couldn't take my eyes off her?

Schmelling called us back into session. A tall, railish man with wild eyes and a bushy black beard and a satin robe joined me at the table. Though at first I assumed him to be of Middle Eastern descent, as I got a better look at him, he appeared to be of more Mediterranean heritage.

"Brother Jeremiah it is good to meet you at last. I am proud to serve in your name." The man put his hands on my shoulders before we sat down. "I will not betray you to the infidels."

"We are joined now by Brother Abraham Townsend of Santa Monica, California, are we not?" Schmelling said. The man nodded. I remembered to close my mouth several seconds after hearing the name Townsend.

"Now, sir, as I understand, 'Townsend' is not your real name, is that correct?" Schmelling said.

"It is my name in the brotherhood, though I was born Alexander Cordopolous. I prefer to be known as Brother Abraham."

"Very well, Brother Abraham it is, at least for the purpose of these hearings," Schmelling said. "Now please tell us, what is this brotherhood?"

"We of the Brotherhood of St. Townsend go out in the name of our most holy prophet here and do good works in his name. We honor his memory and keep it holy." He lifted his hands and spread his fingers as he spoke. I rubbed my eyes and looked at Corrine, who was typing away.

"What exactly are these good works that you do?" Cordoba said.

"We do many things. We minister to the suffering, we lead

305

the lost into the light, we heal the sick. We do all these things in the name of our blessed prophet, the most holy Brother Townsend." His hands were back in the air.

I scanned all possible exits out of the room. If only there were a diversion...

"How many people are in this brotherhood?" Cordoba said.

"We are legion."

"Mr. Townsend, do you endorse this brotherhood? Have you given them your blessing, your permission to use your name?" said Schmelling, addressing me.

"No, Senator, this is the first I've heard of them."

"You're saying you're not even aware of this cult following you have, even as this man sits beside you and claims to go out and do works in your name?" Cordoba said. "That's a bit unlikely, don't you think?"

"Senator, my whole life is unlikely. Don't you think?"

Corrine made a subtle fist-pumping gesture with her left hand, the one on the opposite side of her body from the panel.

"Do not cast your derision on the most holy, bless his name." Brother Abraham pointed a finger toward Cordoba. "We are his disciples in spirit, if not anointment. If Brother Townsend, bless his name, says he had no knowledge of us, then it is so."

"So you say you go out and heal in Mr. Townsend's name," Jameson said. "How's that working out?"

"We heal the inside."

"What does that mean?" Jameson said.

306

"We heal the spirit, the mind, the soul. The body is but a vessel. It passes away with time and is forgotten. What is the body to us? We are here to bring purity. The body will follow when the soul is pure."

For the first time since the hearings began, I understood the blank stares on the faces of the panel. After a painful period of time multiplied by a factor of ten, Cordoba, bless his name, finally shrugged off the stupor.

"So you go out and tell people you're going to heal them. Do you charge them?" Cordoba said.

"We do not ask for earthly rewards for our services. We do accept gifts given in a spirit of love and charity to continue our ministries." His arms had to be getting tired.

"How much have you received in the amount of these gifts given in the spirit of love and charity?" Cordoba said.

"As the numbers of the grains of sand by the sea and the stars in the sky are known only to our lord, so only He knows how greatly we have been blessed." Brother Abraham lifted his arms obediently again.

"Brother Abraham, does your organization have 501(c)(3) nonprofit status?" Jameson said.

"Your words mean nothing to me. We are not of this world," Brother Abraham said.

"Well if you decide to join the rest of us on Spaceship Earth, you might want to look into that before you get into trouble with the IRS," Jameson said.

Schmelling dismissed Brother Abraham and Cordoba asked me again if I had any knowledge of other such groups operating in my name. I told him I did not.

"Next up we have the Reverend Barry Wendell, of The People's First Church of the Healer, Harlan, Kentucky," Schmelling said.

I'd never seen The Rev. Wendell before, but growing up I'd seen his type. Polyester pants at least an inch too short, button-up shirt that rode up on the protruding belly, too much hair all on one part of the head, enough cologne to make a pig sneeze—he had all the markings of one of those small-town radio preachers of the stomp-n-spit variety. Harlan was also only some two dozen miles from my hometown.

"Reverend Wendell, thank you for coming to our proceedings," Schmelling said. "You say your church is a faith-based, laying-on-of-hands ministry that preaches the gospel and casts out demons. What is your association with Mr. Townsend here?"

"Your Honor, prior to the coming of the healer, we were a Pentecostal church of the word of God, Bible-based, praise God, not unlike many other small country churches across this great land of ours, praise God. Then this man appeared, praise God, and we knew we were in a new age, praise God. Not the New Age with the hippies with the long hair and beads and the worship of Satan and witchcraft and the false prophets, no, praise God! A new age with—"

"Reverend Wendell, can we tone down the rhetoric and speak in a normal voice? We can't be here all night while you preach to us,"

Schmelling said.

"I'm sorry, Your Honor," Wendell said.

"I'm not a judge. Please stop calling me 'Your Honor,'"
Schmelling said.

"Yes, sir. As I said, when Brother Townsend here appeared
with the gift of healing, we knew we were in a new age and he was
the messenger of this new age, and we had best prepare for the
Second Coming while there was still time. We took up a love offering
and went forth to preach to all the peoples and to lay on hands and
heal them, as Brother Townsend has shown us to do."

The Rev. Wendell's talk erupted into a lilting litany of
nonsense words, prompting Sen. Schmelling to order him to be quiet.

"Now, Reverend Wendell, you say you and your congregation
practice healing?" Schmelling said.

"We have, Your Honor, I'm sorry, Senator, by the grace of
God we have followed the example shown by Brother Townsend
here, and we have gone forth and cast out the demons making people
sick." Rev. Wendell had already lathered up a sweat.

"Is there a Mary Jane Cobb here?" Schmelling said. There
was movement in the back of the gallery and a tiny woman in a
brown dress picked her way through the seats in front of her and
made her way to our table. I rose and helped her into the seat beside
me, putting myself between her and Rev. Wendell.

"Mrs. Cobb—it is *Mrs.* Cobb, isn't it?" Schmelling said.

"Yes, senator, I'm Mary Jane Cobb, or Mrs. Joe Cobb, of
Harlan, Kentucky."

"Why are you here today, Mrs. Cobb? Do you have some connection with either the Reverend Wendell or Mr. Townsend?" Schmelling said.

"I've never met Mr. Townsend, but the Reverend Wendell here told me he could cure me of cervical cancer. He told me I had to have faith in him and the Lord and I would be healed. He said the only way I could be healed was to show I had faith by quitting my treatment with my doctor," she said.

I winced. I saw where this was headed.

"Did you do as he asked?" Cordoba said.

"Yes, I did. I quit my treatment with my regular doctor. Reverend Wendell told me he had to put his hands as close to my cervix as possible in order for it to work, to get right up in there, you know, *up in there*," she said.

Whoa. This wasn't going where I thought at all.

"You're saying the reverend told you he had to put his hand up your vagina, Mrs. Cobb?" Jameson said.

"Yes, sir," she said.

"Mr. Townsend, if this woman had come to you, would you have had to touch her in her private area to heal her?" Cordoba said.

"No, Senator. Touching her anywhere would have worked," I said.

"Did you let the Reverend Wendell touch you in the way he said he needed to touch you, Mrs. Cobb?" Cordoba said.

"Yes, sir. I didn't want to, but he said it was the only way and so I let him do it. It was very rough; it hurt. Then he got so excited

310

doing it he told me I had to let him have sex with me." She was crying now. "I was so scared and so ashamed I just let him do it."

The Rev. Wendell was looking at the table. Mrs. Cobb wiped her eyes and a female page brought her more tissues.

"Were you healed, Mrs. Cobb?" Cordoba said.

"My next Pap smear came back negative. They told me they couldn't find any sign of the cancer." Mrs. Cobb was still wiping.

The senators looked back and forth at each other. Rev. Wendell, head still down, was grinning and nodding.

"So you're saying he did, in fact, heal you?" Schmelling said.

"No. I never really believed the results, but I was so ashamed of what I had done I took pills and tried to kill myself. My husband found me and called the ambulance. In the hospital they saved me from the poison, but they told me I had cancer and it had spread. I told them about the Pap smear and they checked the lab. They said the lab messed up and gave me the wrong results. Now my cancer is in an advanced stage because I stopped my treatment. I won't live to see my daughters graduate high school."

Mrs. Cobb lost all semblance of control and exploded into a wall of sobs. Pages ran over to hug her and try to comfort her.

"Mr. Townsend, is there any way you can help this woman?" Schmelling said.

I've never healed anyone on television, but I leaned over and put my arm around Mrs. Cobb and whispered, "It's all right. Everything is all right."

She regained control of her emotions as she felt the cleansing

311

effect throughout her body. She straightened up and sat erect and took a deep breath.

"Mrs. Cobb, do you feel better now?" Schmelling asked.

She continued to daub at the tears around her eyes, but a smile had worked its way onto her face, surprising her as much as the rest of us.

"Why, yes. I—I feel clean. Refreshed. As if I'm many pounds lighter." She looked around. "I can't describe it just yet."

Rev. Wendell, meanwhile, stared ahead like a man who suddenly realized he was standing on the freeway in front of oncoming tractor trailers.

"Mrs. Cobb, you're free to go. It's up to you what you want to do from here, but I would advise you to press charges against Reverend Wendell," Schmelling said.

Over the next two hours four more people who claimed to be healing the sick, either in my name or inspired by me, testified before the panel about their activities. By the time Schmelling called it a day, neither Corrine nor anyone else could protect me from the reporters who flocked to me. Up until that point I had always refused to perform for the cameras, but Schmelling and Mrs. Cobb put me in an unwinnable position.

The flare of constant camera flashes blinded me and the jumble of questions spilled forth in an unintelligible hum unlike anything I had encountered. The media made up just the first wave; outside the Capitol steps the streets and sidewalks were thick with the crush of people waiting to get a glimpse of me, to touch me, to ask

312

my blessing. D.C. police formed a human barrier around me, shepherding me into a cruiser which took me to my hotel.

There I faced the infotainment crowd, the celebrity photographers and glitzy reporters who shouted questions about my diet, my sex life, my workout regimen. Hotel security flushed me through to the elevator, where I bolted to my room and collapsed on the bed.

Two hours later the phone rang. As always, it was Sid.

"Jeremiah! I just found out what Cordoba's angle is," he said. "That girl that was killed in the accident in Bedford, that was his granddaughter, and he blames you for not going to her first! This whole thing about healing for profit is a sham; he just wants revenge because he thinks you should have saved her. Are you listening?"

I sat up and rubbed my eyes. "I'm here."

"There's more. I never knew this, I don't know many people did because they had different last names, but Judge Remington is Cordoba's ex-wife. That's why she dismissed your case; that was her granddaughter, too. She knew Cordoba was going to go after you, so she didn't want to stand in his way. She probably should have just recused herself and let another judge have it, but I don't think she plans to stay on the bench much longer."

The click of the lock opening and the light from the hallway alerted me to the presence of someone in my room. It was Corrine.

"Hey, I took the liberty of lifting your extra key last night." She closed the door behind her. "Oh, I see you're on the phone."

"Jeremiah, are you listening to me?" Sid ranted. "Cordoba

313

may send someone, probably a pretty young girl, to—"

"I'm sorry, Sid, I have to go." I hung the phone up. Corrine hit the lights and I flinched at the brightness, squinting at her as she yawned and stretched, thrusting those breasts out again.

"Well, you're the real deal now, although some of the Web sites are running conjecture you're a fraud and the whole thing with the lady with cervical cancer was staged."

She tossed her jacket on a chair and climbed up onto the foot of the bed and sat on her knees. "Poor Jeremiah. It just gets better and better, doesn't it?"

"Maybe it would be better if I were just a fraud. No matter what I do, I'm always a disappointment to those who expect me to fix the whole world's problems."

"Don't ever say that. You're a good and decent man who always tries to do the right thing. I mean, look at you, you don't lie, drink, smoke, gamble, do drugs. In fact, you only have one vice."

I watched her lick her lips. "Don't do this. Not now. I'm too tired."

"This," she slid her skirt high up on her thighs and spread her knees far apart, "is that one vice. You can't say no to it. Most men can't"

***

No matter how hard I stared at it in the dim light from the bathroom, the ceiling above the bed refused to change.

The naked young woman beside me cooed and stretched, her eyes still closed. The guilt that washed through me and quickened my

314

pulse didn't care that physically, at least, I was calm and relaxed. Corrine was absolutely correct about my one vice. I was well on the way to becoming a sex addict. Indulging my addiction, however, had released enough tension to allow me to sleep for a short while.

Her body was warm and smooth against mine, a fixture of serenity against the chaos outside. I could have spent hours tracing my fingertips along the gentle curves of that perfect skin, exploring each fold and crevice, kneading her breasts and buttocks with the care of a potter.

It was all so wrong.

I tried to picture Amanda lying beside me in this same bed, her body flowing into the same contours, but the proportions were all wrong. Over the years she had grown fleshier, older. Still sexy, but not as firm as the Lolita in my bed. Trying with all my might, the only figure I could conjure to replace the one I saw in the shadows was a very young Monique.

Even Amanda's face refused to come to me now. It was a face I had adored for years but only recently had I earned the right to take it in my hands and kiss it and run my tongue along its cheeks, gently sucking her closed eyes and making the woman behind those eyes moan.

Now that face would not come when called. It threatened to appear indistinctly, like some star cluster that could only be seen out of the corner of the eye, but eventually it yielded to another face: the face of Samantha, as she leaned her forehead against mine while sitting in my lap that day. So alike and yet so different in all the most

315

important ways, that visage crowded Amanda's away. Had my wife ever existed at all?

"I was pregnant once."

The voice startled me more by its presence than by what was said. Corrine's liquid body flowed into place around mine, matching each bend the way water fills a twisting tube.

"I knew that," I said.

"Oh, I forgot. You can tell exactly what's going on in a person's body."

"Just about. So what happened?"

"I was only sixteen and stupid, stupid to ever go out with this guy in the first place, stupid to let him screw me, stupid to not take any precautions, stupid to listen to him afterward. God, I didn't want my parents to find out. They'd be so ashamed, so disappointed in their little girl. I missed two periods and I took one of those pee-on-the-stick tests and called him, all crying and all that. He said he knew a guy who could fix it."

I didn't speak.

"So anyway, he knew a guy, all right. This guy apparently had been going to be a doctor but he only took two semesters of biology and dropped out. David, the guy that got me pregnant, took me to the guy's house and stayed upstairs while we went to the basement. He had all these surgical tools laid out on a table with a white tablecloth in his basement and it was just so horrible. He said he needed to get me loosened up so it wouldn't hurt so much, and he said the best way to do it was to have sex with me. Here I am stupid

316

and scared and crying, so I just let him do it. Only he just sticks it right in there, all hard and rough, with no foreplay whatsoever and me all dry and it hurts like hell. I'm screaming in pain and he thinks it's because he's such a good lover and he just keeps going and thrusting harder and harder and it hurts so bad. We weren't even lying down. He just leans me up against a wall and pulls my panties down and starts fucking me with my dress pushed up. He laughs and says, 'At least we don't have to worry about getting you pregnant.'"

I pulled my arm out from under her and rolled over onto my back. I said nothing.

"It hurt so much I was numb for what he did to me afterward. He took care of it, all right. I was bleeding all over the floor of his basement and he and David panic and they roll me up in a big piece of plastic, like what you put on the carpet when you paint a room, and they put me in the backseat of David's car and drive me out of town to a convenience store with a pay phone out away from the building where nobody in the store can see it. David calls 9-1-1 from there and tells them there's a girl bleeding to death and they get in the car and drive off."

There were no tears. She recounted the story as if describing her summer vacation.

"So they come with the ambulance and take me to the hospital and they sew me up and give me lots of blood and ask me what the hell I did such a thing for. They tell me I'll live but I'll never be able to have children because of what that butcher did to me. Of course, they have to call my parents to come get me, so they find out

317

everything anyway. They find out their daughter is just a lowlife slut who now could never give them grandchildren because of what she went and did."

"That's terrible," I said.

"I've learned to deal with the fact I can't have kids, but I always think about the man I'll someday marry. What if he wants kids? What can I tell him? Do I tell him the truth up front about what I did and hope he'll understand? Do I hide it from him and let him wonder why we can't get pregnant? Do I try to marry a man who already has kids or try to adopt?"

Corrine glanced up at me, probably wondering why I didn't jump to her rescue. I said nothing.

"I mean, if you and I did wind up being together, and you wanted children—"

"That's what this is all about, isn't it?" I turned away from her. "The whole reason you befriended me, seduced me, serviced me, everything. You didn't feel like you could just come up to me and ask; you felt you had to barter for my favor?"

She feigned hurt. "That's not it at all. I do care about you. I said I loved you. I just thought—"

"Do you remember when you came on to me yesterday while you were stoned?"

"Barely."

"Do you remember what I did to you?"

"Of course, you put your hand on me and...oh."

"'Oh,' is right. I didn't just cure you from being stoned, I

318

healed your scarred uterus as well. I saw it the moment you came up to me at the Capitol. You were the victim of a botched abortion. I didn't know the details, of course, just that everything was all hacked up inside you and you couldn't carry a pregnancy."

"Wow."

"So you see, you didn't have to come after me with your legs wide open. It was already taken care of even before you climbed on me last night."

"You make it sound so —"

"Dirty? Deceitful? Whoreish? If you know me as well as you claim, and think I'm so noble, you'd know I don't take advantage of people. I'm not an extortionist; I don't demand money or pussy in exchange for my services. I do it because I genuinely want to help people."

Corrine pulled the sheet up over her chest. I've never understood why women suddenly become so modest after being so entirely without inhibition.

"So what happens now?" she said.

"What happens now is you put your clothes on and get the hell out of here. I don't want to see you again, not as friends, not as lovers, not as two people who've been intimate. Get out now."

"We still like each other. It doesn't have to be this way. I can still be here for you."

"I never should have let you in here, meaning in my bed, in the first place. I can't believe I broke my vow to my wife like this."

"It's not like she's going to do anything about it."

"Now."

Corrine dressed and scampered out the door, leaving only her bra behind. I cut it to ribbons with a pair of scissors and flushed the remnants.

CHAPTER FOUR

I didn't sleep or eat the rest of the night. After pacing the hotel room for more than an hour, I could no longer stand the feel of my own skin. In the shower I tried to wash away any stray molecule of Corrine, scrubbing my privates until they bled.

I called room service for a change of sheets. When the housekeeping crew arrived, I made them take away the armchair from the previous night.

"Do you want to change rooms, Mr. Townsend?" the night manager called up to ask.

"No. I like the view."

I didn't care if the reporters were squatting in the lobby, I had to get outside. I took the fire exits to the Dumpsters behind the hotel and started walking, hair still wet, genitals sanded to a bloody pulp.

The air was that of a city with too many fossil fuel-burning vehicles, but it was not the stagnant murk of my room. I had to breathe, to walk fast, to think, to lose myself.

I had to find where Amanda dwelled. I needed to know she was still there with all the clutter, all the rhetoric, all the trivia and detritus that rattled around in my head these days. The real Amanda, not generic remembrances of women accumulated over a lifetime of media images and clumsy groping.

I needed to liberate the memory of the woman I had grown to love through years of intimate friendship, the counselor whose wisdom once spoke to me more clearly than my own conscience.

I needed her forgiveness. I did not know where to look.

With head bowed, my legs carried me through foreign streets and alleyways until I wound up on a seedy little avenue of broken windows, pawn shops and liquor stores. A weary neon sign directed my attention to a fortune teller, although the letters actually spelled "ortune elle." I fought back a hint of a smile and decided to see what Ortune Elle could tell me.

Ortune Elle was a thin, late fortyish woman with boot black hair, jangling earrings and waxy red lipstick. Someone apparently must have surgically implanted an unlit Virginia Slims between the forefinger and second finger of her left hand. From the rasping voice, however, even the most casual observer would conclude it was too late to bother not lighting the cigarette.

"Lost love, eh?" A tiny head popped up over a glass counter at the back of a narrow shop with worn wooden floorboards. The counters along either side of the center aisle carried ancient knickknacks ranging from Kama Sutra figurines to New Age crystals. A thick layer of dust covered the premises, as if a drywall ceiling had exploded.

"That's a pretty good observation. Isn't everyone who comes in here looking for a lost love?" I maneuvered around boxes on the floor. "I'm not seeking wealth or fame."

"Fame you already have." Ortune Elle flicked tarot cards over with an experienced wrist. "Wealth doesn't seem to be in the cards for you."

"How do you know I have fame?" I pulled a small wooden chair to the table where Ortune Elle gazed at the cards.

She glanced at a black and white television on a two-drawer filing cabinet. "The great spirit C-SPAN knows all and shows all. I read it in the tea leaves and the pages of the *Post*."

I smiled without meaning to. "So what do the cards tell you?"

"That you're searching for someone dear." She studied the arrangement. "They do not tell me, however, where to find what you seek."

She sighed. "The cards are for amateurs. Have a cup of tea."

I accepted the still-hot cup before me. She must have made it before I walked in.

"Yuck. That's awful." I set the cup back down. I wanted to rub a sponge on my tongue.

"Taste isn't really what we're looking for, is it?" She took the cup and stared down into it. "Odd."

"Odd?"

"Odd. The leaves tell me you are searching for something you cannot find."

"Isn't that why you search for something? If you could find it, there'd be no need to search, right?"

"No, no, that's not what I meant. What you search for cannot be found."

I sighed. "Well, thank you for your time."

323

"You're not giving up so easily?"

"No, but the answers obviously aren't here." I stood to leave. "What's the charge?"

"No charge unless I help you. We have other options. Tarot cards and tea leaves are toys. I have more powerful means of finding what you need. I will not charge you if I do not find the answer."

I sat back down. I had nothing but time to kill anyway. "So what's next? Crystal ball?"

Ortune Elle snickered and waved a limp wrist my way. "What do you think I am, a gypsy looking into a gumball machine? No, I must consult with Na'Peth."

"That would be..."

"Na'Peth is an extra dimensional entity who sometimes chooses to speak through me. He is very ancient and very knowledgeable, if a bit surly when bothered."

"You're kidding, right? I thought channeling went out with mood rings and pet rocks."

"Hmpf. I do not deny there are fakers and charlatans out there. That man on TV today, Brother Abraham, now he was a phony. Looney. The man was obviously mentally ill."

"You got that vibe, too?" I hadn't meant to use that particular word, but Corrine's memory was still fresh.

"Oh, please. The whole lot of them. You, you are gifted in ways I cannot begin to see. You see things others do not. Like my lung cancer."

I shifted in my chair.

"Yes, you see it. I see it in you. Even my doctors do not see it, for I have not been diagnosed. They say it is only a benign mass, but you and I, we both know otherwise, don't we?"

"I saw it," I said. "I still see it. What surprises me —"

"Is that I know you know. That is my gift, to know things others do not. I take my responsibility very, very seriously. Yet I cannot see the thing you wish to find, and that perplexes me. As a professional, I want to dig deeper. Na'Peth is the only way."

"How long does this take?"

She laughed again, then hacked up something yellow she spit into a napkin. "Silly boy, it takes time to prepare. I cannot do it alone. My sister must be here to ask the questions while I am under the spell. You have not eaten."

"That's not prophecy, that's my stomach growling. Where's your sister?"

"She can be here within forty-five minutes. In the meantime, I suggest you visit the café across the street. The food there is quite good."

***

Forty-five minutes later, with a belly full of the best hamburger I'd eaten in five years, I returned to Ortune Elle's, where the air stung my eyes with the odor of incense. Ortune Elle had been joined by a round woman in a tie-dyed head scarf, ruby red sweater and layer upon layer of beads.

"This is my sister, Janice." Janice didn't even make it to five feet when she stood to shake my hand, but she tipped the scales at

325

somewhere around two hundred fifty. The face under the folds was radiant, however, and the eyes were pools of joy. Here was a contented soul if ever I'd met one.

"Palmetta told me a little about what you are looking for," Janice said.

"Palmetta? Oh, you mean Ortune Elle?" I said.

The sisters looked at each other blankly, then laughed.

"That's what my sign says, isn't it? That's brilliant," Elle said. "I think I'll start calling myself that. Oh, we do need to help you."

We sat back down around the round table, though Janice's bulk skewed the seating arrangement. She made me think of lavender, but it was hard to distinguish scents through all the incense.

"It does not take long to enter the sleep," Elle said. "If Na'Peth is there, he will answer shortly. Do not be surprised if the voice you hear is not my own. Na'Peth sometimes chooses a terrible voice, so be warned."

I'd be lying if I said the hairs on my neck weren't on the march at that point. I could hear my pulse in my ears, though I didn't really expect anything out of the old fraud. My stomach gurgled, prompting me to wonder if the extra helping of french fries had been wise.

Ortune Elle closed her eyes and her head began to swivel and jerk. The sharpness of some of the neck movements made me flinch. They had to hurt.

After several moments of bolting motions, the head flopped forward. I heard a roach crawl up the wall.

326

Janice leaned forward, her juggernaut breasts resting on the table. "Na'Peth, are you there?"

"I have asked you not to call me by that name. Who disturbs my meditation?" The voice came from Elle's lips, but the sound was pure music, notes from a steam calliope.

"I mean no disrespect. Your true name is unknowable to us. We call you only that which you have given us." A strain appeared in Janice's own mannerisms.

"My true name is not for your lips. I reveal it to those whom I wish. The day will come when all will know it. Why have you disturbed me?"

I could have been listening to a merry-go-round speaking.

"There is a man among us who seeks his true love, now lost to him. Even her memory is denied him. His heart carries a heavy burden." Janice was perspiring now.

"She has not crossed over!" The voice went up an octave but retained a windy quality. "Yet she is not of your world, either. I cannot see her at all."

I thought I sensed a note of pity, but how can one tell when spoken to by a carousel?

"Then there is no hope for his quest?" Janice said.

"I did not say that. The answers he seeks cannot be found here. They are within him, if he knows where to look."

"How can she be in neither your world nor ours?" Janice said. "Her essence cannot simply cease to exist."

"She does not exist because she has been displaced. The

327

space she once inhabited is now occupied by other forces. These trespassers must be made to surrender and leave before the woman can return from the nowhere to which she is banished."

I jumped out of my seat when Elle's head, still resting on her chest, ratcheted around to face me and the eyelids opened, revealing only the whites of the eyeballs.

"You know what must go," the voice chimed.

Elle spasmed and jerked until her eyes rolled back into position. She blinked and clamped a hand to the back of her head.

"Oy! That kills my neck," she said. "Was it helpful? Did you get answers?"

"I'm afraid Na'Peth wasn't of much use," Janice said. "Perhaps I asked the wrong questions."

"Na'Peth?" Elle said. "I don't know who that was speaking through me, but it wasn't Na'Peth."

CHAPTER FIVE

I got back to the hotel at something after 2 a.m. No reporters remained in the lobby, so I caught the elevator back to my room and fell onto the bed. I didn't for an instant believe in channeling, any more than I believed in the legend of the Wandering Jew, but I had no explanation for what happened at Ortune Elle's that night. Yet Na'Peth—or whatever that was—had given me the freedom to allow myself to relax for a while, in spite of the swirl of images racing through my head, and I was asleep in moments.

By 8:15, after a solid six hours of sleep, my body had recharged itself enough to drag me through another day. The hearings resumed at ten, so I still didn't have to rush to get ready. I grabbed the telephone and called Roanoke. The voice mail system provided by the hotel, which had a capacity of 37 messages per guest, was full. I took that as a sign I didn't have to worry about listening to any of them.

"Samantha? I'm fine...Sorry about that. The voice mail system was full, so I didn't take the time to go through and listen to all the messages...No change? I wish she could just wake up and realize where she was...Yes. Yes. Listen, I need you to do a favor for me this morning. I want you to e-mail me a picture of Amanda...No, any picture will do, so long as it shows her face clearly. Please do that as

329

soon as you can...No, no problems, I just need a little reminder of who I'm fighting for...Listen, here's the address..."

Then I headed for the shower. I yelped as I peeled my underwear away from the pulpy mass that now hung there. I wondered if I might have done some permanent damage, but the water cooled the fire. The shower beat against my neck and back in a pulsating stream, soothing and helping me sort through the chaos in my head. I still couldn't picture Amanda clearly, but I realized there was hope.

The truth was, Amanda hadn't gone anywhere. I had simply crowded her out with guilt and shame, and until I could come to terms with that, I would not be able to draw on her memory for strength.

A hotel employee knocked at my door with the breakfast tray as I was toweling off. I snarfed the food far too quickly for any sense of enjoyment, but I wanted to get down to the lobby where the hotel provided Internet kiosks.

After shaving, drying my hair and dressing, I headed for the lobby. The kiosks were in a nook just off the elevators, so there was no need to go into the lobby to confront the usual menagerie of reporters. Still, a morbid urge forced me to swing by and take a peek. Though I didn't need any more encounters, I actually felt a twinge of disappointment when I saw not a single camera or pad in sight.

Then I glanced at a newspaper on a table in the lobby and saw the reason: the U.S. had bombed another nation accused of harboring terrorists. The reporters no doubt had been dispatched to get local reaction to the event, thus pushing me into the category of yesterday's news.

A fresh bounce in my step carried me back to the Internet kiosks. I had no idea what the charge to my credit card would be, but I didn't care. I needed to see Amanda. I logged on and went to my e-mail inbox, which, like the voice mail system, was at capacity.

Please, oh please, let it be there.

There it was. The final message before the memory allotment was filled was from Samantha, with an attachment. The photo attachment loaded much more quickly than I expected and within moments the face of my wife smiled out at me from the screen. A tear began to fill up my eye as I pressed my fingertips to the two-dimensional cheek on the screen.

"Forgive me," I said.

Another burst of inspiration struck and I minimized the photo, then logged on to the Web site of a Lynchburg radio station. The station had interviewed Amanda a month before our trip to New York and made partial audio transcripts of all its interviews available online. I scrolled down the list of transcripts until I found the one I wanted, then double-clicked on the link. As the file loaded, I pulled a set of headphones off my iPod in my jacket pocket and plugged them into the terminal. Within moments I had the face and voice of my beloved beaming to me.

"So how do you think your husband has carried the burden of publicity and the extremely high expectations of him as word of his exploits has grown?" the interviewer, a man with that generic,

331

always-on radio voice, asked.

"Oh, I've always had the utmost confidence in Jeremiah to do the right thing." Amanda's voice was pure silk, the words themselves honey. "He's one of that rare breed of men who genuinely has a conscience and a very exacting code of ethics he never varies from. I've never known him to do anything but the right thing."

My beloved, if only you knew.

"What about other women?" the interviewer said. "He's certainly earned his share of notoriety, which seems to excite a particular sort of woman. I think you know the sort I'm talking about, the sort which wouldn't care he was already married. Do you ever worry he'll be tempted to stray into the arms of another?"

"Does any woman ever know exactly how her husband will react in that situation? You're right when you say Jeremiah has become well-known, and, the truth is, he's a very attractive man. That's something I don't tell him very often, but he can turn the ladies' heads without even being aware of himself. That's what I think I find so intriguing about him is he doesn't think of himself as sexy or good-looking; he just is. I find that very charming when a man can just walk into a room and be sexy without even knowing it, without trying to do anything at all. That's my husband to a fault. Other women do notice that as well, because I've seen them look at him, but, of course, I don't say anything to him about it. As to whether I worry about him going astray, I think Jeremiah is as human as the next man, probably more so. The way he was raised, he was

332

taught to be very respectful of women and, as a result, he has a very hard time saying 'no' to women. It's not so much I worry about him going astray; I worry some woman might come on to him so aggressively he may not know how to stop her. If that were to happen, I'd certainly be hurt at first, but I'd probably wind up laughing and saying, 'Oh, well, that's just the way you are.'"

God bless you, my love.

I logged off and pulled off the headphones. A feminine hand extended a tissue to me.

"You look as though you could use this. I always have plenty for my children." A self-assured brunette in her early thirties wearing a Gap sweatshirt and jeans, she had two small girls in white cotton dresses in tow, the younger one hiding behind her mother's leg. "Aren't you the man on TV in those hearings?"

"I'm afraid so." I accepted the offered hanky.

"Mister, why are you crying?" the bigger girl asked.

"Hush, Caroline, that's not nice. He just misses someone he loves very much," the woman said.

"That's right," I said to the girl. "I miss someone very much."

"Oh. Do you have any children?" the girl said.

"No, we lost our little baby before it could be born."

"That's real sad. I'll pray for you."

"You do that, honey. I'll pray for you, too."

The woman nodded and turned away, leading the girls by the hands. I took a deep breath. When you spent too much time in the spotlight, I reminded myself, it became easy to forget what real people were like. These were the people I was meant to be with, not entertainers, politicians, reporters and various so-called "movers and shakers." I remembered a line by the character George Bailey from the movie *It's a Wonderful Life*, spoken to the evil Mr. Potter: "Just remember this, Mr. Potter, this 'rabble' you're talking about, they do most of the working and paying and living and dying in this community..."

I wondered what George Bailey would have thought of the world I lived in. Of course, he had real backbone. He never let Violet Biggs seduce him into ruining furniture in the motel in Bedford Falls.

CHAPTER SIX

The only people who spoke to the panel that day were a pair of elderly women who told the story of how I brought their sister out of a coma. Although the U.S. bombing raid held the headlines, I wound up as a guest on a cable TV call-in show. After going over the day's events and asking me how I felt putting D'Artela in his place, the host, a grumpy former newspaper columnist named Chris Jennings, opened the floor to questions.

"Yes, hello, Jeremiah, this is Marge from Scranton," the first caller said.

"Hi, Marge." I tried to look comfortable on the leather couch that made up the bulk of the show's set. "What can I do for you?"

"I just wanted you to know I've followed your exploits since you revived that kidnapper in Lynchburg a few years ago, and I thought it was just great what you said today about making people's lives better, and we're all pulling for you. My question is this: If you were in a situation where there were a whole lot of badly wounded or injured people and you had to act really fast, would you go to a triage system of trying to save those who could be saved and perhaps letting others go? I'm an emergency room nurse and I've always wondered about that."

"Well, I suppose I would have to rank the victims in some

335

way, but I would probably do it a little differently." I watched the way the director was nodding along off camera with everything I said. "Since I usually have a better chance of saving people than, say, an ER doctor, I would prioritize those who were the worst off, since they might only have a few minutes to live. Then I would go to those who were less badly wounded."

"Isn't that a little like what you did with the children who were hit by the car in Virginia earlier this year?" said Jennings.

"Pretty much. One girl took the brunt of the impact and was already beyond saving, so I rushed to help the other children and then the driver of the vehicle, who had suffered a diabetic seizure."

"Wasn't there some controversy there, didn't some people claim the first girl was still alive and you could have saved her had you gone to her first?" Jennings said.

"There are always people who second-guess anything you do, but in that incident, yes, there were some people who felt the girl could have been saved. I realized that, unfortunately, she was already dead. I truly wish I could have saved her."

"I seem to recall the eyewitnesses saying the girl's body appeared to jerk and writhe when you touched her, almost as if there was some spark of life still left in her. Is it not possible she was indeed still alive, and she could have been saved had you gone to her first?" Jennings said.

"I am by no means infallible." I tried to decide between crossing my legs or putting my right foot on my left knee. "I do have an extremely accurate ability to sense a person's condition, and I

336

sensed the girl was dead."

"What about the way the body spasmed when you touched it? Has that ever happened to you before?" Jennings said.

"No, that was a first. The girl was dead."

Can we get on with it?

"Okay, our next caller is Ryan from Texas. Go ahead, Ryan."

"Hey. Jeremiah, you da man. Listen, I been drinkin' a lot, I mean, a lot more than usual, and lately I been throwin' up a lot of blood. At first I thought it was nothin', but my ex-wife says I need ta see a doctor. It's real nasty, bloody puke and—"

"Ryan, I hate to interrupt, but I think I can answer that question. Yes, by all means, you need to see a doctor right away. Wouldn't you agree, Jeremiah?" Jennings said.

"Absolutely. It may already be too late, but go now. Put down the phone this instant, turn off the TV and go."

"...Hi, Jeremiah, this is Fran from Richmond, Virginia, not too far away from Lynchburg. Have you ever thought about writing a book? I have a cousin who's a writer, and she would love to sit down with you and put your story down on paper. She says her spelling's not very good, but that's what they have spell-check and editors for, right?"

"...Hey, guys, this is Duane from Reno, Nevada, and I was wondering what you think about a sixty-five-year-old woman who absolutely refuses to go to the doctor. I keep telling her, 'Ma, ya need to go every year at least for a Pap smear and a mammogram,' and she's like, 'Oh, there's nothing wrong with me; why waste all that money?"'"

"...Jeremiah? My name is Eduardo. I'm calling from Miami, Florida. Is there any chance you can come down here and look at my brother? He's got this rash all over his abdomen and groin area..."

"...Hey, Jeremiah, this is Francine, from Savannah, and I just think you are so incredibly sexy. I'm real sorry about what's happened to your wife and all, but if you ever need a shoulder to cry on..."

"...Yeah, this is Ralph, from Boise, and I don't think you guys really dealt with that so-called preacher from Kentucky. That man is a pervert and a sex offender and should be banished from the pulpit..."

"...This is the Rev. Fred Coldtree from Vermont, and I just want to know who do you think you are, going around and healing people without calling upon the name of God. Are you aware of the wonderful gift Jesus gave you when he died on the cross for your sins?"

"...This is Rachel from Boston, and I would just like to say while I don't agree with some of the views from the people who've testified at these hearings, I do have a question about how you decide who to help and who not to help, and I would just like to know, and I'm sure a lot of other people out there would like to know, too, is how you make that decision."

"That's a good question, Rachel," said Jennings. "Tell, us, Jeremiah Townsend, Miracle Man of Virginia, how do you make that call? Just what is the criteria someone has to meet before you step in and help them?"

338

"First of all, I don't think I've ever consciously decided not to help someone who truly needed me, except in cases where the person has specifically asked me not to do so. An awful lot has been written about my grandmother, who raised me as her son, and how I allowed her to die because she asked me to not step in. The only people I've ever flat-out refused are those who come to me with requests that have more to do with personal vanity than actual quality of life considerations."

"So if a woman came to you and said she couldn't get dates because her nose was too large, you wouldn't help her?" Jennings said.

"It would depend, I suppose, on whether she was grossly disfigured—"

"Disfigured in the eyes of whom? One woman's nose is another woman's schnozzola, is it not? Aren't you making a judgment call there; aren't you playing God, as some have proclaimed?" Jennings said.

"If she were disfigured, say, in an accident, and asked me to help her, I would probably try to do so. If she's just born with a large nose, I'd have to say no."

"What about fat people? Obesity is a genuine health problem, so it could be argued—"

"I'd advise them to go on a diet and lose weight."

"What about morbid obesity, where the person is in imminent danger of death if the problem is left untreated?"

"That's still a lifestyle choice and something that happens

over a very long period of time with plenty of opportunity to take action before the problem becomes so extreme. No one suddenly gets that big unless there's a tumor involved. There is help available for the morbidly obese, such as gastric bypass surgery and other forms of treatment."

"So you're saying you only step in for cases where all other avenues have been exhausted, where you're the last hope a person has?"

He had me there. That's one point I'd never been able to adequately defend against.

"No, that's not really the case, either. I've healed plenty of people who've come to me with broken bones and sprained ankles. I'm not going to get on a plane and fly across the country to cure someone with a cold or heal a bunion."

"So they have to come to you, make a pilgrimage to Lynchburg, right?"

"That's not what I'm saying at all." He had me and was making me squirm. "I've always struggled to determine just what my responsibility in helping others should be. Some decisions are easy, like whether to help an entire village being devastated by an epidemic. Others are more difficult, such as whether I should just let everybody line up and come at me. Physically there just aren't enough hours in the day, in fact there aren't enough hours in my lifetime, to meet with each and every person on the face of the earth."

"I sense you're getting a bit testy with this line of questioning, but you still haven't really answered the caller: how do you decide

340

who to help and who not to help?" Jennings said.

News of retaliation against U.S. forces for the previous night's bombings finally bumped me off the program. An assistant director was evidently going to apologize to me until the seas ran out of salt, but I assured her I didn't mind at all.

"Well, I really am sorry we had to end your appearance so soon. We received more than seven hundred e-mails while you were on. Would you like to see them?"

"No, that's all right. I really need to get going," I said.

"Some of them might be important; they might be from people needing help who don't have any other way of reaching you."

"I'm sorry, but I'm just not in a position to help everyone out there. I can't save the world," I said.

"Have you helped anyone today?"

***

I went back to the Italian restaurant where Corrine and I had had lunch that first day, not for the quality of the food but for the solitude. I don't know how many stanzas of "Santa Lucia" one can stand, particularly when played over such a branches-on-the-window-pane sound system, but that was certainly the place to find out. As I toyed with my pasta, I began to visualize how a chart of my day's highs and lows would have resembled the classic bell curve.

The woman's face that peered out at me from the photo in my wallet was that of a stranger. It didn't match the mental image I tried to assemble of Amanda because the pieces weren't there and the mental reception was bad. It was only in the previous hour I even remembered I carried a picture of my wife with me, but the face was so alien it could have been some insert that came with the wallet.

"She's pretty." The waitress looked over my shoulder. "Your wife or your sister?"

"A long lost love," I said. "Very long lost."

"That's too bad. Hey, abstinence makes the heart grow fonder."

"That's what they say. Or something a lot like that."

"You're the guy on TV, right?"

"I never realized so many people watched C-SPAN."

"C-SPAN? Are you kidding me? That's boring beyond words. I saw you on the Jennings show. You looked pretty uncomfortable on there, especially the part when he asked you about how you make choices."

"Choices. I've made some pretty bad ones along the way."

"I hope the lady in the photo wasn't one of them."

"No, she was a good one. The best one of all."

"Then why is she a long-lost love instead of a current flame?"

"Because I lost her, that's why. I made a bad choice."

"Then you can make a choice to do whatever it takes to get her back. Isn't anything worth fighting for anymore? I mean, you guys kill me. Don't men have any balls these days? Every man I know just gives up on the women they say they love. Would this woman you're gazing at so longingly just give up on you?"

"Absolutely not. She'd move heaven and earth and drive a golf cart through hell if she had to."

"Then why don't you get off your ass and go find her?"

"I've tried. I don't know where to look."

"That's bull crap. More often than not in cases like these the answer is somewhere inside you."

"You're pretty perceptive. Do you always give advice-to-the-lovelorn to your customers?"

"I just always felt a calling to help people. I guess my name has a lot to do with it."

"What is your name?"

"Charity. Charity Love."

CHAPTER SEVEN

Day four of the hearings brought Reba Myers to the table. I didn't recognize the name at first, until she identified herself as Mrs. Winston Myers, the widow of the store owner murdered by the kidnapper. Though only in her late fifties, the history of her life was written deeply in the lines on her face.

"Mrs. Myers, we can understand the pain you must feel over the loss of your husband, but what is it you want from Mr. Townsend or from this panel?" Sen. Schmelling said.

"I want justice, is what I want." Mrs. Myers said. "My husband is dead because an evil man who deserved to die wasn't allowed to do so. He was given a second chance by this man, and with that second chance he took away my best friend and my children's father. As far as I'm concerned, this man is an accomplice and I want to make sure he doesn't go unpunished for what he did. I want to know he won't go around saving other murderers and rapists so they can go out and kill again. I want him to know what he did to me."

"I believe the judge who dismissed your suit said Mr. Townsend was only doing the same thing the doctors in that situation were trying to do," Sen. Jameson said. "Doctors can't be sued for what a patient does after leaving their care, except possibly where the doctor is treating the patient for some psychological disorder."

"The murderer was already dead, I tell you, or almost there," Mrs. Myers said. "He was beyond saving with their means by the time this man got there. I've read the reports and he was flatlining. He was dead."

The hall was quiet.

"This man," she continued, pointing at me, "this man here, he went beyond what the doctors could do. He went beyond medical skill, into whatever black magic he practices, and he not only saved that bastard, he revived him completely, to a point of such good health he was able to forcibly escape the hospital and go out into the world and kill someone. That someone was my husband. My point here is, even if the doctors had been able to save him by medical means, he wouldn't have been in any shape to go out and do what he did, not for a long, long while. He would have been in jail before he was physically able to terrorize people."

"Mr. Townsend, Mrs. Myers has repeatedly said here the man in question was dead when you arrived," Sen. Schmelling said. "Is that true? Was he indeed dead at the time?"

"No, sir, he was at a point where his heart and other organs had ceased to function, but brain death had not yet occurred. Otherwise I could not have saved him."

"He was very close to brain death, was he not?" Sen. Cordoba said.

"That is correct," I said.

"So, in effect, he would have died had you not intervened?" Sen. Cordoba said.

"Yes."

"You see? Even he admits it," Mrs. Myers said. "He admits he and he alone is responsible for that monster going back out into the world and murdering my husband."

"Mrs. Myers, please, I don't see what you can possibly hope to gain from hammering on that same point. The nail is in the wood already; in fact, it's ready to fall out the other side by now," Sen. Schmelling said. "What is it you want?"

"I want," She made a great effort to make it appear as if everyone should already know what she wanted, "some assurance this man is not going to continue going out and turning dead killers loose on society to kill again."

"Mrs. Myers, this is not a court of law. We don't have any power to forbid Mr. Townsend from doing just that," Sen. Schmelling said. "I don't know any way to grant your request."

"Then I'll go to court again. I'll keep going until I find someone to listen to me," she said.

"Mr. Townsend, let me ask you this: Would you have healed that robber so completely had you known what he was going to do?" Sen. Jameson said.

"I don't understand the question," I said.

"Why, it's very simple: Would you have fixed him all the way up had you known what was going to happen?"

346

"Senator, I can't heal someone part of the way. It's all or nothing. If I'm able to heal someone, they're completely healed, not just feeling better and on the road to recovery."

"Then let me put it this way: Would you have healed him had you known he was going to kill this woman's husband?"

"I can't answer that question because there's no way I could have known that was going to happen," I said.

"I know that, but let's pretend you could. Would you have healed that man had you known he would go out and shoot this woman's husband?"

"Senator, I was there at the request of the Lynchburg police. I was only doing what they directed me to do."

"You could have refused them, could you not?" Sen. Jameson said. "Please answer my question: Would you have healed that man had you known he was going to go out and shoot this woman's husband?"

"If he can't answer that as many times as you've asked him, then his answer is yes, and he would do it again," Mrs. Myers said.

"Mrs. Myers, please. Let Mr. Townsend answer the question," Sen. Schmelling said.

"I guess my answer is no. No, I would not have healed him had I known what was going to happen. Then again, had I known it was going to happen, I would have warned the police and the hospital security to keep an eye on him so he couldn't escape, so he would never have gotten loose. So the point here is moot."

"You probably would have helped him escape and bought

him the bullets," Mrs. Myers turned to face me while the TV cameras rolled. "Where were you when my husband lay dying on the floor of his business just because he happened to be the one behind the counter? There was no miracle for him. Then the robber wound up getting shot to death anyway, so basically you saved him just long enough to allow him to take one more victim with him. That was real good work there."

"All right, Mrs. Myers, that's enough. I think you've made your point," Sen. Schmelling said.

"No! I haven't! Where was he when my children and I needed someone to heal us from the grief that's eaten away at us for almost six years now? Do you know I still have to run the store and look at the spot where my husband died every single day of my life?"

"That'll be all, Mrs. Myers. You're excused," Sen. Schmelling said.

With a look that would curl steel, Mrs. Winston Myers stood and stared at me for several long seconds, feigning a lunge in hopes of making me flinch. I simply stared ahead at the panel members. I was never oblivious to her pain, but I saw no point in confronting her. Finally, as security guards approached, she spun and lumbered off.

"Mr. Townsend, do you still assert you have never once accepted money or favors for your services?" Sen. Cordoba asked. The question stunned me; I thought we had moved beyond that point.

"That's right, Senator. As I said repeatedly on Monday."

348

"Well, we have a Ms. Corrine Necessary we'd like to speak with. Come on over, Ms. Necessary," Sen. Cordoba said.

I had managed to not notice Corrine all morning as she sat and recorded the proceedings. Now another young woman came over to spell her and Corrine stood and sauntered to the table. The slit in her long skirt opened up for a good show of leg as she walked and a nearby cameraman, I noticed, caught every flash of skin as the skirt flared going by.

"Now, Ms. Necessary, you are employed here as a transcriptionist, is that not correct?" Sen. Cordoba asked.

Why is he suddenly running the proceeding?

"That's correct, sir," she said.

"Over the course of the last few days did you come to be involved with Mr. Townsend in any way?"

"Yes, sir. We were involved in a relationship earlier in the week."

"What sort of relationship?"

"Sexual."

I don't think a day went by during the hearings something didn't cause the ambient noise level to rise, and this was no exception. Sen. Schmelling had to shush the assemblage.

"When you say sexual, are you referring to sexual intercourse?" Sen. Cordoba said.

"Yes."

"Were there any other sexual acts that occurred during this relationship?" Sen. Cordoba said.

349

"I performed fellatio on Mr. Townsend," Corrine said, without so much as a blush. I think I may have caught the tiniest hint of a smile at the corner of her lip.

There went the buzz once more. Sen. Schmelling had to play teacher again and quiet everyone down.

"Was that as a matter of foreplay to the intercourse or was it an act in and of itself?" Sen. Cordoba said. I wasn't sure why that mattered.

"No, that was a stand-alone act," Corrine said.

"Did you swallow?" Sen. Cordoba said. The bastard was getting aroused by talking dirty in front of everyone.

"Senator, please, that's enough," Sen. Schmelling said. "Ms. Necessary, don't even answer that. That type of information is not relevant and does not need to be disclosed in this situation."

"With all due respect, Mr. Chairman, I am getting to the relevance here," Sen. Cordoba said. "Ms. Necessary, what was happening while you were performing oral sex on Mr. Townsend?"

"He was on the phone with his mother-in-law," Corrine said. Sen. Cordoba made a big show of rolling his eyes and tossing papers into the air. "She was telling him, I could hear, about how worried she was about her daughter, who's in some sort of coma or something."

Well, that was certainly going to endear me to the crowd.

"Now, Mr. Chairman, back to the relevance of my question as to whether Ms. Necessary swallowed while servicing Mr. Townsend: The following day Mr. Townsend called room service and

350

had them take away a certain heavy armchair that was in his room. It so happens that armchair was taken to a local laboratory and tested for any residual body fluids. Shall I tell you what was found?"

"I don't think that will be needed," Sen. Schmelling said. "I think all of us remember what was found on a certain intern's dress a few years ago." That brought a polite chuckle from the room.

"Ms. Necessary," Sen. Cordoba said, "did Mr. Townsend perform any favors for you in exchange for the sexual services you rendered to him?"

"He healed me of a long-standing condition I suffered from."

"I see. You provided sexual favors to him, and in return he used his abilities to heal you?"

Corrine didn't actually reply to Cordoba's question. Her head moved ever so slightly, as if she meant to nod but stopped herself.

"Ms. Necessary, please answer the question," Sen. Schmelling said. "Did he heal you in return for sexual gratification?"

Again Corrine was silent, her eyes wide, her lips clenched.

"Has he threatened you in any way if you speak out against him?" Sen. Cordoba said.

"No."

"Then what is the problem?" Cordoba said.

"I'm sorry." She started to cry, then turned to me. "I'm so sorry. I don't want this to happen."

"Just tell the truth," I said.

"What truth, Ms. Necessary? What is the truth?" Sen. Jameson said. "Did he or did he not exact sexual gratification from you in return for healing you?"

"No. It wasn't like that. He didn't even know." She put her face in her hands and sobbed.

"Wasn't like what? What didn't he know?" Sen. Schmelling said. "What are you talking about?"

"He didn't know I was going to come on to him." She sniffed and wiped. "I just...I was the aggressor. I was just showing him around town, keeping him company, it was all platonic, and then when he was on the phone with his mother-in-law, I took all my clothes off and started...well, I unzipped his pants, I put my head in his lap, and it went from there. He didn't ask me to do it. I just started doing it."

"He could have asked you to stop, couldn't he?" Sen. Cordoba said. "He could have refused."

"I suppose." She regained control. "He didn't and I just kept doing it until it was too late. It was my fault."

"So after accepting your services, he agreed to heal you, is that not right?" Sen. Cordoba said.

"No. That's not right. It turns out he had already healed me; I just didn't know it. I got stoned earlier that night and I was wearing just a bathrobe and coming on to him and he rejected my advances and somehow made me sober all at once, but he also healed my condition. That was before I ever...did the thing I did to him."

Sen. Cordoba saw his case losing its momentum.

"You then had intercourse, did you not?" he said.

"Not until the following evening. I came onto him again. I

352

went to his room, took off all my clothes and climbed on top of him and took his clothes off. He never really resisted, but he didn't really participate, either. He never even rolled me over. I was on top the whole time. He never even thrusted once, I had to do all the work. He just kept asking me not to do it, telling me it was wrong."

She was crying again.

"Ms. Necessary," said Sen. Estelle Cartwright, an African American woman from Georgia, almost in a whisper. "What you just described is the act of rape on your part."

"Oh, that's nonsense!" Sen. Cordoba said. "He's lying there naked, he's all aroused, the damn thing is sticking up like a flagpole, and she climbs on it and you call that rape? He had a hard-on, for Christ's sake! That means he wanted it. Besides, he could have pushed her off at any point!"

Sen. Cartwright turned with all the wrath a righteous woman could muster and spoke very slowly: "Senator Cordoba, arousal, or the lack thereof, is not a requirement or a condition of rape. Nor is the victim required to physically resist. As you well know. If the sexes of the two participants had been reversed, and if it had been a man who had removed a woman's clothing against her will, and had gotten on top of her and continued having sex with her over her protests, you know very well that would have been considered rape."

"Mr. Townsend is a married man. He should never have let her into his room," Sen. Cordoba said.

"That may well be, but that's not for us to judge," Sen. Cartwright said. "There's also no law against two consenting adults having sex with each other, even if one of them is married. How old are you, Ms. Necessary?"

"Twenty-three," Corrine said.

"Then she's of consenting age," Sen. Cartwright said. "He did not give her his consent. She mounted him and raped him, and I think Ms. Necessary realizes that now. Don't you, Ms. Necessary?"

Corrine clapped her hand to her mouth and nodded. Streaking mascara gave her face a clownish look.

"Mr. Townsend here has every right to press charges against Ms. Necessary," Sen. Cartwright said. All eyes turned to me.

"I have no wish to do that," I said. "We both made a very big mistake."

"Speaking of a very big mistake," Sen. Cartwright said, like a Southern Baptist preacher getting his second wind, "how did that armchair just 'happen' to get to a lab to be tested, Senator Cordoba? Who authorized that? That's something I would like to know. I think we'd all like to know that."

"I resent the implication I somehow arranged all this, that I covertly sent Ms. Necessary over to seduce Mr. Townsend in order to set him up," Sen. Cordoba said. "What would I have to gain from that?"

"I think we'll leave it up to the Ethics Committee to look into whether Senator Cordoba had a hand in any of this," said Sen. Schmelling, who finally decided to resume control of his own hearing. "Before we move on, I'd like to allow Mr. Townsend a chance to speak on his own behalf as to his motivation and conduct."

"Senators, I can only say I allowed myself to be placed into a very compromising position." I didn't realize the pun until it was too late. "As a married man, indeed, as an ethical man, I should have more strongly resisted this young woman's advances. She is a very attractive young woman, but it is I who have difficulty saying no in such situations. In fact, she pointed this out to me in a rather visual manner. As to whether what took place was technically rape or not, I don't wish to make a case of it. Suffice it to say I think we both made a mistake and we have both learned a lesson."

Corrine nodded vigorously, eyes closed.

"What about the mother-in-law's comments on the phone while these two were...fornicating?" Sen. Cordoba said.

"Hearsay," Sen. Schmelling said. "Pure hearsay. I think we've all had enough of this."

I knew I had had enough.

"Senators, may I ask what is the point of these hearings?" I was unable to control the impatience in my voice.

"Why, to look into allegations healers are charging people for services they are unable to render," Sen. Cordoba said. "We're investigating frauds who take people's money and leave them no better off. In some cases, in fact, they're worse off because they go off their medicine, thinking they're cured."

"That's what you told me earlier in the week. Over the course of the past four days, I think it has become all too clear I have had no part in any of this. I don't endorse anyone healing in my name or who claims to be associated with me in any way, nor did I have any previous knowledge of these people you've talked about. What this has turned into, it seems, is an attack on my character and moral judgment, and, quite frankly, I'm very tired of it. You dragged this young woman out here," I indicated Corrine, "in order to shame and embarrass me in front of the entire country and have probably cost her her job here as well. All to prove a point you could not prove."

"Mr. Townsend," Sen. Schmelling said.

"I'm not finished, Senator. You also brought Mrs. Myers up here to blame me, again, for the death of her husband, even though a court of law has already refused to listen to her claim. In her case there is no allegation I accepted anything in return for the service I rendered on behalf of the Lynchburg police."

"Mr. Townsend, if you'll let us continue…" Sen. Schmelling tried again.

"I see no point in letting any of this continue. I don't see…"

Something was wrong.

"Does anyone else smell that?" A sweet scent—the closest correlation I could come up with was honeysuckle, though that wasn't quite it—had wafted into the building. I had smelled that exact aroma recently, but I couldn't place it.

Wait. Africa. This was the smell that permeated the second village, the one where death had not yet hit.

"Mr. Townsend? Is something the matter?" Sen. Cartwright said.

"We've got to get out of here," I tried not to let the panic make my voice rise. "We've all just been poisoned. This is the smell I noticed in the second village in Africa. Senators, everyone, we have to clear this building. If you have an emergency protocol for clearing the building, you need to put it into effect *now*."

"Are you sure?" said Sen. Schmelling, but everyone in the chamber had started rising, along with the noise level, forcing him to call the hearing to a halt. Before anyone could make it out of the chamber, I was knocked to the floor by a concussive force that set off alarms and sprinklers. Now people were panicking.

"We've been attacked!" someone said, as chaos and confusion replaced all sense of order. On the floor my head ached as I tried to keep everything from going dark in front of me. I knew I needed to do something; I just could not focus on what that was.

I put a hand to my scalp and felt it was wet. When I drew it away, I saw a bloody smudge on my fingers, nothing too serious. People were screaming all around me as someone on the public address system was urging everyone to remain calm. The Senate chamber had become a bastion of babble, as words like "explosion," "terrorists" and "bioterrorism" floated above the din.

I tried to evaluate my immediate surroundings. I had been thrown against the large wooden table where all the speakers sat facing the Senate panel, knocking the table over in the process. One wall of the chamber had been blasted inward, leaving a jagged hole with smoke pouring into the great hall. My vision was still blurred from the blow to my head, but I tried to scan the vicinity for injuries. As I stood to my full height, my head throbbed and I sank back to my knees. I wasn't even aware of the presence behind me.

357

"Here you go, Mr. Townsend. Everything's going to be all right." I turned to see a dark-headed young man in a U.S. Marines uniform kneeling over me. As he touched my skull, my head stopped hurting and my vision began to clear.

"Sergeant Lucas," I said. "You're part of the 'protocols' Dr. Wheatley spoke of, aren't you?. I should have known."

"I've been keeping an eye on you. Hope is outside, doing whatever she can. Orders?"

"We've got to alert the Eleven. This is too big for the three of us."

CHAPTER EIGHT

As Lionel and I made our way outside, I pulled the headset Dr. Wheatley had given me out of my coat pocket and placed it over my head. It was time to put his protocols in place.

"Go see if you can help anyone injured by the explosion. Right now I'm more worried about containing the spread of the pathogen," I told Lionel. "Dr. Wheatley is standing by with the African antibodies and he's got WHO and the CDC working overtime to produce more. Tell Hope to get the word out to the Eleven; have them split up and get to every hospital in the area. I'm trying to get through to the White House now."

"What about Warren?"

"Tell him to report to Dr. Wheatley. He'll know what to do."

"Roger." With that, Lionel sprinted off into the crowd with that renowned world-class speed of his, leaving me to the most important task. I tapped the right earphone on my apparatus three times and waited for the computerized voice to ask for my pass code.

"Nightingale." I heard a moment of static and a soft drawl answered on the other end of the line.

"Mr. President, the egg has hatched. The foxes are in the henhouse, but the farmer's on his way with the sack."

I had a hard time saying all this with a straight face, even with the solemnness of the situation before me. I had suggested an alternate code, but mine had been overruled.

"How bad is the breach?" the voice on the other end said.

"We won't know for a while yet, but if the situation in Africa is any indication, this thing is capable of spreading over a pretty wide area. I'd advise grounding all air traffic over the city, with the exception of Bluebird One; we have no idea how high into the atmosphere the spores can travel."

"Will do. Keep me posted. You will get any and all resources needed. Oh, and don't worry about Senator Cordoba. I'll handle him."

"He's in your own party."

"Doesn't matter. The man's got a vendetta, and I will not stand for this kind of behavior. You just do your job and I'll do mine."

Before I could acknowledge and sign off, Capitol security guards were grabbing me by the arms and dragging me down the same front steps where I'd had my picture taken all those years ago on a high school trip.

"Sir, there are wounded over here, but a young Marine seems to be healing them just as you would," said one of the guards.

"That's right. He's the real deal. Let him have full access to any and all injuries you can get him to."

"I thought you were the only one who could really do that," he said.

"Not anymore. The field's actually getting pretty crowded

now. Now, if you don't mind, I've got some other duties to handle."

The guard saluted me and I continued down the steps, tapping the headphones again.

"Dr. Wheatley? What do you know so far?"

"We've got the National Guard and the Virginia and Maryland state police sealing off all roads in and out of D.C.," Dr. Wheatley said. "The president has just given the order to reroute all air traffic away from the city and has grounded everything at both Dulles and Reagan. Captain Robertson is standing by in Bluebird One. There's some pretty good cloud cover coming in from the west, so I think we have a decent shot at washing this thing down as low as possible. In fact, it's starting to drizzle now."

This was good news indeed. After pouring over reams of data since our Africa mission, Dr. Wheatley had come to the conclusion the spores could be knocked out of the sky by rain. The area where the pathogen was released there was mired in a four-month drought, so the spores could travel freely. Capt. Robertson, the pilot from that mission, was prepared to seed the clouds over D.C. with dry ice to coax some moisture out of them if necessary.

"I'd send him up anyway. If your theory is correct, we need to wash as much of this stuff away as possible."

"Mr. Townsend! I need you over here!" Lionel called from the top of the steps back toward the Capitol.

I started to tell him to handle it, but something in his face made me sprint back up the steps.

"She's asking for you, sir." He pointed to a woman sitting

361

outside the building cradling a young boy in her arms. I could see from several yards away the boy was dead, apparently struck by debris from the initial blast.

"They were close to the wall when it blew. I tried, but I couldn't help him," Lionel said.

The woman looked up at me as I approached. It was Mrs. Myers.

"Please," she said. "He's my grandson. He's all I've got left. Can you help him?"

I shook my head. "I wish I could."

She didn't cry. I sensed she had long since lost all capacity for it.

"What about me?" She looked at the sidewalk as she spoke. "Can you heal this hole inside me? Can you make the terrible emptiness go away? Can you numb me to the pain?"

I sat down beside her. There were a thousand things I needed to be doing, a hundred places I needed to be at once, yet none seemed as pressing at the moment as this. The person I had least been able to help in the last six years was Mrs. Myers. Still I could do nothing for her.

"I don't know why these things have to happen," I said. "I certainly don't know why they have to keep happening to you."

"You never met my husband, did you?" She pulled the boy's limp body closer.

"No."

"He would have liked you. He never liked people who just

362

rushed around, never any time to talk to anyone. He liked people to just be."

"Mrs. Myers, I—"

"Didn't he, Robbie? You remember how your granddad used to sit on the porch and talk to you, don't you?"

She was talking to the dead boy now, nodding his head forward with her hand. "When we get home, I'm going to make you and Granddad a big chocolate cake, with white icing, just like you like it."

As I silently stood and turned away from Mrs. Myers, I realized she had gotten exactly what she wished for. The hurt was gone.

***

The rain came down harder now, not a deluge by any means, but hopefully enough to wash the spores away. Hope, Lionel, Warren and I had set up camp at the National Mall and were healing everyone who came to us, whether they thought they were infected or not. This was exactly the scenario I had meticulously avoided all these years, a take-all-comers approach to using the gift. Now I saw no other way to prevent a pandemic.

The rest of the Eleven—so called because they all had been eleven years old when I had healed them of whatever affliction they had, eleven of them in all—were stationed at the hospitals in the area and were healing all who came to them.

Not every eleven-year-old I ever healed acquired the power, and I don't know why these eleven did. There were some mysteries I was not meant to solve.

The solutions to other mysteries, however, were there to be seen by those who had eyes.

"Never should have been chosen, eh?" said a quivering voice from behind me as I watched an old farmer's goiter shrink at my touch.

The man behind me looked as old as the grave itself, but his eyes shone clear and bright through the rain.

"I'm sorry, sir, but you'll have to get in line if you want to see one of us," I turned back to the line in front of me.

"Oh I can wait. I can wait forever if I have to," the voice behind me said.

As I turned back around, the proverbial scales dropped from my eyes.

"It's you! Why can I never recognize you at first?"

"Don't feel bad. Most people never notice me at all. I try not to stand out too much," the Old Man said.

"Look, I've got a zillion things to ask you, but I'm pretty busy right now." I turned back to face a crowd that was now absolutely still. It was as if someone had hit the pause button on the entire world. Even the raindrops hung mutely in the sky.

"I think we can spare a few moments to talk," the Old Man said. "You've earned a break."

He was right. I was physically and emotionally drained, exhausted beyond the point of being able to rest. I sank into a folding chair and the leaden anchors that were my arms fell to my sides.

"So why me? What is this all about?" I said.

"I told you. You were the right one at the right time. The world needs somebody like you every now and then."

"Well I didn't ask for any of this. I wish you'd go away and let me live a normal life. I'm fed up with this dog-and-pony show."

"Are you? Nobody forced you to do any of this. You could have walked away at any time, you know. Changed your name. Moved away, become a hermit. Holed up in that bookstore of yours. You didn't. You went forward and did everything anyone could have asked of you. Despite all your complaints and your whining, you've performed superbly."

"I've also screwed up majestically, more than a few times," I said. "Monique, Mama, the whole thing with the hospital in South Carolina. It's not like you gave me a handbook when you gave me this assignment."

"No, but I thought the arm-tingling was a pretty good idea. That was supposed to warn you whenever you were about to do something really off-key. Let me ask you this: when you resisted your own best impulses and refused to heal your mother—your grandmother, of course—as she wished, did your arm tingle?"

"No, but I felt really sick to my stomach and I—"

"I don't care about any of that. The important thing is the warning signal in your arm. Your arm didn't tingle because you were doing the right thing. You obeyed her wishes, no matter how much it hurt you to do so. Her time was up and she knew it. So don't go dragging that guilt around anymore. The fact is, you're the single greatest healer of the past two millennia. I should know."

"Oh please. I've had it with all the comparisons to him. I'm not Jesus Christ reincarnated."

The Old Man shook his head. "No, you're certainly not. The real Christ would never have cheated on his wife, assuming he had been married, like that book implies."

"How would you know, unless—no, you're not him, either," I said.

The Old Man smiled. "No, but I'm flattered to even be mentioned in the same breath. You could figure out who I am if you really wanted to."

"I already know who you are."

His eyebrows shot up. "Oh?"

"I think I've known it somewhere in the back of my mind all along, but you gave it away with that book you were looking at that day in the bookstore. It was on the legend of the Wandering Jew, and you seemed quite interested in it. That's who you are, isn't it? You were there at the crucifixion; you're the one who mocked Christ, now cursed to spend your days wandering the Earth, never to die, never to rest. Quite a lonely existence, I would think."

His expression did not change. Clearly he had heard this theory before.

"For the record, I never mocked him. That little bit was added centuries later. Actually, I've been many things during my journeys. Yes, I was at the crucifixion. I was also the voice who led

366

Mohammed into the caves where he received the Koran, and I helped Martin Luther nail his objections to the door of the church. I also rode with Charles Darwin aboard the Beagle and helped him catalog many new species.

"My wanderings go back well before the crucifixion. I spent a number of years along the shores of the Mediterranean, telling the story of Odysseus and other great heroes of legend, until someone finally wrote them down."

"You're saying you were the poet Homer? He lived—well, I don't know exactly when he was supposed to have lived, but it was a long time before Christ. He was supposed to be blind," I said.

"So I was, until I came upon a certain tradesman in Nazareth. That, you see, was where I became interested in the gift of healing, passing it on wherever I could, though I lacked the gift myself."

"Okay, now you're creeping me out. So who are you really?"

"No one of consequence. Just someone who felt pity for a pillar of salt."

"Lot's wife? Who would...wait a minute, I get it. You were one of the angels who told them to flee the city, weren't you?"

"I didn't agree with what happened to her. I tried to go back and help her, and I was punished for my disobedience, just as you were punished when you charged into that hospital, full of hubris. I was blinded and left to wander the land. Those were harsh times, those Old Testament days. I've been wandering ever since. Let me tell you, immortality isn't something I would wish on anyone. That's one 'gift' I will not pass on."

"I thought I had it bad," I said.

"I would trade places with you any day. Your journey will eventually come to an end. Mine goes on forever, no matter how weary I get, no matter how I tire of seeing the sun rise and set a hundred thousand times, and a hundred thousand times after that."

His eyes looked into the distance, through the veil of unfallen raindrops, but his thoughts were far beyond the horizon.

"You were the voice that spoke through Ortune Elle last night, weren't you?" I said. "She was right, that was no 'Na'Peth.'"

He winced at the name. What on Earth—though I guessed this was something clearly not of the Earth—could make an angel so nervous?

"You're fortunate I was able to intercede for you, before you got its attention. There are forces out there you don't want to deal with, forces that extract a terrible price from those who do have dealings with them, as 'Ortune Elle,' as you call her, will someday learn. Never say its name again. You may succeed in summoning something you don't want."

"So what's going to happen? With this plague, I mean? What's going to happen to the world?"

"You're the one who's always saying the world doesn't need saving, yet you go on trying to save it anyway. You also say someone has to get sick and die or else the whole world gets sick and dies," he said.

"Damn it, I am so tired of everyone throwing that quote back in my face! I would never have said it if I'd known it would be repeated back at me every day for the rest of my life!"

"You were right when you said it. It's the most profound thing you've ever said, believe it or not. The time will come very soon when someone will have to die, or else the whole world will indeed get sick and die," he said.

"So that's it? That's my purpose, my great unfolding destiny, to simply let someone die?"

"Why does everyone in this day and age think they have some destiny? Are you all Calvinists? You have a gift, an ability to enrich people's lives and lift them up. You do the best you can with the talents you are given. That's all anyone can do."

He could see I was becoming angered, but I wasn't about to let him leave. I grabbed his arm before he could pull some disappearing trick.

"Wait! What about Amanda? How can I get her back? How can I save her?"

"You know the old saying: 'Thrice betrayed, forgiveness delayed.'"

Suddenly the air was vibrant with commotion as the world around me went back to moving again. The Old Man was gone.

"Wait!" I screamed into the rain. "I don't know that saying! Who said it? What does it mean?"

The people in the enormous line before me simply stared like cattle at a passing jet. The rain was falling and we were all healing everyone who came to us, a line that stretched as far as the eye could see. Looking out into the infinite mass, it seemed my journey would never end either.

***

I was wrong, of course. Some two hours after the Old Man left me—or it could have been two days, it was impossible to tell—there was a commotion on the grounds as the sea of people before us parted to accommodate a military vehicle that came roaring up to me. Two soldiers with automatic weapons at the ready jumped out of a Humvee and ordered me into the vehicle.

"What about all these people?" I gestured out at the masses.

"They'll have to wait, sir," said one soldier. "We've got orders to transport you to a higher priority assignment."

I clambered into the vehicle with some assistance. I don't know if it was the years or the mileage beginning to catch up to me, but I certainly wasn't as nimble as I once was. People were booing as the driver shifted the Humvee into gear and many started beating on the sides of the car, demanding I come back out. The driver had to carefully negotiate through the tens of thousands of souls now filling the National Mall like water pouring into a leaky boat.

"So where are we going?" I said.

"I'm sorry, sir, that's on a need-to-know basis."

"Don't give me any of that need-to-know shit, soldier. I wasn't born yesterday. Obviously you have a pretty high-profile subject who needs to be healed. If you want my cooperation, you'd better fess up."

"We have a suspect in the attack, someone pretty high up in the organization. Very high up. His ego got the better of him. Instead

370

of watching the whole thing from the safety of his hideout, he thought he had to see it in person. He went down in a firefight and we need you to revive him before it's too late. We can cripple the organization with the names and info he could provide."

"I don't suppose either of you ever worked for the Lynchburg PD," I said.

"Why do you ask?"

"This situation has a very familiar feel to it."

Far too familiar. The Humvee drove to an airfield where a military helicopter was ready to lift off. Physically, climbing aboard the bird was a good deal harder than it had been six and a half years ago. Mentally and emotionally, however, the present journey was far worse.

My left arm was tingling.

We flew to a military hospital where I was ushered into the ER. On the table, going into cardiac arrest, was a man I had seen just two days earlier.

It was Brother Abraham, suffering severe trauma inflicted by multiple gunshot wounds.

"What are you waiting for? Fix him!" said a tall FBI-type with severely cropped hair and an overbite. "He's flatlining!"

"Who is this man?" I said.

"He's a Croatian national with a background in microbiology. We believe he's responsible for isolating the compounds that created the plaque spores and is very possibly the highest-ranking member of the organization that created it. Now fix him, Goddammit!"

"No," I said.

"What do you mean?"

"I mean I refuse. This man is an agent of death, responsible for the deaths of hundreds, possibly thousands of others. I saved a murderer once before, only to have him go out and kill once more; I will not do it again."

"We can cut the organization wide open from the top down with this man!" the agent said. "If you let him die, we will lose that opportunity."

"You'll just have to lose it, then. I've never in my life refused to help someone in dire need, but I'm doing it now. I will not help this man."

I winced and yelped as the cold steel of a gun barrel drilled into the back of my skull and my right arm was bent behind my back.

"You will fix him, you son of a bitch, or I will blow your fucking head all over the walls of this hospital. Is that what you want? Is it, punk?"

I wish I could relay that I stood my ground with courage and dignity, that I told the agent where to stick his machismo threat. All I could think of was the fact I would never see Amanda again. My saga had come full circle; I was right back to the point where I had to decide whether to save a dying criminal, only this time my own life depended on it.

"I won't do it," I said, the words having to maneuver their way around the heart now throbbing in the back of my throat.

I closed my eyes and braced myself as I heard the agent's

372

weapon cock. It wouldn't hurt for long once he pulled that trigger, but that thought did nothing to reassure me. My breath came so fast and furious I was on the verge of hyperventilation.

"Put your weapon away, Agent Mooney."

"Sir, he—"

"I said put it away! That's an order! This man serves at the discretion of the president himself. Do you want to explain to the president why you murdered his special envoy? The man responsible, both directly and indirectly, for saving every single person in the greater D.C. metro area from this plague?"

"No, sir," Agent Mooney said. I was shaking uncontrollably as he removed the barrel of his pistol from the base of my skull and handed his weapon to his superior. My heart almost fibrillated when I saw who the superior was: the former Lt. B. Devon, the LPD officer who fetched me to save the kidnapper all those years ago. His daughter was never found.

"I'm so sorry about your daughter, sir." My words sounded, to me, anyway, at least an octave above my normal register.

"So am I, son. So am I."

The doctors and nurses in the ER had been so busy watching our little drama that hardly anyone noticed "Brother Abraham" had passed away.

My left arm had stopped tingling.

CHAPTER NINE

I heard my name being said by someone far away, as if in a dream. I later realized I had been dreaming for almost two days. I sat up in an unfamiliar bed in a sparsely furnished bedroom I had never seen before.

I squinted in the darkness until I realized it was only dark because the blinds had been drawn. An amber hue glowed around the edges of the window. I took inventory of my limbs to make sure they were still functioning, then found the floor with my right leg first, then my left. I stood on those creaky limbs, stretched, and made my way to the window where I drew the blinds and looked out onto a walled courtyard of some sort. From the sun's position I guessed it must be at least mid-morning.

"Man, is it morning already?" a man's voice said from the corner of the room.

"Sid? What are you doing here?"

He rubbed his eyes and sat up on the couch I had not noticed was in the room. His remaining hair forked off at garish angles.

"I've been waiting for you to wake up. Never known anyone to sleep for two whole days." His was not a pleasant visage to wake up to.

"So I must have dreamed all that about the plague spores and trying to heal everybody at the Mall and the FBI trying to get me to heal some maniac. Thank God for that. Where are we?"

He shook his head. "No dream. It happened all right. You and Warren and the Marine and that little hottie Hope were out there at the Mall trying to heal everyone in sight, trying to do the one thing you always said could not be done, heal the whole world. You were right all along, it couldn't. After they hauled you away to try and save Brother Abraham, all the other healers collapsed, one by one, from exhaustion and had to be carried away. People were screaming and crying and demanding you be brought back out, given drugs to bring you around if necessary. It got pretty ugly. That's why you're here."

"Where is here?"

"A shelter, a halfway house, if you will. For your own safety. Jeremiah, I don't know how to break this to you, but the life you knew is over."

"What are you talking about?"

"This whole thing, this healing power, the hysteria it creates, it's out of control. You've become the biggest thing on the planet. Everyone—and I mean everyone—wants a piece of you, wants you to make them immortal, heal them and all their family members. They're making pilgrimages to Lynchburg from all over the world, bringing their sick and elderly with them. You see where I'm going with this, don't you? It's what you've always feared," he said.

"What about the plague spores? What's happening outside?"

"The foundation, the CDC and WHO are still administering the antibodies as fast as they can make them. I understand there will probably be some casualties, because it's just not possible to inoculate everyone, but at least there's a chance. I hear the rain washed a lot of it away before it could spread too far, but the city's still in quarantine. Nobody's getting in or out for a while."

"Everybody knows about me now," I said, more to myself than to anyone else.

"Everybody. They all know and believe. You can't ever go back to your house, to the bookstore, to the life you had before. People are starting to worship you, and they won't ever leave you alone. When you die, your body will be carried off and enshrined and memorialized. Do you understand what I'm saying?"

"You want me to hide out here, wherever this is?"

"You can call it hiding if you want, but the fact is your old life is gone, your old identity. You can't just be Jeremiah Townsend, the mild-mannered bookstore owner who heals people on the side anymore. This is way beyond Dr. Wheatley's ability to keep you anonymous. The foundation can't protect you anymore; you have to drop out of all knowledge, assume a new identity, move out of state, get into some sort of witness protection program, something. You know, being Jewish, I was never really into the whole Jesus thing, but I understand even he had to get away from it all once in a while. He didn't have to deal with mass media and modern transportation."

I sighed. My body was rested, my psyche was not. A lifetime of unbearable responsibility will do that. I think I had always realized my life would someday come to this point, though I had fought to push that point as far into the future as possible. There were so many people I would never be able to see again, so many friends and faces that would be lost forever.

Not that there was much hope of hiding for long. As long as I had these abilities, I would have to use them. I would be discovered again. It would be so simple if I could simply walk away from it all, the way the Old Man said I could do.

"It's not just you, either. The others, the ones you called The Eleven, they've been found out, too," Sid said. "Hope's been asked to pose for *Playboy*. So has that Corrine chick. Guess which one's already accepted?"

"What about Amanda?" I said.

"Last I heard there was no change. You can bring her with you, of course, wherever they put you. God, Jeremiah, I don't know what it'll take to bring her around, if you can't do it."

"Thrice betrayed, forgiveness delayed," I said.

"What does that mean?"

"I wish I knew. I'm just sorry Hope, Warren, Lionel and all the others have to go through this same thing. They're all so young; they're not supposed to be weighted down with burdens like this."

"From what I understand, they were no younger than you were when you started," Sid said, fighting to bring his tangles of hair under control.

"Yes, but I was still pretty much anonymous when I was at the age they are now. My little 'coming out' party didn't happen until much later."

"That reminds me. They all want to see you later. They're

having a meeting of some sort today at two."

"What time is it now?"

He rummaged around in a duffel bag for a watch.

"Here it is, eleven thirty a.m. Time for a shower, lunch and some sightseeing before you go."

"So where is this meeting? For that matter, where are we?"

"We're at some sort of secret government enclave, that's all I know. Hell, for all I know we could be at Camp David or Area Fifty-one. They asked me to come here to fill you in on everything, but they insisted on blindfolding me when they drove me here. I don't even know what state we're in, but considering the quarantine, I guess we must still be in D.C. somewhere."

I wasn't as hungry as might be expected for someone who hadn't eaten in almost three days, but my bladder was full beyond reason. After a lengthy purge, I opted for a long soak in the tub rather than a shower. No matter how hard I tried to feel sorry for myself, my thoughts kept drifting toward Amanda. It was looking more and more like I would never see her—at least not the way I remembered her—again.

During my leisurely bath I began to realize just how hungry I truly was. When I emerged back into the room, I found a tray with fruit and sandwiches.

"At least we have room service here," Sid said. We helped ourselves to everything on the table and were soon rooting around for any hint of a hidden stash.

I found a change of clothes in the closet and looked back out at the courtyard. There were no signs of life.

"So where is this meeting?" I said.

"They're supposed to be coming here, last I heard. I hope so, because I have no idea how to get out of here. I wandered around for a while when they first brought you in, but the place makes no sense. Too many corridors and stairways for my tastes."

"So you're not a prisoner here, then?"

"Neither are you. You're here for your own protection, is the way I understand it."

"You know, I have no idea how I got here. I have no memory of being brought here or where I was when I fell asleep last. I just woke up and here I was. Isn't that strange?"

"Not really. You were exhausted beyond all feasibility when they brought you here. For the record, you walked in under your own power, but you were babbling something about Lot's wife and the Wandering Jew. Now that's an old legend I haven't heard of in a long, long time. My grandmother used to tell me that story when I was little. It was a big deal in the old days, in Europe."

"It's no legend. I've met him. He's not a Jew, he's an angel who got his wings clipped, so to speak."

"You meet the darndest people in this job, don't you?"

CHAPTER TEN

I found the three of them sitting in a large drawing room with a stone fireplace and plush chairs. The room was lined with rich mahogany woodwork and heavy red drapes that must have served for hundreds of hide-and-seek sessions over the ages. Hope, in yet another sundress, sat on a Queen Anne couch. Lionel, in a polo shirt and dress pants, stood with perfect posture off to one side while Warren, in a T-shirt and sweatpants, slumped in a matching armchair.

The whispers trailed off as I wandered in from the hallway. Hope gave me that natural smile she always carried. Lionel offered a respectful nod, and Warren just smirked.

"Welcome back, sleepyhead," Hope softened the mood. "Glad you could join us."

"I'm sorry. I feel like I've let you all down. I never wanted this to get so out of control. I shouldn't have dragged you all into this."

"Sir, we weren't 'dragged into' anything," Lionel said. "We all volunteered to help in any way we could. We were given these abilities for a reason, same as you."

"Now that reason seems to be gone. That's what we wanted to tell you." Hope sat up straighter. "Our powers are gone. So are everyone else's we talked to. We were wondering if you still had yours."

I nodded. Earlier, the moment I first realized Sid was in the room with me, I detected he had a touch of indigestion and acid reflux. Now, looking out at my three most faithful disciples, I sensed Hope was suffering from cramps, Warren had a minor rash on the bottom of his foot and Lionel had a small cut on his hand. If my diagnostic abilities were there, I still had the power to heal.

"I'm afraid so," I said. "I'm happy for the rest of you. This means you should be able to get on with your lives after all."

"What are you going to do?" Hope walked over and took my hand. "Some of the people are saying you're going to have to go away and assume another name. Where will you live; what will you do?"

"I don't really know." I was aware moisture was forming behind my eyes. "I'll be all right, though. I always have."

Hope hugged me and put her head on my shoulder. "I'm not so sure this time. This all just seems so wrong. You shouldn't have to run away and hide because you can do remarkable things. What about your wife?"

"She'll be with me, wherever I go." I was not at all sure of myself on that one.

"Aunt Charlotte said you could live with her." Warren laid one hand on Hope and his head on my other shoulder. "Nobody knows about her."

"I couldn't ask her to do that, no matter how good her intentions." I was now hugging them both. "I have to go somewhere far away from everyone I've ever known. I've hurt too many people as it is."

"Sir, you've done nothing but help people." Lionel stood closer but was not part of the group hug. "Look at me. I'd be hobbling around on a prosthetic leg if it weren't for you."

"Yes, but I've had my failures, too." I disengaged myself from Hope and Warren. "Look at Monique. Look at Amanda. Look at what almost happened to the three of you. They say you only hurt the ones you love. I guess I'd have been better off if I'd never gotten close to anyone."

"Don't say that!" Hope was now crying. "You deserve to love and be loved just like everyone else does."

"You sound like Corrine. Look where *she* got me."

That silenced her. The four of us stood looking at the floor for some time.

"So what are you all going to do?" I finally said.

"I'm going to finish my tour and then go to medical school," said Lionel. "I still want to work with amputees. You've given me some ideas about tissue regeneration. Maybe someday I'll figure out how it's done."

"Attaboy. You've got the drive and determination to do it. It shows."

"I'm still looking at colleges," Hope said. "I know this sounds kind of silly and girly and everybody wants to do it these days, but I want to write children's books."

"Sid said something about—"

"About me posing for *Playboy*, I know. Well, I told them no thanks. I don't need *that* kind of exposure."

That brought chuckles from the rest of us.

"Oh come on, you guys. I didn't mean it that way. Well, I guess I did. I understand Corrine has agreed, so you all be sure to rush out and grab your copies, so you can all see her show her butt. Again."

"If I ever have a daughter, I hope she turns out as well as you did," I said. "Always keep your clothes on."

"What about you, Warren?" Hope said.

Warren shrugged and glanced at the floor.

"My grades aren't too good," he said. "I didn't get to go to school much when I was little, so I was always behind the other kids. I like to draw, and my teachers say I'm pretty good, so I may get to go to art school. If I can get in."

"You can illustrate my children's books," Hope said. "We could be a team."

Warren grinned. "I'd like that."

"Well, you all made up the best team any Miracle Man could ask for. I'm still not entirely clear how or why things happen the way they do, but if I had been consciously trying to choose people to help me out, I couldn't have chosen any better than you guys. And gal."

"I don't mind being one of the guys," Hope said. "Just don't ask me to sit and watch football."

***

We said our good-byes and Hope, Lionel and Warren made

their way back out into their own lives. The last one had barely filed out of the room when the gloom of isolation I'd carried for so long fell back upon me, and I sat on the couch with my face in my hands.

Now is it okay to feel sorry for myself?

There was no answer. No Old Man. No Sid. No Amanda.

Where was Amanda? Now I had distanced myself from Corrine, I could recall my wife a little better. I could see her face a little more clearly in my mind, but it was still blurred, as if obscured by a curtain of fog.

I found a staircase and followed it down to another sitting room, not unlike the one I'd just left. There was a note by an old-fashioned candlestick telephone, the kind Andy Taylor had in the Mayberry courthouse.

The note consisted of three words: Ring for transport.

Within half an hour I was on a helicopter out of the D.C. area, quarantine or no. Someone very high up, I assumed possibly at the White House, wanted me kept happy. The pilot, another FBI-looking chap with close-cropped hair and sunglasses, had instructions to fly me anywhere I wanted to go in the continental U.S.

I hadn't seen a newspaper in days, since before the attack.

"So what's going on the world?" I said.

"The world goes on," he said. "I suspect it always will."

A regular chatterbox this one. We flew to Richmond, refueled, then headed for Roanoke, where a nondescript van waited to take me to Samantha's house. Traffic was light at the Roanoke airport, and twenty minutes later I was as close to home as I was going to get for a while.

Samantha hugged me at the door.

"I didn't think we were ever going to see you again," she sobbed. "Oh, God, Jeremiah, I didn't want to lose you, too."

"How is she?"

"No change. There's someone else here."

My first thought was Sid or the Old Man. As I entered the back bedroom where Amanda lay, the shrunken figure turned to face me caused me to flinch, for the second time in less than a week.

"Hello, Jeremiah."

"Monique? What are you doing here?"

"I don't really know. I was just drawn here. I feel like, somehow, I have a part in all this." The words wheezed past her lips. "I keep hearing this saying in my head: 'Thrice betrayed, forgiveness delayed.' Do you know what it means?"

She sat down in a chair beside the bed, staring at the lump of sweat, skin and hair that was now my wife.

"At first I didn't, but seeing you here now, I think I do. The three great betrayals in my life, at least the ones committed *by* me, rather than *against* me, were against you and Amanda. The only problem is, you two were the ones who had to suffer for them. I betrayed you by doing this to you, against my own better judgment. I betrayed Amanda twice, the first time when I left her in the limousine, the second time—"

I stopped and glanced back at Samantha, standing in the doorway.

"Go on," she said. "The second time…"

"The second time was when I slept with Corrine." My cheeks burned with shame.

"So we're supposed to forgive you for what you did to us?" Monique said.

"I think so."

"Amanda's comatose," Samantha said. "She can't forgive you."

"Well, for the record, I've already forgiven you," said Monique. "Just this week, when I saw you at the hearings. I realized I just couldn't keep on hating you any longer. I felt better, but it by no means healed me of what happened."

I put my hand on her shoulder.

"I forgive you, too, for asking me to do something we both knew was wrong. For not asking me to put it all back."

Monique straightened up and clamped her hand over her mouth.

"Ow! Ow! Ow ow ow ow!"

"What's wrong?" Samantha said.

"My teesh are coming baff in," she said, through closed fingers. "Ow! And my wips! Thew're woosening!"

Samantha stood with her jaw open as the husk in front of her melted and straightened and flowed into an entirely different shape. The front of Monique's sweater had even started to swell.

"My boobies are back!" Monique shouted, clamping her hands on the rich orbs which now thrust against her sweater. "Look,

386

Jeremiah, feel them!"

I glanced at Samantha. "I don't think I'd better—"

"Oh, go ahead," Samantha said. "These *are* unusual circumstances."

Obediently I cupped my hands over her breasts and gave them a little squeeze. They felt as firm and resilient as they had all those years ago.

"I've...I've got to go look at them." She rushed out to find a mirror with some privacy. "I've got to go out and buy some bras!"

"All those years," Samantha said. "You could have fixed her a long, long time ago."

"She didn't want me to. She felt shame and loathing, toward me and toward herself."

"If this had never happened, you might never have met Amanda." She looked toward the bed.

"It would have been better for her if I hadn't," I said.

I thought she was going to slap me.

"Do not ever say that again. I know my daughter and I know she loved you—loves you—very, very much. I don't understand what's happened to her, but I do know she would not trade the time she's had with you for the world, coma or no."

"I wish we knew what she would say." I took Amanda's limp hand in my own. "I love you so much, and I can only ask you to forgive me, if not for me then for yourself."

Her hand squeezed mine. Then squeezed it again.

And squeezed it a third time.

AFTERWORD

Editor's note: The preceding chapters were found among the personal effects of Jeremiah Jerome Townsend. As the whereabouts of the author remain unknown as of this publication, the following text was added by Amanda Townsend, the wife of the author. In order to protect her privacy, however, she no longer uses this name.

By Amanda Ogden Townsend*

I know he is out there somewhere, and he stills loves us.

As of this writing it has been almost three years since I last saw the man who has dubbed himself The Reluctant Messiah. To me he is just Jeremiah and he remains the love of my life. I know he has given so much of himself, sacrificed his health, his sanity, to try to do the right thing with this "gift" of his. I never thought I'd see the day when I actually put that word in quotes, but that's the way he always said it. You could hear and almost see the little marks around it whenever he used it in the context of his healing ability.

I know there are those who must wonder if I ever forgave him for his affair with Corrine. God yes, I forgive him, a thousand times and more. I'd forgive all the sins of mankind itself if it would bring him back to me for just one moment. Re-reading the previous chapters—something I find myself doing more and more these days—I am struck by how empty of passion those encounters seem, as if he were simply going through the motions in someone else's dream. It's as if they simply used each other the way one uses the lavatory, without regard for how the fixture must feel. I know he never felt that way with me.

Am I not raising the child of their union? Kari has become the most precious thing in the world to me. She looks so much like her father. I wonder if it will be necessary to tell her the truth about her mother, though I realize in my heart she has the right to know. Her mother has made many mistakes. I hope she finds her way some day.

It hasn't been easy, reconciling oneself with the reality of forced obscurity. Everyone seemed to think the only way Kari and I could ever escape the demands imposed upon Jeremiah was to disappear and assume new identities. I can no longer practice law; that was felt to be too public, too easy to slip back into the public eye. Now I toil away in a sea of cubicles, one more faceless drone in the hive. We have a comfortable income thanks to a trust set up by Dr. Wheatley and Sid. The one thing we do not have is Jeremiah. Apparently he felt his presence was too great a danger for us, even in this idealized reality that has been created for us.

I never saw him after I awakened from my coma. I collapse into tears each time I re-read his account of how I never said anything to him but "You left us." I don't remember any of that. My last real memory of him was in the limousine on the way to the awards banquet.

His account of the past four years of our lives together is basically accurate, as far as I can tell, except for the part where I tried to divorce him while in a near trance-like state. I don't believe that ever happened. If I was truly in the state he describes—and my mother and several other people have confirmed that I was—I could not possibly have generated any such divorce document, valid or otherwise. No such paper has been found, and I have no idea why he came up with this fabrication. Perhaps he felt a need to justify leaving me to open the bookstore. In any case, I forgive him of this little discrepancy as well.

As to where he is, I have my theories, but I truly do not know. There have been a number of reported sightings, most of which can be easily dismissed. One woman claims she saw him descend from the clouds in the skies over Istanbul. The tabloids claim he has been spotted all over the world. He has become quite the hitchhiker, according to a number of accounts.

I believe he is very close to here, although I cannot publicly note just where "here" is. I think he is keeping watch over us. At nights I swear I hear the floors creak under his feet. There have been times I have felt his phantom touch just behind me, but he is never there when I turn around.

He is close to us. I know it. He is watching over us and will come if we need him. If only he knew just how badly we need him now! Kari needs a father and I need a friend.

* Mrs. Townsend no longer uses this name. Her new identity is not being made public in order to protect her privacy.

THE END

About the author

J. Butler Cox is an award-winning journalist and feature writer with a knack for creating ordinary characters thrown into extraordinary circumstances. He holds a master's degree in English from Lynchburg College in Virginia, where he successfully defended his thesis on the work of Ray Bradbury, and a bachelor's degree in Mass Communications from Emory & Henry College, also in Virginia. As a reporter at the Greeneville (Tenn.) Sun, he was the first person in the paper's history to win the Tennessee Associated Press Managing Editors' Malcolm Law Memorial Award for Feature Writing. He has also won numerous Virginia Press Association awards for reporting and feature writing.

When not spending time with his wife and son, he enjoys bicycling, hiking, and motorcycling along the Blue Ridge Parkway.